DOUG ... **T**

UNDERCURRENT

MAGNUS

'He laid the package on the table. Then, like a small boy looking at his birthday cake, he prowled round it. For a flickering second he was back to his childhood. He could recall sitting at the foot of the Christmas tree with his two brothers as they had stacked and re-stacked the parcels. This was different. No pretty ribbons, no fancy wrapping. Just brown paper, stark, thick and decorated only with bold black writing. Gingerly he turned it over, studying every inch. Scarcely daring to breathe, he put his ear to it, listening, expecting to hear the tick-tock of a nasty timing device.'

WHAT THEY'VE SAID ABOUT HIS BOOKS

DOUGLAS STEWART
UNDERCURRENT

MAGNUS

Published by
Magnus Books Limited
67-69 Chancery Lane
London
WC2A 1AF

Production management by Snell Print

Typeset in 10/12pt Palatino by
Character Graphics, Taunton

Jacket Artwork and Design by
Ken Vail Graphic Design

Printed in Great Britain by
BPCC Paperbacks Ltd
Member of BPCC Ltd

The moral right of the Author is asserted.

A CIP catalogue record for this book is
available from the British Library

ABOUT THE AUTHOR

Born in Glasgow, Douglas Stewart spent his childhood in Kent, attending Cranbrook School before reading Law at Durham University. Following Articles of Clerkship in London, he became a solicitor in the West Country, remaining there for about fifteen years, before returning to London in 1984, where he is now a partner in a Lincoln's Inn law firm.

He is also a successful and widely-read author. In the mid 1970's Douglas started writing novels to counteract the boredom of the Christmas television schedules, originally using the pen-name Cameron Ross. He now uses his own name and *Undercurrent* is his sixth novel. Beside his full time role as an international solicitor and the ever-increasing demands of writing, Douglas enjoys most sports, particularly cricket and hockey, travel, wine and fishing, besides being a regular broadcaster on radio and television. He is married with two sons.

DEDICATION

*This book is dedicated to all those who have to combat, defy
and defeat the dangers, ingenuity and menace of
international fraud at sea.*

ACKNOWLEDGEMENTS AND THANKS

I am indebted to so many people from the world of shipping for their advice and guidance that it is impossible to name them all individually. Specifically, however, I must mention the co-operation of Eric Ellen who (despite what is said in this novel) is and remains the Director of the ICC International Maritime Bureau. His guidance has been invaluable as have been the skills of agents, editors and others who have been good enough to give up their time to help me. Bill Snell, in particular, has given enormous guidance. Last, but not least, I am grateful to my wife, Penny, for the endless hours during which she has toiled at the word processor.

AUTHOR'S NOTE

This is a work of fiction, although set in the real-life world of the ICC International Maritime Bureau. The characters are fictional and bear no resemblance to any person living or dead. Whilst the investigations carried out by the International Maritime Bureau can be dangerous, the methods used in this book and the action of the characters are strictly fiction.

'Present day Piracy is increasing in many parts of the world. These criminals will attack vessels, both in port and at sea without showing any concern for the crews who are their victims.'

Eric Ellen Q.P.M.
London,
June, 1992

PART ONE

RYME LADY

Chapter 1

Something had gone wrong, badly wrong.

'Do you think we've been double-crossed?' enquired Tommy Muir, ship's radio officer, his voice low and conspiratorial. He was whispering to Captain Scutar as they sat in the stern of the lifeboat. Beside them was Jed Tewson, the engineer.

Rory Scutar, Glasgow-born, strained his eyes against the sun and shook his head gently. Around them, the sea was empty. The small white boat, carrying the nine crew and three officers, bobbed on the perpetual swell of the Malacca Strait. The nearest land was the west coast of Malaysia, some twenty-three miles away. Twelve pairs of eyes had been endlessly scanning the distant horizon, seeking the first glimpse of rescue. *Ryme Lady*, their cargo ship which they had abandoned at dawn, had gone.

They were alone, frying in the searing heat, their lips parched, their throats dry, their brains becoming addled. Despite sunglasses, their eyes were screwed up against the glare from the shimmering surface.

'Should have been picked up long ago,' continued Muir. He enjoyed carping. 'We've been at the rendezvous point for over four hours.' He looked at his watch again and then at Tewson, seeking support from him. 'Being roasted alive wasn't the plan,' he muttered as Tewson stayed silent. The mainly oriental crew were inscrutable, saying little but in some faces a mean sullenness was developing. They too realized that something had gone wrong.

'We'd better feed the bastards. They're getting restless.' These were the first words Scutar had spoken for a while. The Scottish rasp in his voice was roughened by a lifetime at sea. The touch of granite evoked images of storm-tossed Atlantic nights and an endless stream of Gitanes. His creased, weather-beaten face told its own story of too much whisky drunk alone in a small cabin.

At first, booze had been a relief from his broken marriage. Later, he'd sought refuge in whisky to numb his hatred of Brads, the owners of *Ryme Lady*. He checked his gold watch and scowled. After forty years at sea, they'd given it to him, along with a pat on the head. Nice. Just as if they owned him.

Gold it may have been, inscribed it certainly was but to Rory Scutar, the watch was scant recompense for a lifetime of dedicated service. A word of thanks and a smile would have been more welcome. It's presence was a constant reminder of the owners - of Sir Archie Crawford and his son Edward.

Except the watch wasn't two-faced.

The scowl lingered as he imagined them - fat, bloated and safe back in England. He checked the time again. When he spoke, it was with more confidence than he felt. 'It'll be all right. No doubt they've been held up.'

Scutar was well aware of the dangers. The International Maritime Bureau had emphasized the piracy problem in the Malacca Strait. 'It'll be all right,' he repeated, almost to himself.

'Still nothing, sir.' Tewson put down the binoculars. 'That's nearly seven hours. We're in trouble.'

'This lot'll have us,' agreed Scutar, 'if they get the chance.' He patted his pocket and felt the reassuring outline of his small pistol. 'Brought yours?'

Tewson and Muir nodded affirmatively. 'I'm not going before them,' said Muir, his young face strong with determination. 'We can't wait much longer. They'll mutiny at nightfall.' He studied the map. 'We could cut our losses and head for Malacca.'

'No, laddie, not yet.' The Captain's smile was paternal. He looked down at the small suitcase beside him and felt reassured as he patted it gently. 'Aye, that's better than a pension from Brads after forty years at sea. Dinna forget, we get the other half from the rescuers. Canna miss out on that.' The words, delivered in broad Glaswegian were decisive.

'Give it an hour. That's what I say. Then we move on.' Muir was a touch rebellious himself now.

'We'll see.' Scutar was non-committal as he watched one of the crew urinating splashily over the side. Even Scutar was worried now, yearning for the shade, thinking of his stuffy, cramped cabin on *Ryme Lady*. Would he miss her? Would he hell! Tewson edged across and spoke in a whisper to him. 'Couldn't refuse that type of offer, could we? Not that sort of money? Sets us up for life.' The weasel-like eyes, piercing even behind the Polaroids showed the avarice which ran deep. 'But there's one thing - I mean, surely you know ... you must know who set this thing up? Who paid us to ...'

'No, I don't.' The response was brusque but as if to soften it, Rory Scutar patted his case. 'Why worry? Why sniff at a chance to do down those bastards back in Bristol ... and be rich as well.' His Scottish accent emphasized the word *bastards*, showing the depth of feeling.

'You've always hated them?'

Scutar lit another Gitane and coughed again from the bottom of his ragged lungs. 'You see ...' His voice trailed away on hearing the shout. Suddenly everyone was pointing. On the distant horizon was a speck. Tewson looked through the binoculars. 'It's the right size, sir. Looks like a small fishing smack.'

It was forty minutes before the crews were able to wave to each other excitedly. A further twenty passed before the creaking blue and brown fishing boat was alongside them and the vessels were lashed together.

The small Malaysian skipper, in his late thirties, smiled his greeting, his teeth prominent. 'Captain Scutar? Welcome.' His few words were accented in a mix of Chinese and Malay. His complexion was sallow, his face more Chinese than Malay. He'd been born on the boat. It had been his life ever since. Day in, day out, come storm or fair winds, he'd been out in these waters. Usually it had been fishing, initially helping his father but, after he'd died, as the elder son he'd taken command. Just occasionally they'd carried a light cargo, sometimes human, sometimes cocaine. The profits were better.

Scutar led the transfer, keeping a firm grip on his suitcase and other personal belongings. 'What kept you?' The only response to Scutar's question was a shrug of the shoulders. He understood English well enough but he spoke little. Though the British had ruled Malacca and had left a permanent legacy, his education had been at sea rather than in class. 'Och! It disna matter. You're here now anyroads.' Scutar answered his own question before following the Malaysian's pointed direction to the for'ard deck. It was small, cramped but welcome after the lifeboat. His crew joined him to perch on boxes, fishing nets and piles of rope, their suitcases and personal effects stacked together in front of the wheelhouse. Astern, the lifeboat was firmly secured, ready to be towed back to port.

'When do we get the rest of our money?' asked Muir.

'Relax laddie. You canna spend it yet anyway. He'll pay us before Malacca. That's a few hours away. D'you fancy a wee dram?' As he spoke, Scutar fished an un-opened bottle of 'Famous Grouse' from his holdall and filled a couple of plastic beakers. 'Let's drink to success. And a happy retirement.'

Behind them, the three Malaysians entered the wheelhouse, six feet above deck level. The boat was only twelve metres long, typical of the region. Through the windows the skipper could see its every inch. The weathered timbers reeked of tar and fishy brine. The deck was bloodstained from the tons of fish which daily had been gutted en route to port.

As he looked round, the skipper could see the lifeboat, whilst in front and below were the rescued crew. Already, they were sprawled about, some of them nearly asleep. Ahead lay the truck journey to Bangkok. There they would each find beautiful women to fondle and good food in abundance. And after that? They were on their own, their separate futures an undiscussed secret.

The skipper fired the diesel and the bows creamed frothily through the gentle swell. The Malaysian waited a few more minutes and then, satisfied at what he had seen, nodded a command. His two crew ducked down and produced machine guns from a cupboard.

It was turkey-shoot time.

'What the ...' said Scutar as the staccato of bullets started to spray over his crew. He never got to finish the remark as the endless stream of bullets played without mercy across him, across each of them. Back and forward, forward and back, the Malaysians scattered the bullets like children with hosepipes. For a few moments, there were screams of terror and pain but then the noise died away. Even after the last of the bodies had stopped twitching, the Malays fired on, long after there could be no survivors.

Laughing at the fun, all three approached the obscenity. One of them grabbed Tewson's corpse. He stripped it of clothes and belongings and in seconds had looped a noose round the bloodied head, its features locked in a bemused, quizzical look. Then he turned to the stomach, slitting it open as if he were gutting a fish. With a flourish the two of them picked up the corpse and swung it overboard.

Though it was too early for the sun to set, the late afternoon sea turned crimson as the bloody innards spilled into the ocean. Another body followed in similar fashion. Then another, each tethered behind the boat on forty yards of line. The Malaysians knew it wouldn't take long for the first shark to appear. The Strait was notorious for its man-eaters. As the entrails were sucked out into the water, the gory slipstream was a generous invitation.

While they waited, the Malaysians moved from corpse to corpse searching for valuables. Jewellery, watches, pens and wallets, some of them bloodstained, were tipped into a sack. Each crew member had been carrying US$2,000, the officers US$100,000 apiece and Scutar US$200,000, their pay-off for co-operation with the paymasters. Double that had been assured to each of them on docking in Malaysia - a false promise, the price of treachery.

Unknown to Captain Scutar and his crew, their pay-off had been guaranteed to the Malaysians as reward for mass murder. The spoils were high. So were the risks.

One fin appeared, lured by the bloody slipstream. Then came two more, the triangles cutting swathe-like through the surface. It was the awaited signal for the remaining bodies to be flung overboard. Soon the water was alive with feasting sharks ruthlessly destroying the evidence of the massacre.

On board, it was business as usual - time to clean the decks, scrubbing, hosing, swabbing. At last, when the skipper was satisfied, he ordered the lifeboat to be cast adrift. Only then did he restart the diesel motor, chug-chugging at a steady eight knots on its homeward journey. He looked at Scutar's gold Rolex before putting it into a drawer. It was 5.15 p.m. Then he glanced behind. All that remained was the lifeboat, a distant speck of white on an empty sea

The small historic town of Malacca nestles on the west coast of Malaysia, south west of Kuala Lumpur and four hours by road north of Singapore. Dominated by its fishing fleet, Malacca also shelters a flotilla of small boats which ply the Strait between Malaysia and Sumatra. The architecture tells of Dutch invasion, of an English influence and now of the Chinese community who rub shoulders with the Malays.

In the Chinese quarter it was long past midnight when the three fishermen emerged from the shabby interior of the small restaurant where they had celebrated their new found wealth with giant portions of chicken rice. The skipper and his nephews were still dazed at their good fortune. Their laughter and voices were loud, a reaction to the slaughter of just a few hours before.

Ready for sleep now, the trio entered the darkened narrow street. Close by were the muddy brown waters of the Malacca River just across from where they were standing. Upstream was the faded glory of the Majestic Hotel, itself a symbol of the English colonial past. Laughing and joking they carried the heavy sack with their spoils through the shadows towards the skipper's car. The old Datsun was parked close to the narrow strip of trees and bushes which bordered the riverbank. Except for their own voices, everything was silent. The last of the children who had been playing out of doors were now inside. The fishing fleet had sailed an hour before. Chinatown had gone to bed except for a few gamblers in smoke-filled parlours. The still night air was warm, the temperature up in the high seventies and in the humidity the cloying smells of durian fruit and salted fish hung heavily.

As the skipper led the way across the pot-holes, his nephews carried the sack between them. For a moment he fumbled in his jeans' pocket for the car keys, his thoughts still full of the day's events. One thing would certainly change! He would buy a new car. A white Toyota. And a new boat. Or perhaps he'd retire. Yes, maybe that would be nice. That ... and a trip to Bangkok!

So ran his thoughts as he pushed the key into the lock, before a rustle and movement from the rough ground behind made him falter. He turned, startled. There, he saw a figure with a masked face. Then two more emerged from the shrubs on the bank, the silencers on their guns muffling the shots as they fired. Three bullets tore into the fishermen at point blank range. Each fell, crumpled, beside the battered old grey saloon. Pausing only to pick up the sack, the killers ran to their car, parked just along the street. Seconds later, without drama and without any unnecessary noise, the vehicle slipped away into the night.

Somewhere a dog howled. Then there was silence.

Chapter 2

In Barking, close to Docklands in London's rapidly changing East End, lies Maritime House, the headquarters of the International Maritime Bureau. Housed in a modern building of no great style or pretention, the Bureau came into being to combat the rising tide of crime at sea during the 1970s. Sinking ships, disappearing ships, piracy, swindling boat-people, murder and theft were the daily occurrences which had led to its creation.

The multi-million profits from stealing cargos or from scuttling ships were a temptation. The chances of getting away with it had made that temptation irresistible. To a large degree, insurers had shrugged their shoulders, paid up ...... and raised their premiums rather than spend fortunes on proving the frauds which they suspected.

National police forces had found it hard to get funding to combat these crimes and so, as part of the International Chamber of Commerce, the International Maritime Bureau had been formed. Through the '80s it had gained credibility in a string of successes, the result of painstaking investigations, contacts and tip-offs.

Originally the Bureau had been under the directorship of Eric Ellen. The stamp of success came from him. His legacy, following his own elevation, was a smooth-running machine, a Bureau which had the ears of Governments worldwide. Shipping companies which had joined knew that if they were struck by fraud or piracy, then the Bureau's expertise was instantly available.

The mantle of directorship had now fallen on Walter Corbin who had continued the tradition of success. Yet it had not all been success, could not always be success - a thought which was uppermost in Walter's mind that morning as Anna, his secretary, busied herself around the room doing his filing whilst he spoke to the chairman of Brads on the telephone.

'Sir Archie - it's six weeks since *Ryme Lady* disappeared. Yes ... I know the name of Brads now stinks ... but you don't make it easy for us. Yes. Six weeks too late.' He coughed politely. 'Sometimes we're retained within half an hour of the loss. It helps.' Walter Corbin's understatement was typical. 'Nevertheless, I'll put two of my best men on it. But I just wish you'd brought us in earlier.' It was a familiar reprimand.

'I know. I know. Don't tell me. We've debated it ad nauseam d'ya see.'

For a moment Corbin was tempted to reply explosively but instead he kept his exasperation in check. 'I'll put Art Lemman and Gavin Blair onto it. Lemman's American and tough as they come. Blair is English, with a calculating brain.'

Sir Archie, 130 miles away at Brads' headquarters in Bristol was pleased. 'Say 12.30 tomorrow, over lunch?'

'I'll tell them.' Walter Corbin put down the phone and turned to Anna. 'Sometimes I despair. Brads are in deep financial trouble. *Ryme Lady* was lost in dubious circumstances. Now their credibility in the City is below zero. What do we hear from them? I'll tell you! Nothing! Nothing until six weeks too late, by which time the criminals have covered their arses. Unless, of course, Brads themselves are the criminals.'

Anna, who had been with the Bureau since it started, nodded sympathetically, her dark, curly hair bobbing as she did so. 'I suppose Brads have been told that the insurers won't pay out for the hull. And the cargo? And the cargo insurers? No pay-out I presume? Anyway, did the cargo even go aboard?'

'That'll be for Art and Gavin to find out.' Corbin looked at Anna and felt that she was about to add something but then she turned away, busying herself with her filing. He admired the neat lines of her pale green suit and white shirt. He'd learnt a great deal from her. She was the point of continuity between the days of Ellen and his own tenure of office.

'Art and Gavin? Do you think that's wise?' said Anna, a few moments later, without facing him. She pushed shut the drawer of the filing cabinet and picked up a yellow folder, all the while carefully avoiding his eyes.

'Because of Kuantan? You mean about Theo?' Although Walter spoke as though he were questioning her, he knew the answer. Feelings in the Bureau about the murder of Theo were still running high.

'They only buried him three weeks ago. Art hasn't forgiven Gavin yet for what happened. I'm not sure he ever will. Theo was Art's greatest friend.'

'Yes. It wasn't a pretty end.' Walter spoke slowly, his words guarded. Although forty-two years old, he had the maturity and looks of someone ten years older, his hair almost completely silver now and his moustache whitening to match it. 'I know what Art thinks. But he's not really thinking. It's all emotion. He's blind to the facts.' He shook his head, his teeth just slightly bared in irritation. 'I know the truth. Look .... what happened to Theo wasn't Gavin's fault.'

'Try persuading Art, not me.' She turned to face him at last and her eyes carried the warning of her words. 'Sometimes I hear more than you. He's not going to like it.' At times like this Anna wished that her old boss, Eric Ellen, was back. He'd have understood, would have listened to her, anxious to understand every nuance. Not that she underestimated the wisdom or tenacity of the new man. It's just that he wasn't the old one. She'd been used to being the eyes and ears of what happened in the office.

Walter rose angrily from his desk, knowing that she was right, knowing that he had a problem. He walked to the window and stood for a moment, gazing out across the developing East End. The skyline was a sea of cranes, reflecting the hopes and aspirations that the old derelict wharfs and warehouses could, once again, be rejuvenated into a vibrant community. The recession of the 1990s had seen the greatest hopes fading with liquidations and uncertainty. Up river and out of sight, the giant complex of Canary Wharf was a sharp reminder of high hopes and even higher disappointment.

His eyes were on the grey horizon, on the scudding clouds and scattered swaying trees far below. His thoughts were on Theo, the young investigator who had been Art's protégé until murdered whilst investigating the scandal of the Vietnamese boat people in Malaysia. Theo had been working on it with Gavin Blair but Walter was sure what had happened had not been Gavin's fault. Yet Art was convinced that Gavin was a coward. 'Art's paid to do a job. He'll do it. He's a professional.' Walter wasn't sure whether he was talking to convince himself or to convince Anna.

'There's something else as well ...' said Anna but Walter was already turning to his desk and ready to face the problem.

'Just wheel them in, can you. I want Art first.' Despite the fact that he had only one lung left, the Director lit yet another cigarette. Outside, a police car wailed as it sped down Linton Road and into the drab anonymity of the Greater London hinterland in which Barking lay. He flicked open the file regarding Theo's death, saw the picture of the fresh-faced man and then the one of his mutilated corpse. With a sigh Walter pushed it aside. People came cheap when the profits were big enough.

After he'd landed the job, Eric Ellen had told him that life in the Bureau was tough - not just tough decisions, though there were plenty of those, but danger - danger whether investigating stolen cigarettes in the Mediterranean, sinkings off Hong Kong or drug related crime in the Caribbean. 'You don't join the Bureau as a sinecure,' Ellen had said to him. 'You don't join the Bureau if all you want is to die in bed.'

Tell that to Theo's widow.

Art had joined the Bureau before either Gavin or Theo and had been hand-selected by Ellen in the early days. At the time, the Director had been working in a joint operation with the US Drug Enforcement Agency on a bust at Norman's Cay in the Bahamas. He needed careful handling.

Walter's thoughts were interrupted by the knock on the door and there he was. Lemman. Art Lemman. Thirty-eight years old. Square built, rugged, New Jersey born and a hard drinker, he was the iron man of the Bureau. The two bullets still inside him from a job on Staten Island were too dangerously positioned to be removed now.

'Art! Good morning. Take a seat.' The last part of the greeting was unnecessary as Art, casual in approach and casual in clothing, seated himself as if the room were his own. Though he acknowledged that Walter was his boss, it was only just. There was irreverence in his attitude. To him, Walter was still the new boy, the person brought in to replace the irreplaceable Eric Ellen. 'There's a new job. *Ryme Lady*. Owned by Brads of Bristol. Complete disappearance whilst en route from Singapore to the Middle East.'

'I remember.' He pulled a packet of Camels from his bomber jacket and lit a cigarette with a throw-away lighter.

'You've got it. Further north than the usual piracy strip. That, as you know, is closer to here.' As he spoke, Walter jabbed at the large globe on his desk. He was pointing to the Phillips Channel, a narrow stretch of water at the foot of the Malaysian peninsular. Cargo ships and even 200,000 ton vessels were equal quarry there. Marauding pirates thought nothing of grappling aboard a low-lying, heavily laden tanker under cover of darkness. 'Doesn't sound like the work of pirates to me. Not if it sank. Could be like the *Isla Luzon*. She was hijacked for the cargo. One of the crew died.'

Art *looked* thoughtful but even during their comparatively short time working together, Walter had realized that Art thought far too little. 'If it's an *Isla Luzon* situation, then *Ryme Lady* will have changed her name by now, either at some foreign consulate or just with a lick of paint.'

Walter drained the last of his coffee as he nodded approval. 'If *Ryme Lady's* been stolen, any number of linked crimes will follow. Anyway Art, this is a two-man job. I'm putting you to work with Gavin Blair. I think he's ...'

'Gavin Blair? For Chrissake! You think I'd work with Gavin? Look, that scumbag killed ...'

Walter raised his hands in protest. 'You know that's not true. You want to *believe* it to be true. But it's not. There was nothing, absolutely nothing, that Gavin could have done.'

'Got some coffee? I need some.'

The conversation broke down as Anna was summoned to bring coffee, and lots of it, for both of them. Even after she'd left the room, there remained an uncomfortable silence as each man wondered what next to say. Corbin knew that Gavin was suffering from a crisis of confidence.

'I'm telling you,' continued Art, his New York accent sounding more nasal in his anger. 'If I'd been there, Theo would still be alive today. He's shit-scared.' He stopped to stub out his cigarette with determination. 'No. It's worse than that. Gavin is scared of his own fart. Because of him we spent a day in the Cotswolds burying Theo. Because of

Gavin Blair, Theo had his throat cut and his balls stuffed in his mouth.'

Art rose sharply, eyes flashing. He stood still for a few seconds. He wasn't small - 5' 10" according to his passport but his broad shoulders and hefty frame took away from his height. In recent weeks he'd gained a few pounds around his waist but otherwise he remained a formidable figure. As he snorted defiance across the desk at Walter, the Director was put in mind of a bullock - full of strength but not always sure what to do with it.

Art walked across the spacious room, pausing by a reproduction table which was full of trophies. There was a silver statuette presented by a grateful ship-owner, photos of Eric Ellen meeting the Prime Minister and of Walter shaking hands with the American President. Art looked at none of these. Instead, he picked up a small framed photograph of a Vietnamese child, forlorn and frightened, sitting in the stern of a fishing boat. 'Gavin let her down. Let everyone down. Left Theo exposed.' He turned in a sudden movement, then advanced on Walter in accusation. 'And now you want me to work with *him*?'

Walter looked away but only for a second. 'I do. And it's an order. You're the precise team I need. It could be rough but it's going to need cunning too. It's going to need subtlety.' Though he wasn't saying it, Walter's message was that Art lacked that quality. The American understood and if he'd been less emotive, would have agreed. As it was, he looked sullen as Walter continued. 'There's boardroom politics involved at Brads. Sup with Brads and you sup with the devil. Now, for that, I need Gavin as well. His time as a lawyer was not wasted. His logic, his questioning are assets which we'll need.' Walter thought wrongly that he was getting through. His smile would have convinced most.

'Fuck logic. Fuck questioning. The man's a goddammed coward. I won't work with him.' Art's raised voice could be heard by Anna at her desk in the room next door. On her face was an I-told-you-so look.

'You're going to. And you're going to make a damned good job of it.'

'I'm resigning. Goddammit! I'm resigning here and now.' Art thumped his fist heavily into the palm of his other hand.

'That's a great way to repay the Bureau.'

'But ...'

'No buts.' The Director was brooking no argument now. 'Just remember. You were flung out of the Drug Enforcement Agency. If it wasn't for the Bureau, you'd be dragging your ragged arse down Skid Row. Eric Ellen gave you a chance when you needed it most.'

Walter stood up, so that the two men were only a few feet apart but divided by a mile in temperament, size, appearance, outlook, background and purpose. 'Look. If you want to repay me by walking out just when we've lost a good man ... fine. You just walk. And if you walk ... do you know what?' Walter paused, looking at Art, noticing just a slight defensiveness in the strong yet raffish features. It showed around his lips as he half turned towards the door. The pugnacious face, eyes deep-set beneath heavy brows, revealed momentary weakness. 'I'll tell you. If you walk out, you're walking away from trouble. Walking away from life, from responsibility.'

He took another step towards Art, pointing an accusing finger, making clear just what he was thinking. 'So who does that make a coward?' He spat out the words. 'Maybe your references were right. Maybe you were just a pig-ignorant, womanizing hard-man.' Tall, lean, the Director advanced again until they were just inches apart. Art's swarthy features were close to his. Art's black wavy hair tumbled down to his ears. The short but heavy sideboards had just a fleck of grey and his face, though clean-shaven, had a tinge of shadow. A trace of damp glistened on Art's forehead and Walter noticed a mix of garlic and Camel cigarettes on his breath.

'I don't run ... not like Gavin.' Art's face was set cold, hard as granite.

'You want a reference now then? Know what I'd say?' The Director spoke with a slow mechanical rhythm, emphasizing every word. 'I'd tell them that Art Lemman ran like a coward even *before* the first hint of danger.' He enjoyed throwing back Art's earlier expression. Walter shrugged as he turned away and strolled back to his desk, the body language showing that Art was dismissed from the room, dismissed from the future of the Bureau. If that's what he wanted. 'Ok Art ... carry on. Just drop out again. Go back to the bourbon, the women. Chuck away everything you've achieved.'

The American, who had his hand on the door, stopped instantly. Thirty-eight years old, nearly twenty years in the cocaine war, the pictures of his past raced through his mind. He froze momentarily, weighing up the implications of Walter's challenge. Slowly he raised his eyes. The rounded face lengthened slightly, the dark eyes flickered and then slowly a smile started to form and changed into a rueful grin. 'I guess you're right Walter. You'd better get Gavin in.'

'No. I'll see Gavin alone first.'

'Sure.' Art opened the door and his shoulders filled the doorway as he left the room.

Walter closed the door and returned to his desk, nervously adjusting his tie as he did so. There was no doubt about it. Art's hatred of Gavin bordered on the irrational. The death of Theo had cut deeper than it should. He sat for a moment, fiddling with the brass desk calendar. At times like this he wished he could spend more time in the field himself. Office politics were more exhausting.

He ran his hand nervously through the carefully

groomed hair, leaned back in his chair and closed his eyes. In repose you could accept that he was only forty two, but, under pressure, the taut muscles and the creased forehead added ten more. Nevertheless, the lean foxy features, the dark eyes and the well-defined chin made him an attractive man, assets he'd never bothered to exploit.

He thought back to the interview with Art. There was no certainty that Gavin would want to work with him. He rocked forward and pressed the buzzer on the intercom. 'Anna - can you get Gavin Blair in please.' Once again he sat uneasily in the recliner, fingers drumming restlessly on the black moquette.

The knock at the door brought him back to the immediate situation and he leaned forward, elbows now on his desk. He picked up his gold pen and when the door opened, he looked relaxed and confident. The elegant tailored suit, the immaculate cuffs, the silk, lightly patterned tie and the soft leather shoes completed the image which the Director needed. Indeed it was not just an image, it was reality. Head of the International Maritime Bureau was a position which opened doors in all continents. Sometimes however, those with whom Walter Corbin had rubbed shoulders were less scrupulous than their image and status might foretell.

'Morning Gavin. Help yourself to coffee. Anna brought some in a few minutes ago. How are you feeling?'

'May I sit down?' Gavin's diffidence contrasted with the breezy informality of Art's earlier arrival. 'How would you be feeling? Look ... if you want me to resign, I've heard the rumours around the place. I'll go quietly.'

Walter's hand shot up in protest. 'Look. That's not on the agenda. Theo wasn't your fault.'

'Then start convincing some other people, Art Lemman for one. He's really been putting the poison in.' In contrast to the casual slacks and Reebok approach of Lemman,

Gavin who had just turned thirty one was wearing a navy blazer, with silver buttons and grey flannels. Unlike Art, his face didn't look as if he'd lived a thousand lives and suffered a thousand and one deaths. It was a face which spoke of breeding, of culture.

Walter looked Gavin up and down and liked what he saw. People did. Though he was tall, angular and clean cut, there was nothing languid about him. His appearance created an impression of nervous energy and cool determination. 'Look,' Gavin continued. 'I know I've had your full support. But sometimes people won't accept the truth. Not even Janie. After the funeral I got back to the flat and found that she'd gone. Everything. Buggered off.' As he spoke, his eyes were lowered in a moment of shame.

'But you were getting married, weren't you?' As he looked at Gavin, the Director judged that it wouldn't be long before someone else succumbed to Gavin's good looks. His face, dominated by the dancing, wide-set eyes and smiling mouth, was friendly, kind and yet forceful.

Gavin nodded his head in agreement. 'Next May. Not now. The note simply said 'Goodbye'. I haven't heard from her again. No idea where she is.'

'I'm sorry. Bad at any time. Even worse when you've been together for so long ... and coming at the same time as Theo. Anyway, let's get to the point. I'm putting you and Art to work. Together.'

Gavin's laugh was full of irony. 'Me and Art? You think Art'll work with me?' He paused to examine his fingernails whilst he weighed up what to say next. 'Murderer. That's what Art called me. A murderer.' Gavin spread his hands helplessly.

Corbin shrugged. 'Well, whatever ... but he's agreed. It's working in the Far East again. Nothing to do with boatpeople. Least, I don't think so.' He pressed the buzzer and almost at once Art appeared. For a moment they looked at each other, face to face for the first time since Art had called Gavin a fucking murderer. Art looked up from his 5′ 10″ to the 6′ 1″ of the Englishman. 'You and me a team. That's what Walter told me. You've heard?'

'I'd heard.' Gavin let the words sound neutral. As he often did, he ran his hand over his strong sandy hair. It was neatly cut, swept back and just covering the tops of his ears.

Hands in pockets, thumbs tucked over the rims, Art moved confidently round the room until he had his back to the window. 'Ever faced a gun, Gavin? A loaded gun?' The words came out slowly but were followed by a rapid withdrawal of his right hand from his pocket, as if he were aiming to fire. The fingers pointed accusingly across the room. Gavin's face said no as he looked away. 'Huh!' came the grunted, dismissive comment from the American.

'Listen, the pair of you.' Walter intervened. 'There's no room for sniping,' but Art brushed aside the Director's interference with a flourish as he threw off his bomber jacket and raised his faded green shirt.

'Want to see a scar?' The scar tissue of a bullet hole high on the left side of his chest was revealed. 'A .38 revolver. Fort Lauderdale. I stopped that trying to save a friend. See, I didn't run. I didn't run Gavin boy. And if you and me are going to be a team,' he snarled with contempt at the very notion, 'then there's no room for running. Not this time Gavin.' He made Gavin's name sound despicable. Walter was about to intervene again but a chopping movement from Gavin's left hand said it was probably better for the showdown to take place now.

'Now you listen.' Gavin's tone was clipped, very English. 'Not easy for a loudmouth braggard like you. *Nobody* could have saved Theo. And let me show you something.' As he spoke, Gavin slipped off his jacket and pulled up his own shirt. 'Let me show you this.'

'Ain't nothing there. I don't see no scars.' Art played dumb.

'Oh yes. I'm wounded all right.' He motioned towards his heart. 'I'm scarred. But my scars are invisible. They're real and just as permanent.' Gavin turned and started to tuck in his shirt once again as Walter came between them like a referee at a prize fight. 'Sometimes it hurts more to run than to stay.'

Walter saw the glint of tears in Gavin's eyes. His hands, his voice were both shaking with emotion as he relived the murder in Kuantan. Walter spoke. 'That's the last word on the subject. The matter's closed. Agreed?' He looked at each of them in turn.

Slowly at first but positively nonetheless, Art found himself extending his hand. 'Shake hands the English way, dear boy. Kiss and make up.' Art's voice was mocking as if he couldn't bring himself to be entirely gracious. For a moment, Walter thought that Gavin was going to spurn the gesture. But no. Walter saw Gavin's mind at work. It was deliberate. He was letting Art sweat a bit. After leaving the American uncertain for almost too long, Gavin moved forward. Then they shook hands - the soft elegant hand of Gavin contrasting with the weather-beaten hairy fist of Art Lemman.

'With hands as soft as that you should be advertising a soap product,' said Art. He was half-joking, half still determined to emphasize his contempt for the soft-centred man in front of him.

'And you,' retorted Gavin, 'you're acting like someone from a soap. No. Maybe not. You haven't the brains to remember your lines.' The three men were standing almost huddled together, but then, as if by mutual assent, all three took a step backwards from the brink.

Walter rubbed his hands briskly. 'Right. Glad to see you're friends. We've work to do. Starting now.' He returned to his chair as Art and Gavin each took a seat at opposite corners of the mahogany desk with its inlaid leather surface.

'Can't even get it up, can you?' Art hissed quietly in the direction of Gavin. A look of puzzlement came over Gavin's face. It was as if he wasn't sure what he'd heard or if he'd even understood what he thought he'd heard. If the Director noticed the comment, it didn't show as he busied himself with the projector. Onto the screen flashed the first picture.

'This is *Ryme Lady*. 9,000 tons deadweight. Length overall 140 metres. Beam 18 metres. Draft 8.2 metres. Mixed cargo carrier. Fifteen years old. Coming up for an expensive special survey. A bit of a rust-bucket. Owned by Brads. Disappeared in the Malacca Strait about six weeks ago.'

'But unlikely to sink in a calm sea?' suggested Gavin.

'Agreed. And the sea was calm.' Walter came as close to a grin as he ever did, his eyes warming behind his reading glasses. 'It would sink if the crew pulled the plug out, flooded the engine room, reversed the pumps.' He flicked on the picture. 'This is Singapore, where she loaded. Stashed full of electronics. If they went aboard. Worth about $60 million, all in containers. The rest was mainly bulk tapioca.' He paused to let the point sink in. Ageing ships with high value cargo were always suspect. 'There were no Mayday calls. No trace of any crew. No lifeboat.'

Gavin nodded. 'Should have happened in the Bermuda Triangle. A Marie Celeste without the ship,' he volunteered. Art's grunt was dismissive. He'd heard stories of the Bermuda Triangle and had believed none of them. His creed was facts - facts stacked on facts, a creed which rarely prevented him from delivering his opinions without waiting for the facts to formulate.

Walter felt pleased. The tension was easing. He preferred to be dealing with fraud rather than feuding. 'Brads had chartered her to a company called Mentocca,' he explained. 'Mentocca is owned, run and masterminded by this man.' He flicked forward the picture. 'Carl Klodinsky. A self-made New Yorker of Eastern European extraction but brought up in the States since the age of nine. Now aged forty eight.'

'And Brads?'

'You'll find out tomorrow. They're an old established company. Three vessels left now out of a recent fleet of eight. Two without *Ryme Lady*. Run by establishment people who've fallen on hard times.'

'The worst sort. A nest of vipers?' There was relish in Art's voice. To him there was nothing better.

'Let's say vipers whose silver spoons are a little tarnished.' Walter admired his own eloquence. 'Questions. Did she founder? Or was she scuttled? And who did it? As for why ... $60 million has disappeared. Add to that the insured value of the hull. One million. Far more than its scrap value. And maybe Brads couldn't afford the spell in Dry Dock for the special survey. No income, just expense. But high stakes, especially if it meant losing an entire crew. Any ideas?'

Gavin, trained as an English barrister and admitted to the Middle Temple, paused to weigh up the most appropriate response. Art, still trained to shoot from the hip, proceeded to do so. 'Ageing rust-bucket? Company short of money. It's goddammed obvious. Brads paid the crew to sink it. The modern conjuring trick. Turning rust into cash. Robbing the insurers. That's the scam.'

'A crew scuttling their own ship and getting wet feet? Worse still - all drowning. Come off it!' Walter's eyes, grey and cold, were unusually severe and penetrating. 'The insurers aren't satisfied and aren't paying out.' He looked at Gavin who was stroking the side of his cheek, a mannerism he'd picked up at the Bar. 'Gavin?'

'Maybe she hasn't sunk at all. Maybe she's just changed her name with a lick of paint. With a new identity, she could call in at some small port. Selling the cargo for quick cash is easy. With an insured value of $60 million, you could sell it for 20, maybe 30 million. Then ... ' Gavin tried to develop his theory from other similar incidents. 'Then ... anchor up somewhere. The crew disappear. Everyone wins but the insurers. Everyone that is except for Brads. Even they win if the hull insurers pay out.'

'Twelve men just disappear?' Walter looked dubious. 'Let's move on.' The picture on the wall changed. 'Those three are Scutar, Muir and Tewson. The officers. Scutar was coming up for retirement. Lifetime with the company, a pension to look forward to. Nothing much known about the two youngsters. Nothing adverse anyway.'

'I'd say the cargo never went aboard.' Art's tone was equally dogmatic about his new idea. He changed and discarded theories like catwalk models change clothes. 'Or wasn't on board when she sank. Ship sinks. Big insurance claim put in for non-existent cargo. Clean up $60 million if there never was a cargo.'

'But why no crew? Why no Mayday?'

Art was cornered and it showed. The obvious theories didn't make sense. 'Maybe the lifeboat leaked,' he suggested in desperation. 'Anyway ... who stood to gain from the lost cargo?'

'That depends,' suggested Gavin, 'on whether the cargo ever went aboard. Any sign of it being flogged on some remote quayside?' The answer came with a shake of the Director's head in denial. 'In that case,' Gavin continued, 'Klodinsky, as the charterer, wins if the cargo never went aboard. The insurers pay him $60 million for a cargo which was never lost. What's more, it may never have been purchased.'

'You're right.' Walter looked pleased. The chemistry

40

between Art and Gavin was dangerous but it might work. If they'd give it a chance. 'Klodinsky's over in Paris at the moment. Gavin, I want you to question him. Art, I want you to cover the Far East.' Walter's invitation was rewarded by Art sneakily helping himself in the darkness to the Director's last cigarette as Walter flicked on the picture. 'Let's take a look at Brads.'

A picture of Sir Archibald Crawford appeared on the wall. Aged in his late sixties, he looked precisely what he was - the end result of Eton, the Guards and too many business lunches with the *chaps* or *the boys*, as he called his friends in the City. Nevertheless the picture didn't tell the whole story. 'Chairman of the company. War hero in Burma. Rows of medals. Escaped from a Jap prisoner of war camp.' Walter rattled off the details from the notes in front of him. ' Slaughtered several guards with a home-made stiletto. Survived eight weeks alone in the jungle. He's a crack-shot - won an Olympic gold medal in Helsinki l952. Now he's looking for retirement.'

Walter clicked the control again. 'This is Edward, Sir Archie's son, aged thirty two. Also educated at Eton and then the London School of Economics. He's Chief Executive ... or acts as if he is. There's no love lost between father and son.'

'Piggy face,' said Art. 'Smug, second-generation wealth. English Ivy League.'

'Third generation at least. Don't go judging by appearances though. Don't underestimate him. Nor Sir Archie. Both clever, as is,' he advanced the picture, 'Edward's sister Susannah. Quite a stunner too, isn't she?'

Art wolf-whistled as he stared at the picture of Susannah Crawford. 'Wow! Is that class or is that class! Who's balling her!'

'It won't be you Art. Keep your hands off the clients. She's the Financial Director. She's got brains and looks.

Educated at Roedean and Cambridge. My crib-sheet says she has to divide the warring factions of father and son. It's believed she has a lover.'

Art Lemman rubbed his hands in anticipation. 'Boy! Does she need me!'

'I said no.' Walter's face was unusually severe. 'Just remember. $60 million is worth a few corpses. In this job … it's grapes by the bed if you're lucky, a wreath if you're not. And you make your own luck.' Neither of the listeners needed reminding. Once seen, the pictures of Theo could never be forgotten.

Art rose to leave but squared up to Gavin as he did so. The two men's faces came close. 'Too late to tell that to Theo. Still, it was a decent burial. What they found of him.'

Walter Corbin sat alone after they had left the room. The truce was uneasy.

Chapter 3

At the White House, in the quietness of the Oval Office, the President of the USA studied the report. When Cormack O'Brien had finished , he removed his glasses and rubbed his eyes. It had been a long day in a long week in a long year. Glasnost and the rapid thaw in East-West relations had not made the burdens of office significantly easier. Just different. The Gulf War had been a triumph but the Middle East was still troublesome. Gaddafi, out in Libya, was still smarting from when the Reagan Administration strafed his country.

Outside, in the Rose Garden, the autumnal sun was still warm with just a slight breeze. For a moment, the President's thoughts turned to the evening. Soon he'd be flying up to New England for a spot of relaxation on the boat. Tomorrow there would be golf and maybe a cook-out in the evening. He rubbed his chin thoughtfully before returning to the decisions awaited by the two men sitting in front of his desk, his Secretary of State, Bob Merchant and CIA Chief, Ralph Gill.

'It seems I've got to go there. Is that your reading of the position, Bob? Cut out questions of *like* or *want*. They don't come into it. It's a matter of obligation. Ought I to be in Lumbola for their celebrations? That's the only question. The answer seems to be yes.' The President did not sound enthusiastic.

'Mr President, even forgetting wanting or liking, does the President of the United States of America really have to go to a tiny Third World country in West Africa?' Merchant paused to watch the reaction. 'You know what they used to call it?' He saw the President shake his head. 'The white

43

man's graveyard. Mosquitos like hornets. Disease most everywhere.' Merchant was big, physically reassuring, with a strong accent from his home state of North Carolina.

'Pack your First Aid. You'll be coming too,' laughed the President in his own droll manner. He enjoyed watching the look on his Secretary of State's face. 'I've read the briefing papers. Sampopo and Lumbola may be small countries, blips on the West African coastline, but hell, they are both merging ... and emerging. Strategically this new country they're creating, called Lupopo, will be of great importance to us.' He sipped from a glass of grapefruit juice. He was aware from the files in front of him that arab extremists had been causing trouble in black Africa, organizing local uprisings here, demonstrations there, all the while seeking to undermine lawful regimes. 'We don't want fundamentalists dominating this new baby. Look at the CIA local station reports ... I mean just on that evidence alone ...'

Ralph Gill, as the new Chief out at the CIA's Langley HQ, was visiting the Oval Office for the first time but seemed comfortable enough. 'This new republic of Lupopo *will* be strategically important. What worries me is security if you visit. These African countries haven't got the ... er ... sophistication.'

The President replaced his glasses and rose from his chair. He strolled thoughtfully round the room. Death held no fears for him. The adrenalin provided its own armour-plating. He had been in office nine months now and knew that in that time security teams had been working day and night, sifting through the warning threats, the tip-offs, the false leads, in order to maintain the democratic rights of the constitution. He knew that every time he stepped on the streets there was a risk of the one lone nut. Yet it had never got to him and whenever possible he'd plunge into a crowd for a friendly word or to shake an outstretched hand. It was

44

this open style which had helped him win the election - that and his statesmanlike physique and powerful oratory.

O'Brien had always been a Washington insider, had been brought up in Great Falls in a political family. As a child he'd vacationed at the Kennedy family home at West Palm Beach. He'd understood the meaning of the word assassin. 'Lincoln was shot in the theatre, just the other side of the block. When I was fifteen, Jack Kennedy was killed in Dallas. I was about twenty-one when Bobby was shot in Los Angeles. Ronald Reagan was shot within spitting distance of here.' His laugh was deprecating. 'Maybe I'll be *safer* in Africa.' He could afford to laugh. It was, after all, his own life about which he was joking.

'Security is a problem, Mr President,' repeated Gill.

'Security is *your* problem, not mine. You can't operate a presidency by running scared. If the mineral wealth of Lumbola is as good as reports suggests, we want access to it and to the port of Dakalla. According to these reports, Dakalla could be a key security base for us. But not if we don't show up at their big celebration. Just because we don't have to worry about Iron Curtains any more; just because we've done some hard thinking about the Middle East doesn't mean we can ignore Africa. A base in Lumbola would be attractive.' He glanced at Merchant's face and saw that he was still unconvinced. 'Look, Bob, I know what you're thinking but your own reports show that even the Chinese are making a big play. Gaddafi is working on the politicians in his own way. What's more, they say you could smell Castro's cigar in Lumbola within minutes of the announcement that the new state was being created. Both the UK Prime Minister and the French President are expected to follow my lead.'

'Castro's a busted flush. The CIS won't be there either.'

'Too preoccupied at home. All the more reason for us to get our card marked,' O'Brien tapped the CIA report, 'despite the swamps, malaria, and galloping diarrhoea.' With a casual, easy walk, he circled the room casting an occasional glance at the personal items which he'd brought to the Oval Office. As a lawyer with one of the big three law firms in DC, he'd had a major international practice before moving into politics following the death of his father. He knew all about Africa, understood the stresses and strains in Europe and had advised Third World governments on everything from immigration to irrigation.

By the time O'Brien had circled the room for a second time, his mind was made up. Cormack O'Brien was a reasonable man, renowned for being a good listener and ready to appreciate the other side of any argument but Merchant and Gill knew that nothing would shift him now. They looked at their President, tall yet slim, only the skin round his eyes showing the weight of the world's burdens. He paused to lean against the desk in front of his Secretary of State. 'Smile Bob! You'll enjoy this trip. Needn't even pack the Special K.'

'If you say so, Mr President.' Merchant's voice and tone showed his reluctance. 'So let me remind you that whilst Lumbola was a French colony, Sampopo was English. Both became independent about thirty years ago. Now they're to become Lupopo. Dakalla will be the capital. That's where the celebrations will take place - at the Palace. What Lupopo will lack is experienced management and a skilled workforce. The other thing we'll need to do is to cut out the corruption, the bribes. Once it starts, it's unstoppable.' Bob Merchant spoke with his slow drawl and as he did so he was flicking through Ralph Gill's report. 'See here. If the reports are accurate, then the uranium and other precious metals alone'll justify your air ticket.'

'I see you're coming round. But uranium? With Glasnost, the uranium would barely justify using my Frequent Flyer upgrade.' They all laughed. It was an in-joke among White House staffers that before becoming President he'd travelled 220,000 miles in a year and could have gathered a lifetime of Frequent Flyer bonuses. Now, he had free travel anywhere in the new presidential 747. The previous Air Force One, an ageing 707, was now at the disposal of the Secretary of State.

'Can I get back to security, Mr President? What we recommend,' suggested Gill, 'is that you land at Dakalla for the Independence Day celebrations, attend the banquet in the evening - that's the only local food you'll eat - and then fly out.'

'Fish heads and crocodile stew? Fine by me but just make sure there's plenty of steak and cookies on board. But hey! That's some schedule! Ronnie Reagan would have taken a week over it.'

'Not in West Africa, he wouldn't. Anyway, we want you in and out quick. Damned quick. Not everyone wants Western influence, let alone *our* influence in West Africa. By keeping it brief you just might avoid ...'

The President laughed. 'Malaria?'

'No, Mr President. Being blown to bits by some extremist. There've been rumours.'

Chapter 4

The city of Bristol has a long tradition of ships and seafaring.

It was from here that John Cabot sailed in 1497 and on landing in North America believed he'd found Asia. In Bristol too, the Society of Merchant Venturers was founded, exploiting the discovery of North America. The port flourished, exporting wool and leather. Wines, tobacco and cocoa beans were the imports.

Nearly 500 years later the city still thrives, its nautical history still evident. Isambard Kingdom Brunel's iron steamship, *Great Britain*, launched in 1843, is a reminder of the past as is Brunel's Clifton Suspension Bridge, which has proudly spanned the Avon Gorge since 1864.

Not far from the bridge, towering some eighty metres over the Avon, stands the offices of Brads - or British and Dominion Shipping to be precise. The company mirrored the changing faces of commerce in Bristol. Housed in a Georgian terrace of classic design, the building exuded stability.

A glance at the cars outside the offices would have suggested that the old shipping company was prosperous. A Mercedes 350, a Porsche 928 and a Three Series BMW stood in the car park. A second look would have shown that all were over six years old. Inside the building, the visitor could only be impressed by the reception. Its spacious grace was enhanced by the decor. In the corner stood an eighteenth-century grandfather clock. Around the walls were classical statuettes, paintings of storm-tossed tea clippers and a model of a giant tanker. Again, a second look would reveal the other part of the story. The leather on the chairs was faded, cracked and worn. The telephone system was outmoded. The carpet, fawn in colour and rich in quality, should have been replaced years ago. Threadbare in places, scuffed and dirty all over, it told a tale of a great company fallen on hard times.

Up the staircase, lined with heavy oak banisters and portraits in oil of past generations of Crawfords, the present owners were locked in discussion in the boardroom.

At the head of the Regency mahogony table was Sir Archie Crawford. On either side of him at the twelve seater were Susannah and Edward. At every place was a blotter, notepad and sharpened pencil, whilst in front of Sir Archie was a gavel. Above their heads was a thirty piece chandelier which threw its light into every corner of the panelled room.

Through the generous casement windows was a glimpse of the elegance of the Clifton Bridge. Around the walls were portraits of arrogant, haughty-looking Crawfords - former Lord Mayors of Bristol, Sir George Crawford and Sir Anthony Crawford, MP, VC. The wall at the end of the room was dominated by a painting of a schooner battling through Atlantic rollers though in the 1990s the storms were more likely to take place in this room. The harsh realities of high interest rates, an ageing fleet, unsympathetic bankers and a difficult market dominated their discussions. Recession was hitting them hard. Now, where once had been pride there was pressure, where once had been profit there was loss.

'That's settled then,' said Sir Archie. 'Two of Corbin's top people arrive tomorrow.'

'Should have done it weeks ago,' said Edward. The snap in his cultured voice matched the contempt in his eyes as he stared at his father. Similar in physique, nevertheless more than the generation gap divided them. The telephone call had been the culmination of a festering row about company policy ever since *Ryme Lady* had disappeared. As if to haunt them, a model of their missing vessel stood on top of a mahogony chest. 'I told you we shouldn't rely on our P and I Club.'

Sir Archie scowled. 'Not much point being members of a Club unless you let them handle something like this.' It was the voice of the old school.

'Not much point joining the IMB and not involving them,' Edward was quick to retort. Traditionally companies like Brads were members of mutual insurance groups, termed P and I Clubs which investigated losses. 'The whole rationale of the IMB is shipping fraud. We've put up with six wasted weeks and our credibility's shot. The bankers are on our tail. Creditors are closing in. If we don't watch it, the company's going to be sold up.'

Susannah, who had been listening to the regular sparring between her father and brother, felt the need to intervene. 'Come on, Edward. There's no point. Daddy persuaded us not to bring in the Bureau. We all agreed to leave it to our Club. After all, ship-owners have always relied on their Club, so what's the point in having an inquest now? Let's just face where we are.'

She flicked open the papers. Her thoughts were of how many hours they'd debated this, compared with the scant time given to the plight of the crew or their families. Though she was only twenty-nine, she had plenty of business experience. After graduating from Girton College, Cambridge, she'd served accountancy articles with Touche Ross. She'd been well trained, particularly in crisis management, insolvency and liquidation. These skills were all required now as Brads reeled from its adverse cash flow. 'There's today's computer print-outs. A net outflow of funds. A balance sheet supported by mortgaged ships with a dubious value, one of which has now sunk. No cash payment for it. Who knows what the security's worth in this market?' Her smile was forced as she looked at her father. 'Visiting the bank is more painful than going to the dentist.'

'Credibility - that's the problem d'ya see?' said Sir Archie, as he leaned back in his chair and exhaled the smoke from his stubby Havana cigar. 'I know what people are saying around the Baltic Exchange and in the City. They're saying we sank her. That's why insurers won't pay out.'

'Not much point in us sinking her and not getting any insurance money. Doesn't make sense.' Edward reached for his fourth chocolate biscuit of the morning. None at all.' As always, he was dogmatic.

Susannah nodded her agreement. 'If we'd been paid out, then it would have made sense. Pay off the mortgage and use the rest to tide us over.' She pointed to the Profit and Loss Account. 'Look at our income. It's a nightmare. We can't go on with both *Cerne View* and *Adber Arrow* lying idle. It's a matter of credibility. People are worried that we'll sink another one and so they won't charter with us. Oh ... did you hear that Captain Scutar's wife is demanding a Board of Trade Enquiry?'

'Yes. I'd heard,' said Sir Archie 'but I doubt she'll get one. Ships do founder. Ships do sink. Crews are lost, especially in the Far East.'

'There's only one answer.' Edward was emphatic. 'With no income from *Ryme Lady*, no pay-out from insurers, we've got to get some charters, get some income. Three vessels, that's what we *were* down to. Now only two. Not even two the same.' Edward looked with loathing at his father as he sat, toad-like, hands joined across the expanse of stomach. 'Your great idea, your master-plan,' he spoke contemptuously, 'of moving into the oil market was none too special, was it?' He stared down his father. 'There's *Adber Arrow* lying off Piraeus. 180,000 tons of useless deadweight. Losing money by the second. We've got to get an oil cargo for her. As for *Cerne View* ... ' His voice trailed away as he imagined their other vessel laid up and rusting down in Piraeus. Edward's heavy eyebrows nearly met as he looked across at Susannah and then at his father. 'Ironic, isn't it. Our charter brokers say the only interest in chartering two ships comes from Klodinsky's Mentocca group. *He* trusts us. Well ... I for one am not flattered or deceived.' The look on his face said that his father most certainly was. Even Susannah felt that she was under fire for not giving him the support. She sighed as she watched Edward preening his hair. How she hated being stuck in the middle. 'I don't trust Klodinsky. You mark my words. He knows the truth about *Ryme Lady*.'

'I'd give us just days to get a charter. Otherwise our bankers will ... ' Susannah's voice broke, preventing her from stating the obvious.

'Yes. We all agree about that.' Sir Archie eyed the clock and his thoughts turned to lunch. 'If I hadn't feasted the manager down in Corn Street so often, we'd already have receivers in. As it is, the bank's Head Office in Leadenhall Street want us to sell up the options.' It was the first time that Sir Archie had raised this touchy topic. The horrified looks from the two listeners said it all.

Edward's florid face blanched. The lower of his two over-smooth chins trembled. Susannah sucked in breath sharply and gazed again at the balance sheet. She knew better than anyone that Brads' development site was the jewel in their crown. The land was the only asset which was not depreciating and even that was barely holding its own.

'What! Force us to sell our options now?' Edward's tone was incredulous. 'That's mad. Typical bankers. Only worried about their own bottom line. Write off billions in South America and then squeeze people like us who've been with them for generations.' He helped himself to coffee as he spoke. 'I suppose this is Jason Meers at work. Miserable little creep. An Open University degree and a closed mind. Ideal qualities for a banker.' Edward sat forward, so that his stomach was pressed against the rim of the table. The podgy hands were clenched into tight white fists, masking their usual bloated pinkness. 'If there's a forced sale of the options we'd be nailed to the floor on price.'

He thought of the prime development site on the Bristol waterfront, close to the Floating Harbour. 'It's the best undeveloped fifteen acres in the city. Planning permission's just round the the corner.' The intense green eyes, a legacy from his mother, flashed angrily. 'I know those bastards' game. The bank'll take over the options themselves and then make a killing. How long is it before the options expire?' The question was asked of Susannah, who was the detail person. Edward had little time for that. He preferred the role of strategist, a position which brought him into perpetual conflict with his father. The old man prevented change, was suspicious of expansion.

'Fourteen months. If we can't raise five million pounds by then, the options lapse. With planning consent, getting a loan will be easy, but not otherwise. Not bankable, they say. If we can just hold on ... we'll get that consent within six months. Then that land will be worth a large fortune, even in the present market. It'll solve everything.'

'I'm sorry, Susannah,' Sir Archie spoke kindly as he looked at his daughter who had inherited all her mother's beauty, grace and elegance. 'I met Jason Meers at the Atheneum Club last night. Far from putting up any funding so that we can exercise the option, the bankers want us to scale down, d'ya see? The stark choice is to sell a ship ... or sell the options.'

'Over my dead body,' barked Edward, thumping the table. 'That bastard Meers. Never supports you when you need it. Pontificating in his suede shoes and golf club tie.

Kicks you when you're down. Sell a ship! In this market! Don't make me laugh. It just shows he knows nothing about shipping. Hah! Plastic boats in the bath's all he's fit for.' Sir Archie as he listened found it hard to disagree. Instinctively though he found it hard to agree either. 'As for the option,' continued Edward, 'just in case you've forgotten, it was me who spotted the site. Screwed an amazing deal out of the owners.' The rounded face and snub nose were unattractive, whether in repose or in anger.

What Edward said was true. 'No, we haven't forgotten. You've never let us.' Sir Archie's handsome features, his skin bronzed by the Barbados sunshine, broke into a sardonic smile. His eyes narrowed beneath the crinkled, brown skin. He flicked a speck of ash from the front of his crisp white shirt. The strong face under the well-groomed silvery hair froze into a sneer of hatred. When he spoke again, Sir Archie's voice was almost a growl. 'It's you who's blocking us dealing with Klodinsky - the one person who would take both ships on decent charters. It's *you* who's ruining our cash flow - *you* ... the great positive thinker.' The barb was sharp and it struck home. Edward was always rubbing in that his father was too negative.

Edward looked furiously at his father, hating the smirk which he saw but the irony of the role-reversal was not lost on him. Usually his father was cautious, slow to see opportunities, let alone to exploit them. Now it was Edward who was using his veto to prevent a life-saving charter deal. Deliberately he decided to ignore the sally. 'There's another possibility. Our brokers are sniffing out some charterer. Wants to send a cargo to Lumbola in West Africa. Meantime, the options stay. No way will some toadying friend of Jason Meers pick them up cheap through a shady bankers' deal.'

'Well ... we'll never sell a ship. Not in the present market. And that,' Sir Archie finished with a triumphant jab of his cigar across the table, 'brings us back to Walter Corbin's Bureau. If his boys can show we didn't sink *Ryme Lady*, we'll get the insurance cheque. Then our chartering prospects would improve. It wouldn't just be Klodinsky. Until that happens ... we're shot to buggery. That's why I say we should do a deal with Klodinsky today.' His face and voice rose as he showed his exasperation. 'It's money. Why wait? Why risk everything?' He stubbed out his cigar and paused while the clock finished chiming twelve. 'Come on Edward or we'll miss the Paris flight.'

'You're both going to see Klodinsky?' Susannah's surprise was genuine. 'Daddy, why are you going too?'

'Because I don't trust Edward. Klodinsky's our life blood. His name on a bit of paper would be a transfusion. We can question him about *Ryme Lady*. You're condemning Klodinsky without any evidence. I'm prepared to deal with him. Anyway ... there's nothing else I can usefully do here this afternoon.'

'And that goes for most days,' snapped Edward. 'Waste of time. For both of us. We're *not* chartering to Klodinsky. He knows what happened to *Ryme Lady* and, for my money, he's the one that sank her. After all ... he'd have cleared 60 million if the cargo never went aboard. That's worth killing Captain Scutar and the crew for, isn't it?'

Chapter 5

To the accompaniment of an angry toot from a following vehicle, the taxi containing Sir Archie and Edward, pulled up outside Klodinsky's office in the Avenue Rapp. They got out, paid the driver and stood momentarily in the Paris drizzle. Sir Archie was wearing an expensively-cut, navy-blue overcoat. Edward was in a belted fawn trenchcoat which emphasized the indulgence of his stomach. A passer-by would have recognized them as father and son without a second glance. The similar build and the way they moved were the clues. Recently however, Sir Archie had developed a slight stoop though he remained a fine looking man. Edward, in contrast, was unprepossessing, missing out on the looks of both his parents, having to use snappy dressing to give an illusion of style.

Edward enjoyed the good life, gold cufflinks and Jermyn Street handstitched shoes and suits. The shirts were monogrammed, the ties only of the finest silk. He dined fashionably and was regularly to be seen at Le Gavroche, Lasserre, the Waterside Inn or Le Cirque in New York. His bachelor pad, close to the office, was lined on one wall with vintage wines which he hoarded, counted regularly and drank in quantities of which neither his liver nor his doctor approved.

'Klodinsky's on the third floor,' said Edward looking at his notes. With the wind gusting and drizzle and darkness falling, Sir Archie hastily followed his son into the building.

'Now remember, Father,' said Edward imperiously, 'no hints of our desperation. Play it my way. We'll probe a bit, make him feel uncomfortable. I'll winkle out his back-

56

ground more deeply than before we chartered *Ryme Lady*.'

'We'll grab his money and run,' said Sir Archie in sharp response. 'We've got no choice.'

'You'll be quiet! We'll play it my way.' Edward slammed shut both argument and the lift door at the same moment.

Twenty minutes later Sir Archie and Edward found themselves standing in the now driving rain. The air was full of the tooting of horns as the French drivers angrily fought their way home, pushing their Renaults into gaps which were never there, switching from lane to lane with mounting impatience. Yet there was not a taxi in sight as Edward struggled to put up his umbrella, the two men huddled close beneath it.

'Pleased with yourself?' growled Sir Archie. Though he couldn't see his father's face, Edward recognised the sneer of contempt. 'You told me to leave Klodinsky to you. That's what I did. I'd say you've all but signed our liquidation.' Sir Archie turned sharply. His fury was all too evident. His face was contorted with wrath, drips of water in danger of steaming on the puce complexion. 'Probing and winkling ... pah! Baloney!' The rasping growl came from deep within. Edward stared him out, fixing his eyes on his father's shadowy features. 'God knows what your education taught you. It certainly wasn't tact or commonsense.'

Edward's voice was raised. 'Bollocks! I thought it went well. Good meetings are short meetings. I don't give a fig for Klodinsky's feelings. I really let him have it! I'm telling you - his success was all too quick. Too brash.' He paused to watch his father's expression, to make sure that he was listening. 'He's a ship-sinker and I'm going to prove it. With the help of the Bureau.' He shook his head. 'Klodinsky's just candyfloss. Too good to be true.'

'Come off it. Granted his offices are vulgar in their ...' he searched for the word '... their opulence but he's entitled to his luxury.'

'No. Not that - his offer. Doesn't make sense. Why does he want to charter both ships from us on such generous terms? He doesn't need to be generous. We need the money. So I say beware of Klodinsky bearing gifts. Mark my words - if he charters from us, we'll regret it.' They walked a few paces further before Edward stopped, transfixed. 'My God! I bet he's found out about the options.'

'Oh! For God's sake! How could he? He's just a good businessman. He can see a profit if he charters. I can see a profit for him ... and salvation for us.'

'It's the options. That's the key. I bet he's heard somewhere. Suppose he charters from us and then screws us - maybe fixes another sinking.' Edward glanced up and down the road in frustration. Still not a taxi. There was no reaction from his father except that Sir Archie threw a good two inches of cigar into the rain-filled gutter. 'Another sinking would destroy what little credibility we've got. We'd have to liquidate or sell up the options on the land. That's when Klodinsky'd pounce. Pick up Brads' shares cheap and control the options, whether we like it or not. The five million option fee he'd scarcely notice. Pin-money.' Edward's voice turned nasty. It matched the hatred in his face. 'And as for you. You'd charter to anybody. One day I'll tell you why. Now .... is not the time.' Edward wiped some rain from his face and then moved forward to hail a passing cab into which they bundled, eager to be out of the rain.

'*Defense de fumer*,' said the driver, glaring at Sir Archie who was about to light another cigar. With obvious irritation Sir Archie stuffed it back in the holder. It did not improve his mood. 'Handle Klodinsky! What a joke! You think you're street-smart, don't you! Well, I'm telling you: Carl Klodinsky is streets *ahead* of you. He's offering us money, a lifeline if we charter to him. We've got to take the deal, discuss it with these fellas from the IMB.'

'Only sensible thing you've said.' Edward was not one to be flustered.

'And we'll do what they recommend,' said Sir Archie. It was a command.

Edward shook his head. 'We'll listen. Then we'll decide. That's final.'

The cab turned off the Avenue Bugeaud and went through the Place Chancelier Adenauer. Then it turned into the gravel drive of the chateau which housed the St. James's Club, just off the Avenue Foch. The Citroen swung round the fountain and pulled up at the steps leading to the entrance. A commissionaire appeared with a giant umbrella and led them inside to the tiled reception.

'Dining here tonight?' Sir Archie's question was certainly not an invitation and there was only a slender veneer of politeness.

Edward started to walk up the sweep of the majestic staircase, past the magnificent floral display which dominated the landing. 'No. I'm dining at the Tour d'Argent.'

Sir Archie didn't show it but he was relieved. He didn't want to share his son's company. 'Anyone I know?'

'No. And you?'

Sir Archie's face revealed nothing of his inner thoughts, which were of the brothel which he had visited regularly for many years. 'I'll be dining here, then ... er ... I'll be going out. Take the air. That's if the rain stops. The cab to the airport will be here at 8.30am.'

Two hours later as Sir Archie was enjoying *Sole Véronique* in the Club dining room, Edward was in a traffic jam about a hundred yards from the restaurant on the Quai Tournelle. Susannah, back in Bristol, was having a quiet drink with a friend. Charles de Penichet was rather older than her with latinate features. Although she hadn't known him long, she'd come to love, no - that was the wrong word, admire his style. He had a ready laugh, easy banter. He was interested in the affairs of Brads and had a well-travelled worldliness about him. When they danced, his sure-footedness and the firm grip around her waist made shivers run up and down her spine.

As they sat in the red velvet intimacy of the small bar, they clinked glasses of *Kir Royale*. Seated on a comfy sofa, he had his arm draped around her bare shoulders. For the past few minutes he had been trying to lift Susannah's spirits. 'Things can't really be that bad,' Charles de Penichet said soothingly.

'I'll tell you after tomorrow's meeting. Daddy and Edward get back to meet these top people from the Bureau.'

'Tell me about them,' de Penichet's voice was soft, kindly, inviting confidences. 'Top people may mean nothing. From what you're telling me, time's running out.'

She looked at the candle which was spluttering by their drinks. 'Brads' future is about as short as that candle's. Daddy and Edward just don't get on. Their philosophy is different. Their lifestyles are different. Their policies are different.'

'But their objectives are the same ... the salvation of Brads surely?' Charles' face was serious and caring. He pressed his hand on hers.

'Oh yes. I suppose so. But Brads has become a shameful thing, like a cat without its pride. You see, Daddy used to run the company so successfully. It was easy then. You didn't have to be that good to succeed. Times are harder now. The old boy network isn't enough. He's yesterday's man.' She turned her head and gave a nervous laugh but her tone was serious as she continued. 'Now Edward knows it all. Well ... He knows it from the book. Doesn't understand people. That's where Daddy scores.'

'They ought to be a good team.'

'You'd think so but it just doesn't work.' Her face looked sad. 'Our problems aren't just about ships. Daddy understands ships. Our problems are about cash flow and balance sheets. Daddy doesn't understand any of that. To cap it all, we've got to have sufficient money to exercise our valuable options.'

De Penichet looked at her sharply. 'Options? You haven't told me about that.' He drained his glass and delicately popped a gherkin into his mouth. 'Tell me more.'

Susannah shrugged. 'There's not much to tell.' So locked was she in her thoughts that she scarcely noticed de Penichet's hand tightening its grip across her shoulder. Neither was she aware that he had moved just a fraction closer to emphasise togetherness.

'I'll tell you what. The table's ready. let's talk through there.'

Later, much later, when the coffee was being served and Charles was soothing her with his gentle voice and dancing eyes, on the other side of the Channel, Sir Archie had just entered the luxurious *salle d'attente* of the brothel on the Avenue Victor Hugo. The Madame who had let him in, disappeared and returned with Chantelle, clad in a brief leather outfit with black boots. She greeted him warmly, just as one would a long lost friend. 'Sir Archee! So long time! Why you not come?' She pouted as she leant forward to kiss him with lips which were narrow and hard.

'You look as wonderful as ever, Chantelle.' He pulled her close to him. Her perfume prompted memories of previous visits. God! If only she were in London and he could see her more often. Better still. In Bristol. 'You're right though. It's been too long. I've been all over the place - Africa, the Far East, the USA, Barbados, everywhere but Paris.'

Chantelle led him down the corridor and into her boudoir where along the wall were canes, whips, masks and a giant thonged crucifix. 'We 'ave fun, *n'est ce pas*?'

'Just like the old days.' Sir Archie's eyes rolled in pleasure as he re-lived some moments from the past.

Chapter 6

Gavin Blair manoeuvred the open Mercedes to the left for the Bristol exit. It had been an awkward journey down the M4. The delays for central barrier repairs had added half an hour and had done nothing to ease the tension with Art. He glanced at the clock. 'We'll just about make it. We've caught up a bit of time.'

'You've done well,' responded Art, his first friendly words in two hours. Throughout the journey he'd been sniping, carping and griping about Britain, the British Government, British roads, British weather (despite the fact that it was a beautiful sunny morning), Walter Corbin, *Ryme Lady* and lousy, stinking Brads.

Gavin had tried to humour him, hoping that they'd get a rapport. Despite it all, Art had remained 5' 10" of misery and they were no more a team than opponents in a tug-o-war. Art's irrational behaviour suggested deeper problems, not necessarily connected to Theo. Nothing made sense. Gavin tried again. 'This is where my legal career ended.'

'Failed attorney, weren't you?'

'I was a barrister. My father sat in the Court of Appeal. My family was steeped in the law but it didn't run in my blood. I never liked it, the politesse, the whole concept of litigation as a lawyers' game. So when the end came I wasn't unhappy.'

Art was scarcely interested. 'So how did the end come?' They were on the M32 now, speeding on the elevated section through the suburbs.

'At the Bristol Crown Court, in front of Mr. Justice Cawder, I was claiming big damages for a poor sod who'd been brain damaged. It was an easy case in front of anyone but Cawder. He'd already given me three hellish days when he asked me, "but Mr Blair, what is your best point?"

"M'Lud," I retorted. "That was my best point." I'm telling you, Art, it was a good point. It was a winner. Well, this Judge who had spent twenty years as a barrister getting rich on brief fees from insurance companies, wasn't going to have it. "Mr Blair, I've been listening to you for half an hour. I'm none the wiser."'

Art seemed interested. 'So?'

'Well I debated for a split second. The case was lost anyway. Should I say it? Well, I did. I looked up at the Judge and, using a hackneyed phrase, brought my career to an end.

"M'Lud. You may be none the wiser. You may never, ever, be any wiser. You are at least better informed."' Gavin laughed at the recollection. 'You can imagine - the old boy's horse-hair wig jumped nearly a foot in the air and his face turned puce. "I've had enough of your insolence, Mr Blair," Cawder said. "I shall be reporting you to the Bar Council." As I was a condemned man anyway, I thought I'd get in the last word. "If I may say so, Your Lordship, that's the only correct decision you've taken all week. I do congratulate you."'

Art's laugh was coarse and guttural but with a sign of respect in it. 'You said - *screw you* ... to a High Court Judge?' He shook his head in appreciation. 'But ... it was you who got screwed?' Even as he was speaking, Art was seeing Gavin in a different perspective.

'Yes. I was chucked out of my chambers. So I burned the wig and gown.' He glanced across at Art and saw that the respect was genuine. 'I really enjoyed that! Then I found the job with the Bureau.' His voice faltered. 'The only sad thing is my father's never spoken to me again.'

'Sonovabitch! That's some tale!' There was respect in the

voice. Art could relate to this. Gavin had certainly never expected such an appreciative audience. Art the player, the punchy New Yorker, the where-it's-at man had actually showed real respect.

'Did I ever tell you how I came to join the Bureau?' Art asked while signalling to Gavin to turn off the dual carriageway towards Clifton.

'Tell me.'

'We were on a drug bust. Off Norman's Cay - a small island about forty miles from Nassau. A joint operation with the IMB and the CIA. The Agency was headed up by a real regular guy called Matt Rees. Well, drug-runners were hijacking cruisers and yachts, killing the crews and then using the vessels for the coke run.' Art's face broke into a grin at his recollection. 'Hell! Was that some shoot out! Three dead, seventeen arrests. For a while I was on a high. Then I realized I was sick of the lousy life, lousy drugs, lousy drug-dealers, lousy chicks, lousy, stinking Miami.'

'So that's why you joined?'

'And for more danger, keeping in the fast lane.' He hesitated, as Gavin was quick to notice, even though he was concentrating on manoeuvring the white sports car through the narrow streets of Clifton.

'No other reason?'

'You mean you hadn't heard?

'No. What?' Gavin wasn't sure if he had or hadn't.

Art looked discomforted. Volunteering didn't come easily. 'I was fixed ... framed by as big a sonovabitch as you'll ever meet. I went from hero to kicking boy in less than a minute.'

'But the Bureau still took you on?' Gavin wasn't sure what to believe.

Art's confidence had returned. 'Sure. Eric Ellen believed me. I was pretty much down at the time.' He glanced out of the window and saw that they had pulled up outside Brads' offices. 'Let's go and sort out these assholes.' Then he grasped Gavin's arm. 'No. Hold it! Just remind me about Brads. Keep it simple. Remember, I'm the dumb one.'

'Sir Archie holds 60%, Susannah and Edward got 20% each when their mother died. Without *Ryme Lady*, all they've got is the oil tanker, *Adber Arrow* and *Cerne View* which is a mixed container and cargo vessel. Both in hock to their bankers.'

'That'll do.' Art picked up a perspex folder. It contrasted with Gavin's slim black briefcase in which everything was in place, from pens to mobile phone, from dictaphone to paperclips. The briefcase was like his brain - well-ordered with the facts neatly marshalled. His appearance too was conventional: a navy blazer, club tie, grey flannels and highly polished black shoes with tassels. Art, in contrast was wearing a pale lemon coloured shirt, open at the neck. His brown leather jacket was frayed and losing its colour. A pair of marble-washed jeans and cowboy-style boots made up the rest. A close observer like Gavin would have noticed the built-up heels. Gavin judged that, in his bare feet, Art would lose nearly an inch.

They waited in the faded refinement of the reception, Art looking out of place as he bustled round like a blow-fly. In contrast, Gavin stood quietly by the window, cool, languid and balancing every move like a Grand Master.

'Good morning, gentlemen,' said Sir Archie's secretary, as she descended the staircase. 'Won't you come up?'

'Ain't never been called a gentleman before. That's their first mistake,' muttered Art to Gavin as he lit his fourteenth Camel of the day. They filed up the oak staircase passing the line of Crawfords in oils on the way.

Forty minutes later the visitors had examined the models of all three vessels. They'd studied the photographs of the crew, had checked *Ryme Lady's* cargo and had pored over the complex insurance papers. 'I can see why the insurers won't pay out,' prompted Gavin. Everyone nodded.

'So who's the big shot round here?' asked Art. The five of them were standing at one end of the room, beside the fireplace, whilst a young waitress, traditionally dressed in black with white apron, busied herself with laying out lunch on the boardroom table.

Sir Archie laughed. 'If you mean who calls the shots, it seems to be Edward. He's Chief Executive. Sometimes he even forgets that I'm still Chairman.' Sir Archie downed the rest of his gin and tonic and glanced round. 'Anyone else need a livener?'

Art's glass was quickly proferred for another scotch. 'No. I meant the shooting.' He nodded in the direction of the photograph of Sir Archie with an Olympic gold medal.

'That was Father. When he was younger,' said Susannah. 'Clay pigeons at the Helsinki Olympics.'

'Long ago, too long ago,' growled the Chairman, apparently embarrassed at receiving the attention. 'But Edward's been a bit sporty too.' He pointed at a picture of his son holding a pair of crossed oars.

'Cambridge?' enquired Art, though Gavin had already realized that there was no way that Edward could ever have made any Varsity team.

'No. Just at school. Never made it to Cambridge.'

'Sounds as if *Ryme Lady* could have done with some oars. Judging by the last surveyor's report, she was on her last legs. And they weren't sea legs either.' Art laughed at his own joke. As usual his laugh was coarse and throaty. It was followed by an embarrassed silence during which Art was not embarrassed at all. '*Ryme Lady* was just a disaster waiting to happen,' Art concluded as the tumbler of highland malt appeared.

'I wouldn't put it quite like that, old boy,' said Sir Archie, masking his anger with a patronising tone and an arm outstretched to pat Art's elbow. 'Shall we sit down? The table's ready.' If Sir Archie had hoped for urbane civility to break out, then he was mistaken.

Art flipped open his napkin and then thoughtfully eyed the swirled glass of whisky. 'How *would* you put it then? If she didn't fall apart because of rust neglect, then she sank because someone wanted her sunk. Was that you? You need the cash.'

Sir Archie's mouth dropped just a fraction before the disciplined muscles round his jaw held him in check. 'The crew were our responsibility, our friends, d'ya see ... Captain Scutar ... been with us since he was a lad.' The response came through clenched teeth, eyes and mouth narrowed at the same time.

'I'd say it was Klodinsky who sank her,' Edward intervened. 'Father and I met him in Paris yesterday. He wants to charter our other two ships. He's offering big money. Too big. Father wants to deal with him but I don't trust him.' He looked defiantly at his father. 'Klodinsky's come up from nothing, a Polish boy who went to New York. Now, he's worth millions from chartering.' He paused to fill his mouth with a generous slice of smoked salmon. 'He's cut corners,' he explained, waving a knife as he spoke. 'If that cargo never went aboard *Ryme Lady* at Singapore and insurers can be persuaded it did, he'll net a cool 60 million. That's how you get rich quick. Like Klodinsky.'

'So long as you don't get caught,' said Sir Archie. 'No, I didn't mean that.' His backtracking was hasty. 'Edward's got it in for Klodinsky. We need charters, d'ya see. I'd say he was our only real hope.' The conversation was broken up by the arrival of the waitress.

'How would you like your steak, sir,' she asked Gavin.

'Medium rare.'

'And you, sir?' She turned to Art.

'Rare. And I mean rare! Just cut off its horns, wipe its ass and slap it on a plate ..... ma'am.'

Susannah gave a quiet smile but Edward's face showed his utter contempt for the brash New Yorker. 'I'm seeing Klodinsky in Paris tomorrow,' commented Gavin in a damage limitation exercise 'and Art's off to the Far East.'

'And Corbin? He's the Director. What's he going to do?" We expected him, not a couple of his gofers.' Edward put down his glass and glared at Art. 'Especially when one of them has the manners of a pig and the intelligence of a mule.' Edward's tone was sharp, his public school vowels clipped and terse.

Gavin was back on the defensive. 'The Director's jetting off to Puerto Rico. Cargo of cigarettes has disappeared.' The response was civilised, the type of straightforward explanation which his upbringing had instilled into him.

It cut no ice with Art who grabbed his fork and pointed it at Edward. 'Now look here, you asshole. You just listen to me. Brads' fleet sure ain't the P and O Group, not exactly an Evergreen Line. *Ryme Lady* was a heap of shit. Your company's nearly bust. Despite that, you've got us - the best team in the Bureau. So just one more remark like that, Crawford and you'll wish you'd never stopped playing in your rowing boats.' Every word was accompanied by an aggressive stabbing motion of the fork, the gap across the table narrowing as Art leaned forward in final emphasis. Edward shifted uneasily under the glare and lowered his eyes to avoid confrontation.

Sir Archie sought for the right word but it was Susannah who broke in. 'I'm sorry Mr Lemman. Edward can be a bit abrasive. We're glad you're here. We need the help.'

'You've got a lot to prove. Firstly I want ... ' said Edward sullenly but the waitress returned, stopping him in mid sentence. As the young woman busied herself round the table, Edward's moment had passed. Genial chit-chat prompted by Gavin lightened the atmosphere and Edward's point was never made. Instead everyone concentrated on the excellent steaks and crisp salads.

Later, after the main course had been cleared and the cheese had arrived, the port was doing the rounds. Gavin let it pass him by. 'Are you sure?' queried Sir Archie who could not envisage anyone turning down his beloved port. 'It's Fonseca '66. Laid down when we could afford to buy it.'

'Driving,' said Gavin, full of apology as he shook his head.

'And I'll stick to scotch,' said Art, so that Susannah rose to get the decanter. For a moment all eyes were on her, the visitors both admiring her tall shapely figure. With her elegant walk, she seemed full of assurance, a hallmark of Roedean. Since the Bureau photograph had been taken, she'd had her hair cut short so that it fitted tightly round her oval face. Her hooded but alert eyes made it easy to forget that she had all the hard-nosed cynicism of a city accountant. *Not someone to cross* had been Gavin's assessment. Beautiful she certainly was. but with the cool, distant allure of a television newsreader, someone to admire from afar. Everything about her appeared reasonable, her life seemingly as well-balanced as one would expect from a chartered accountant.

In contrast to Gavin, Art had been trying to guess what Susannah had on underneath her red suit. Tights or stockings? Matching red bra and pants? Or black silk? Not wearing any rings either. Just a heavy gold bracelet which looked large on her slender wrist. 'Anyway, if we don't charter to Klodinsky, we face receivership or liquidation,' said Susannah as she returned with the malt.

'Damned bankers.' Edward's hatred showed itself through the white of his knuckles as he clenched his fists.

'Got us by the balls. Castration imminent.'

'The Profit and Loss Account's so bad I even dream in red now.' Susannah's smile was desolate.

'I'll tell you what Klodinsky's game is.' Edward spoke as if everything which was about to follow would be fact instead of opinion. 'He sank *Ryme Lady*. Destroyed our credibility. He charters again - both our ships. Then plays silly buggers ... not paying up for the charter. We kiss good-bye to our cashflow. The bank sell us up. In steps Klodinsky to buy up our shares cheap. Picks up the option.' He turned to Gavin for support. 'I want you to prove it.'

'The brokers say not,' said Sir Archie. 'Oh ... there's some vague talk from the brokers that someone might want to charter *Cerne View* for a run down to Lumbola and Nigeria. I'm not convinced.' He popped a juicy, purple grape into his mouth and eyed the cheese lovingly. 'Won't anyone else have any of this cheese? The Stilton's quite delicious.' Times may have been hard, carpets may have been frayed but the food was worthy of a Michelin Three Star.

'I'll give you a scenario,' interjected Art, flourishing his tumbler. 'Brads had the most to gain. You sank it, fixed it with Scutar or the engineer. You assumed your insurers would pay out. They usually do. Bye-bye rust-bucket, hello cash. I'm told that *cash* is a rare commodity round here. There was no other charter lined up for her. No income. Just the expense of a special survey.' He pointed at each of them in turn. 'You sank her.'

Sir Archie roared with laughter, head thrown back. 'I wish we'd thought of it. Then again ..... I'm not so sure. Cracking idea if insurers do pay out.'

Susannah frowned. She never did like her father's extravagant approach when he had been drinking port. 'Scarcely a cracking idea,' she said contemptuously, 'for the crew or their families.' Her tone was curt.

Art was impressed and his raised eyebrows showed it.

He gave her one of his rare smiles, warm and seductive. The reward was just a slight colouring of her cheeks. Stockings, he decided. Silk underwear. Black probably. It would go well with the rich huskiness of her voice. 'In murder cases, cops always check out the family first. I don't see ships no different.'

Gavin had been watching Edward closely. He'd seen the blood run to the man's cheeks and had noticed a tic start to twitch angrily beneath the right eye. Then Edward stood up, as if to make a speech.

'I think the time's come for some straight talking. Our Chairman should resign. He's led the company into the wilderness. Our Chairman,' he repeated the words with obvious contempt, 'won't run Brads as a modern enterprise. Now we can only write cheques by special courtesy of snivelling little bank clerks with cheap suits and shoes from a supermarket dump-bin.' He gave a derisory laugh. 'They call them *managers* these days.' He walked round the table and stood behind Sir Archie's chair and continued speaking as if his father were not there. 'Our Chairman, in days when shipping was easy, was a success. So why is he so inept, so increasingly inept?' He looked at each of the listeners in turn. 'I'll tell you.' He paused for dramatic effect. 'He's not inept. Running the company into the ground is just a deliberate policy. He *wants* this mess.'

'Why?' Gavin's question was quickly put.

'Because he wants to do me down.' Each word was said slowly, with calm deliberation. Like watchers at Wimbledon, the eyes of the listeners all switched now to the seated man at the head of the table. Behind him stood Edward, smug and defiant, his arms folded. Sir Archie slowly put down his cigar and glass of port. Then he adjusted his heavy, black glasses, pushing them back up onto the bridge of his nose, before turning awkwardly to face his son. 'At any time your remarks would be an outrage. In the

71

present circumstances ... I demand your apology or your resignation.'

'You, Mr Chairman, can get stuffed. I'm not resigning. Art may be right. Perhaps you wanted *Ryme Lady* sunk. Or didn't care. Now you're hell-bent on chartering to Klodinsky.' He pointed a stubby finger towards his father's head. 'You can win either way. Charter to Klodinsky and sell your Brads shares at the top. Alternatively, enjoy seeing Klodinsky destroy the company and me at the same time.' He jabbed his finger in accusation and his voice rose to a rasping crescendo. 'And you? You'd retire to your brothel in Paris to have your bum spanked.' Edward moved towards the door as Susannah gasped with horror.

'Is that a resignation? Shall I have it minuted?' Sir Archie was unruffled whilst Gavin sat spellbound, his eyes now turning to the son. What Edward said was making sense. He had a point. Sir Archie could win either way if the charters were struck with Klodinsky. Art too sensed that matters were coming to a climax. The entire room was silent except for the ticking of the clock in the corner. No one moved.

'No.' Edward grasped the door handle and started to open it, then changed his mind. 'Go on. Go on, Mr Chairman, sir.' The words were said with mock deference. 'Tell them about Mother, about how she died.' Watched by everyone, he marched across the faded Axminster carpet to the casement window, from which Brunel's bridge could be seen. 'A fall ... a nasty, long fall to the rocks from the Clifton Bridge.' His arm shot out in a sudden, fierce gesture, his finger pointing accusingly at his father. 'That's if you didn't throw her.'

The late afternoon sun glinted on the sweeping curves of the Clifton Bridge. Art and Gavin looked over the parapet, staring down at the confusion of rocks to their left and to the relentless flow of the River Avon, 250 feet below.

'Susannah's a deep one. What did you make of her?' Art threw his cigarette end into space and watched it tumbling until it disappeared from view.

'Friendly but calculating. Dispassionate. Don't-touch-me notices clearly displayed.' He cast his mind back to the nastiness of the last few minutes of their stay. 'She'd need the hide of an armadillo working with those two.'

Art nodded. 'That ... but maybe more.' He was looking down at the cold greyness of the mighty river which was nearing the end of its long journey to the sea. Soon it would meet the Bristol Channel. The wind ruffled his hair, showing just a hint of baldness at the crown. 'Suicide or murder?'

'I can't even guess. It's history. Probably irrelevant.' The north-easterly wind made Gavin shiver. 'Let's go back to the car.' He looked down at the dark and menacing rock formation. For a second he imagined the smashed bodies which had lain there - anguished wives, tormented husbands, worried solicitors and bankrupt dealers. It was a favourite spot. But in which category had been Lady Ingrid Crawford?

'And the other two? Scumbags, the pair of them.' Art paused to throw a stone over the bridge.

'Sir Archie's nobody's fool. OK ... he's old fashioned - the cut of his suit, the way he talks, his confidence in the power of the 'old boy' network. But there's gunmetal in that character. As for Edward?' Gavin quickened his pace towards the white coupé, parked on Sion Hill. 'He gets a bit of my sympathy. He's greedy, a product of the Thatcher years but he's frustrated.' He glanced across at Art to make sure he was still listening. He was. 'He's got to turn Brads round. If he doesn't, he's the loser. Not his father. Sir Archie's lived the good life, selling ships, just like the family silver, to keep himself in pampered comfort. Running down the business to spite Edward. Now there's nothing left. So it's down to Edward to fight to survive. Got to turn things round. Just like a supertanker, it's taking too long.'

'Well ... I've seen straighter corkscrews than those three. I didn't *like* any of them.' Art flung his jacket carelessly into the back of the car. 'I guess they're talented. Maybe it's their personalities which have screwed them up. I've met nicer folk in San Quentin jail.'

Gavin nodded thoughtfully as he fired the engine into life and swept off towards the motorway. They fell silent but it was not the leaden, brooding silence of the morning. As he accelerated up to seventy, Gavin was feeling relaxed and weary, happy to be saying nothing and feeling that perhaps a common bond was developing between them. No sooner had they hit the M4 than the phone rang. Art picked it up. 'Hello.'

'Gavin Blair?' The female voice at the other end was questioning.

'No. Wait one.' Art handed over the phone. 'Sounds just my type. Tell her you've got a hunk of real meat beside you, just waiting to pleasure her.' Art chuckled to himself.

'Gavin Blair. Who's calling?'

'I'm assistant to Carl Klodinsky. Claudine Flubert. He asked me to call you. He can't see you in Paris tomorrow. He's gone to his yacht in Cannes. He'd like to meet you there. There's a 9.30 flight, Heathrow - Nice. I'll meet you at the airport. Can you do that?'

Gavin had been admiring the accent. It was American with an undertow of French. Even over the phone there was a silky sensuousness to the voice. 'I'll be there. Bye.' He put down the receiver. That voice!

He explained the new plan to Art who was envious. 'Jeez! Cannes, you lucky bastard.' Then his face brightened. 'Still, Singapore should be interesting. Beautiful women, soft brown skin.' He reclined the seat a few more degrees and stretched. 'Yes ... I guess I'll enjoy myself.'

Chapter 7

The British Airways flight to Nice had landed a few minutes previously and Customs and Immigration had been a brief formality. Gavin, with only an Antler carry-on bag, had been one of the first through to the main concourse. There, he was faced with the usual battery of people, many of them holding names scrawled on tatty cardboard. Among them all, towards the end of the line, one stood out.

Claudine Flubert was clasping a smart white clipboard with Gavin's name printed on it in heavy black type. Even without that help, he'd have assumed that she had to be the owner of the voice which he'd heard whilst speeding past Swindon the previous day. She, however, seemed uncertain and her eyes were still flickering over the arrivals as Gavin moved towards her. This gave him the advantage of taking in as many details of her as possible.

Twenty-four. Maybe twenty-six, he decided. Perhaps 5' 7" tall, her skin was fresh, clear and tinted by the sun. Her eyes were invisible behind a large pair of red shades which matched the red necklace, bracelet, belt and shoes. The shortish, white, cotton dress hung loosely over her trim figure, giving her a cool appearance for the hot day outside. Her hair was mid brown, bordering on blonde, with highlights. It was without curls, cut short and shaped almost like a helmet. Though her eyes were hidden, her face promoted an image of sharp intellect whilst the small pouting lips expressed an invitation which the rest of her demeanour did not.

'Hi! I'm Gavin Blair.' As he spoke, he was able to take in the delicate pinkness of her lipstick and her fragrance of Georgio.

The hand which she extended was slender, well-mani-cured and varnished to match her lipstick. Her handshake was firm and cool but the smile was friendly. 'Welcome to paradise. I hope you like the sunshine, Mr Blair.'

'Call me Gavin. And yes ... I love the sun.' He watched as she removed her glasses, a movement which was without any purpose for, as soon as they were outside, she replaced them. However, it gave him the chance to admire her more fully. Now he could see the steady evenness of her green-eyed gaze.

Outside it was scarcely paradise. The air was heavy with the smell of aviation fuel mixed with the fumes from count-less taxis. These were jockeying for position, weaving impatiently in and out of the travellers.

Claudine led him to the car park where the metallic blue Rolls Royce Camargue awaited them. The chauffeur gave a respectful nod and touch of the cap as he took care of Gavin's bag. Inside was a cocoon of coolness, the air smelling of leather with just a touch of perfume. Gavin and Claudine each sat in a corner, turned slightly towards each other. She crossed her stockingless legs and waggled her foot in neat circles.

'No doubt it's been said before but I just love your accent. Where are you from?' enquired Gavin.

'Oh yes, I'm always being asked that,' Claudine replied without irritation. 'I was brought up in Manhattan by French parents. I worked for Carl there but then he moved me to Paris. I now run the *Paris scene*, as he calls it.'

'You're not running his office today.'

'Carl doesn't like the rain,' she replied with a laugh in her voice, as if that explained everything. 'The forecast for Northern France was cloudy. That was it. He decided to fly down yesterday. Tonight he flies off for oh ... somewhere or another.' Her voice trailed away. It was obvious she knew and that it wasn't her role to tell him.

'And where does Mr Klodinsky spend most of his time?' Gavin watched as Claudine re-crossed her legs and carefully adjusted the hem of her dress. 'Most anywhere but avoiding Nigeria and Central America.'

'Do you often travel with him?'

'Not so much since I came to Paris. I used to get everywhere. The best of everything.'

Gavin laughed. 'Lucky to have such an interesting life.' He was rewarded with a smile.

'Sure it was glamorous. It was fun too. Living high on the hog, first-class hotels, Concorde till it became boring. Famous people, vital meetings ... everything on the run. But now?' She lowered her eyes. 'That's in the past. Now I'm in the Paris office. I deal with owners, insurers, cargo, charter paperwork. Not much glamour now.' Her smile was sad as she spoke. 'Maybe I peaked too soon.'

Gavin wondered if there was just a trace of bitterness as well as regret. Was she out of favour with Klodinsky? A discarded mistress perhaps? 'And Mr Klodinsky? I suppose, like most successful people, he isn't always easy. Pretty demanding.'

'I didn't say that.' There was a touch of annoyance in her voice and her hands rose in protest.

He looked away, watching the thunderous traffic all around as they hit the autoroute. He'd have to remember not to push her too hard about Klodinsky. Not if he wanted to keep her on-side. 'Sorry, no offence meant.'

'I guess I'll forgive you this time.' It sounded pompous but not the way she said it. She was enjoying watching him, well aware of his dilemma. Klodinsky had briefed her well. Be polite ... but keep him defensive. *Stay on top*, had been his parting words. She looked restlessly at her watch as the chauffeur paid the toll for the autoroute and then accelerated without effort westwards past Juan-les-Pins and the turning for Cannes. 'I'm sorry! I forgot to offer you a drink.'

She reached forward, emphasising the outline of her breasts as she opened the mahogany faced cabinet. 'What will you have? I haven't looked after you very well.'

He looked at the array of sparkling glasses, neatly held by little clips. In the mirror-lined cabinet were refrigerated beers, champagnes and cocktails. Claudine wondered why he was taking so long over the choice but Gavin had been puzzling about why Claudine was so defensive. Did she, or rather did she and Klodinsky, have something to hide? For someone so clever, with so much beauty, so chic and so full of self-confidence, she seemed overly defensive.

'Some champagne perhaps? Claudine prompted. She pronounced it *purr-apps*. Gavin loved it.

'Why not! Sounds delicious.' For a moment, he thought of Art. He wouldn't have been so polite, so predictable. He'd have said something outrageous. And got away with it. He watched as she poured the vintage Laurent Perrier. 'Are you settled over here?'

It was her turn to pause, as she reclined to stare briefly out the window. She shook her head slowly. 'No. *Pas encore.*'

'But why? Paris is ... Paris. Everyone loves it.'

'I guess I miss New York, my friends there. I don't get to travel so much. More responsibility. That I like. I've a good team and Carl has provided me with a small apartment overlooking the Seine.' She glanced across, her eyes momentarily fixed on him. 'I just get lonely. I'd give anything to kick leaves in Central Park. I'd kill to smell bagels on 7th Avenue. As they say ... give me Manhattan.' She sipped at the chilled glass thoughtfully. 'My French relatives are dead. I've made no real friends yet.' Her expressive face showed her sadness.

'In Paris? You'll meet somebody soon.' Gavin hoped that he sounded convincing, despite the emptiness of his own life since Janie had disappeared..

'Perhaps. For now Paris has no charm for me. Sure, it's full of beauty but you need to be able to share it.'

'Sounds as if you left someone important in New York?' Gavin didn't want to pry too much.

'Matter of fact, I didn't.' She laughed in a self-deprecating way, throwing her head back as she did so. 'Someone left *me* there. That's why I volunteered for Paris.' She turned to look at him and then changed the subject. 'Your star sign. Don't tell me. It's my hobby.' She thought for a moment, looking him up and down. His physique was pleasing, muscular yet lean, slim yet well-built. 'You haven't said much. Not about yourself anyway. Now that tells me a lot. It tells me you're a good listener. You need to be that with me around.' She laughed again. Her lips pursed and her brow furrowed for a moment. She could have listed a few more characteristics which she had noticed. She could have explained the clues he'd given but instead she went straight to her conclusion. More impressive that way. 'An Earth sign. *Absolument*. You're Taurus.'

'That's amazing.' Gavin's open face beamed in pleasure. 'Some party trick. 16th May.'

They both laughed as Claudine emptied the bottle into their glasses just as the Rolls was leaving the usual crawl on the Croisette at Cannes. Ahead lay the quay. 'There's the yacht ... and that's Carl.'

Gavin looked where she was pointing. There he saw the elegant swept-back lines of a vulgarly expensive, spanking white gin palace. No quarter had been given to class or discretion. This was money - big and brassy. It broadcast 'I've-got-loadsa-bucks'. 200 feet long, it had a pair of engines big enough to fly the Atlantic, let alone sail it. Carl's *Polish Princess* was ostentation beyond luxury. Above them, the sky was now clear blue, the air clean, the midday sun warm on their heads. 'Does it have a diamond-encrusted bottom and a chiming loo-roll?' suggested Gavin as they walked towards it. He was rewarded with the biggest smile which she'd yet given him. She was about to reply with her own sardonic quip but decided that her boss was too close.

Klodinsky was standing at the stern, clasping the railings by a red and white lifebelt. He was 5' 4" tall, barrel shaped with a balding head which had eclipsed his neck during the past forty-eight years. In contrast to the pink wasteland of his head, his chest was covered in thick black matted hair which luxuriated from shoulders to stomach. The blue and white shorts divided the rippling rolls of his stomach from the short, stubby legs. The face had a watchful wariness about it, the jowls were heavy. The remnants of his black hair hung wispily round his ears. His eyes were tucked in beneath the intimidating sweep of his eyebrows. He could look angry without even trying and yet, when he smiled, there was a genuine warmth which was capable of disarming even the most ruthless interrogator. From around his body came several glints of gold, as thick and chunky as its owner.

'Good journey, Mr ..... ' said Klodinsky, ushering Gavin. It was a deliberate snub.

'Gavin Blair,' prompted Claudine.

'That's right, of course. Welcome aboard, Mr Blair.'

Chapter 8

Art's jumbo circled above the vastness of Singapore's Keppel Harbour on its final approach into Changi Airport. The port, one of the busiest in the world, was visible as a profusion of lights in the early evening sky. Shadowy outlines of oil tankers, cargo vessels and container ships could be seen everywhere. Some were waiting, some docking and some departing. And from there, he thought, as he looked down at the rows of docks, was where *Ryme Lady* had commenced her final voyage. In those waters, she had loaded with her hi-tech cargo. Or hadn't.

He looked inland and saw the high rises, tall needles of light, each one a symbol of the international prosperity which had replaced the colonial image. Today's Singapore was unrecognisable from the city which Sir Thomas Stamford Raffles had founded nearly one hundred and eighty years before.

Two years had passed since Art's last visit but, even in that time, there had been changes, more skyscrapers, more efficiency. 'Efficiency Rules OK?' would have been the graffiti message everywhere if the disciplined Singaporeans had been permitted to let loose with their aerosol sprays. Though cricket was still played on the Padang in front of Government House, the lingering vestiges of Raffles' city were ever harder to find, tucked away in the ethnic areas of Chinatown or Little India.

Feeling rumpled, crumpled, jet-lagged and with a bottle of bourbon circulating in his bloodstream, Art stood up to file out of the plane. Near the exit, crisp and with that cabin staff plastic smile was Carole. She'd looked after him on the flight. Mechanically she was going through her goodbye procedure until it was Art's turn. As he grasped her on each shoulder, she momentarily recoiled. Her reaction was not quick enough to avoid him kissing her on the lips. There was no response. 'Now you won't forget,' mumbled Art. 'The Mandarin Hotel. We've a dinner date.'

Looking embarrassed and flustered, Carole was relieved to see that the next passenger was still struggling with his hand-luggage. 'Thank you for flying with us, sir,' she said in a matter-of-fact way. Her voice then dropped to a hissing whisper. 'Not unless I ring we haven't.' Her voice rose again. 'I'm glad you enjoyed your flight, sir.'

'I'll fly with you anytime. Just any time.' With a wink and a leer, Art moved on. He'd always been lucky on flights, sometimes a hostess, sometimes a passenger. He reckoned to have perfected the technique. Give them a bit of banter, tell them about the unremoved bullets. Chuck in some bullshit and a generous topping of promises of the high life. In his sober moments, which even he had to admit were more isolated these days, he realized that his strike rate had been falling. But that didn't matter. 'Home or away, Art finds a way,' he muttered to himself as he joined the moving walkway.

After clearing Customs, Art spotted Ho Shi Li who was Lloyds' Shipping Agent in Singapore. The two men had never met but Art was aware of Ho's excellent reputation built up over thirty years. After brief pleasantries the BMW was speeding them along the dual-carriageway towards Orchard Road. Outside, the temperature was still nudging ninety. The humidity was like being wrapped in a steaming wet blanket.

Ho's English was good and there was little he didn't know about fraudsters in the Far East. In the 1970s, he'd played a key role in the *Ferit* investigations when even the complacency of the marine insurance market in London had become concerned about the multi-million losses in the Far East.

'Any news yet? asked Art.

'A breakthrough, I think.' His style was precise, neat, consistent with his well-cut suit made in Little India. The man's brilliantined hair completed the dapper image. '*Ryme Lady's* empty lifeboat has been found. Drifting off the West Coast, near Malacca.'

'Had it been used?'

'I think so. I don't know. No one does.' He paused whilst he switched lanes on the busy highway. 'What took place? Pirates maybe.'

Art grunted dismissively. 'Maybe she didn't sink at all, just changed her identity. Cast her lifeboat adrift.'

'It happens.'

'But not if the lifeboat was *used*.'

The black limo crossed the Benjamin Shearer Bridge. Then it dropped into the heart of the city, an army of sparkling towers. 'Tell me this,' Art continued. 'Did the cargo go aboard? If so, then did *Ryme Lady* put into some small port and secretly offload, before being scuttled?'

'There's no evidence of that. No buzz of illegal cargo sales. No sign of the ship. No sign of the crew. Everything checks out.' Ho's face, silhouetted across the car, radiated his own confidence.

'If the cargo went down with the ship, then it wasn't fraud. No point. Not unless you're only in it for the hull insurance. So ... my guess is it never went aboard.'

'Care to check that out now?' There was a staccato in every sentence. He spoke with the rhythm of a metronome. 'Want to visit the cargo sellers?'

'At this time?'

'If we go straight there. The Pi Fau Pang Export Co. is not far.'

Moments later the chauffeur drove the car into the

83

underground park beneath the office block off Shenton Way. On the sixteenth floor was the suite of offices of the Pi Fau Pang Export Company, whose appearance was opulent, legitimate, permanent. Ho spoke to the Chinese receptionist in mandarin. After a few moments' explanation and an internal telephone call, Ho confirmed to Art that Mr Tsang would see them in a moment.

'These guys? What's the background?'

Ho hesitated for a moment. He didn't want to be unfair. 'Nothing known against them. They've traded for three years. Fast movers. Very successful. The documentation for *Ryme Lady's* cargo was in good order. So you want my view? Sound, beyond reproach.'

They were standing by the window, looking across the lights of the city. Art's head was throbbing. The flight was catching up with him. Impulsively, Art went over to the receptionist. 'For Chrissake? What's the delay?' His voice was raised, his tone hectoring. Only the opening of a solid wood door prevented a tirade of abuse.

'Mr Tsang will see you now.'

An hour later Art and Ho had leafed through the box-file of papers relating to the shipment of goods. $60million of Singapore's finest computer equipment, videos and televisions had apparently been loaded. The destination had been the Middle East. The Arabs were back in the market again after the Gulf War.

Mr Tsang had been delighted to co-operate, clasping his hands piously as he had watched them. As necessary, he had summoned up paperwork which they wanted, had answered questions with calm efficiency. Tea, juice and minerals had been provided. In short, Mr Tsang had been the perfect host during their unexpected visit.

'Is this the lot?' enquired Art.

'It's enough. The cargo was shipped. All checked aboard. All the signatures obtained.' Mr Tsang's moonlike face broke into a smile of satisfaction. His eyes were stead-fast behind the lunette spectacles. 'After that, Mr Lemman, the problem is not ours. The insurance was in place. It's the charterers - Carl Klodinsky's company - who were in charge. End of story.' Again Art was fascinated by the man's English, spoken in machine-gun delivery.

Art thumped the desk as if it belonged to him. 'Why is everyone so goddammed complacent!' He stood up sharply. 'The cargo insurers haven't paid out. Neither have the hull insurers. I suppose you don't care, do you? You've been paid. Have the insurers been here, asking questions?'

Mr Tsang's grin seemed to split his face completely this time. He enjoyed the frustrated anger of the American.

'Sure. Plenty of questions. Same answers.'

Chapter 9

The cruiser's skipper and four man crew had skilfully manoeuvred the floating gin-palace away from the quay. Then the Australian skipper gave the engines a bit of throttle and, moments later, they had left the shelter of Cannes Harbour and were making thirty knots through the deep blue water of the Mediterranean. The boat powered forward, its bow high in the water, its flags fluttering brightly, the spray gleaming in the morning sun.

On the upper deck, Claudine was sprawled out in a black bikini, a large white sunhat tipped forward over her face. By her side was a book on astrology, a selection of sun oils and an expensive leather make-up bag. On the deck below, Gavin, having changed into a blue casual shirt and white shorts, was seated with Klodinsky. The breeze swept through Gavin's thick sandy hair, masking the temperature which was hovering in the high seventies. In contrast, the tufty remains of Klodinsky's hair fluttered above the chunky black stems of his sunglasses.

'I've told the skipper to cream it down to San Tropez. There we can swim from the boat. Relax a little. Then eat. We'll talk later.'

Gavin nodded in agreement, stretching out a lean arm, still bronzed from his spell in Kuantan. The movement took in the luxury which surrounded them. 'It's some lifestyle you've got. Rather different from my life in Barking. Down there, it's all graffiti, unemployment and the smell of jellied eels from the shop by the Tube Station.' His nose wrinkled in memory of the other world, the real world he'd left behind.

'Well, today at least you're here.' Klodinsky's tone was

friendly, a continuation of the disarmingly welcoming approach which he had adopted ever since Gavin had arrived. 'I've fought for this. Worked hard. I enjoy the sun, the sea. *Money* itself is not important to me. I enjoy its power. Take this cruiser. It cost me over 10 million bucks. Besides paying the crew, the fuel costs $200 an hour. So what? I'm single. I don't want to die rich. Anyway,' he helped himself to a black olive, 'it's good for me. 'Nothing personal but if you weren't here, I'd have time to think. Clear skies and a sea breeze - nothing better for taking tough decisions.' He pointed towards the bow. 'Ever jet-skied?'

Gavin looked at the two jet-bikes lashed to the deck. 'No.' It was a no which meant that he'd like to try.

'It's easy. Let's race before lunch.'

The cruiser was anchored, bobbing just slightly on the swell. Gavin took his place for lunch under the blue and white striped awning at the vessel's stern. Klodinsky stood at the foot of the sheer steps leading to the roof deck. 'Joining us for lunch, Claudine?'

'Thanks, but no. I'll grab the sun while I can.' The voice was muffled and Gavin felt disappointed at the refusal. Klodinsky merely shrugged and then sat down, noticing as he did so that Gavin was massaging a large bruise on his right hip.

'Jet-skiing's not as easy as it looks, is it?' consoled Klodinsky who, only an hour before, had been saying quite the reverse. Despite the mask of Klodinsky's face, Gavin was sure that it had been deliberate. 'You'd soon get the hang of it.' He poured champagne for them both. 'You did well for a novice.' Klodinsky's tone was pleasant. Too pleasant.

As he listened, Gavin thought of the jet-skiing. Humiliating. Couldn't even kneel on it, let alone stand up like Klodinsky. He'd been battered, bruised and nearly drowned but the real pain came from Klodinsky's patronizing tone. Now Gavin knew. It was all so clear. Step by step, he'd been out-manoeuvred since his arrival.

He watched Carl amble across the deck and put on a yachting cap. Though it fitted him well, his wiry black hair stuck out sideways, making Gavin want to laugh. Yes ..... he thought. You're a clever bastard, Carl. You're one-nil up because it's your boat. Two-nil up because of the jet-skiing. Three-nil up because you've been so damned nice. He squeezed lemon onto the lobster and admired the Salade Nicoise which was ready to follow. 'Right now, put me down as an aching, battered and bruised novice.' He could still hear Klodinsky's laughter. Guffaws of it had accompanied Gavin's attempts to master the jet-ski at twenty five knots.

'Now - *Ryme Lady*. That's why you're here. What's your game? No *impertinent* questions, I hope. Ah! ...' He stopped as a member of the crew appeared, carrying some messages. Gavin could not be certain. If he'd had to put money on it, he'd have said that Klodinsky had deliberately started the conversation, having spotted the crewman approaching.

'Some faxes have arrived for you. I'm sorry to interrupt your lunch.'

'Goddamned paperwork!' He dismissed the uniformed youngster with a flourish of his hairy hand and then read the messages. As he did so, his finger made circles in the hairs on his stomach. Then, he scribbled notes in heavy black writing from a gold pen with the thickest of nibs. 'Sorry about this,' said Klodinsky but the tone didn't suggest that he was sorry at all. Indeed, Gavin wondered whether it suited his host to fragment the conversation. It kept Gavin on edge, kept him wrong-footed. 'Claudine!' he shouted. Seconds later, both men were rewarded with the view of Claudine's firm, brown legs as step by step they descended the ladder. 'Type up these messages for me, can you?'

'I'll do it now.' She smiled at them both. 'Enjoy your lunch. Looks good. I'm sorry I turned it down now.' Gavin thought he detected a fleeting sharpness in the flash of her eyes as she patted her slim, golden brown stomach. 'I needed to keep an eye on this,' she added as if an explanation were necessary. She wandered off with a casual but provocative wiggle. Gavin watched his host's reaction. Did Klodinsky find her figure of interest or was the obsession with balance sheets all-consuming? Had they a relationship? Or was it purely business? So why should I care? Why? Because she's so bloody gorgeous, that's why, he told himself. Whatever Klodinsky thought, he said nothing though his eyes lingered on her black bikini bottom until she was out of sight.

'Where were we? Oh yes. *Ryme Lady*. You're from the International Maritime Bureau. The IMB - Incompetent, Moronic and Bumbling. That's what they call it, don't they?' Klodinsky didn't wait for a response. 'I've heard of it, of course. Full of failed detectives and shipwrecked sailors. Which were you? Shipwrecked or failed?' Klodinsky picked up his glass and clutched it like a baboon with a banana.

Gavin laughed nervously. 'I was ... and am a lawyer.'

'A lawyer!'Carl's face and voice showed that he viewed lawyers as he did rodent exterminators. 'Lawyers, lawyers, lawyers! The world's full of them. Crawling everywhere like maggots out of rotten meat. Lawyers breed out of filth. So they become filth.'

Gavin shrugged off the insult with a laugh. 'Anyway, don't underestimate the Bureau. You just might regret it.' Gavin put down his cutlery and held the glass of champagne by its elegant stem. 'When *Ryme Lady* disappeared, your company had chartered her. Apparently she sinks in calm seas, with no Mayday and no survivors. $60 million worth of cargo entrusted to an old ship like *Ryme Lady*. Now to me that prompts a thousand questions.' Gavin debated whether to say it and then decided to continue. 'Like maybe there was a quick fix.'

'Or like maybe there's a solid company offering cheap rates. Brads ... a good tradition in English shipping. Times are rough. My brokers screwed a good deal. OK. *Ryme Lady* wasn't new. She wasn't ready to sink either. You know that's true.' Chomping at his crusty bread, Klodinsky put his elbows on the small circular table, seeking to intimidate the listener with the fierceness of his eyebrows. He wiped his mouth with a flourish of his pink napkin.

'All that crap being talked, for God's sake!' He continued. 'Too much talk and too little thinking.' Klodinsky pushed aside his plate, having somehow managed to devour the lobster claw and salad whilst working and talking. He stood up and flipped open his cigarette pack and lit one. It was a mechanical gesture. 'You suggesting I wanted *Ryme Lady* sunk? Is that what you've been thinking?' Deliberately, as Gavin thought, Klodinsky notched up the New York Jewishness in his accent. 'Gavin ... may I call you Gavin? You take my wine. You take my hospitality. And now ... you're sitting there thinking that I sank *Ryme Lady*. You think I fixed a crewman ... the engineer maybe. Think I'm a murderer.' He waved his podgy arms in the air like a conductor reaching a crescendo. 'So you should think that? So you do me an injustice.' His jowls quivered, his eyebrows met in a frown of rare intensity. Then he laughed. Suddenly, unexpectedly. It was a laugh which showed that life was full of irritating absurdities. Like the International Maritime Bureau asking ludicrous questions.

Carl looked down beside him and then bent forward. From a small case he produced a slim folder of papers.

'Take a look. That's me. That's Mentocca, my group of companies. My pedigree: accountants, the best, lawyers, vermin though they are, the best. Chartering records for the '70s and '80s - the best.' He pointed to a pie-chart and a graph. 'That's our growth. That's our share of the Far Eastern market. Now look here ... er ... Mr ... er ... Gavin. I didn't build up that reputation by sinking ships. I don't *need* to sink ships.' He turned his hands palms upward in a gesture of openness. 'I don't want to play the bogus cargo game. I'm rich. Can't you see that? It's coming in so fast that my accountants can't even count it. Just one word from you and your one-horse Bureau and there'll be so many lawsuits flying around, it'll be like an eclipse of the sun.' He accompanied the threat with a fierce jab of his fork into a piece of steak.

Gavin met the man's stare with equanimity. If Klodinsky wanted him to flinch, then Gavin wasn't giving him the pleasure. 'You see, Carl, we have a shared interest.' Gavin deliberately slipped in the Christian name for the first time. 'You want your name cleared. The Bureau want the truth, want justice. So, apparently, do you.'

Klodinsky's laugh was mocking. 'Justice! Keep looking kid.' He clasped his hands behind his head. 'But yes, I want the truth. It's your tone. I don't like it. If you'd asked me to help you then ... fine ... that's good, Ok by me. But no. You threaten me, insult me, insinuate.' He tossed his cigarette angrily over the side.

'You told Brads you guessed the cargo must have shifted so that *Ryme Lady* capsized.' Gavin looked sincere but cynical. 'That doesn't wash, Carl. Not in a calm sea, not without a Mayday. And you know it. Now, tell me this. Why do you want to charter two more ships from Brads? It's risky, isn't it, with their reputation shot?' Gavin's sarcasm was obvious. 'Unless of course you know better. After all, it would suit you to sink them, wouldn't it? Only last year you told the Wall Street Journal that you were thinking of moving into ownership, thinking of diversification. So what better than kicking Brads into the gutter? Then pick up the company on the cheap from the liquidator. In the meantime, you pick up Brads' options.'

'Hey! What options? Don't give me all this! I don't need it. Options? What options? Buy Brads? Give me a cheap toy for Christmas any time. But Brads? Don't make me laugh. I just wanna earn bucks from chartering ships. Brads have the capacity. I've dealt with the Crawfords, Sir Archie mainly, for years. Now, I'm offering them a fair charter rate, generous even. Sure as hell, no one else wants to risk cargo with them.' He bit off a piece of celery with sharp precision and Gavin noticed the glint of a gold tooth as he did so. 'But buy Brads!' He laughed. 'I could massage Brads' profit and loss account all day long but where's the pleasure?'

'Are you kidding me or kidding yourself? You don't have to sink Brads' other ships. Just charter them.' Gavin stretched out his own hand and cupped the palm. 'Then you've got Brads right there. All in one basket. Your basket. You raise a phoney dispute. Don't pay. You'd find a pretext.' He made his hand into a fist. 'Squeeze Brads into submission. Kill off their cash flow.' It was Gavin's turn to lean forward so that their faces, both hot and perspiring, were close together across the elegantly laid table. 'Yes ... another little toy for your Christmas.'

'Dream on!' It was said in a mocking tone and without rancour. Gavin was disappointed. He'd wanted to push this man. Push him as far as he could.

'You've picked up other companies on the cheap. Like Calmex Steamship, for example.' There was silence. The Bureau's file of clippings had been right. He'd struck a weak spot by mentioning the Texan company which had filed for Chapter Eleven protection from its creditors. Klodinsky had bought it cheap amidst a flurry of allegations only three months before. He looked hard at his host, who busied himself with cramming an over-large lump of cheese into his mouth. It was time to be rude. Time to get a reaction. 'You're a corporate raider, Carl, a pirate without the eye patch, just waiting to unfurl the Jolly Roger.'

This was too much for the American who pushed his chair back with an irritated sweep and beckoned a crewman. 'Weigh anchor, will you. We're going back to Cannes. Fast. Our guest is in a hurry to leave.' He turned to Gavin. 'The interview's over. You'd better get changed.' He watched as Gavin stood up and then paused by the doorway. 'You've got a lot to learn.' Klodinsky's face was purple with anger.

Gavin's face hardened, his eyes narrowed and he sucked in his cheeks with a sharp intake of breath. Even his broad nose seemed to narrow as he set his face in a look of fierce determination. He was about to reply but thought better of it. Don't get mad, get even, he told himself. With a rapid movement, he left the deck, striding through the saloon, richly furnished with heavy white leather chairs, jade and marble *objets d'art* and littered with expensive hi-fi toys and a mirrored cocktail bar. Centre stage was a huge vase of flowers, specially flown in from Paris to fill the saloon with colour and perfume.

He descended the stairs to the cabins. They were lined either side of the corridor and he was about to enter his own when he paused. Impulsively he pushed open the door opposite and saw that it was Claudine's. Lying on the bed were her white dress, her underwear and red shoes. On the dressing table were her make-up and jewel box. The single bed had obviously been slept in.

He pushed open the next door and his face lit with pleasure when he saw that Klodinsky's bed had also been used. The room was cluttered with Klodinsky's bits and pieces. There was his clothing, his paperwork, his spectacle case and his aftershave. Gavin was just about to close the door when he saw, lying on a chair right beside him, a file marked Brads.

He glanced over his shoulder, his stomach knotted with guilt. He was alone. Quickly he flipped open the file. At once he almost dropped it. There, staring at him, was his own photo. A recent one too. Taken outside the Bureau. It had to be recent. He was wearing his new raincoat. He flipped over the page. There followed photographs of Art, Sir Archie, Susannah, Edward and Walter Corbin. Then there were details of Brads' fleet. Quickly he flicked through the chapter headings. *Option Agreement*, *Profit and Loss Account*, *Balance Sheet*, *Pen Pictures*. Christ, he thought, Klodinsky's been doing his homework. There were enquiry agents' reports on Sir Archie, Edward and Susannah. They too had been followed.

Fingers trembling, he turned back to the page on Sir Archie. His breathing was tense, his nerves taught. Trying to concentrate and to listen out for someone coming was not easy. All was quiet except for the steady roar from the engine as the cruiser buffeted its way towards Cannes. 'Excellent War record. Unhappy personal life. Wife Ingrid died 1988. Inquest returned open verdict but talk of murder persists. Are rumours well founded? Wife had three known lovers (See below). He, known to be highly sexed. Regularly visits brothel on Avenue Victor Hugo, Paris. Not to be underestimated. Man of drive and energy despite his years. Reluctant to see his son Edward take over. Facade of ...' Gavin heard footsteps behind him. Panic-stricken, he put down the file and retreated the two steps into the small passage between the various cabins.

'I'll get changed.' The voice unseen was Claudine's. She appeared just beside Gavin in the small gangway and looked surprised. 'Oh, it's you.' Her tone was not unfriendly. There was just a slight frown of puzzlement wrinkling the otherwise smooth flawlessness of her skin.

Gavin reddened and shifted nervously from foot to foot, a sheepish grin on his face. 'Where's the loo?' It was the best he could think of to cover his embarrassment. 'I can't find it anywhere.' The question seemed to allay any suspicions which Claudine might have felt.

She laughed. 'You mean the john? You should have guessed. After all, you *are* on a boat with a diamond-encrusted bottom.' She winked at him and smiled generously. 'There's one *en suite* for each cabin. Gavin grinned stupidly. She pushed open his cabin door. 'Look. That mural slides back. On the other side is your own mini-gym, a restroom, jacuzzi, sauna. You name it. It's all there.'

'You're right. I should have guessed.' The grin changed to a smile.

Claudine's voice was hushed for a moment, slightly conspiratorial. 'Carl tells me you're leaving. I'm sorry.' Her slightly aquiline nose, which gave a firmness to her features, softened when she smiled.

'Me too.'

'I wanted to join you for lunch but Carl had told me to decline. He only offered as a gesture.' Gavin found it easy to guess why he'd not wanted any witness to the conversation. As they stood looking at the brash mural of a reclining nude, he wanted the moment to linger on. He hovered, not wanting it to end, intensely aware of her fragrance, a pleasing mix of sun oil and perfume. 'Didn't my horoscope predict a sudden departure?' Gavin's eyes twinkled.

'Yes,' she said simply. 'I knew there'd be trouble.' It was no answer, as Gavin appreciated, but he let it pass as she continued. 'But I'm still sorry. I was hoping we could have had a twosome for dinner up in the Old Town. Carl's got to fly off this afternoon.' Her mouth gave away a moment of sadness. 'I don't think I can do that now. Carl would go ... you know. Maybe some other time. The stars are good for us.' Then she pulled the door shut and was gone, leaving Gavin to wonder just what his horoscope had predicted. He let out a sigh and headed for the luxury of the multi-pulse shower and fluffy monogrammed towels.

Gavin walked down the short gangplank onto the quay-side. In the mid-afternoon sun it was busy with jet-setters joining or leaving their tax-haven-registered yachts. Mingled with them were the bystanders, the sightseers, the curious, all anxious to rub shoulders for a moment with a lifestyle which was beyond them and yet so tantalisingly close. 'Thanks for the ride. No doubt I'll be seeing you again,' said Gavin as he avoided shaking hands with Klodinsky.

The American's face said *I doubt it*. For a moment their eyes met and not a great deal of warmth passed either way. Klodinsky's eyes were glazed, defensive and discreet. His clothes were not. For docking he had put on a garishly multi-coloured beach shirt, lilac Bermuda shorts and green sneakers.

'One final warning. I shall be watching, waiting for one false word. Just one innuendo against me.' He shook his head decisively. 'Give me the chance and you'll find my lawyers bite.'

'Legal rottweilers are they? Let them try.' Gavin's hair, still wet from the shower, stayed firmly in place as he rocked his head back in an exaggerated laugh. 'If you think you can deflect me by threats, then you'd better think again.'

'Don't count on it. I'm warning you. Be careful Mr Blair.' Klodinsky's face had a knack of showing anger well. Dark brown anyway and heavily wrinkled, the penetrating glare from beneath the awesome eyebrows completed the ferocity.

Gavin shrugged, turned away with a fixed grin and strolled along the quay, sensing the hostile stare in his back.

The farewells had attracted a share of interest and he could also feel the eyes of the curious upon him. After fifty yards such thoughts dispersed. What next? Where to go? Had it been a success? Or a disaster?

Impulsively, he took one last look at the touch of luxury which he'd enjoyed. Klodinsky's rainbow-hued clothing had disappeared. Up on the sundeck, Claudine was leaning on the rail and looking in his direction. He waved and was rewarded with an instant response, a quick, nervous wave, as if she felt guilty. He continued walking, glancing back occasionally, until the vessel was out of sight and he had reached the Croisette, where he hailed a cab.

'Nice Airport', he commanded the driver and continued the debate in his own mind. So why did Klodinsky have photographs? Why deny that he knew about the options? His own file showed that he did. Why have a file at all on Brads? Impressive research. Pity he hadn't finished reading it.

At the airport, he approached the British Airways desk. 'I'm sorry sir.' The young woman sounded sympathetic. 'Would you like the bad news or the bad news? You've just missed a flight to London. Our next one is in four hours. It's over-booked and there's a long wait-list.'

'So how do I get back to London,' he enquired.

'I suggest you get routed via Paris. You'll pick up a flight from there quite easily.'

Gavin thought for a moment. 'Fine. Do that please.' He waited whilst she organized the tickets.

'You'll get the seat allocation at Air Inter, just over there. You're a bit early for the flight. You might get a good seat if you try now.'

'Thanks.' He was about to take her advice when, on impulse, he decided to ring the Bureau in the hope of catching Walter before he left for Puerto Rico.

'Sorry Mr Blair,' said the duty officer in Barking. 'You've

just missed Mr Corbin. Not ten minutes ago. You'll get him in San Juan, tomorrow.'

'Thanks. See you.' He wandered aimlessly round the concourse towards the Air Inter desk. Since Janie had walked out, his flat had seemed uncomfortably empty and the prospect of flying back to London over the weekend was unwelcome. Ok, their relationship had deteriorated. Ok, he'd had to devote more time to the Bureau than either of them would have wanted. But hell! Simply to walk out! No explanation. Just a scribbled *goodbye*. *That* had hurt. Not a word from her ever since. Not then, not ever. He wondered where she was, wondered if she were happy. Had she found someone else? Not that it mattered. She was just history, a sexy, sultry, moody, selfish piece of history. Such were his thoughts as he joined the queue for seat allocation.

'That's the Athens check-in over there.' The familiar voice brought his thoughts to an end. He turned and saw Claudine directing Carl Klodinsky to the check-in further down the Departure Hall. Neither of them had seen him. He saw Klodinsky nod his head in acknowledgement and then put his arm briefly around her shoulders before kissing her lightly on the cheek. It was an affectionate gesture rather than an amorous farewell. Seconds later he had got his ticket and in his pale blue suit, strolled towards Security with a corpulent gait, his small Gucci case in his hand.

Alone now, Claudine headed for the Paris queue. There she saw Gavin and looked startled. 'Hi!' he called. 'Let me save you queueing. I've been routed via Paris. Looks like we're on the same flight. If you've got a ticket, I'll get us two seats together.'

Claudine, still looking surprised, gave a quick smile, her cheeks dimpling and her eyes softening as she did so. 'Of course. But I thought ...'

'So did I.'

Art's evening in Singapore had not developed the way that he'd wanted. Having said goodbye to Ho, he'd checked in at the Mandarin Hotel, whose twin towers dominated Orchard Road. He'd showered, clearing his head under the torrent of the high jet stream flow. Having started to towel himself down, he was looking forward to a slug of scotch. It had been a while. The telephone killed that pleasing line of thought. 'Ah! Carole,' he said to himself as he hurried towards the phone. He'd been telling himself that she'd be in touch.

'Hi!' The enthusiasm in his voice died as he realized that it wasn't Carole after all. 'Oh, it's you Ho.' His tone changed to irritation. 'What do you want?' He didn't mean to sound curt. 'Sorry. I was expecting a date!'

'Excuse me for disappointing you. I hope I'm not going to spoil your evening. But here's something! I was checking out some old reports. The day *Ryme Lady* went missing, the crew of a fishing boat were murdered in Malacca. At the time it wasn't significant. Now? With the lifeboat being washed up near Malacca, there just could be a connection. It may be nothing but ... the timing's interesting.'

'Agreed. I'd better go there. But how?'

'Drive up the West Coast. It'll take four hours or more. Or you could fly to KL and then drive south from there in just over an hour. If you hurry, you'll catch the last flight out tonight.'

'Kuala Lumpur? Jeez! I guess I knew there was a reason I hadn't unpacked!' He laughed sardonically and thought for a moment of Carole with her wide smile and slender waist. Hell, probably she wouldn't ring anyway. 'And Ho ... thanks for your help. Appreciate it.'

Art had barely checked out of the hotel when Carole telephoned. 'You say Mr Lemman's just checked out? Ten minutes ago? Did he say where he was going?' She paused. 'He didn't? No message. Oh thank you. Thank you *very* much.' Her face was taut as she put down the phone and reached for a cigarette. 'Bastard,' she muttered under her breath as she would have done about an awkward first class passenger. 'I bet he does that all the time.'

Chapter Ten

In the White House it was early morning. The President had just dismissed his secretary from the room with a smile. Now he was alone with Ralph Gill from the CIA. 'Any advance on the jaunt to Dakalla?'

'Well in hand, Mr President.'

Cormack O'Brien removed his spectacles and rubbed his tired eyes. He'd been reading too many reports overnight. 'Still concerned about security?'

'No more than anywhere else. Security'll be tight, Mr President. Your Secret Service team will take charge of your motorcade and your personal safety. The Lumbolans are dealing with security in Dakalla generally.'

'I want a briefing paper on this merger.' The President sat down, closed his eyes and clasped his hands in front of his chest as he was lost in recollection from the past. 'I've spent time in Africa. Nothing is more racist than two African tribes. No hatred is more intense. They can make black and white in Mississippi seem like best buddies.'

Gill nodded thoughtfully. 'Not everyone's happy. There are a few shit-stirrers. We'd told you that.'

The President replaced his glasses and fixed Gill with a cool stare. 'Then, to use your phrase - who's stirring the shit-stirrers? That's what counts. Talk to London, will you. Work with them. More coffee? I guess we need to keep a close eye on this.'

'Rest assured, Mr President, we are. And thanks but no for the coffee.' He closed his file. Inside was the report which had arrived from Dakalla the previous evening. It read *Security - fears of unrest during celebrations. Hard to guarantee safety*. There was no point in alarming the President with detail. His men were working on it. Anyway ... there always was talk, there always would be threats. The difficulty was knowing which one to take seriously.

The taxi containing Gavin and Claudine was crawling slowly around the Peripherique, the clogged road circling Paris. Friday evening rush hour represents the height of Gallic confusion. Tempers are frayed. Horns are blasted. Engines overheat. Collisions take place with ever increasing frequency. The wail of ambulances are a constant backdrop. To all this, Gavin and Claudine were oblivious as they headed for the Champs Elysées.

During the flight a warmth had grown between them over champagne and canapés. 'And you're quite sure about dinner tonight?'

'Yes,' replied Claudine. 'Not tonight. I'm very tired. Carl is so exhausting. Like a small child. But lunch tomorrow?'

'Call my hotel in the morning. We'll fix something. I got the last room at the Chateau Frontenac.'

'There's one condition,' her voice hardened but her hand brushing lightly against his arm softened the impact. 'No more of those questions like on the flight. If you want a friend ... that's one thing. If you want a witness ... then count me out.'

'Understood.'

Having studied the map, Art had decided not to fly to Kuala Lumpur. Instead, he hired a Proton through Reception and within an hour was leaving Singapore Island behind him. Traffic was light on the causeway linking Singapore to Malaysia and across the border, the streets of Jahore Bahru were quiet and empty. The contrast from the bright glitzy cleanliness of Singapore was hard to believe. It was as if he'd turned the clock back. Political uncertainty and the growing influence of fundamentalism in Malaysia contrasted with the squeaky-clean single-minded materialism of Singapore where even chewing-gum was now banned.

Moments before there had been the high rise blocks. Now he was speeding instead through darkened shanty towns. Up the coast these gave way to small communities, fishing kampongs, the houses on stilts briefly lit by his headlights. The road was good but the overnight traffic, mainly timber lorries, was heavy and progress was slow. By 2.00 am he'd crossed countless rivers, creeks and flat uninteresting scrubland before turning westwards from the main highway. Ahead, the straight road was empty, the kampongs deserted. He was alone, passing through areas of deep humid forest, sinister and threatening. He thought of the story of the lorry driver who'd stopped to urinate and had never been seen again. All they'd found was a contented python with a bulging waistline. It was not a place to break down and he felt more comfortable when the first lights of Malacca flickered into view. Though only a small port, it was the first place of substance since leaving Johore Bahru nearly three hours before.

At 4.15 am, the girl at the Ramada front desk was surprised to receive a new guest but was cheerfully welcoming. He booked a call for 8.00 am and then collapsed exhausted on the bed, his head still full of the throbbing of the engine which he'd hammered too fast through the black night. For a flickering second he wondered whether Carole had phoned, about what was happening in London and how Gavin had been getting on. Then sleep overcame him. Unusually, he hadn't needed the help of the duty free.

At 8.00 am and refreshed by the depth of his sleep, Art was eager to get to work. A couple of telephone calls later, he'd got a meeting fixed with the police. Outside, the morning was less than invigorating, the air humid, the sky overcast with heavy black clouds threatening a deluge at any time. As he sauntered through the ancient town, hands deep in the pockets of his black jeans, he was oblivious to Malacca's history. Though each street contrasted with its neighbour, Art noticed none of it. Only Chinatown stirred him. It was all bustle, noise, the air heavy with tempting aromas from the many cafés and food shops. Other than a glass of orange, he hadn't breakfasted. Yes, he'd look forward to a good Chinese meal.

The police inspector was waiting at the bridge over the river at Jalan Hang Jebat. He was short, slightly built, olive skinned and looked efficient in cap, white shorts and shirt.

'Right on time,' said Art, tapping his watch appreciatively. 'I'm Lemman. Art Lemman.'

The police officer replied in English, spoken with a curious accent. The high pitch of the voice didn't help. 'Inspector Manuel D'Silva. Where would you like to start? Where the murders took place?' He saw the American's nod of agreement and together they walked slowly through the exhausting, steamy heat of Jalan Laksamana where children played noisy and exciting games in the dusty streets.

'You speak good English. Better than mine! How come?'

'My ancestors came here three hundred years ago from Portugal. They say about two hundred of them married local girls. So I have European blood. Here in Malacca we are mixed. Very mixed,' he chuckled. 'My grandmother was English.' The little man turned to look at the chunky figure beside him, the small brown eyes sincere and friendly. 'One day I want to visit Portugal. The dialect which we speak here is Cristao - it's like Portuguese was spoken four hundred years ago. I want to see London too – Buckingham Palace, Arsenal Football Club.' If he'd expected to be offered a conducted tour by Art, then he'd have been disappointed. The American was scarcely listening.

As D'Silva was talking, they were passing the Majestic

Hotel. Other than its name, Art could see nothing majestic about it any more. D'Silva pointed at the faded arched gateway briefly. 'English history,' he cackled. 'The rubber planters used to go there for cocktails at sundown.' He gave another derisory laugh. The small hotel, with its fading blue paint but grand sign conjured the image of gin and tonics and the voice of Noel Coward somewhere in the background.

'Monument to a failed empire,' growled Art. 'So tell me about the three fishermen.'

'The owner, Mansur Ibrahim, was a married man, aged about thirty eight. The two crew were the unmarried sons of his brother. His brother died many years ago.'

'And the two widows?'

'The brother's wife left here many years ago. As for the owner's widow? She's gone back to her mother in Kuala Lumpur.'

'A rich widow?' The implication was obvious.

'No!' The denial was emphatic. 'Most fishermen here make little money. Some of the traders, like Mansur Ibrahim, do better. Mainly the small boats here bring in charcoal. Once it was spice, gold and drugs. That's all changed.' He stopped to point at a small café. 'That's where they ate.' The windows were dripping in condensation, the name written above the door was in Cantonese. It looked precisely what it was: a place for the locals to congregate, to set about *Yong Tau Foo* or *Laksa*. It was cheap with no frills. A few people were sitting at the Formica-topped tables. 'There were no witnesses. The owner says they ate well. According to him they were laughing a lot. Also, they were carrying a large bag.'

Art's face showed his interest. 'Was it heavy?' he said quickly.

'Witnesses say yes. When they'd eaten, they walked across to here. Where we're standing. It was well after midnight. Mansur Ibrahim's car was parked here.'

'They were shot here?'

'All three. The bag was never found. The killers took it with them. We know the motive must be theft. As to the killers, we are getting nowhere. Someone heard a car drive off.'

'Did this Mansur guy normally carry much money? Or smuggle drugs ?'

'Drugs are a possibility. His reputation was not good but we'd never caught him.'

D'Silva waited patiently whilst Art walked over to the café and imagined the last moments of the three fishermen, elated by whatever was in the bag. The streets would have been quiet, the night dark. Twenty-five paces further on there must have been at least two killers waiting. The surprise must have been total. 'Were the fisherman armed?

'No. So ... shall we go and look at *Ryme Lady's* lifeboat?' Without waiting for a response D'Silva started to lead Art through the narrow streets, past temples, mosques and ancient ruins. At one point he paused and pointed to a rock by the river. 'Big lizard, eh!' The lizard was more like a baby crocodile, at least three feet long and utterly motionless, perched a few inches above the chocolate brown opacity of the water.

Down by the mouth of the river, the inspector chattered away about the ancient junks, high-bowed and with raised poop decks, their white sails lowered to lie drunkenly across the bleached blue paintwork. Near the sea, the river was no longer lined with houses, low, dark and with tin roofs. Here the river was wider, maybe eighty yards across instead of the twenty yards further up. Beside the moored junks were a few small fishing boats. 'The main fishing fleet is upstream. Many, many boats, small and purple-painted all of them. Only the larger ones are here. That one there was used by Mansur and his crew.' He was pointing to a larger boat than Art had expected, not as big as the junks but a sturdy, firm, sea-going vessel, ideal for plying to and from the Sumatran coast.

'Can we go aboard?'

D'Silva shook his head firmly. 'No. We searched it at the time. Nearly seven weeks ago. We found nothing. No drugs, nothing suspicious. The bag. That's the clue. Whatever was in there would explain everything.' The Inspector could see from Art's face that he was weighing up the possibilities of getting aboard, with or without consent. 'I don't recommend you go aboard without consent.' The warning was serious if understated.

Art laughed. 'Me? No way! That's your job. Now, where's the lifeboat?' He watched as D'Silva hurried along the path to a shed with a rusting red corrugated iron roof. He unlocked and opened the door of the old store. Inside, amidst the musty gloom and the smell of damp rising from the earth floor, Art saw the spanking white of the lifeboat and the name *Ryme Lady*. He felt a slight shiver go through him. He leaned against the boat, grasping the woodwork near the stern. It was a solid, even eerie reminder that Captain Scutar's crew were more than just names. D'Silva flicked on the light.

'It was used?' Though Art was asking the question, he was already forming his own judgment.

'Crumbs of food. Pipe tobacco. A used match. A can opener. Empty beer cans.'

'Interesting, but proves nothing.'

'And fingerprints. At least nine different sets. When we've finished checking it out, Brads will be told.'

'Motor been used?'

'The fuel tank was only half full.'

'Any blood?'

'Not that we found.'

107

Art opened up and had been examining the cowling. Then he sniffed the engine, studied the plugs. 'The motor was used. Could the crew have put ashore?'

'Yes. Weeks ago. The lifeboat was washed up yesterday. It wasn't there before. The man who found it lives at the spot. As you see, it was undamaged. No reason to abandon it.'

'Not unless they were rescued.'

'By whom?'

'By the dead fishermen.' Art scrutinized the policeman's face. It was obvious that D'Silva, charming though he was, had no idea about ships and shipping fraud. Had he done so, he'd have known the significance. The tranquil olive brown of the inspector's features remained unruffled. If he was surprised or even shocked at the suggestion there was no sign. There was a slight shrug of the shoulders that said it was possible.

'Checked Mansur's boat for fingerprints? To see if they match?'

'No.' The intonation was that it had never been considered.

'Jeez! What do they pay you guys for!'

The police inspector was unabashed. 'Sure. We'll check it out.' The man's cap bobbed up and down in positive reassurance. Art didn't believe him. To the Malaccan police, *Ryme Lady* was an irrelevance.

About twenty minutes later, Art had finished his inspection and the giant bolt was slammed back across the door and the padlock replaced. Outside, Art stood thoughtfully. As his eyes re-adjusted to the brightness, he gazed seawards. Who knew that the bag was worth killing for? What was in it? Drugs surely ... or money. Payment for a boat-people operation? Unlikely. 'Good meeting with you, Inspector. Be sure and let me know about the fingerprints.'

'I will.'

Art did not believe him. Malaysia was not Singapore. Muggings, brutal attacks and murder were a daily feature and he reckoned that the files on the fishermen and *Ryme Lady* had been closed already.

He was right.

Art looked at the fishing boat. Moored amongst five others, getting aboard was not going to be easy. He felt the surge of adrenalin at the challenge. A quiet smile played round his lips. Tonight there would be action, danger. It would be just like the old days in Miami.

Chapter 11

Wearily, Claudine put down her bag. The expensively furnished apartment, high above the Quai Louis Blériot, overlooked the Seine. She glimpsed the lights from the factory opposite as she closed the heavy curtains. Even then, the noise of the wind-driven rain could still be heard as it beat against the picture window.

She sighed long and hard. Her face, so radiant when she'd been with Gavin, now showed her sadness as she looked around the comfortable cocoon provided by Carl. She'd found Gavin such fun, quick-witted and eager to make her laugh. If only ... She sighed again. Around her, the minute attention to detail showed the efforts of interior designers. Carpets matched curtains, curtains matched covers. The pictures matched the room. Yet it was not home and never could be. Home was New York. Home was a tawdry apartment at Lexington and East 73rd Street. There she had her own things, her own friends close at hand. Here, the opulent luxury which Carl had provided seemed only to emphasize that she was not her own person ... that she was alone.

Only her bookcase was a comfort. Though she had graduated from John Hopkins' University in Baltimore, there was no evidence of that. The volumes, large and small, all showed her love of astrology which she had studied on a vacation course at Columbia Greene Community College. Tonight though, she was too tired for that. She kicked off her shoes as she slumped into the depths of the leather sofa. Curling her legs up beneath her, she reflected on the day. In her hand was a glass of vodka-tonic, tinkling with ice and sharpened by a twist of lime. Had Carl reached Athens yet?

Had Gavin gone out to dinner? Why had she accepted his invitation to lunch? What did she make of him? Did she like him? Yes. Physically he was attractive, pleasing to her. Intelligent ... yes, he was certainly that. Interesting and funny too. Yet there was something calm and reassuring about him. Steadfast. Yes. That was the word. He didn't come on heavy. None of that Wall Street jargon and hype. In different circumstances he'd have made a good prop, an antidote to her own life which she planned through the planets.

She drained her glass, re-filled it and flopped onto the sofa. She yawned and stretched. If only she and Gavin could have ... Her thoughts were interrupted as the telephone rang. 'Claudine Flubert,' she said. Instantly she heard Carl's voice, slightly muffled and distant down the line. 'Ah, Carl! How was the flight? Excellent. And Athens?' She nodded her head as she agreed with his response. 'Yes. It always was a filthy city. But we had some good times there.' She heard his throaty laugh of agreement.

'And you?' Klodinsky enquired.

'Guess who flew back with me. Gavin Blair. Yes ... Mr Blair. He'd missed the London flight and so flew via Paris. He's weekending at the Chateau Frontenac Hotel.' Even as she was speaking, she could sense the developing scowl on her boss's face.

'Well, just remember,' Carl rasped, 'Keep your big mouth shut. I don't want that man prying into my business. I don't need that kind of hassle.'

Claudine was hurt at the suggestion. 'Cool it, Carl! You don't have to remind me. I know the way you operate - big deals in small rooms, everything discreet and low profile. Just relax.' She spoke slowly as if to reassure him. 'I've not told him anything but it's just possible that ...' her voice trailed away uncertainly.

'Go on.'

Her voice was faltering. 'I was going to say that he may take me to lunch tomorrow.' Her face puckered as she awaited the expected blast. It came in no more than a split second.

'No! No! No! Claudine no! I cannot agree. I cannot trust him. You ... I can trust but ... well, heck, the man's got charm. Know what I mean?'

Her voice was hard for the first time. 'I know precisely what you mean Carl. But you don't own me. I can take care of myself. I'll do what I want. And ... ' her voice lost its edge, 'don't worry. I won't be indiscreet. My loyalty is to you.'

She sensed that Carl was lighting a cigar as she heard nothing but sucked breath coming down the line. She imagined his fat cigar, glowing red to match his anger. 'Ok! Ok! I told you that I trusted you. Make me believe it.' The line went quiet and she wondered whether he'd slammed down the receiver. He hadn't. 'He's no friend of ours,' he growled.

'So why did you call?' She changed the tack of the conversation.

'I've fixed a meeting to check out Brads' tanker in the morning. It's down the road, anchored off Piraeus.'

'*Adber Arrow*?'

'It's a neat deal. Better still, there's no sign of anyone in the market for *Cerne View* either. If we can charter the pair of them, it'll be like a can-opener to the real soft underbelly.' There was a pause and the voice was brighter again. 'Say, check me out for a fool! Claudine, my love, you go ahead. Date this guy. Do what you like. Suck what you like, just so long as you suck out of him the last drop of what he knows about Mentocca and Brads.'

'Oh sure!' Remarks like that made her puke. It showed how Carl really saw her. Worse still, it showed her what she'd become. Though she sounded approving, she saw in stark terms the developing dilemma of loyalty.

'Things are looking good,' Carl concluded, 'but ...'

'But not for Brads.' She finished his sentence with a laugh. She'd heard Carl's pet phrase so often before. This time, no sooner had she said it than she felt guilty. Why should she feel so gleeful at Brads' expense? She wriggled uncomfortably on the sofa. Again, she sensed a conflict within her. God! She was sick of Carl's double-dealings and yet ... yet everything she was, everything she had was down to him. His influence was stamped on her like a brand on a steer's rump.

'You still there?' Carl's voice brought her back to the present.

'Oh yes,' she stumbled. 'I'll be in the office on Monday. Talk to you then.' She put down the receiver. Her face was white, her emotions drained. She knew it. Every muscle and sinew told her. She was trapped in a way of life whose appeal had faded. Money, manipulation, smears or whatever it took were Carl's motivations but since she'd moved to Paris she couldn't be sure. Was she *in* or *out*? Was that the way Carl saw things? She'd have to look up her books again. Had the stars really predicted such a muddle?

Her green, almond-shaped eyes filled with tears. In the floor to ceiling mirror behind the sofa, she could see them rolling down her cheeks and wished she hadn't looked. They'd been good years with Carl, hadn't they? As she wiped back a tear, she had to admit they had. Though only eighteen when she'd started as his runner, her ambition had let her be manipulated to become Carl's mould of whatever he'd wanted. She'd recognized from the start that her beauty would help. *I like you, I like your style*, was what he'd said. Like had become turn-on, turn-on had become infatuation. Within six months she was getting special deliveries of roses and jewellery. By then she was nineteen. His wheeling and dealing enthralled her, as did the travel, a stream of executive jet flights and first class hotels with only the best rooms of course.

She topped up her glass and stared moodily at it. On one trip they'd stopped-over at Mauritius. After a long dinner with champagne and roses specially flown from Europe, she'd given in to his persistent wooing. Now, as she sat alone, the rain beating down outside her Paris apartment, her head shook in revulsion as she recalled the occasion. Quickly she drained the vodka at the memory. Had to get you out of my system, he had told her straight as they lay across the bed. To him she was just like a charter deal, a company take-over, a game to play and win. And he had.

Ever since, she had filed the incident in a deep dark locker. So had he. Never again did he seek to seduce her, never again did he refer to the occasion. Sometimes her recollection of the incident made her feel ashamed, sometimes angry and occasionally just a little wistful, for he'd been a good lover, gentle, yet as commanding as his character predicted.

After Mauritius, he had continued to treat her well, in some ways even better, but the obsessional flowers and jewellery had stopped. Indeed, their relationship had blossomed until her role in running his office was indispensable. Maybe that had been the trouble. Maybe she'd got to know too much. Her horoscope had predicted it, had warned that something big and dramatic was going to happen in her life.

It had.

The big event was a summons to his penthouse office and the chance of promotion to run the European end of the Mentocca empire. He had sold it to her as a great opportunity. The reality, though, was different. Now she was away from the hub, no longer his alter-ego. Now, in New York things happened and were happening which she didn't know, wasn't told about. Yet somehow she still trusted him. So what was he doing? Was it something too big for him to share with her? It wasn't another woman. Not that, though there had been plenty since Mauritius, one of them even a bit special. Or so it had seemed. Carl had moved her to Paris for a reason. He never did anything without a motive.

She drew on her cigarette and blinked back the tears. How had she ever been inspired by this man? How had she been impressed by his ruthless exploitation? She went to stub out her cigarette in the orange, saucer-like ashtray, selected by the designers to pick out the colours in the curtains, the lampshades and the scatter cushions. As she moved to extinguish it, her hand moved impulsively, missing the ashtray. The burning end bit fiercely into the expensive newness of the white leather sofa. She ground it in, pushing hard against the arm.

'Damn you, Carl! Damn you!'

In Athens, Carl paced restlessly round his penthouse suite which looked across to the Parthenon. His mutterings about Claudine were something similar. He was a worried man and could do without weak links.

Chapter 12

Sprawled on the hotel bed, just across the city from Claudine, Gavin dialled Sir Archie's home number. No reply. Just an answerphone. He left a message with details of where he was staying. Then he tried Edward and was more fortunate. 'I'm glad I caught you. It's been an eventful day.'

'I suppose you're about to have dinner in some chic Cannes restaurant, with or without Klodinsky.'

'Matter of fact, no.' Gavin laughed as he explained where he was and how he'd come to be there. 'So you see, there was no point in staying in Cannes. Even now I expect Klodinsky's put in a complaint to the Bureau. I kicked him in a no-go area. My God, he's touchy.'

'I know.' The laugh showed a shared experience. 'Rogue elephants have nothing on him.'

'Certainly kept me on the defensive. Then when I provoked him ... well, that was it. End of party. Pity. I was quite enjoying his lifestyle.'

'You're not there to enjoy yourself.' The reprimand was said in jest. 'And Claudine?'

Gavin picked his words carefully, like a cat walking on a wet path. 'She seems friendly - even after her boss nearly made me walk the plank. Otherwise she was 100% pro Carl.'

'I've met her. You won't get much out of her. Secrets, that is. Sure you're not just attracted to her legs?'

'I am! I am! Who wouldn't be! And the rest too!' Then Gavin's tone turned serious. 'She holds the key to the enigma of Klodinsky. She's been close to him for years.' Gavin paused, debating how much to tell of what he'd seen in Klodinsky's cabin. He decided to say nothing.

'He's ruthless,' commented Edward, adding 'I just wish you'd give us some quick answers. Did he fix *Ryme Lady*? Do we charter to him or not? You don't seem to be progressing.' Suddenly the tone was serious. 'Don't forget - Brads aren't paying for you to find out the colour of Claudine's underwear. Don't kid yourself she's on your side, even if she does wrap her legs round your neck. What we need to know is whether her boss wants to sink us. Literally. I think he does.'

Gavin felt the blast down the line. Images of their meeting in the boardroom re-appeared and he saw the flabby figure as clearly as if he were in the room. There was however nothing flabby about his attitude. The voice was of the man who was fighting to pull Brads round in the face of entrenched opposition from Sir Archie. It showed and Gavin respected it.

'Leave it with me. She's nobody's fool and ...'

'And you fancy some legover.' Edward interrupted. 'Don't think I can't understand your problem. But I repeat. Don't forget *ours*. Each day is another day lost. Another day's bank interest to pay.' As he listened, Gavin wondered whether to reveal just a little more. Again he decided to say nothing, waiting for Edward to continue. 'I'm sorry, Gavin. Perhaps I've been a bit hard on you. The position's got more complicated since we met. Some brokers in Piraeus have just phoned in the last hour. Remember we said someone was sniffing round about chartering *Cerne View* for the West Africa run - Lumbola and Nigeria? Right ... they're for real. Their clients are called Pinetto Charter Inc. Believe it or not, they're interested in chartering both *Cerne View* and *Adber Arrow*. That's put a torpedo across the old man's bows,' Edward chuckled.

'What are the charter rates like?' Gavin would have been suspicious if the terms had been over-generous in the present market. The answer, when it came, was a relief.

DOUGLAS STEWART

'Not very good. Not as good as Klodinsky's. But then his offer's far too good - a honey-pot.'

'Well ... if rape's inevitable,' commented Gavin as he sipped at a very spicy Bloody Mary.

Edward was irritated. 'It's not inevitable. Not unless you make a balls-up of the investigation. You just tell us quick. Damned quick ... whether to grab Klodinsky's offer. Meantime we'll try and negotiate something better with Pinetto.'

'What does Sir Archie think?'

Edward snorted. 'Think! I didn't know he did! That man's a blind donkey.' It was hard to accept that Edward was talking about his own father. 'Still wants us to charter to Klodinsky.' The exasperation exploded across the Channel. 'I'll try to hold the position. For God's sake, help us and quick. It's urgent, bloody urgent.'

'And it's hard, bloody hard to find out. Just remember that.' Gavin understood the frustration as he sat alone, contemplating the quiet comfort of his surroundings. The sound of silence and an empty glass were poor company and he poured himself another drink, a little less tabasco this time.

The trouble with deliberate sinkings or cargo frauds was the number of combinations of conspirators. Was it shipowner alone? Was it shipowner and charterer in league? Was it the crew, acting alone? Was it the shippers of the cargo? Was it the shippers of the cargo together with one of the others? Was it a *genuine case* without fraud? Was it piracy?' Perhaps the secret lay in that file. If only he'd been able to finish reading it. What did Klodinsky know of Sir Archie, of Edward, of Susannah ... and why did he want to know?

The shrillness of the telephone startled him. He snatched at the receiver. 'Gavin Blair.'

'Hi! Art here.' The voice was faint and there was a slight

echo on the line. 'I'm in Malacca. Any news?'

As Gavin recounted his day, he thought it typical of Art to get him talking first. Then he could blend whatever he had to say with what he'd heard. It gave him the best chance of saying the right thing. Art may have been the hard man of the Bureau but he wasn't dumb either.

'Guess you'll have more for me tomorrow.' Art had listened attentively. 'I was just touching base with you. Nothing vital. I've spoken to the Harbour Master. A real regular guy. English but settled out here and now a Muslim. He was telling me that local currents run mainly north to south. By his calculations, for the lifeboat to be washed up here, *Ryme Lady* was even further north than we'd thought. Well out of the normal piracy zone.'

'I'm not surprised. Anything else?'

'I'm going to do a little ... investigation.' Art explained in a few words his planned visit to Mansur Ibrahim's boat.

'Well take care. Maybe it's just the bad line but I'd say you've had a few.' Gavin was sure he was right but was surprised at his own confidence in talking so freely to Art. Perhaps it was the distance which made him secure.

Art laughed, Jack-the-lad-style. 'I'm gonna have a real ball. I can piss my way through the lock. Take a quick look-see and then it's London for a square meal and a well-rounded date. I'm getting tired of boiled rice. I'm even dreaming of T-bones and French fries.'

'It's dinner time here. I think I'll slip out for a steak and *pommes frites*.' It wasn't what he had in mind but he couldn't resist the wind-up.

Though it was not cold, Gavin pulled the belt tight on his raincoat as he stepped out of Fouquet's into the still crowded Champs Elysées. He was replete with *raie au beurre noir* and a lesser year Chablis. It was nearly 11.00 pm. Parisians were scurrying to their cars, taxis and to the Metro. Their heads were bowed, more against the wind than the rain which had eased. Everywhere there were puddles, flashes of watery reflections on the pavement as they picked up the lights from the car showroom windows and beams from the lines of slow moving traffic.

The Chateau Frontenac Hotel was only a few minutes walk away. Gavin hesitated as he looked at the sky. He'd chance it. Warmed by the excellent meal and more particularly by the Armagnac, it seemed too soon for bed. Ahead lay the Arc de Triomphe, magnificently floodlit, a kaleidoscope of vehicles circling endlessly around it. Beyond the arch lay the Avenue Victor Hugo. Sir Archie's brothel! The words from Klodinsky's file flashed before him. Fine! He'd go that way. It was as good as any.

He was about to set off when he saw a stranger standing a few yards away, just under the restaurant's red awning. Yet the man was not a stranger at all. He was of African appearance, with an ebony-black face and a wide-flared negroid nose. He was wearing a blue denim jacket, dark trousers and a pair of grubby trainers. He was probably in his early twenties. His curly hair had been flattened by spending too long in the rain. His build was wiry, lithe and, as he stood just a few feet away, Gavin knew where he'd seen him before. Hadn't it been just outside the hotel? When he'd set out for dinner a couple of hours before? Coincidence? Maybe. Maybe not.

The man did not seem to be particularly interested in him or indeed in anything as he stood, back against the wall. Gavin set off, briskly striding out for the Arc de Triomphe. His life as a barrister and the desk-bound months at the Bureau had been poor training for instinctive danger but Theo's murder had changed all that. Now, as he stepped out, apparently unconcerned, he was anxious to know if he really was being followed.

On the Champs Elysées the air was rich with the smell of

roasting chestnuts. Around the sellers, small groups gathered, glad of the warmth. Feeling very much one of the crowd, smart and scruffy, scruffy and smart, Gavin thought of Art as he walked. What was he doing now? Had he managed to break into Mansur's boat?

Thinking of Art reminded him that both their photos were in Klodinsky's file. It was not comforting. Especially not if he were being followed. Maybe it was just imagination. He went down the steps into the maze of pedestrian tunnels under the Place Charles de Gaulle. They were narrow, long and busy with vagrants and home-goers. But was there someone there, someone paid to pursue him? He wanted to look round but resisted the temptation. Not yet. On climbing up the concrete steps to join the broad boulevard of Avenue Victor Hugo, he took in the view towards the Rond Point. It seemed an unlikely street in which to find a brothel, this broad highway with its fine symmetrical buildings. Still ... the report probably wasn't wrong. Somewhere above one of these shops or offices was a room, a person who knew more about Sir Archie than perhaps he'd want known - the bum-spanker referred to by Edward and confirmed by Klodinsky's investigation.

He quickened his pace, swinging his arms briskly. Now and again he paused to gaze at a shop front, looking at nothing in particular. The number of pedestrians had grown fewer, the street lights adequate but by no means bright. Was it imagination? No. Somewhere behind him there were still footsteps and yes ... that was a cough. A man coughing.

Even the late night traffic was down to a trickle when a 1200cc BMW motorcycle roared past, accelerating towards the Arc de Triomphe at 80mph. It was the opportunity he needed. Gavin spun round, apparently attracted by the leather clad blonde who was riding it. He caught his breath in shock. Perhaps he hadn't really expected to see anyone.

Yet there was no doubt. He was there: the man in the blue denim jacket, the man from outside the hotel, the man from outside Fouquet's. Now he was just forty yards away, suddenly obsessed with the paintings in a small art gallery.

As his brain sent out messages telling him to hot-foot it, he fought to resist. Not yet. With panic turning every muscle to water, he forced left leg in front of right, right leg in front of left.

Ahead lay the Rond Point. From his past he could remember that it was ringed with cafés and brasseries which just might provide some refuge. So why was he being followed? Was he to be shot, knifed or would it be strangled when he made his first mistake and entered a darkened street? Or maybe it would just be a threat? Oh shit! At moments like this he wondered why he'd joined the Bureau.

Use your assets. Wits before fists! You're not Art! He peered anxiously ahead. Thank God! One of the cafés was still open. Quickly he crossed the street and headed straight for a group of students. There were about twenty of them, noisy with beer, all laughing and drinking under the shelter of the café's awning. With a sudden dart, Gavin cut his way through the throng and into the bar. From there he dived into the men's room where he flung off his raincoat, jacket and tie and ruffled his hair so that uncharacteristically it fell forward scruffily across his forehead. Bundling his belongings inside the raincoat which he tucked under his arm, he immediately joined the students outside, positioning himself in their midst, bottom leaning against a table and clutching someone's discarded glass.

He saw Denim Jacket at once. He'd been taken by surprise once Gavin had rounded the corner at the Rond Point. Now he was loitering uncertainly. He looked down each street leading from the roundabout in turn. Then, quickening his pace, he crossed the road, obviously intent on searching the café. Scarcely glancing at the students, he went straight inside, intent on finding the well-groomed man. Instantly, Gavin was gone, running across the street and hailing a taxi. For a few seconds he just sat, exhausted by tension until relief flooded through and his racing pulse slowed. Denim Jacket had failed. The pleasing thought didn't last. Ok ... he'd failed this time but it wouldn't be for long. Failed to do what?

Worse still ... he knew where Gavin was staying.

Still disconcerted when he reached his bedroom, Gavin double-locked the door. As an afterthought he pushed a chair against it. Then he stripped off and went to bed but sleep was out of the question. The same thoughts kept repeating themselves. Who was Denim Jacket? Who was he working for? And why?

About twenty minutes later he could stand it no longer. He went over to the window and drew back the curtains. Then he pushed open the shutters and looked down. Leaning against a wall, someone in a blue denim jacket was smoking a cigarette.

He closed the shutters and resisted the temptation to grab a drink, to drown himself in an entire bottle. What to do? Pack? Slip out the back way? No ... wait. Think. If Art were here ... what would he do? Well, he'd have a drink for a start. Gavin went over to the drinks cupboard and fixed himself a brandy and ginger ale in proportions which didn't do much for the sale of the latter. And next? Well he wouldn't check out. He'd stay. Dammit. Art'd *want* to be followed ... would *want* a confrontation. That's what Art would do. He'd pick up the little bugger, pin him to a tree and beat the hell out of him. Find out what his game was.

Suddenly in the warmth of the room the idea excited him. Be macho, he told himself. He pulled on his clothes and hurried down to the lobby. By the time he reached there, he could feel the chill night air blowing in and the idea didn't seem quite so good. Come on, he told himself. Be like Art!

He went through the doors and into the darkened street.

It was empty.

Denim Jacket had gone.

When he awoke Gavin lay in the quietness of the bedroom, realizing that nothing had changed. His mouth was dry and his limbs ached after an uneasy night. By the door, he could still see the chair, jammed under the handle, where he had replaced it. Now, it appeared incongruous, absurd. There was a crease of worry across his face. What had it all been about? Denim Jacket? It all seemed unreal in morning light. He eased himself out of bed and stood beside it.

Gently he stretched to his full 6' 1", the muscles rippling as he raised his arms high towards the ceiling, his nakedness emphasizing his well-kept physique. His skill at cricket had benefited from his height, his high action helping his leg-breaks to both turn and lift. On a good day. But that was history since he'd smashed his spinning finger.

He moved towards the window, changed his mind and instead showered in a thunderous force of hot water. Only once he was into the thick bathrobe did he return to the window, throwing open the shutters with a flourish. Outside it was a fine Paris morning, the sky blue, the only clouds high. The sound of distant starlings carried on the autumn breeze.

He looked down, half-expecting to see the familiar figure slouched against the wall. No one. Nothing. It was as if the man had never been there, as if he'd never been followed along the Avenue Victor Hugo, as if the thumping heartbeat and legs like melting candles had never happened. Daylight changed so much.

He felt reassured and rang down for breakfast. 'Eggs Benedict, a pot of coffee and two glasses of orange juice,' he ordered in French, 'and *Le Figaro*.' Until breakfast arrived, he paced the room, wondering what lay ahead. Had he been followed from the airport? Had Claudine told Klodinsky where he was staying? Or Edward? Or Sir Archie? Or Susannah, come to that?

Breakfast came on a well-organized tray and he sat at the round table, feeling deliciously pampered as he scanned *Le Figaro*. Claudine would ring soon. Forget Denim Jacket. It was going to be a good day. And maybe there'd be some good news from Art about the fishermen's boat.

He tipped the coffee jug and was disappointed to find that he'd drained the lot. Of course Art would have sorted out Denim Jacket differently ... but I am what I am. No good comparing yourself with Art. The shrill ring of the telephone made him jump. Great! Claudine! Or maybe Sir Archie.

It was neither. It was the Concièrge, telling him that a *boite*, a parcel, had been delivered for him. Arrived at 9.25 am.

Odd. He hadn't been expecting anything.

Chapter 13

The streets outside the Ramada Hotel were dark. Art, clad in a black jogging suit and loafers, merged with the shadowy surroundings. He chose a route away from the centre, through the narrow back streets leading down to the river. Then he passed the Majestic Hotel and the murder spot. It was 2.25 am. Tonight all was quiet. The restaurant where the fishermen had eaten their last meal was in darkness.

Silently he padded through the Chinese quarter. The occasional figure appeared and disappeared. Somewhere a dog howled its distress. The ever-present sickly smell of the durien hung in the heavy atmosphere, mixing with the odours of yesterday's trash.

He bypassed the bridge at Jalan Hang Jebat but even so he quickly covered the half mile to where the boat was moored, just upstream from the Harbour Master's office. He saw the familiar shape of the vessels involved in the Indonesian trade. From one of them came the sound of laughter and the smell of cooking fish. A chink of light could be seen through the waxed yellow curtains. On deck the cargo of charcoal was ready for unloading.

Just downstream was moored the boat of the murdered men. Lying black and silent, the vessel was just a silhouette against the horizon of the open sea.

From the earlier reconnaissance, Art went straight to the place to board. Piece of cake. Just a short jump to the deck. He landed silently. That was easy enough. Now what? He stood on the deck, the weathered timber creaking under his weight. His hands reached out for the door to the wheelhouse. At first he felt only the gnarled old timber but then he found what he was seeking. The padlock felt cold to the touch as it hung from the latch. With a twist of his piece of wire, the simple cheap mechanism flew apart in seconds. Silently he turned the handle and the door opened.

From within came a variety of smells - stale air, tar, rope and salty spray. In the stillness, the noise of the creaking hinges sounded deafening. Gently, as quietly as he could, Art swung open the door. Then he went in, easing the door almost shut behind him.

He waited for a few moments to see whether anyone had heard. If they had, then they'd done nothing about it. Only then did he put on the torch, its pencil light piercing the darkness to reveal the sturdiness of the wheel, the glint of the sextant, a pile of ropes, a coil of wire, a compass and a couple of windcheaters hanging from a hook on the far wall.

To the left of the wheel was an open door leading to the cabin below. He'd check that out in a moment. For now his thoughts were on the drawers beside the wheel. Swiftly he started to open them, one by one, starting at the bottom. Each was full of charts, old, faded and much used. They showed every inch of water in the Strait between Malacca and the island of Sumatra, seven hours sailing away.

The top drawer was locked but of the key there was no sign. Again, the piece of bent wire did the trick. With a snap, the lock was gone and he opened the drawer. It slid back easily to reveal some more maps. So why had the skipper locked it? What was so different about it? He pulled them out and laid them on the table. Each measured two feet square. He played the torch across each in turn, looking for markings, clues of a link with *Ryme Lady*. There was nothing. Not a mark on them. Disappointed, he was about to put them back.

Hold it Art! The drawer *had* to be locked for a reason. He slipped his hand back inside, feeling, fumbling. Then he touched something right at the back. It was cold and yet familiar in shape. He pulled it out. It was a watch, an expensive Rolex, showing the time correctly at 2.30 am. He turned it over and shone the pencil-light on the reverse. He breathed a low whistle as he read the inscription. 'To Captain Rory Scutar, from the Directors of Brads. Forty years service.'

He slipped the watch into his pocket, then rolled the charts and returned then to the drawer. Interesting! Now for the cabin. He was about to push the drawer shut when a noise from outside made him stop. He flicked off the torch. Through the window he saw a figure approaching along the quay. The man was no more than twenty feet away and heading straight for the boat. Even in the gloom, the menace in the man's face could be seen.

Chapter 14

'A parcel? For me? I'm not expecting anything.' Gavin's surprise was clear to the concièrge. 'You'd better send it up.' He put down the phone and impatiently paced the room, hands deep in the pockets of his towelling wrap. A parcel? Who would send him a parcel? Claudine perhaps. She knew he was here. But why should she send him a parcel?

There was a knock at the door. The young bell-hop handed over the package. It was not much bigger than a large thick book and neatly wrapped in brown paper. In heavy black ink was written the name Gavin Blair, Hotel Chateau Frontenac. Absentmindedly, he slipped the lad five francs and held the parcel in front of him. A million years before, like the previous morning, he would have been unsuspicious. Not now. Suddenly the sunny morning had gone. Memories of the night before descended like a mist, shrouding him in an envelope of fear.

He laid the package on the table. Then like a small boy looking at his birthday cake he prowled round it. For a flickering second, he was back to his childhood. He could recall sitting at the foot of the Christmas tree with his two brothers, as they had stacked and re-stacked the parcels. They'd shaken them, guessing the contents, kidding each other in games of bluff and counter-bluff. Those parcels had been gift-wrapped with coloured ribbons and red bows everywhere.

This was different.

No pretty ribbons, no fancy wrapping. Just brown paper, stark, thick and decorated only with bold black writing. It would make a good Exhibit A at his inquest. What was left of it. Gingerly he turned it over, studying every inch. Scarcely daring to breathe, he put his ear to it, listening, expecting to hear the tick-tock of a nasty timing device. Nothing. Not a tick. Not a whirr.

The folds in the brown paper were held down by sellotape. Opening the parcel would not be easy. *Le Guide Michelin* perhaps? A token of friendship from Claudine? Or was it more sinister? He studied the writing. Each letter was in capitals, each stroke thick and forceful. Something about it troubled him.

He sat down on the bed, thinking about the writing. And then it came to him. Klodinsky's yacht. Lunchtime. The dark brown of Klodinsky's hand. In it was a pen. He'd scribbled notes in thick, harsh, black strokes. But Klodinsky was in Athens. True ... but he could have used a courier ... no problem.

In spite of his better judgment, curiosity overcame fear. He returned to the table and delicately started to peel back the sellotape, first one end and then the other. Carefully, he turned over the parcel to peel off the last sticky strip, fingers all of a tremble, chest heaving with the shortness of his breath. Every second he expected the deafening roar of an explosion and the searing pain of his chest being crushed by the detonation of the device. Exhibit B, 'Item believed to be part of deceased's brain.'

Nothing happened, not even after he started unwrapping the brown paper, easing it apart as painstakingly as a surgeon separating skin during an operation.

A layer of corrugated cardboard was revealed, wrapped around something which looked very like paper but which was not a book. Gently again, he removed the corrugated cardboard. What appeared was money. No, not just money ... *lots* of money, riches and a note, written in the same heavy black handwriting. Relieved, he stood back and straightened himself. There was a clamminess around his neck and a trickle of sweat running down the flat of his back. Fleetingly, he was tempted to grab the note. Then, conditioned by the pace at which he'd opened the parcel, he decided on caution. Touching only the very corner of the paper, he twisted it open. The note was written in English.

THE EASY WAY
BRADS CHARTER BOTH SHIPS TO KLODINSKY
1,000,000 MORE FRANCS WILL REACH YOU ON SIGNATURE
OVER

Still clutching the note by its corner, Gavin turned it. There, written in one-inch letters, were the words:

THE HARD WAY
DEATH

The plain white paper trembled in Gavin's hand. The word *DEATH* advanced and receded as if he were adjusting binoculars. Then the note fell as he slumped back on the bed, elbows on knees, face in hands, his senses numb.

Once again he thought of Art. Art had faced death. 'Ever faced a gun?' He recalled Art's words at the meeting in Walter Corbin's office. Well ... now he was facing death. By a gun? By a rope? By a knife? It didn't really matter much. It was *DEATH* Finite. End of story.

One body ... thirty one years old. One careful owner. Very expendable. One body standing in the way of Klodinsky.

He lost all track of time. It was 10.40 when the numbness passed and he raised his head from his hands and flicked an eye across at the four stacks of notes lying side by side on the dressing table. Reluctantly he went across to examine them, deciding to touch one bundle only. The other three stacks he left for the fingerprinters, not that they would get much help from such old notes. In just one pile there were 250 notes of 100 French francs each. At a rough calculation, there was an immediate 10,000 pounds. All he had to do was to tell Brads that he thought Klodinsky was clean. The deal would then go ahead and there'd be another 100,000 pounds for him. Or so the note promised.

The choice was simple, starkly simple. Just play down his suspicions and advise Brads to sign. What would happen then? Well ... presumably disaster would strike one or other of the ships. Or both of them. Or there'd be a dispute about payment of the charter to Brads. The Bureau would say - *sorry, there's been an error of judgment but of course Gavin Blair had acted in good faith.* The Bureau would never know the truth. Brads would go under. Klodinsky would descend like a hooded vulture to pick up the scrapings ... including the options. 100,000 pounds to the credit of G. Blair Esq's Cayman Islands bank account would be a small price for Klodinsky to pay.

Gavin walked to the window. He shrugged at the nothingness in the street and resumed pacing the room like a restless Bengal tiger. Back and forth, back and forth he went, his eyes lowered. Why was inspiration so slow?

Eventually he managed a smile. Soon it became wider. Then he gave a small laugh. Hell ... he was in no danger at all! Until Brads signed with someone else, like Pinetto, his life was safe. He punched his left fist into the palm of his right hand with a noisy smack of satisfaction. Dammit, that had to be right.

The shrill sound of the phone startled him. It was Claudine. 'I'll be at the hotel at 12.30.' Gavin's spirits soared even higher. They'd celebrate his reprieve together. But how long would this phoney war last?

Unnoticed by Claudine, he watched her arrival in the elegant foyer. Perhaps not quite as tall as he had been imagining, the length and slenderness of her legs had been misleading. Now as she stood, finger on cheek, she was utterly composed. Could she possibly have set up Denim Jacket? Known of the parcel? Looking at her, it all seemed so unlikely.

She'd dressed more formally than he'd expected, especially for a New Yorker. Her navy blue suit was tailored to perfection. In her dress sense, the French blood obviously prevailed. The white ruffled blouse was both immaculate and expensive. The gold brooch on her lapel spoke of a wealthy lover or family inheritance whilst the navy bag slung from her shoulder reached her waist. Today her short hair was styled differently which, while changing the shape of her face, detracted nothing from its beauty. As he took in her pleasing formality, he was glad that he'd gone for a jacket and maroon rollneck. If she was wearing make-up, then it was subtle, simple and scarcely apparent to Gavin.

When he stepped forward from the bar entrance, the movement caught her eye. She laughed rather than smiled her greeting, her pleasure obvious as he walked towards her. *Remember Gavin, this is a dangerous game.* She extended both her brown slender hands for him to clasp and proferred each cheek in turn to be kissed. He brushed his lips softly against her skin and appreciated the fragrance of her delicate perfume, a different one today.

'Claudine! You're looking wonderful. And no trouble getting here?' he asked in order to get the conversation moving.

'Not at all. I came by taxi. But the traffic! Just like New York. The Metro would have been quicker. As for the French drivers ... !

'Lunatics. They drive their *Deux Chevaux* like tank commanders.' They both laughed at the shared image. 'Have you had to come far?'

'Not really. The Quai Louis Blériot isn't far. The view this morning was ... just great.' The intonation left a feeling that she wanted to add a proviso but impetuously Gavin gave her no chance.

'So ... do you feel like walking now? I was thinking of a

restaurant I know down on the Quai Tournelle.'

Quoi! Before lunch! Walk to the Quai Tournelle! We'd be lucky to get there in time for dinner,' she exclaimed. Her voice contained a husky laugh and other guests turned their heads to admire the owner.

'It didn't look far on the map.' Gavin was defensive and shuffled from foot to foot. 'Anyway, what do you suggest?'

'Let's go to Léo le Lion in the Rue Duvivier. It's fun. And not too far to walk.' Her tone was decisive.

'Fine. You're on!' Throughout these exchanges, Gavin's responses had been almost mechanical. The note from Klodinsky was stamped indelibly on his mind. Her presence made it more stark. As they set off she seemed natural, unaffected, ready to chatter, frivolous, friendly and disarmingly open. In contrast he struggled to match her mood, obsessed now that he was outside with looking around, expecting any moment to see Denim Jacket.

He didn't. He wasn't there ... or he'd taken lessons overnight in the art of following. It wasn't till they'd reached the Pont d'Alma that he started to relax and share the conversation. Till then, he'd been going through the motions, saying the right things, looking happy and nodding occasionally but doing so without thinking. As they stood, looking down at the Seine and standing arm in arm, memories of the note were blurred. No point in challenging her about the parcel. Stick to his plan, he decided. Say nothing.

They strolled on, pointing out and sharing the pleasure of the sights. Les Invalides, Notre Dame, the *bateaux mouches* and Eiffel Tower were all at their best in the warm sunshine. Claudine looked downstream. 'My apartment's that way. You can't see it. It's maybe a mile or more. It's got a great view. Maybe we'll have time to see it later.' She paused. 'Say! Isn't that real neat!' The Americanism spoken with a French accent was appealing. She was pointing at a line of barges. They were long, black with colourful red, yellow and white trimmings. 'See those drying clothes on the deck? That reminds me of Hong Kong. Aberdeen Harbour. Papa was there ..... in the French Embassy. I was only seven then but the memories are vivid.'

'Was there ever a real home?'

Claudine squeezed his arm. 'You didn't think we lived on a junk, did you?'

'Something like that. I was wondering,' he laughed.

'Home was wherever Papa was based. I was born in the Alps. After that I never lived anywhere long till I reached New York. I was the only child. Now my parents are retired and living in Bangkok. We're not close. Too much time apart in childhood.' She nearly added that the astrology with her parents had been all wrong, that she had never been close to them.

'So you don't share your apartment with a friend?'

Her laugh conveyed anything but happiness. 'No. I've no one special.' The smile was sincere, the voice believable.

'And Carl?' He glanced sideways at her, anxious to see the response. The shake of the head was dismissive. Do me a favour, were the unspoken words. He believed her or wanted to anyway.

At the far side of the bridge, Gavin stopped. Deliberately he took in the view from all 360 degrees. If Denim Jacket were there, then he was well hidden - tucked in amongst the throng enjoying the change in the weather.

They continued walking to the Rue Duvivier. It was a small street, unfashionable, notable more for its mediocrity. It's brightest feature was the golden sign of the restaurant swinging above the entrance. Léo le Lion was a bistro, small intimate and inexpensive. Inside, the air was rich with the smell of prime Charolais beef sizzling on charcoal. The best tables, tucked in the nooks and crannies, had gone but le Patron was able to find room close to the window.

There they seated themselves opposite each other and over glasses of white port studied the menu.

As they sat at the tiny square table with its red cloth and simple cutlery, Gavin puzzled over Claudine's multi-layered personality. Now, as she studied the menu, she was radiant, sophisticated and very much the successful PA. Superficially she had everything - an apartment by the river, right through to the pearl necklace and the lavish gold jewellery. The trappings hung comfortably on her. Nevertheless he was sure there was another Claudine. He was sure there was a vulnerable person hidden behind the assured exterior. Glimpses of insecurity just occasionally flickered. He felt very protective towards her, saw the gentleness in her face when she relaxed. He was sure that she had a feline desire to be stroked but not dominated. It was an interesting balance. 'Chosen?' he enquired.

Her wide-apart eyes were a particular feature. When she smiled, her eyes danced, lighting her face with enthusiasm. 'Let's call the waiter.'

Having ordered, they chatted - just a little about his job and even less about hers. Chateau L'Estephe was served with the thick onion soup. Then came the gigot - deliciously pink lamb, highly seasoned with herbs and served with petit pois. It was then that Gavin started his first tentative probe, hating himself for doing it, hoping he wouldn't blow everything. He drew closer across the table. 'Funny man, Carl.' He tried to make it sound like a throwaway.

'What do you mean?' Her reply was even. With her eyelids lowered and her thoughts apparently concentrating on the lamb, he could read nothing into the response.

'Funny, strange.'

'Yes. I understood that. But your remark ... it irritates me.' She spoke with an angry toss of her head. Her hair, short though it was, bobbed and swayed.

'Well - for a start - although he denied it, Carl knew why

136

I wanted to interview him. Yet what did he do? Only expressed shock horror at my questions.' Gavin spoke with his hands in unison. 'A total over-reaction.' He watched for a sign as to what she was thinking. 'That's one thing. Another is that he keeps a file on everybody. Has photographs taken. Has them watched.'

'So? You find that odd?' Her tone was cool but she had made no attempt at denial.

'Yes. I do.'

'Gavin,' she leaned across the table. 'I thought you were a man about town. You look like it. You don't sound like it. Don't you know anything about the real world, real business? For God's sake! Surveillance, photographing - that's business.'

'Maybe,' Gavin sounded hesitant.

'Well ... don't think you can ask me instead.' The pointed finger was a sharp reproach. 'I'm not allowed to talk about my work.'

'Come on! Admit it! Carl's an enigma. I've read the press cuttings about him. I'm surprised you've put up with him for so long.' He wanted a reaction. There was none except for a flicker of irritation. He had to try again. Push his luck. 'By the way, did you tell him you'd be seeing me?'

For a moment it was her turn to look flustered but then came the denial. '*Mais non!*' She felt ashamed at the lie but remained poised. 'Look, Carl doesn't own me!' There was an angry snap in her voice. 'Sure ... he makes it his business to know everything ... but that doesn't mean to say I *tell* him everything. *Knowledge is power*, that's his creed.'

'From the sex life of Sir Archie Crawford to finding out where I'm staying.' The loaded comment was slipped in and he waited for a denial which never came.

'Why not? You've met him, can see what he's like. He's a machine.'

'Doesn't he ever ... unbend? Or was yesterday a typical

microcosm of his life?'

'I've never seen him different.'

'Not even socially?'

Her face hardened. 'Let's quit it! Question after question. Is this what you want to know? Whether or not we've been lovers? Well, the answer's no.' The denial came easily. She'd denied it so often before. 'I know him well ... by working with him. He's turned on by money or rather by its power. Money, ships and deals. He doesn't want to be liked - he doesn't feel the need. He gives 100%. Takes 200% back. Sucks you dry.' She shrugged her shoulders, as if to say that this little speech explained the entire paradox of her boss.

There was silence as Gavin debated his next question. He never got the chance. 'Don't ask.' Claudine's face was angry. 'Don't even think about asking if he sank *Ryme Lady*.' She raised her voice, eliminating the huskiness. 'You're not interested in me at all. You just want information.' She banged her cutlery onto her plate. The couple at the next table looked amused at overhearing someone else's row. Claudine ignored their craned necks. 'Oh Jesus! Don't you see? I want a friend, not an interrogator.'

'I'm sorry. Really I am. I promise I won't ask about *Ryme Lady*.'

'You'd better not,' she pouted. The fixed thrust of her jaw made her point which detracted nothing from the awesome allure. Then, just as suddenly, her face broke into a sad smile and she stretched a slender hand across the table to touch his arm. 'Gavin, can't you back off? Can't you see *I'm* here because *I* want to be with you.'

'I'm sorry. No more questions.' He looked full of remorse but felt an explanation essential. 'But you must understand - I'm under pressure to get results .... and quickly.'

She nodded her head but then pushed her chair back to

stand up. She leaned forward and kissed him on the cheek, just a reassuring brush. 'It's all right. I'm not leaving you. I've got to make a phone call.' She returned moments later, without any explanation, apologizing for breaking up the meal. 'I've asked for the cheeseboard,' he said and, even as he spoke, the Patron appeared.

The trolley was laden with over forty different cheeses in various stages of readiness. Claudine chose over-ripe goats' cheese which would have asphyxiated an unwary mouse. Gavin ordered nothing except large black coffees and two brandies.

The mood had mellowed. Since she had returned to the table, the tension had eased and conversation had flowed, helped along by the red wine, the brandy and the cosy room. They found themselves touching hands, clasping elbows, grimacing, puzzling and laughing as they shared incidents from their past. Yet despite all of this, Claudine was watchful, sensing that Gavin wanted to say something. At last she could stand it no longer. 'There's something you want to tell me, to ask me. Go on, for God's sake, whatever it is. It's obvious.' She watched as he agonized. His hands clenched and unclenched before he spoke. When he did so, it was slowly and with precision.

'Don't laugh but I was followed all yesterday evening.' He put his head on one side and nodded in emphasis.

'Are you sure?' Her concern seemed genuine, her brow furrowed.

'Positive. By a man wearing a blue denim jacket.' Again he watched for a flicker of the eyebrow, for any sign to prove she'd known all along. For a moment her face was a mask and then came the reaction, a look of apparent shock flitting across her face.

'Did you say blue denim jacket?' She was looking over Gavin's shoulder, through the window. 'Like him over there?'

Chapter Fifteen

Art waited in the darkness of the wheelhouse. A squint through the window showed him that the man had stopped right by the boat.

'*Ho'la?*' Art wasn't sure what the shout was but that's what it sounded like. There was a question mark in the voice, a slight touch of fear. Art saw the man's torch flash towards the partly-opened door to the wheelhouse. '*Ho'la?*' The question was repeated. Again, Art peered through the crack in the curtain and made out the appearance of a youngish man with dark Chinese features. In one hand he held a torch, in the other a gutting knife with a six-inch blade.

Scarcely daring to breathe, still less to move, Art waited, hoping that the man would go away. He didn't. Almost at once the boat shook as the man jumped aboard. In the darkness Art's own face suddenly looked years younger. A smile played round his lips. He was enjoying himself. This was living. It had been far too long since his heart had raced like it was now doing. It seemed years since he'd felt the relentless squeeze of his muscles on the pit of his stomach. He hadn't felt this good since ... since he'd worked on the drug bust at Norman's Cay when he and Matt Rees from the CIA had been holed up, cornered, just like this, pinned down in a hut just off the tiny airstrip.

No! This was better. He was alone! Just himself and a vicious looking bastard with a knife. The meanness of the situation fired his belly. This time he was cornered in three square yards.

The man, aged maybe nineteen or twenty, had looked fit and the knife gave him menace. So what, Art reasoned.

Surprise was the best weapon of all. That, and fifteen years experience. Relishing the man's fear, Art could picture the narrow Chinese face taut with tension. Art knew what the man would do. The inexperienced could always be relied upon to do the obvious. This man would be no exception.

Art moved till his back was to the wall close behind the door. The boat creaked with the shifting weight. But it didn't matter. Not now. Art could hear the man's laboured breathing as he stood close to the door before swinging it open. The hinges creaked noisily. The heavy breathing, short sharp pants of nervous tension, seemed to fill the small space. The beam of the torch shone across the wheel-house, lighting up the charts and the open drawer. He thought back. Come on Art. Which hand was the knife in? Yes. That was it. Definitely. The man had the knife in his left hand, the torch in his right. So the knife would be in the nearest hand. Unless there'd been a switch.

Art waited. He saw the silvery glint of the end of the torch, then the point of the knife. He sensed the youthful figure, adrenalin pumping, every muscle and sinew taut as he stood, divided only from Art by the flimsy wood of the old door. Hold it Art! Don't move yet! Wait! Keep him coming! Wait another second! The whole of the knife appeared. Then the man's fists. The murderous weapon was clutched so that it pointed upwards, ready to rip into Art's stomach or neck.

Now! Art slammed his right hand down in a violent chop onto the man's left wrist. The sudden pain as the hard, striking edge struck him caused a reflex action. The man dropped the knife, emitting a shriek of terror. Even before the knife had hit the deck, Art's left hand shot across to clench the man's other arm in a fierce lock, forcing it backwards. For a second, Art and the man came face-to-face as Art twisted him round. As the torch shone uselessly upwards, it highlighted the terrified features. Instantly

Art's free arm grasped the man's left leg. The stranger, small, lithe and lightweight let out another scream as he felt himself being lifted. For a moment Art held him high above the deck. Then, with consummate ease, he hurled him more than a dozen feet through the air into the chocolate-brown water below.

Cursing his ill-fortune at being interrupted, Art knew he had to run for it. Already there were sounds of movement from the other boats. A large overhead light had been switched on, possibly from the Harbour Master's house.

He jumped back to the quay and started to pound the tow-path, heading up-river for the hotel. In front of him, two men emerged from a boat, alerted by the screams. Before they'd had time to get their bearings, Art was up to them. Like an American footballer charging for the touch-down, he took them on the run. Using his weight, he barged between the pair of them, brushing the men aside like flotsam. Behind him, he could hear shouts as other people appeared but by then he was 75 yards away. A glance round revealed they were more concerned for the men who were picking themselves up than to involve themselves in hot pursuit.

This was just as well. Art's body was no longer built for speed. As he gasped and panted through the streets, he regretted the bourbon, the beer and the cigarettes. Still he kept on pounding, gritting his teeth against the pain which clamped across his chest. He never paused until he reached the multi-storey car park. Seconds later, the small blue Proton, already loaded, was spiralling down and into the night. It would be a long drive back to Singapore.

In his pocket, Captain Scutar's watch showed that it was 2.50 am.

Chapter 16

At first Gavin didn't react. Claudine repeated what she'd said. 'A blue denim jacket - like him out there?'

This time Gavin turned to follow her look. Beyond two pigeons dancing in a shaft of sunlight, stood Denim Jacket. He was leaning in a doorway at the foot of the building opposite. The single glance gave Gavin a polaroid image of the chipped wrought ironwork by the first floor window. Beneath it hung the gas lamp over the door. Beneath that was Denim Jacket, one foot raised and pressed against the wall. While smoking a cigarette, he was examining the ends of his long black fingers.

He spoke through clenched teeth. 'Yes. Just like that. Wait here!' His face was grim. The unanswered questions raced through his mind. How the hell had Denim Jacket found him? Had he been followed all along? Had Claudine's telephone call tipped him off? Or had she been told to get him to Léo le Lion at all costs.

Pierre Chouen stopped looking at his fingernails as a sudden movement attracted him. He looked up and saw Gavin approaching the door of the restaurant. For a moment he was confused. His instructions had been clear. Being spotted didn't matter. Avoiding a confrontation did. So ... should he wait? As the Englishman bounded onto the pavement, Chouen was convinced. The man's clenched jaw and angry eyes threatened serious violence. Chouen waited no longer. As Gavin crossed the road, Chouen was off.

Gavin's red wine, brandy and pommes frites were a handicap. Chouen, with his ten yards advantage and eco-nomic build, was quick as a whippet. Soon he'd extended the gap to fifteen and then twenty yards. Though much larger than Denim Jacket, Gavin was no slouch either. Years of circuit training, countless afternoons chasing leather on the cricket field and pumping iron at the health club had kept him in trim. His muscles were in good shape. Like a juggernaut, once he had his own momentum, he was able to keep pace. All the while he watched the pumping elbows ahead of him. The African's strides were short but effective as he rounded corners and sidestepped the dawdlers in the Rue de Grenelle. Gavin's were larger but more cumbersome. His highly polished black shoes had to fight for a grip compared with the Nike trainers which sped Denim Jacket at a lively pace.

The roar of traffic and the hoot of a barge meant they must be nearing the Seine. Maybe Denim Jacket would get stuck, trapped by the surge of insane drivers approaching the bottleneck of the Pont D'Alma. Similar thoughts must have been going through Chouen's mind. At the junction of Bosquet and Université, he faltered. A decision taken, he changed pace to turn right and away from the river, weaving and dodging between the pedestrians.

The hesitation, the moment of indecision, cost him yards whereas Gavin had no need to think, only to follow. That and to watch those heels, those arms and never to lose sight of them. Ahead lay a busy junction. Again Denim Jacket hesitated before turning sharply into a side street, almost completing the square from the restaurant. Panting though he was, Gavin knew that he could match the man, pace for pace, the gap between them dropping to ten yards with three quarters of a mile behind them.

The last turning had led them into a quiet, narrow, residential back street. There was no one about. Suddenly as he looked ahead, Chouen realized that it was a dead end, that he was trapped. Should he turn round? Or what? The indecision showed before he turned impulsively through a gateway to a magnificent, eighteenth-century mansion. It was large enough when the great green doors were open to receive a coach and four. Now they were shut except for an inset pedestrian entrance through which he hurled himself with little more than five paces separating himself from his pursuer. He was still trying to slam the door shut as Gavin struck it with a full-blooded charge. The force of the impact sent Chouen sprawling, his legs flailing in the air.

Gavin jumped, landing across Chouen's prone figure. His knees crunched into the pit of the man's stomach. Chouen's eyes rolled large and white. He gasped as twelve stone of packed muscle slammed his navel into the ground. For a second they lay there, Chouen with his arms pinned to the flagstones, Gavin kneeling astride him.

The sudden intrusion awoke the owner of the house, Marc Valmain, who had stripped to the waist after lunch. Warmed by the afternoon sun on his first floor balcony, he'd quickly fallen asleep. The rude awakening did not please him. The sight of a black man and a white man wrestling by the fountain in his courtyard down below was an outrage. He went inside and called the police. Then he went to the cupboard and picked up his shotgun - the one he used for hunting wild boar in Normandy.

Down in the yard, neither man had yet spoken. Chouen was unable to do so as his cheeks pumped like bellows. Gavin wanted to vomit as he fought for breath in air soured by the musty stench which rose from Denim Jacket's quivering body. Blasts of stale breath and garlic filled Gavin's nostrils as he glared down at his prisoner. As he tried to fix Chouen's frightened eyes, he saw rivulets of sweat running down from the high cheekbones. Chouen's bull neck glistened with a sheen of perspiration. The open mouth was full of rotten, blackened teeth.

'Who are you? Who are you?' He shouted the words, in french. All the while he was forcing Chouen's shoulders to the ground. The African said nothing. He'd understood though. Now he kept his large aubergine-coloured lips firmly shut. Ok chum! Have it your own way, Gavin thought. He gripped Chouen by the slender shoulders and shook him, banging the man's black head against the concrete yard. 'Who are you? What do you want?'

At that moment Marc Valmain strode through his front door. Still dressed only in a pair of shabby, green trousers, belly hanging over his belt, he looked at the two men. The sight of smashed pot plants, the pride of his Italianate courtyard, angered him even more. 'What's happening?' he roared in french. His face was as purple as the claret he'd been knocking back. He advanced a few paces closer, then took aim, surprisingly steady considering the liquidity of his lunch. Gavin looked up and saw the end of the barrels just above their heads. There was no doubt. The owner was ready to blast off at the slightest sign of trouble. The skull-like face, almost devoid of flesh and hair was ready to enjoy any excuse to pull the trigger. Behind the rimless spectacles, the man's eyes were unflinching.

The rights or wrongs were of little interest to Valmain, who garbled something too fast for Gavin to understand. The tone was sharp, aggressive. However, the upward motioning of the gun he understood with ease. Reluctantly he got up, releasing his victim as he did so.

Chouen too struggled to his feet. In gasped-out french he pointed accusingly at Gavin. Whatever was said seemed to be effective. Valmain peered over his spectacles in Gavin's direction and nodded grimly. Gavin heard the word *gendarme*, accompanied by aggressive lunges with the gun. Again, the message was clear. Step by step he was forced to retreat towards the gate at gunpoint whilst Chouen stood, hurt but triumphant, shoulders slumped and hands in front of him. With a final flourish of the gun, Gavin was pushed back into the street. Immediately the door was slammed shut, followed by the sound of a bolt.

After a moment of hesitation he walked to the corner where he decided to wait. Claudine would have to be patient. No doubt Denim Jacket would be given a glass of something and then sent packing. Then he'd get him. At that moment he heard the wail of a police siren. A blue Peugeot, all flashing lights and punished tyres, appeared and slewed by him into the cul-de-sac and stopped outside the green doors. Bugger it! Gavin didn't hesitate. It was time to leave. Corbin wouldn't take kindly to him being arrested for assault and criminal damage.

En route to the restaurant he brushed himself down and did his best to tidy his hair. Even so, on arrival, he cut a curious figure. His jacket and trousers were filthy, his shirt soaked with sweat, his face dirty and dust-stained from the scuffle. He slumped into the seat opposite Claudine who was the picture of relaxation. 'Only the silver medal I'm afraid.'

He watched as she stubbed out a cigarette and looked at him quizzically. 'Tell me.' She could see that he was scarcely triumphant.

He pointed to his matted, damp hair. 'I need to tidy up ... that and a large beer.'

'That'll keep. What's it all about?'

'I was hoping that maybe you or Carl would tell me.' Even as the words tumbled out, Gavin regretted them. He hadn't meant to sound so bitter.

'Me? Carl? Are you mad? We haven't had you followed. Look, Gavin, when it's just you and me I'm having a great time, a real ball. When it's me and your Bureau ... count me out. You know what really hurts? That you don't trust me.' She grasped her designer bag, slung it over her shoulder and rose to leave. 'I've got better ways of spending my time.' Her tone was resentful.

Gavin stood up and moved to bar her route to the door.

Then he placed his hands on her shoulders. 'Look. I'm sorry. Don't go. Please. Don't you see? I need explanations. Someone had me followed or someone knew I was here. Carl has to be a suspect.' For the second time he fixed his eyes on her, urging his sincerity. 'Please stay.'

She looked up at him. Her eyes were doleful, full of reproach. 'I suppose you're right.' Her oval face showed her inner turmoil. She sighed. 'Get cleaned up. Then we'll talk about it.'

When he reappeared he looked not much smarter but a shade cleaner. She patted her own hair into place as they went into the empty street. 'Let's walk to Notre Dame,' suggested Claudine.

'So far? After I've just run the marathon, fought three rounds and bloody nearly had my brains blown out.' His tone was joking but she got the message.

'*Mais non!* You English! No stamina. No wonder Napoleon won the Battle of Waterloo.'

Gavin thought for a moment, looking puzzled. 'He didn't, did he?'

'You *rosbifs* - no sense of humour.' She'd ramped up her French accent deliberately for the leg-pulling as she tapped him on the nose. 'Just keep walking and tell me what's going on.'

He nodded in response, knowing he'd be able to tell her nothing.

They were both under orders.

Chapter 17

At the Bar Figaro, not far from Trocadero, Gavin and Claudine were perched on stools at the marble topped counter. It was 8.00 pm and there was a noisy chatter all around them. Lining the back of the bar was a stunning array of fine wines. They were chatting inconsequentially over a bottle of Chambolle Musigny and nibbling from a selection of olives and cheeses. Life was good.

The afternoon had been a great success. They'd strolled by the Seine, seen an attempted suicide at Notre Dame, walked the high-fashion stretch of the Faubourg St Honoré and studied the soldiers patrolling on the Avenue Matignon. They'd laughed, joked, walked hand-in-hand, sometimes arm-in-arm, but they'd never kissed. Gavin had held back, not feeling that the invitation had been there.

'You see how well we get on,' commented Claudine as she played with the stem of her wine glass, 'when we just talk about this and that and keep the Bureau out of it.'

'Escaping the clutches of the Bureau isn't as easy as you think. It's not a nine-to-five job. It probably sounds daft but it's a bit like a mission. It grabs you and swallows you up whole.'

'Do you miss being a lawyer?' Gavin noticed that her eyes were fixed on him, steady and searching, even though the question itself seemed inconsequential.

'Once a lawyer, always a lawyer,' he laughed. 'It's a state of mind, a discipline. Like a bad bout of flu, it's hard to shake off. The difference is that working for the Bureau, I'm freelance.' He thought for a moment. 'Correction, freelance except of course for Walter Corbin. He's the Director, cool, calculating, with the brain of a Grand Master. His main

149

weakness is he's a bad listener. That apart ... he's pretty bloody good. But, like Klodinsky, he's an enigma too. Hard as nails with a heart of gold.'

'Meaning?' Claudine helped herself to some Brie.

'Gives 100%. Expects 200% back.' He threw back an earlier description of Klodinsky. 'Let's change the subject. We're getting near Bureau-talk. Tell me some more about horoscopes.'

'Fine by me. As I told you yesterday, you're Taurus.'

'Meaning?'

'Taurus people are persistent, conservative, careful, stubborn and steadfast, not known for versatility or imagination. Yet somehow you've got these last two.'

'Thank you ... but that destroys your theory.'

'Not *my* theory and neither is it destroyed.' There was excitement in her eyes, the belief of the zealot shining through. 'I checked your birthday. Your planet sign is Mercury. Mercury in Taurus gives you the versatility and imagination.'

Very convenient, Gavin thought. Somehow you could always fix the rules to fit the circumstances. Nevertheless, he kept his cynicism to himself. 'You'll have to keep on convincing me.'

She clasped his hand. 'That's Taurus for you. Stubborn in the face of the evidence.'

'So what are you predicting for me? That a man in a blue denim jacket will enter my life?' He smiled at her across the top of his glass and was rewarded with a laugh.

'I'm not talking about the rubbish in the papers. It's worth taking seriously. I'm an Aquarian. 5th February. It's a good sign. Doesn't always go too well with Taurus though. We're both too stubborn.' She drained her glass and then looked at the expensive Piaget watch which adorned her wrist. 'It depends though.' She never explained on what it depended. 'It's gone nine. Time for you to take me home. It's been fun.'

About ten minutes later, they stepped out of the cab at the Quai Louis Blériot. Arm in arm, they paused to look over the Expressway at the river view before she led him inside to the elevator. Her apartment block was seven storeys high and spanking new.

'Yours is the penthouse, isn't it?'

'How did you guess?' She seemed impressed.

'It's in your stars,' he teased, though he'd worked out that anything less would have been out of style for Carl Klodinsky. However, once in the apartment, the lavishness overwhelmed him. The hallway alone was bigger than most people's entire apartment. Beyond that was a galleried split-level dining-room. On the far side was a giant sliding window leading out to the balcony which ran the full thirty metre stretch of sitting-room and dining-room combined. Everything was new, everything in the best possible taste. The plushness of the velvet curtains and the expensive sweep of Turkish carpets created an opulent elegance. The blended shades of apricot and cream on the walls, on the lamps, on the curtains were restful. The subdued lighting which was operated from a central console created contrasts of light and shade.

If she noticed his questioning respect, Claudine said nothing. From the control by the sofa she partially shut the curtains and switched on the television. 'Why not fix some drinks? There's some champagne in the fridge.' She disappeared into a bedroom and then decided to take a shower. Strange, she thought a few moments later as she soaped herself. Only yesterday evening she'd felt so lonely, so restless, that she'd downed more than half a bottle of vodka. Tonight, she was singing an Edith Piaf number, something she hadn't done for more than a while.

Meantime Gavin was playing with the electronic controls. Curtains went back and forth, the television switched channels, lights brightened and dimmed and, for all he knew, the fridge was de-icing and the waste-disposal unit was working full-speed at the touch of the buttons with which he was playing. Bored with that, he went round the room studying the expensive ornaments, the statuettes, each of them worth hundreds if not thousands of pounds. Most had a touch of the orient but the rest of the room did not. The mix of plants, chairs and occasional tables were all straight from the most exclusive shops in Paris. Everything was perfection. Everything that is except for the blackened burn mark of a cigarette on the arm of the sofa.

Gavin thought of his own home, the nondescript apartment in nondescript Barons Court. He thought of the furnishings or what Janie had left of them. They were a mix of old and new, trendy and staid, a mish-mash without style. But it was home. It was homely. He looked round Claudine's room again. Despite all the expense and all the luxury, it wasn't relaxing. It was, however, proof of the power of money and a credit to designer chic.

He poured 1983 Laurent Perrier into shapely glasses and wondered for a moment just what Claudine had done to achieve such enormous largesse. Even the champagne was the same as at Cannes. Carl's influence was everywhere.

He slid back the window and leaned on the balcony railings. At one end, beyond the potted shrubs, were stairs leading to her private roof terrace. Up there he found a small, heated swimming pool and a gas barbecue. It was new, unused, unloved and probably unwanted.

He descended the stairs and again rested both arms on the balcony railings, relishing the coolness of the night air blowing in from the river. Why had Klodinsky spent so much on her? Love? Guilt? A bribe? Why such opulence? If it wasn't sex, and Claudine had said it wasn't, then why? Guilt for shifting her to Paris? Or what she knew? Or was she a key player? She certainly didn't seem to bring her work home with her. There had been not a sign of business papers anywhere.

Down below, the traffic was speeding along the Georges Pompidou Expressway and on the river he could see the outline of a small boat chugging upstream. He shivered slightly at the chilly breeze, his mind full of conflicting thoughts. From behind he heard a noise. It was Claudine who'd done a quick change. Now she was wearing a pink mohair jersey with a high collar, clinging white jeans and a pair of flip-flops. 'Some view eh?' she prompted. 'Even the factory over there has it's own beauty at night. And the river ... it's always alive. But I miss New York, even without the view.' She picked up her glass. 'Cheers.'

'Cheers.' They clinked glasses. 'I'd no idea your apartment was ...like this.' He waved an arm in each direction. 'Carl didn't spare any expense, did he?'

'He never does.' He thought she was going to volunteer something else. There was an uncomfortable pause, then she shivered. 'It's cold. Shall we go in?' She led him back inside and they sat down on the sofa. On the table was a pot of coffee and some pizza pieces which she had heated up. On the television, the news was starting and they fell silent to watch as they munched pizza and poured each other glasses of champagne.

'Michel Mboro, Lumbolan Minister of the Interior, was in Paris today,' said the newsreader as a voice-over to a picture of the African statesman. 'Discussions are believed to have included security arrangements for world leaders who will attend the celebrations when Lumbola and Sampopo become Lupopo next month. A spokesman for the Elysée Palace said that arrangements were satisfactory.' There then followed more shots of Michel Mboro, this time shaking hands with the French Foreign Minister at the Quai D'Orsay.

'Did you understand that?' queried Claudine.

'Sort of. The French was a bit quick. It was about Lumbola and Sampopo wasn't it? Not my scene. Should I be interested?'

'Carl's going. He knows the President of Lumbola.'

'Some freebie! Does he do much business in Lumbola?'

Claudine turned and smiled coquettishly before tapping him gently on the end of his nose. 'Naughty! You're not here to question me about Carl.'

Gavin put up his hands in surrender. 'Ok. You win.' He shifted uncomfortably, drained his coffee and put his arm around her shoulder. He was about to probe again but more subtly this time, when the telephone rang. She pulled away from him to pick up the receiver. ' 'Allo, 'allo. 'Allo, 'allo.' On the phone, the Frenchness in her voice seemed more pronounced. Or maybe he was just looking out for it. She held on for a few moments, looking increasingly puzzled. As she returned the receiver to the cradle, she shrugged her shoulders. 'No one there.'

'Doesn't that worry you?'

'Wrong number maybe. Fault on the line. Could be anything. No.' She shrugged again. 'I'm not worried.'

Despite the denial, Gavin wasn't convinced. 'You sound frightened.'

Claudine shook her head vigorously. 'No. I'll be all right.' She was regaining her composure. She sprawled back against him, the mohair tickling Gavin on the neck as he draped his right arm across her shoulders.

'If you're worried, I can stay if you like.' There was a catch in Gavin's voice as he spoke.

'Good try, Romeo.' She kissed him, just briefly, with a mere brushing of their lips together. 'That's more like a Sagittarian than a Taurus.' She took a sip from her glass. 'Turning that phone call into an opportunity. Must be that touch of Mercury in you again.' Her eyes, wide open and innocent, showed that she was teasing him and her fingers playfully squeezed the nape of his neck.

'In England we'd call it old-fashioned chivalry.' He was enjoying the bit of flirting.

'Well chivalry must wait.' The laugh, light and soft, was infectious. 'I want to know you better. My love life has been one long mistake. All the wrong guys.' She looked downwards, eyes slightly ashamed. 'It didn't stop me wanting them. Now ... I need something different. So trust me, take things slowly, then ... who knows?' It was said in a husky whisper. When she'd finished she kissed him on the lips, firmly this time.

'You're right,' he said without enthusiasm as they separated. His body was telling him not to be so bloody chivalrous and to get on with it. 'We need time. So it's lunch tomorrow?'

'If the weather's fine, let's go to the Bois de Boulogne. Perhaps an outside table at La Cascade. But as for tonight ... it's been a long day. I think you ought to go.'

'I'll call round at about eleven. Ok?'

'Perfect. And believe me. I *shall* miss you tonight.'

'Me too.' He put his arms round her waist and pulled her close. For a moment they nuzzled against each other. Then she pulled away with a reluctance which Gavin was quick to notice. It was almost as if she were schizophrenic.

'Until tomorrow.' He leaned forward to kiss her again. 'And watch out for Denim Jacket,' she murmured.

As the elevator descended, Claudine bolted her door and went straight to the telephone.

Chapter Eighteen

'Kidnapped?' Art's grumpy voice was dismissive.

'That's what I said.' Gavin sounded strident as he reported on the Paris trip in Corbin's office. 'I'm telling you. Claudine's been kidnapped.' He was exhausted and the air was full of Monday morning blues. Art's disbelief and flippancy were just making matters worse.

Of the three of them only Walter didn't need some coffee, though his flight from San Juan had only landed two hours before. Art's plane had got in at 6.00 am, after fourteen hours in the air from Singapore. Though Gavin had been closest to home, he hadn't slept for over twenty-four hours.

Between the three men on Walter's desk lay the exhibits. The heavy black lettering of the death threat showed through the perspex of the folder in which it was now carefully protected. The stack of money and wrapping paper were sealed in a polythene bag. In the middle of it all lay Captain Scutar's gold Rolex.

'Oh sure, kidnapping's possible. So's turning water into wine.' Art was irritable. He'd grunted and growled his way through the last twenty minutes. The lines on his face seemed etched even deeper than usual. His eyes were puffy, his hair in need of a wash. If he'd bothered to shave, then it hadn't been a good one. Yet it was Gavin who was more on edge. It showed as his fingers drummed nervously on the desk.

'Tell me again Gavin. More slowly this time. It doesn't make much sense to me.' Walter's voice was patient as he leaned back in his chair and tried to make something of the latest developments. Death threats and kidnapping? Maybe it was believable. Maybe it just had to be believed.

'On Saturday night, I left Claudine. We'd fixed for me to pick her up at eleven the next morning. I went round to her place and she wasn't there. I spoke to the concièrge. She told me that at just before eight, breakfast time, a Citroen had stopped outside. She saw Claudine go out to the car. She was between two men. The way she describes it, they *put* her in the back. Then they got in, one either side of her.'

'Typical concièrge. They see everything,' said Walter. 'Go on.'

'There was a driver in front. She had never seen the Citroen nor the men before. She didn't want to say that Claudine was *forced* into the car. Not in the sense of being man-handled. Just that she thought that Claudine had no choice.' Gavin's tired face pleaded for understanding. It was lost on Art. 'I rang her several times on Sunday. I changed my plans and stayed the night. I phoned again this morning. Still nothing.'

'So? Perhaps she wanted a good lay.' Art's tone was contemptuous. 'Maybe by all three of them.'

Gavin's eyes blazed in anger. 'Why don't you sod off? If you can't say anything more constructive ...'

'Cut it out!' Walter was quick to intervene. 'Anything else?'

Gavin was still scowling at Art as he continued. 'The only other odd thing was a phone call she got on Saturday night. The line went dead. Said she wasn't worried. I didn't believe her then.' He shrugged his shoulders and looked at Corbin. 'It may be nothing.' Nevertheless, he wanted to be taken seriously. 'Believe me, we were getting on really well. I don't think she stood me up.'

'Didn't screw you though, did she? Didn't want your little pink pecker up her. Didn't want you that much did she, big boy?' The tone was contemptuous as Art stubbed out one Camel and immediately reached for his packet to light another. 'Kidnapped - baloney! It was her job. Klodinsky wanted her somewhere without you knowing. Nothing more sinister than that. She hasn't phoned because she doesn't want to see you. Or because Klodinsky won't let her break confidence. For all we know, she's in Piraeus, looking at *Adber Arrow*.'

Art rose from his chair and stood in front of Gavin. 'Look at me.' Gavin's face puckered. 'Admit it. I can see you, Romeo, all starry-eyed and loose-tongued, telling her all about the Bureau.' Surprisingly nimbly he spun round to clinch his argument to Walter. 'And the whole lot's gone back to Klodinsky.'

They fell silent. Walter and Art both saw the sullen despair on Gavin's ashen face. From below came the buzz of traffic, whilst overhead a twin-engined Dash whined on its approach to the City Airport. Corbin thought it was time to intervene. 'Ok. Who would kidnap her? Klodinsky? Why would he? Why should *anyone* kidnap her.'

'I've thought of nothing else all night.' Gavin twisted a paperclip to destruction as he spoke. 'Klodinsky has my photograph, has the top to bottom on Brads. He has me followed. He finds out that Claudine is seeing me, fears she could blow his secret plan. At the same time, he needs my help to get Brads to sign the charter deals. So he sets up the bribe and death threat. But Claudine's a worry. So he has her kidnapped ... maybe even silenced.'

'Klodinsky the kidnapper? Bring on the clowns! What a heap of shit! Look ...' Art slumped forward, resting his head in his hands as he leant on the table. His speech was slurred from lack of sleep, his right eye more closed than his left. He ran his fingers through his dank hair. 'Klodinsky sure doesn't *need* Brads. Brads need him, that's the real time of day. *Ryme Lady* was old. She leaked. She sank. Then the crew were rescued, only to be murdered.'

'There's more holes in that theory than in a lump of gruyère.' Gavin enjoyed his joke and even Art joined in

Walter's laughter. Nevertheless, Art's face showed his dis-agreement. 'No.' The denial was vehement. The pouches under his eyes were larger than usual, his tongue furred, his eyes reddened and sore. The watchers looked on and waited. 'Now, you listen.' He slurped at a cup of coffee, shoulders stooped, brow furrowed, hair sweaty and dishevelled, finger wagging. 'You should thank me Gavin! Don't you understand, you dick-head, that I'm saving your life! I'm telling you that Klodinsky's clean. I'm telling you that Brads can charter to him. I'm telling you to pick up the money. Be rich! Do yourself a favour. I'm telling you to do what Klodinsky wants. Save your own life.'

Gavin was unconvinced. What Walter was thinking was not evident. He was silent, looking at each of them in turn. 'How come the fishermen were killed? That's what I want to know.'

Art defended his viewpoint. 'Been shooting their mouths off. Pure chance. Got mugged.'

Gavin was still uneasy. 'Twaddle! And Sir Archie's wife? Was she murdered?' Even as he said it, he knew that shape and coherence were disappearing from his argu-ment. He wasn't surprised when he saw the hostile glint in Walter's eye as he peered over the top of his spectacles.

'What does that matter?' Walter sounded tetchy. 'Anyway, what have you told Brads?' There was an edge to the question, a rasp in the voice. It was the schoolmaster bringing the class back to the point.

'I haven't told them about the death threat or the kidnap. I've told them I was followed. Sir Archie didn't seem to care. Firstly he wants to know whether to charter to Klodinsky and secondly he wants to know what happened to *Ryme Lady*. No doubt, if we could throw in the address of a Madame Whiplash, with a leather suit who'd spank his bum with a hairbrush, he'd like that advice best of all.' Gavin's flippancy, aimed at a target outside the room, lowered the temperature though no one laughed. They watched as Walter looked at the death threat, turning it over front and back, back and front.

'Let's see what Forensic make of this little lot. I'll get my pal Greenaway down at the Yard to talk to the French police. We play this down, very much down. All of it. Especially the death threat.'

Gavin looked disappointed at the lack of dramatic action whilst Art's hunger was making him increasingly displeased. Breakfast had been a long time ago and he felt ready to demolish a Big Mac. In a slow movement he shifted the Director's silver pen stand and seated himself on Walter's desk. His short, strong legs swung just above the floor and the slight new bulge of his stomach was all too obvious in the grubby T-shirt which he had been wearing since he'd checked out of the Mandarin twenty hours previously. He chose to ignore Walter's glare of disapproval. 'I'm telling you. There's no mystery about the *sinking* of *Ryme Lady*. The only mystery is how she managed to stay afloat.'

'But no Mayday.' Walter's metaphorical slap on the wrist was decisive. This time Walter's disapproving look caused Art to debate whether to shift from the desk but he decided to sit it out and helped himself to the last biscuit on the plate, a bourbon cream which was Walter's favourite. The Director was not amused as he continued. 'It's not unreasonable that Brads want advice.' His eyes looked first at Gavin and then at Art. 'So get your act together. You're like a pantomime horse but with each of you pulling in different directions.'

Art nodded in agreement and pointed at Gavin. 'Sure! And guess who's playing the asshole.'

Gavin met Art's disparaging comment with a cool even look which gradually broke into a smile. Then he put his hands to his ears. 'Art could play a donkey on his own.'

Chapter 19

The meeting in the St James's Hotel in Buckingham Gate had been brief. Gavin and Art both stood by the window in the meeting room, talking quietly. The room was heavy with smoke from Sir Archie's cigars. The plate of sandwiches had been cleared, the pot of coffee was empty. An uneasy peace had broken out between Sir Archie, Edward and Susannah as they prepared to leave.

Edward wanted no misunderstanding. 'You're positive? Brads should not charter to Klodinsky?' He was almost disbelieving in his moment of triumph over his father.

'Right. That's the Bureau's advice.' Art was decisive. Beside him, Gavin tried not to look amazed at what he had just heard.

'Minute that, can you Susannah.' Edward looked across to his father who was furious that he'd failed to persuade the meeting to grab Klodinsky's offer.

'It'll be the death of Brads, d'ya see? You wait.' Sir Archie's voice was less strained now than it had been. In his anger his cigar butt was being chewed rather than smoked.

Gavin studied the three Crawfords. All wrapped up in their own squabbles, none of them knew that he had just signed his own death warrant. He doubted if they'd have been any more grateful if they'd known. 'We're not concerned about Klodinsky. As you've got the Pinetto opportunity instead, charter to them. Edward's already told us that they've improved their offer.'

Edward closed his attaché case and moved to the door. 'It should keep the bankers quiet. Agreed Susannah?'

She nodded her head. 'Yup. If they move fast and start the charter payments soon.'

'What do we *know* about Pinetto?' Sir Archie asked, his voice gruff.

Before Gavin had a chance to comment, Edward had been quick to respond. He wasn't going to let his father re-open that debate. 'Good reports. I had them checked out. Nothing known against them.'

Art and Gavin looked at each other, shrugged their shoulders and it was Art who spoke. 'Let's be clear on this. We weren't asked to compare Klodinsky with Pinetto. Except for Klodinsky, who you deal with is a matter for you.'

'I think you should check them out,' said Susannah, to Sir Archie's obvious delight.

'Pinetto need to know by tomorrow,' explained Edward. 'They want to charter *Cerne View* at once for the West African run and *Adber Arrow* within seven days.'

Sir Archie buttoned up his navy-blue coat with fur collar. His voice showed his resignation. 'It's probably too late, d'ya see. It's Pinetto or bust. But check them out any-way ... let us know. Meantime, get *Ryme Lady* sorted out. We need the hull insurance money.' He shook his head in irritation so that his jowls shuddered. What's more, we've got all these damned Members of Parliament on behalf of the families badgering us, writing letters, some calling for an enquiry.'

Susannah opened her mouth to say something, probably something rather sharp, then changed her mind. She filed the last of her papers into the slim, burgundy-coloured case which she was carrying and the Crawford family left, heading for Paddington and their train back to Bristol.

When they followed, Gavin and Art decided to walk through St James's Park to Trafalgar Square. With no breeze, a few people were sitting on the grass enjoying the morning sun, some even sitting in the shade of the trees. They made an odd couple, Art in his bomber jacket, open-neck blue shirt, slacks and trainers, while Gavin was in a well-cut grey pinstripe, white shirt and club tie. As they walked, Gavin did so with languid, lengthy strides whilst Art's shorter legs had to work hard to keep pace. 'Went better than expected,' said Gavin. 'But if it hadn't been for Pinetto ...'

'It would have been a blood-bath,' Art completed the line of thought.

'Anyway, why the big U-turn? You caught me on the hop.' Gavin had been stunned to hear Art warn against chartering to Klodinsky. Before the meeting the plan had been to tell Brads the facts and leave them to decide which way to jump.

Art cleared his throat. 'I changed my mind.' He made it sound so simple, nothing dramatic at all. 'I just had to respect your views. After all, you had the death threat. Your advice was to defy it. Why should I worry?' Art's tone was almost flippant as if Gavin's life was of no importance at all. 'I guess I came to the view that you were sure you're right.'

'This death warrant thing.' Gavin laughed nervously. 'Probably bluff.'

Art swung up his muscly arm and patted Gavin on the back. 'Sure. Probably bluff. Anyway! So what! Live on the edge, live dangerously. Otherwise go back to lawyering.' It was as if Art didn't take the threat seriously or, if he did, wasn't concerned. 'Say, what about Claudine? Any news?'

'Nothing. It's ripping me apart. The not knowing.'

'Forget her. Women are just trouble.' Art gave Gavin a sideways glance but the listener didn't notice. He was locked in his own private torment.

'No. Claudine was different.'

Art stopped to face Gavin. 'Hey! Cool it! You scarcely knew her. She was a plant, a come-on girl. She'll turn up alive. When it suits her or Klodinsky. Hell, maybe she's the one who's going to kill you.'

'That's a load of ...' Gavin never finished the sentence as, with a sudden movement, Art pushed him to the ground.

'Duck!' cried Art. He watched Gavin crash onto the grass and wrap his hands round the back of his head. There he lay like a corpse. Gradually Gavin raised his head, looking round like a startled rabbit. He saw Art standing over him, his face full of mocking laughter. 'See ... a duck.' Art pointed at the lake as he helped Gavin to his feet. Gavin looked ruefully across at the water whilst he brushed the grass cuttings from the finest worsted. A white duck was paddling towards the bridge.

'Bastard! Christ, that shook me.' Gavin tried to laugh as he picked grass cuttings from his hands but he was too shaken.

'I meant to. You've got to sharpen up. You're not playing softball now. If not ... you'll wake up dead.' He paused as Gavin finished brushing the last of the mud from his knees. 'Come on, I'll buy you a cup of coffee. Last meal for a condemned man.' There was a genuine warmth in the voice, a touch of affection even.

Gavin noticed it, thinking how it contrasted with his earlier sardonic view. 'It's not like you to care. What gives?'

Art kicked an empty Pepsi can. 'Maybe I just respect what you've done. Hell, it would have been no sweat to tell Brads to charter to Klodinsky. Yes, I guess I respect that.' The two men crossed the bridge over the lake and took the path towards the Mall.

'And you know what Walter said, don't you? I don't even get to keep the bribe.'

Chapter 20

Nearly two weeks later, Art was in his apartment. It wasn't home. It was just where he happened to live ... a rented place by Marble Arch. Some days he'd kid himself that he'd move. He never would.

He finished shaving and stood by the mirror in his blue bathrobe. Back in New Jersey, life had been one long move, seventeen broken-down apartments that he could remember, some that he'd prefer to forget. He smiled at himself as he combed out his hair. He turned his head from side to side, admired his teeth, liking what he saw, although the smile faded as he studied the first hints of recession in his hairline. And was that a touch of grey there at the side? He moved his face closer to the mirror and decided he was being over-sensitive. What the hell! Women everywhere still found him attractive. Not *all* women but there were plenty around who loved the rough edge of his tongue, the lived-in look, the sod-em-all attitude. He splashed on a touch of aftershave, adjusted the bathrobe and went through to the living room.

There was the odd personal touch but otherwise the room was just as he had rented it - bland furniture, bland colours, bland lighting, everything plain bland, designed by the landlords to offend no one. A tinkle of glass behind him restored a contented smile and he turned to kiss the petite young woman who was wearing not a lot as she put her arms round his neck after placing a large scotch and ice in his hand. 'Feeling better?' she enquired.

'Not as good as I'll feel after I've had this, honey. Joining me?'

She loved being called honey - so different from *darling*

said with the long vowels of the Sloanes who worked with her in the City. 'Only if you're not coming to bed.' She moved round the moquette chair and sat beside him, stroking his ear. She was twenty-four, slender, 5' 7" tall and with sharp features which took nothing away from her beauty. Her hair was jet black, shoulder length and with a slight spring in it so that it hung well and swayed in unison. Her voice, her bearing, her style spoke of an affluent upbringing and an expensive education somewhere in the Home Counties. Now she worked as an analyst for a firm of brokers, specialising in media-related stocks.

Art pulled her to him and kissed her gently, enjoying the softness of the dark hairs on the nape of her neck and the warmth of her body as she cuddled up to him. 'Supper first? It smells great.'

She pouted in disappointment, uncertain whether he was play-acting or not. She was used to getting her own way and usually took full advantage of her strong personality and seductive charms to achieve whatever she wanted. But not with Art. Perhaps that's why she'd been so attracted to him. He was rough trade by the standards of Virginia Water. Nevertheless, the talkative eyes' deep-set in his rugged features, coupled with a cruel wit and unbridled lust, made it easy for her to forget the spreading stomach, the stubby legs and the rasping New York accent.

'So much for romance,' she mocked him. 'That lasted just twenty four hours after you got back from the Far East.' The moment of irritation passed. 'But you're right. Supper's Lamb Provençale, mixed salad, no potatoes.' She patted his stomach. 'Definitely no potatoes .... but I've opened a bottle of Beaune '85.'

The wine meant nothing to Art. He would have been as happy with a can of Budweiser. She however, like most people working in the City, was familiar with the good and bad years of Grand Crus. 'I didn't say there wasn't time for just a few moments relaxation.' The lines round his eyes creased and crinkled as he smiled before kissing her white, rounded breasts which were spilling over the top of her black negligée. 'You know, honey, there are times like this when I wish we had more time to enjoy each other, more time to share.'

In the short weeks since they'd got together, they'd had more than a few highs and lows. 'You know you wouldn't like it really. You'd get all my aggression. I'd get all yours. We'd fight like mad. Even more than now.'

'And screw like hell.' He nibbled the lobe of her ear. The sex seemed to bridge the vast gulf between them.

'Mmm! That too but ...' The telephone rang and broke the moment. Irritated, Art reached across and picked up the cordless phone.

'Yes?'

It was Sir Archie. 'Look. Sorry to butt in on a chap and all that. Bad moment?'

'Ah! Sir Archie. Well ... matter of fact I've got something warming up here right now.'

'I see, I see. Cooking supper eh? Anyway, won't keep you long. There's been a development.'

'Yah?' Art's mind was somewhere between Sir Archie's baritone voice and the rampant nipple which he was licking.

'Look,' said Sir Archie, 'our agency in New York has had an anonymous call, a tip-off if you like, saying that *Ryme Lady* was scuttled with no cargo aboard. The caller said it was part of a fund-raising scam by the IRA. The informant wants a meeting next week, in New York.'

Art decided it was time to give Sir Archie his undivided attention. 'You could make a lot of bombs, buy a heap of guns with the insurance money.'

Sir Archie, who would be the last one to leave Brads that night, coughed noisily as he put down the glowing cigar.

'That's what I felt, d'ya see. Thought you'd like to know at once.'

'Sure. That's interesting. What about *Cerne View*? And *Adber Arrow*?'

'They're both earning. Chartered to Pinetto. *Cerne View* is picking up a load of containers and mixed cargo in Marseille. Going down the West African coast - destination Lumbola and then Nigeria. We signed that last week.' He paused for a moment.

'And *Adber Arrow*?'

'Signed today. Pinetto's got a consignment of crude oil for her.'

'Right.' Art thought for a moment. So Klodinsky had definitely lost. The fuse beneath Gavin had been lit. 'You alone?'

'Yes. Why?' Sir Archie sounded puzzled.

'I was just wondering. Something different I wanted to ask. Did you murder your wife, Ingrid?'

It was as if the line had gone dead, as if Sir Archie had momentarily stopped breathing. Then the halting tones of the Chairman returned. 'I say. That's a bit O.T.T. old boy. Good Lord no! There was an inquest you know.'

'Inquest baloney. Proves nothing. Why did Ingrid fall from the Clifton Bridge? You don't do that if you're happy. You do it because someone *flings* you over or because you *want* to hit the rocks below. And you're falling a long time. Plenty of time to think. Plenty of time to know you're going to die. So why?' Deliberately, Art had laid it on thick.

Sir Archie picked up the cigar and twisted in his chair. He couldn't seem to get comfortable, wishing now that he'd called Gavin instead. *He* was a gentleman, wouldn't have been so offensive when a chap was only trying to help. 'I don't know. I wish I did.'

Art was unconvinced and said so. 'Ok. I'll tell you why she jumped. It's because she'd found out about your trips to the Avenue Victor Hugo. You'd picked up Aids.'

'Come off it! You ought to be careful what you say. Slander and all that. Someone might be listening. You're talking rubbish. The answer's no.'

'No - she hadn't found out? Or no - that isn't why she jumped?'

'It's no. No to everything.'

'Ingrid had lovers, didn't she. Was Klodinsky one of them?' Art enjoyed switching the attack.

'No to that too. She'd met him. We all had over the years. But Carl and Ingrid lovers? Not that I knew. Other lovers? Yes, maybe but ...... they weren't important to her. Or to me come to that. A fella's entitled to the occasional *dalliance*, wouldn't you say?' He paused for Art to comment but none came. Sounding rather lame, he continued. 'She was depressed, d'ya see. It happens.'

'Now, just look here Mr Chairman.' There was dumb insolence in Art's voice. 'I'm being paid to help you. You're not helping yourself. Cut out the bullshit. Why was she depressed? It's important.'

'Not to the sinking of *Ryme Lady* it isn't.' Sir Archie reached for his glass of brandy and ginger ale, only to find it was empty. A look of irritation crossed his face. He wanted to put down the receiver, to cut the conversation short.

'Then I'm telling you.' The American's voice was menacing. 'She found out you were screwing her younger sister, Chrissie.'

'Chrissie! Chrissie! How in hell's name did you know about that?' Art knew he'd scored as he heard the sharp intake of breath. Down in Bristol, Sir Archie's cheeks turned from their usual fiery red to aubergine. Every blood vessel looked fit to burst. Then Art heard the heavy exhaling at the other end of the line.

'You Ok?' Art prompted. 'Hell, I didn't expect to give you a stroke. Not till I've finished questioning anyway.' As he waited, he rewarded himself with a nibble of an ear whilst his left hand absent-mindedly stroked the softness of an inner thigh. 'Ok. Let me ask you this. How did Ingrid find out about Chrissie?'

Sir Archie spoke slowly. Suddenly his office seemed very hot. He pulled a spotted handkerchief from his top pocket and mopped his brow before wiping the base of his neck. 'I wish I knew.' Sir Archie sounded broken.

'And I wish I could believe you,' snapped the American. 'I'll want to ask about this again.' Art could hear the tension dissolve as the Chairman realised that the inquisition was over for the time being.

'You'll follow up this tip-off?' Sir Archie sounded relieved to change the subject.

'Sure. Leave this IRA thing with me. Goodnight.' Art put down the phone and smiled with satisfaction.

'I don't think I like you,' she said. 'You're a right bastard.' The words were whispered in admiration as she lay across him, stroking his chest.

'It's all guesswork, honey. Won't do any harm. May do some good.' He kissed her perfunctorily. 'All that's made me hungry. Thirsty too.'

'Bed first?' Then supper? It's overcooked by now anyway.'

Outside, the endless hum of traffic from the Edgware Road rose towards Art's sixth-floor apartment. In the near darkness of the bedroom the only sounds were those of the ecstasy of the lovers as they gyrated on Art's circular water bed. It was the only major item he'd bought. 'Oh! Oh! Oh! You big, big boy!' Her voice was breathless and excited when the telephone started to ring, shrill and intruding.

'Let it ring,' said Art angrily. 'What a godawful time to telephone.' From the corner of his eye he could see it was only 8.40 p.m. Still the phone kept ringing. Grudgingly, reluctantly, he stretched out and flicked the phone to receive. 'For Chrissake! Yeh!'

Gavin sensed he'd called at a bad moment as he stood in the phone box at Heathrow. 'How are things?' he said uncertainly, his voice sounding metallic. Gavin wanted to play Art at his own game. Get Art to speak first. It didn't work.

'Till you called, just fine. Whaddya want?'

'It's Claudine. I'm at Heathrow, meeting her. She's just been released.'

'Released? In London? Why London? Why you?'

'Damn you Art! Because she likes me. Can't you accept that? She'd got no friends in Paris. When she phoned she sounded petrified. Hell! It's been two weeks since she was kidnapped.'

'You believe that, you'd believe my old Mom was last year's Miss New Jersey. Now listen kiddo. Don't tell her anything.' He paused for effect. 'Especially don't tell her what I'm now telling you. It's looking like the IRA are in this. Sank *Ryme Lady*. See you tomorrow. And don't call me. I'll call you.' Just for a moment, as he turned over to luxuriate in the welcoming contours of the warm body beside him, he felt a pang of remorse. It didn't last. 'Asshole!' he muttered.

Out at the airport, Gavin smarted at Art's tone. Of all the pig-headed boorish people he'd ever met, Art was the biggest. But if hard-ball was the game, then Art was your man. He looked round him, taking in the bustle of the Arrivals Hall. It all looked innocuous enough, everyone dashing about, hurrying to meet loved ones from flights or the return of business associates. Yet maybe even here was someone watching him, watching everything he did, just waiting for the moment to blast him into oblivion. It wasn't pleasant.

He'd got a few minutes for a coffee before the Paris flight landed. As he went in search of the cafeteria, he realized

just what Art had been saying. An IRA connection. Shit!
That's trouble, Gavin! Now that Brads had signed up with
Pinetto. Oh ... and there was something else. That's right ...
up until now Art had been adamant. *Ryme Lady* had simply
sprung a leak. No fraud at all. Now, with equal conviction,
he says it was the IRA. Probably all crap. 'Coffee please,' he
asked the woman behind the steaming urn. To Art, changing opinions was as easy as changing clothes. The IRA?
Forget it, he told himself. Art's judgment's no better than
an Exocet with a broken gyro. The thought made him feel
better ... for a few moments at least.

Chapter 21

Edward was irritated as he rose from his favourite arm-chair to answer the phone. The dinner had been good but then Thornbury Castle always was. The wines had been excellent, the port had been vintage, the company had been excellent. He'd been alone. Unless she was pretty, he liked it that way - more time to relax, to think and to appreciate the little pleasures of a gourmet evening. 'Oh, it's you,' he said contemptuously.

'I've been trying to get you all evening,' Sir Archie retorted agressively.

'I've been out for dinner. Do I still need your permission before I blow my nose? Anyway, what do you want, ringing at this time?' It was only 11.15 pm.

'Look, we've had this message suggesting an American IRA link.' Sir Archie went on to explain the message received after Edward had left the office. 'Now, if that caller is right, then the IRA must be linked to cargo interests. They'd scoop the pool if the cargo had never gone aboard. I, for one, don't underestimate their ability. They're no Irish joke. So maybe they pressurized Klodinsky or fixed one of the crew.'

'Leave that to the Bureau. That's one for Art Lemman.'

'I've told him.'

'And I can imagine what he said. *Quit dreaming* ... or something more profane.' He paused to test his father's response but there was none. 'So, you're taking it seriously? A totally unsubstantiated tip-off? Well I regard it as tripe.'

'Art Lemman seemed to take it aboard. By the way, do you know where Susannah is? I wanted to ring her.'

'No. What she does out of office hours is not our business. It'll keep till tomorrow. This isn't hot news, certainly not worth calling at this time for. I'll tell you this.' Edward's tone was sibilant with alcohol but his face was mean. It was a look he saved for his dealings with his father whether on or off the phone. 'You're just a tired old man. Tired and bitter. Bitter about Klodinsky. I've said for months you should take the hint and go.'

'I'd retire if I knew the company was in good hands. It isn't. After all, as Chief Executive, you should be doing something about this IRA thing, d'ya see?' Sir Archie's tone was a mixture between sadness and despair, his mind drifting back to when he was Edward's age. By then, he'd been through the War, had seen death, had killed in action. Back in civvy street he'd shaped Brads as international trade started to resume. The pickings had been easy then. Edward had been brought up in a take-it-for-granted world, where money, travel, entertainment, excitement and a plentiful supply of vintage port were always available. 'I'll talk to you again tomorrow.' Sir Archie felt old and tired. Worse still, he felt sad. Perhaps it really was time to retire.

A few miles away Edward hitched up the elasticated waistband of his yellow pyjamas so that they fitted snugly over his indulgent stomach. *Bedtime*, he decided but then changed his mind and walked towards the drinks cabinet. A balloon of brandy was called for. So the old man was convinced there was an IRA connection? He wondered what would happen next, wondered what view the professionals would make of it - that's if you could call Gavin Blair a professional. Edward warmed the glass in his hand, savoured the deep oakiness of the bouquet and then took a generous swig. Now Art was different. He *was* a professional.

As if by a reflex motion, he found that he was topping up

his glass. He wasn't ready for bed yet. Despite what his father had said ... maybe in spite of what his father had said ... he was deeply interested in the future of Brads. He eased himself out of the depths of the armchair and went across the room into the study on the other side of the landing.

The telex machine had been silent whilst he'd been out but the fax had been busy. He picked up the reports on *Adber Arrow* and *Cerne View* and permitted himself a smile for the first time since he'd come in. The Board would be impressed with them. He tipped the last of the brandy down his throat and headed for the bedroom.

He'd bought the four-poster with chintz drapes when in his late twenties, fancying himself as a bit of a stud. Unhappily, no one else had - not Pauline the university lecturer, Mandy the shop assistant from the florists and not Kookie the black girl with the big boobs from the night club on Park Street. Worse still, even Tracey, the seventeen-year-old daughter of his next-door neighbour, who'd been impressed by the flashiness of his credit card lifestyle had sniggered at his efforts between the sheets.

He slumped onto the stack of pillows and lay on his back, looking at the mirrored ceiling, watching the blanket rise and fall over his spreading stomach. How had his father been so successful?

Chapter 22

While Edward had been gorging himself at Thornbury Castle, Gavin had finished his coffee and was pacing the Arrivals Hall at Heathrow Airport. It was ironic. Claudine wanted shelter and safety and here she was, coming to him! Him - the man with the death warrant! Maybe from the IRA too. He shivered involuntarily and thrust his hands deeper into the pockets of his slacks and then looked up at the Arrivals Board again. Ah! The flight was delayed by seven minutes. Just time to ring Walter.

The Director was still at his desk, even though it was nearly 10.00 pm. He listened attentively and without comment until Gavin had finished. 'I agree with Art. Don't confide in Claudine. Bring her to the Bureau in the morning. We'll have a de-briefing. And as for this fairytale stuff about the IRA, what do you mean? Sinn Fein or the Provos?'

Gavin wished that he had thought out his strategy more carefully before impulsively telephoning. 'I don't know. I'm only passing on what I'd heard. Just wanted to bounce it off you. But the New York connection's interesting, don't you think?' Gavin made it sound convincing. 'I mean, Klodinsky's there.' he added.

'So are the Muppets,' Walter snapped angrily. 'Facts, not fantasy. Look, I've got every respect for the IRA but I just don't think it's their scene. You've got a lot to learn. Would you know a red herring if you saw one, let alone sniffed it six inches from your nose?' It had been a long day. The Director realized that he'd been too hard on his young protégé. 'Look Gavin. Just take it one step at a time. Test every fact against another fact. You'd do well to remember the advice I had from a schoolmaster, a wily old bird. He told me never to believe a word children said and then to divide even that by half to get some idea of the truth. Just remember that. In this game nothing is ever what it seems.'

'I will.' Gavin noticed that the Paris flight was now in Customs. 'I'm sorry, Walter, I must dash. Claudine's coming through now.'

'Not so fast. She can wait. Unless you start making some real progress on *Ryme Lady* soon, you'll be out. Back in that wig and gown - that's if any solicitor would be stupid enough to send you a brief. Tell me, Gavin, what have you really found out about Pei Fau Pang? What dockside enquiries have you made about sales of the cargo? What are the Salvage Association doing? Who's behind Pinetto? Have you checked out whether any arrangements had been made for *Ryme Lady* to be re-chartered? What deposits had been paid for bunkering at her next destination? You know, refuelling and so on? Was she really *expected* at her next destination? What's the buzz round the Baltic Exchange? Those are the things that I want answers about. Not tales of disappearing women and rhubarb about the IRA.'

'My enquiries aren't complete but ...' Gavin was unable to finish as Walter interrupted. He'd wanted to explain that arrangements *had* been made at Jeddah for bunkering; that some engine spares *had* been ordered for delivery there. Facts ... and hard ones at that.

'Sorry to interrupt you but I wanted to tell you something.' The tone in the Director's voice commanded instant attention. 'Lloyds' Intelligence Services in Colchester have told me that a ship, similar to *Ryme Lady* but flying a Panamanian flag, was seen in the Med. Now she's disappeared. So what conclusion do you draw from that?'

'If it's *Ryme Lady* then it means she didn't sink.' Gavin laughed as he stated the obvious. The Director seemed unamused at the joke.

'You see I'm ahead of you, *Mr* Blair.' The tone was patronising. 'But you're being paid to be ahead of me. And that goes for Art too.' The last comment restored a smile to the listener's face. Walter was about to put down the phone when he added. 'And remember, don't trust this Claudine woman. She may be a plant. Keep your mind off her. Better still, keep your hands off her too. '

Still seething, Gavin left the phone. Hell, surely he was entitled to run his own life. What with Art and now Walter! There was defiance in his step, an irritated look on his face as he hurried across the open space. Then Claudine appeared, walking slowly, downright forlorn. Suddenly he felt foolish, wondering just what he was doing. They hardly knew each other, just a few fleeting hours together. Maybe Walter was right.

Claudine was carrying a small blue suitcase. She'd tried to smarten herself but remained unkempt. He'd seen sights like her thumbing lifts after a weekend under canvas at a pop festival. Then she saw him. She faltered in her step and a wan smile appeared. Her eyes were tired, her face waxy and pallid. Gone was the fresh skin. Along with it had disappeared the bronzed glow of good health. Her face looked drawn whilst her hair, though tidy, was lank. She was almost unrecognizable from the radiant personal assistant who had greeted him at Nice Airport in her white dress. The worn, black jeans and T-shirt completed her broken-down image. What's more, she'd lost weight - a few pounds at least judging by the hollowness which had appeared around her cheekbones.

She passed the end of the barrier and dropped her case, flinging her arms round him, like a small child. Her shaking body said everything that she wanted to say. He let her cling to him as long as she wanted, before bending to pick up her case. 'Come on. I'm taking you home.' He put an arm round her shoulder and they set off.

'Thanks for being here. There was no one else.' It was all she said as they walked to his car. They attracted the occasional glance because they made an unusual couple, Gavin in an expensively-cut green blazer, yellow roll-neck and slacks; Claudine, still sexy but jaded.

As they sped down the fast lane of the M4 into London she sat silently, her eyes open but lifeless. She took in little of the developing skyline, scarcely noticing the colourful new buildings by the Chiswick Flyover. If she noticed the reassuring hand on her thigh, then there was no sign.

At Hammersmith Broadway they cut off down the Fulham Palace Road, turning off before Putney Bridge into the maze of back streets near Barons Court. Gavin stopped outside the mansion block which was home. Before leading her upstairs, he locked the car, failing however to notice the solitary figure in the parked vehicle across the street.

After they had gone in, the man picked up his car phone and started to dial, able at the same time to study the whole of the front of the dull, red brick building. He saw the light come on in the fourth floor room, saw Gavin pull across the curtains without looking down. In the quiet drabness of London W.14 the agent settled down to wait. As a professional, he knew it was best to sit quietly, not even smoking, slumped behind the wheel, alone in a line of anonymous saloons which bordered both sides of the one way street.

Only when the clock on the dashboard showed twenty to midnight did the fourth floor lights go out. He weighed up the situation, looked up and down the street. It was empty. Maybe it was clear now. No, best wait. Give them time to fall asleep. Just in case.

It was 1.30 when he made his move, opening and closing his car door with the faintest of clicks. With the experience of years, he slipped into the darkness.

Chapter 23

Gavin's apartment was less distressingly drab than its neighbourhood. The front door was black and solid, protected by a single lock. The corridor inside led on to the kitchen-diner, the sitting room and a couple of bedrooms. The rooms were warm from the central heating but Gavin switched on the electric fire - anything to stop Claudine shivering. She was perched on the edge of the rocker in the sitting-room, arms clasped in front of her, her head resting on her hands. She stared mindlessly at the electric bars. 'Make yourself at home,' he said. 'I'll get something to eat.' The furnishings, some old, some new, were sparse. Janie, with an angry flourish, had taken all the womanly personal touches which so easily transform a room but Claudine never noticed anyway. The eyes which had been so lustrous were glazed as if she had seen life in the raw and had decided to lock it out for ever.

When Gavin returned from the kitchen he found that she had not moved at all but she accepted the bowl of game soup, declined the wine and smiled an acknowledgement at the offer of a hot drink. Gavin's coffee and her smile were equally weak. He seated himself on the arm of her chair and watched as she picked at the wholemeal bread and played with the soup. If she were acting, then it was an Oscar-winning performance.

He tried but quickly realized that small-talk was out. Drained of energy, exhausted from stress, she had nothing left to give. It was a time to wait ... she'd tell him what she wanted to say in her own time.

'Come on.' The soup had long since gone cold. 'It's time you went to bed.' He stroked her cheek and spoke softly.

'It'll all seem different in the morning. Just you see.' She nodded in response. Child-like she followed him into the spare room where she sat on the bed and opened her blue suitcase. Inside there was almost nothing - a change of underwear and a make-up bag which she had obviously intended to use on the flight but had never got round to. There was just one stocking. No other clothing. Gavin knew then that she'd packed in a panic. 'I'll be in the next room. Let me know if you want anything. But you're completely safe. No one knows you're here. Not unless you've told anyone?'

'No. I've told no one,' she whispered. He pecked her on the cheek and slipped out of the room, closing the door behind him. In his own room he took time to settle. I mean, she's alive. Miraculous. But why? And how? And why come to London? And what of the death threat? When was that going to happen? Tonight? Next year? Was he safer with her here? Or in more danger?

The agonizing continued till long after one, when he fell into a fitful slumber. It was over half an hour later when he realized once again that he was awake. Something had disturbed him. He lay still, looking at the digital alarm by his bed. Yes ... there it was again. The squeak of the boards outside his room. Someone was there. Then the handle started to turn. He felt transfixed with fear. But then he realized. Claudine! He found he'd been holding his breath and exhaled mightily in a huge sigh of relief. Thank God for that!

'Claudine?' He croaked anxiously.

Chapter 24

The scrambled line from London had rung a few moments previously in the Langley headquarters of the CIA. Set deep in the Virginian countryside, not many miles from the White House, out along the Potomac, Langley was the eyes and ears of the American Government. The caller had been Sir Jack Castleton, Ralph Gill's opposite number in London. The two men had yet to meet, following Gill's recent appointment and the relationship was typically uneasy, the inevitable kind where Sir Jack was a long-standing respected figure and Ralph Gill was the new boy - but in the bigger job.

'Sure, we must meet up,' said Gill without much enthusiasm. 'Lumbola. Is that what we're talking about?'

Sir Jack Castleton suppressed his irritation at the brusque, almost dismissive tone. 'That's right. Just wanted a word about security. It's the end of next week. Our PM arrives Saturday morning.'

'President O'Brien arrives the previous evening,' acknowledged Gill. He spoke as if he were giving away a state secret rather than something which was public knowledge. 'What's your worry?'

'Just wondered what you'd heard. You understand ... that it's not our show. Lumbola never was British.'

'I know,' said Gill irritably.

Sir Jack didn't like the way the conversation was going at all. 'We're told that the French are doing their own thing to look after their President. But overall ... security seems to be under the control of the Lumbolans. The Ministry of the Interior.'

'Sure. The rules are that the Lumbolans do general security, crowd control, public buildings and so on. We're putting security round O'Brien as tight as a mouse's ass-hole. No doubt you're doing the same.'

Sir Jack Castleton coughed politely. 'Of course. We've had a team in there for days, checking out the Palace, the route to the Palace and the parliament building.'

'And?' Gill made even the single word sound bored and laconic.

'No problem.'

Gill was puzzled and he looked at the wall clock for the third time in mounting irritation. What in hell's name was this chap wasting his time for. 'We're happy too. I've got Matt Rees as my man down there. Well ... good talking to you, uh ... Sir Jack. Keep in touch.'

'But Mr Gill ... I haven't told you why I called. Aren't you interested?'

'Go on.' The peremptory command was not mellowed by the transatlantic distance.

'I'm told there's trouble brewing. Not, I hasten to add, against the PM or the President. Just trouble. Our people in Sampopo hadn't picked up the vibes at all but I've had a man in Dakalla, Harvie Jameson. He's a veteran of the Congo, Cyprus - even goes back to the Mau-Mau in Kenya. He can sniff trouble. Says there's something in the air.'

Gill made a note on his pad. 'West Africa's full of smells, but tell him to keep sniffing. I'll pass it on to Matt Rees. Appreciate your call.' Gill stroked his chin thoughtfully before opening his file. Though he had said nothing to Sir Jack, the reports coming in from Matt Rees were the same. Nothing confirmed, nothing concrete. Just an air of unease.

Chapter 25

He sensed rather than saw the door opening. 'Claudine?' He repeated, his voice full of sleep.

Then there was a movement. 'Gavin?' Claudine's voice was soft to the point of timidity, apologetic for the intrusion.

'Over here.' His own voice showed relief as he searched for the bedlight. 'Come on in.' Quickly she did so and he realized that, like him, she was totally naked. He shivered as her body, cold and goose-pimply, slid in beside his warmth. At once he wrapped himself around her, enveloping her in his body heat. My God, she was thin, nothing like the bronzed beauty with the luxurious curves on the yacht in Cannes.

'Please hold me. Hold me tight. I'm so frightened.' She spoke haltingly, half into the pillow as he clung to her. 'I'm so confused. I don't understand. Who did it? Why me?' As she spoke, she was nuzzling backwards into him.

'I've been so worried, felt so guilty,' Gavin prompted, not answering her questions at all. 'I kept thinking it was all down to me. I felt so helpless. And it's been nineteen days.'

'Nineteen days!' Though her response was wooden, she sounded surprised.

'Yes. It's Thursday. Two and a half weeks they kept you.'

'Thursday.' She paused, her mind trying to assimilate this new information. 'I'd no idea. Time meant nothing. I just kept thinking they'd kill me.' She started to sob. Gavin felt the tears dripping onto his arms. '*We'll kill you, kill you and dump you*, they kept saying.' No questions, Gavin decided. Just let her unburden herself at her own pace.

'The Bureau think you just stood me up. I never believed it. That day in Paris ... we came a long way. I could tell ... we

184

had something special.' He shifted position slightly, increasingly aware that his caring and protective instincts were being overwhelmed by a stronger surging emotion which was hard to conceal. If she noticed, she said nothing.

'That Sunday morning, I had a phone call from a man. Said he was speaking on behalf of Carl. Wanted me to fly to Athens at once. About the charter. It sounded genuine. I was told to be ready in fifteen minutes. When the bell rang, I went down. I'd planned to ring you from the airport. As the chauffeur opened the car door, two men appeared from behind. Before I knew what was happening I was in the back seat with one of them on either side. The chauffeur drove off. *Mon Dieu!* The next moment ...' Her voice faltered and the shaking started again. 'The next moment, they stuffed something in my mouth. I was blindfolded. They held something over my face. Then I went unconscious.' She broke down again at the recollection.

'You don't have to talk about it. Just lie quietly.'

'No. I must. I want to tell you.' And she did - speaking with her face still almost lost in the pillow. His left arm was round her neck, his right arm clasped across the gentle rise and fall of her stomach. 'I don't know where they took me. Somewhere in Paris. Near the Metro. I could feel the trains passing underneath. I was kept in a dark room on my own. Someone came in to see me each day. Every time, it was the same questions.' Her voice broke down and her shoulders started to heave. He pulled her closer to him, proud of his masculinity, yet ashamed of his fierce sexual arousal. Yet still she continued her unburdening, her mind locked in memories of her own private hell.

'You don't have to go on.' Yet he was desperate to add some more pieces to the jigsaw.

'No, it's all right.' She sniffed loudly and then blew her nose on his offered handkerchief. 'The questions were always the same. Why had I been so friendly with you?

What had I been telling you? What had you been telling me? What had I said to you about Klodinsky? What had I told you about Klodinsky's plans for Brads? Oh ... about chartering *Cerne View* and *Adber Arrow*? And something else ... about an Irish connection. What had I said about *Ryme Lady*? About documents?' Gavin felt her delicate fingers grip his arm. 'I just kept shouting at them. "*Non! Non!* It wasn't like that at all."'

Gavin knew this to be the truth. 'But would you recognise them, these men?'

'I barely saw them. I would recognize their voices. They always wore masks ... green ones with devil faces.' Her nails dug into his flesh at the memory and he had to prise her hand open. They fell silent as Gavin soothed her gently and made calming noises into her ear. Yet he himself was in turmoil at the unanswered questions which still nagged him. As if she had read his thoughts, she continued. 'They didn't hit me. One of them used to stroke my breasts. Nothing more.' She shuddered at the recollection. 'It was just the threats. If I didn't tell them the truth they said they would put me into a sack and throw me into the Seine.'

'And then ... ?'

'Suddenly, today they came into my room. As usual it was dark, the windows shuttered. I was lying there, bound up hand and foot. They picked me up and bundled me into the car and eventually pushed me out in the street. A passer-by found me blindfolded and gagged. He freed me and I found that I was in the Quai Louis Blériot. So I went home. I sat there ... shaking and sobbing, scared to be alone any more. I'd no one to turn to. In the past I'd have called Carl but after those questions - how could I? Not now. My only friends are in New York ... or there was you in London.' She wriggled slightly. 'So I chose you.'

'Because I was nearer?' Gavin hoped there was more to it than that.

She squeezed his muscular arm which was stroking up and down her rib-cage. 'Because I trusted you. Being held prisoner like that ... you get not to trust anybody. That Saturday in Paris ... I became very close to you. As I lay on that damp bed, tied up, mouth gagged, I kept thinking about you, about things you'd said.' Her body was warm now, her shaking had stopped.

'You'll feel better now that you've told me. We'll find out what was behind it.' He spoke with more confidence than he felt.

'I don't care,' she said with decision. 'I'm free. That's what counts.' She sought out and kissed his lips, just a gentle touching. It held a promise of much to come. 'Soon ... when I'm feeling better, we'll make love.' She kissed him again. 'We'll make love as if we're the people who invented it. You see.' Seconds later she'd fallen into a deep slumber in his arms. Gavin however couldn't sleep. There were too many unanswered questions. For one, Klodinsky had never reported her missing. The French police had agreed to reveal nothing publicly, preferring to wait for Klodinsky to contact *them*. Nothing. Not even after nineteen days. And then her release. Why had she been freed? He stroked her shoulder lightly. She stirred and gave a gentle sigh but didn't awaken. Her release? God! Why hadn't he thought of it before? It was so obvious. Brads had just signed the second charter to Pinetto. Klodinsky had lost. While there was hope, he'd wanted her out of the way. Now it made no difference.

That made sense. She was the one person who could have dished the dirt on the Klodinsky empire. So, like a pawn from a giant chessboard, she'd been removed. Until today.

In the stillness of the room and as the hands of the clock moved round to 4.20, Gavin nodded in satisfaction.

It made sense. The blurred picture was coming clearer.

Chapter 26

In the morning, he took Claudine on the District Line Tube as she hadn't wanted to be left alone. Together they'd jostled with the City types, all reading the *Financial Times*, until the pin-stripes had got out around Mansion House. For the rest of the journey out to Barking they'd had seats through the endless grey concrete of the East End. There, he'd pointed out Maritime House before leaving her by the shops. 'Here's some money. Kit yourself out, buy what you want, something to wear into the Bureau and something special for tonight.' On the journey he'd told her that he was taking her away for the weekend - to Wickham in Hampshire for the Annual Reunion of the Society for the Preservation of the Frog. He kissed her goodbye but she seemed reluctant to leave him. 'Go on. You'll be safe out here. Nobody will find you in Barking, for God's sake! Come to the Bureau in an hour or so.' He kissed her again.

A few minutes later, he joined Walter Corbin and Art Lemman in the Director's office. Outside, a squally shower had replaced the scudding grey clouds and the windows were being buffeted but in Corbin's office there was an air of calm. 'It wasn't easy to achieve,' Walter said with satisfaction as he pointed towards the telephone, 'but the French police have been persuaded to close their file on the kidnap. My old mate Greenaway has some good connections over there.' Corbin then turned to Gavin. 'Right. Give us the full details. Is she real ... or is she a plant?'

The man who'd spent the previous evening watching Gavin's apartment saw them head for Barons Court Tube. He'd taken no chances. Only after seeing them get on the eastbound line did he return to the mansion block.

Gaining entry to Gavin's apartment was easy. With all the experience of the professional he went through every room, every drawer, every cupboard. Here and there he photographed something. Always he was careful to replace the papers precisely as they had been, anxious to leave the place apparently undisturbed.

In the sitting room he photographed a notebook in which Gavin had been scribbling the previous evening. The invitations on the mantelpiece he also photographed - the one to the Annual Reunion of the Society for the Preservation of the Frog, together with a couple of wedding invites.

The whole search lasted nearly an hour. Nothing had been missed. Satisfied, the man slipped out through the door and hurried towards the one hour developers on the Earls Court Road.

The lingering perfume of Giorgio was still evident in Walter's office even after Claudine had left. Indeed, the whole room still seemed to be filled with her presence, such was the impression which she had made. Gavin had not enjoyed the previous forty minutes. Before her arrival he had painted the picture of the waif-like girl, confidence destroyed, a nervous wreck, sick from worry and in desperate need of rehabilitation rather than a grilling by the Bureau.

It hadn't quite been like that.

Claudine had spent her time well. Dressed now in a white shirt, with a high ruff neck, a red suit, black stockings and red shoes, she'd looked like a Vogue model. Her hair carefully coiffeured, her make-up restored, she was barely recognizable as the person who'd been scared to leave him just two hours before. Even her cheeks didn't look so hollow.

Gavin had introduced her as she joined them round the Director's desk. He'd smiled at her reassuringly but Walter, old smoothie that he was, had made her feel at home by lots of hand-kissing and *enchantés*. For a few minutes it was *toujours politesse* but after that, with the cups of coffee handed round, she'd faced a battery of questions. To Gavin she came across as telling the truth but he wasn't so sure what impression she'd made on the others. As she'd left the the room it had been the seductive wiggle in the tight red skirt which had left the biggest impact on Art. 'Wow! But coloured red for danger! She just has to be a set-up! I mean, hell Gavin, she looks as if she's just checked out of a five star hotel, not been chained up like an animal for nineteen days. Like I mean, you still believe in the tooth fairy as well.'

'I believe every word she said.' He found he was over-stating the position. The stridency showed, yet Walter, as he looked at Gavin, could see the transparent honesty showing through. 'If you'd only seen her last night. I just wish you could have done. You'd have known she was genuine.'

'Klodinsky never reported her missing. That's what troubles me. We've got to work on that,' pondered Walter.

'That's because he was holding her. That's why,' said Gavin. It was special pleading and he knew it.

It was scarcely a surprise when Art dismissed his views with a contemptuous snarl. 'It's Gavin's fatal charm. And his body. That's what she's after. Oh no! She's not a plant. Wouldn't dream of going through his files.' He scoffed at Gavin, his chest puffed out with self-importance. 'Look, she's a loyal Klodinsky girl. Worked for him for years in New York. Moved specially to Paris against her wishes because that's what Klodinsky wanted. Do you really believe that she would set off for Greece after a phone call from someone she didn't know.' Art could see that Walter was still undecided. He tapped an unlit cigarette on the packet and then put it in his mouth with a swift movement. 'Klodinsky's no fool. Quite the reverse. If he'd kidnapped her, he'd have reported her missing just to cover it up.' This time Art saw that Walter was impressed. Even Gavin looked shaken at the logic.

'I'm on the fence,' said Walter. 'I'd like to believe her. She's a sweet kid. Just say that her innocence is not proven. Tell her nothing, show her nothing. I'd like to think she was genuine.' His sermon was addressed at Gavin. 'What's more, don't let those legs and that smile beguile you.' He fixed Gavin with a penetrating stare. 'And I'll repeat what I said: keep your hands off her. No pillow talk.' He'd said it for effect and was rewarded by Gavin's cheeks colouring. 'If it's not too late ... ' Walter let him down gently, satisfied that he'd got to the truth of the position.

'What about New York?' enquired Art. Are we going to follow up this IRA business?'

'We've no choice. You'll fly Monday. Claudine mentioned something about the Irish. Brads want it checked out - not surprisingly. We just can't afford to ignore it. Gavin, you'll stay in London. Plans for Claudine anyone?' His tilted head and the slight rounding of the mouth suggested he knew the answer already.

'I'm taking her to a gourmet dinner and a quiet weekend in Hampshire. It's the Annual Reunion of the Society for the Preservation of the Frog.'

Walter's mouth downturned and he examined his stapler in minute detail. 'Wonderful!' He responded without conviction. 'Whatever, just be sure that she's back in Klodinsky's office in Paris on Monday. That's where we need her. An eye and ear person.' This was Walter the crafty, the silvery fox with the ruthless guile and a lifetime's experience.

Gavin jumped from his chair. 'She's not a plaything to be

used by the Bureau. No. I'm not agreeing to that.'

'Wipe the love out of your eyes, buddy boy.' Art was always ready to add the extra gallon of petrol to a good blaze.

'Those are orders. She doesn't trust her boss any more. She trusts you. Let's use it?' Walter Corbin showed that the discussion was ended as he shut the file. 'Art,' he continued as an afterthought. 'You're a bit of a gourmet. Know a Big Mac when you see one. I want you to go to this Frog thing tonight as well. Go through Claudine's things. Check her handbag, her diary, the lot. Watch her like a hawk.'

Gavin was still seething at having to send Claudine back to Paris. Now this ... it was just too much. 'You're a bastard. You're both bastards. Why can't you leave her to me? I can deal with it.'

'Bastard I have to be. Bastard you have to become. People out there want you dead. Don't you forget that. Your life's in danger. I want Art with you until Monday. Orders.'

Gavin looked out at the driving rain, watched the trickling patterns of water running down the panes. The temperature had dropped and the driving rain had turned to sleet. The skies were leaden and as heavy as his burden. He stared mindlessly at the drab scene, aware that they were watching him. No doubt they were wondering if he would resign. That had been his impulsive, instinctive reaction, the kind which had led to him leaving the Bar. No. That wasn't the answer. It was a time to duck and weave. Even when he turned to face them, he didn't speak at once. He sipped his coffee and helped himself to a biscuit as he looked at Art. 'I can get you a couple of tickets for the dinner. Do you want to bring a girlfriend?'

Art thought for a moment, his hand picking at the wood on the edge of the Director's desk. His eyes reflected the debate in his own mind. The decision seemed to take even longer than it should have done. 'No ... no, I don't think so. Business and pleasure. I've got a job to do.' The dig at Gavin was not lost and Walter fought to conceal his smile. They were at their best when needling each other. It kept them thinking, kept them debating. That way they'd unravel the truth. 'Sounds as if you three are going to have a great weekend. Have fun.'

Art looked at his watch. 'Time for a bourbon. Anyone joining me?' There were no takers.

Chapter 27

With London's weekend rush for the grouse moors, the fishing, the windsurfing, the place in the country all starting at lunchtime, the Friday afternoon drive through south west London to the A3 was painfully slow. On a good day, Gavin might have taken one and a half hours through the beautiful rolling hills of Surrey and Hampshire to reach Wickham but today he could tell it was going to be two and a quarter, mainly as a result of the stop/go snarl between Putney and Kingston.

Art's scowl when he'd arrived at Gavin's showed he'd no intention of squashing up in the back of the Mercedes. Though Gavin hadn't wanted to do so, he'd had to admit that Art was ill-designed for the limited space. So Claudine was sitting, knees bunched up to her chest, whilst Art luxuriated in the front. Both Art and Gavin kept a watch out for a tail but they saw nothing. Art's foul humour kept conversation desultory and all the small talk which Gavin wanted to share with Claudine had to wait for later. 'You've packed your best togs, have you? Black tie and all that,' enquired Gavin of Art.

'Sure. Don't worry. I've got the gear. I'll be on best behaviour. Like you told me.' Art smacked his own wrist in penance and resumed his scowl and the occasional glance behind. Claudine he'd deliberately ignored until both he and she had fallen asleep leaving Gavin to drive the last twenty five miles locked in his own thoughts.

Wickham is typical of many small towns of similar size in southern England. Around a large Market Square stood buildings from different centuries, each style reflecting the ongoing stability and prosperity of rural Hampshire. The women shopping, the retired men putting in time, all seemed to have a similar Tory party worthiness in a town at peace with itself. The Bear Hotel, on the south side of the Square, was mainly Georgian, all burnished red brick. Tinted floodlights lit the entrance and the facade was freshly-painted and welcoming. Inside, the rooms were spacious, airy and light - beautifully proportioned and entirely suitable for a high quality country hotel. As an old coaching inn, The Bear had been frequented by Charles Dickens and had been lavishing hospitality for two hundred years. Few were as rowdy as the bunch who met annually in the private dining room in honour of the Frog.

'I can't think you'd be in a safer place anywhere,' volunteered Gavin as he and Claudine entered the bedroom and closed the door behind them. 'Rural England and really anonymous. You can put your nightmare behind you.' He joined his hands behind her neck. 'Believe me. You'll soon forget what you've just been through. We're in for a great evening.'

Claudine moved closer to him, clasped her hands round his waist and kissed him. 'Gavin, you're wonderful! It's such a beautiful room,' she said as she looked around her.

'And you were just great this morning,' he replied. 'Corbin was impressed. As for Art? Who knows? He'll come round.'

'I keep thinking there's a nice man inside that body, if only he'd let it come out.'

'He's had a rough life.' It was an inadequate explanation of Art's boorishness and he knew it.Why was Art so bitter, so resentful?

'A whole weekend here! You just make me feel so safe, so happy.' She kissed him on the cheek. 'Now I'd better get unpacked. I've got a few more things this time.' And she had. Last night's empty suitcase was now bulging and reinforced with a second overnight bag.

Down in the Square, a Vauxhall Cavalier had parked a few minutes before. The driver got out, stretched and strolled towards the paper shop. He smiled inwardly as he walked past the Mercedes. It had been a doddle. Just some careful planning and the benefit of modern technology.

Seated round the table were ten couples plus Art. Ten of the men were in dinner jackets and black bow ties. The women were all wearing expensive-looking outfits, many of them specially purchased for the occasion. The voices were rich and plummy, the atmosphere refined only in breeding rather than behaviour. The Society had been formed eight years before. Gavin, James and Paul had been the founder members and had laid down the rules and invented the tradition. Formal dress was essential. When Art appeared in his American-style tartan tuxedo with flashing bow tie, it had been something of a shock.

'Your black tie, I see,' Gavin had said, feeling somewhat responsible for his guest.

Art responded by pressing a button in his pocket and the bow tie revolved in a whirr of coloured lights. 'People pay for my brain, not for my attire.' Before Gavin could enquire as to what brain, Art turned to James Charlesworth who was Chairman for the evening. 'Delighted to be here, I'm sure.' Art's smile was disarming and his accent mockingly English.

James was far too good a host to offend. 'I rather wish I'd had the courage to wear something like that,' he replied. 'Might make it obligatory next year. Anyway, Art, make yourself at home' It was an invitation which was wholly unnecessary.

The menu always started with frogs' legs. This year it had been followed by Beef Wellington, Crèpes Suzette and a dazzling array of French cheeses. Inevitably the Chablis was from the Grand Cru Grenouille vineyard and the

Chambertin was Clos-de-Bèze '79. The wine was intended to flow freely, the conversation to be lively, witty and never obscene, a point Gavin had emphasized to Art even before the journey. As the port arrived Gavin looked across to where Art was sitting, a few seats away. His voice could be heard, somewhat louder than before, as he called for a bottle of bourbon. He was well fired-up, his eyes flashing laughter and excitement, his bow tie revolving in unison.

In contrast, Claudine had been quiet at the start of the evening. She had looked stunning in a simple white evening gown with a slimline cut. She'd been lucky though to be seated next to the Hon. Gilbert Sedgeway whose urbane charm had put her at ease. By the time the cheese had arrived they were locked in animated discussion.

Just as Gavin was giving her a smile of encouragement across the table, there was a sharp rap. James Charlesworth stood up. 'I will ask Alison who, if I may say so, is looking absolutely stunning tonight, to make the draw. Indeed ladies, you are all looking younger and more beautiful than ever.' There was much table thumping of approval and Art's bow tie rotated in appreciation. Alison Sedgeway stood up and held the pint pewter tankard in her hand. In it were, purportedly, the names of all the men in the room. If there were no guests, then the names of all the men went into the tankard. If there were a guest, then the other names were removed. Alison played up the moment and rummaged her hand in the tankard before completing the draw.' And the winner is ... Art Lemman.' There were roars of laughter. Everyone round the table, except Art and Claudine, knew that the whole thing was a fix.

Someone from the foot of the table shouted, 'What does a Yank know about *The Wind in the Willows*?'

There were calls of 'On your feet' and 'Can Americans read?' Everyone was agog as Art stood up to receive the script of Toad's speech.

'Congratulations Art. Here's the script. First, you drink this.' James thrust a tumbler full of brandy across the table.'Then you read Toad's speech. Any mistake and you have another drink and start again.'

'Sure sounds straightforward.' Art grinned up and down the table, threw back the brandy and picked up the script.

'The Toad came home!

There was panic in the parlour and howling in the hall,

There was crying in the cowshed and shrieking in the ... hall,'

Everyone in the room shouted in unison. 'Wrong! It's *stall.*' Art nodded sheepishly and accepted the next brandy, throwing it back with gusto.

'The Toad came home!

There was panic in the parlour and howling in the stall.'

Again came the hoots of laughter. 'No. The first time it's *hall.*'

Art steadied himself for the third slug of brandy. 'Gee. Wouldn't you let me sing *The Star Spangled Banner*?' But of course he knew the answer would be no. It was twenty minutes before Art was able to get through the four verses without a mistake.

The Chairman rose to speak. 'No staying power, these Americans.' He looked across at Art who was alternating between lolling back to his left and then to his right. He'd loosened his flashing bow tie, had undone his shirt button and was breathing hard, trickles of sweat glistening from his forehead to his chin. 'That must be a record. Twenty minutes for four verses. But anyway, ladies and gentlemen, that concludes the evening, except for the toast. Ladies and gentlemen - I give you *The Frog*.'

Everyone except Art stood up. 'May we all preserve it,' they responded in unison. Art did his best to beam his support as he struggled to remove his tartan jacket. All of a sudden the room had seemed so hot.

The evening was over, the ladies disappearing to get their coats, the men chatting among themselves or prodding Art without success. 'We'd better take a look at him,' Gavin said to Claudine. Art was now slumped, head in his arms, breathing heavily. Beside him lay the four verses. 'Doesn't look too special, does he?' Gavin peered anxiously, before pouring a glass of iced water over him. Other than an irritated shake of the head, there was no improved sign of sobriety.

'Gavin, I wonder if you can do me a favour.' The words were accompanied by a tug on the elbow of his jacket. Gavin turned. It was the Hon Gilbert Sedgeway, now wearing an expensive overcoat, his wife, Alison, beside him. 'I know this is a bloody cheek but I left my car lights on. Now it won't start. We've got a baby-sitter to get home. Can I borrow yours? I can return it first thing.'

'Fine, so long as Alison drives. You're far too pissed. Not as bad as Art though.'

'Hardly,' chortled Gilbert. 'Never had any intention of driving, old boy.' He watched as Gavin produced the keys to the car.

'Help yourself.'

'It's the Mercedes, isn't it?' said Alison.

'Yes. Just outside and down to the left. I'd come out but I ought to shift my guest.' He poured more iced water, this time from a jug. It ran down Art's back inside his shirt and trickled in freezing rivulets down either side of his ears and across his forehead.

'Want a hand getting him upstairs?' enquired Gilbert.

'A crane would do better,' Gavin suggested. 'No. You get on. We'll sort him out. If we can't, we'll just leave him here. I shouldn't want his head in the morning. Actually not even at any time.' The four of them laughed as they exchanged kisses of farewell, leaving Gavin to heave at Art's dead-weight. It was hopeless. His head simply rocked from side to side. His eyes opened briefly before alcohol again won the day. 'It's a waste of time. Let's go to bed.'

Claudine looked doubtful at leaving Art but Gavin steered her to the door. Together they left the debris of the room, the pushed-back chairs, the wine-stained table cloth, the half-empty glasses, the smell of cigars and in the middle of it all the slumped figure of Art in his tartan smoking jacket which he'd failed to get off.

Upstairs their room smelt fresh and clean after the staleness of the dining room. It was quiet too. The stillness of the night air, now that the gale had blown itself out, filled Gavin with a sense of peace. The comfortable, chintzy furnishings, the four-poster bed, the bathrobes, the thick towels, the expensive soaps all added to the ambiance. He pulled Claudine towards him. 'You were wonderful. I could see you were enjoying yourself.' She looked up at his face, admiring the strong features.

'Yes. Once I got to know them. It was just ... 'She never ended the sentence. The room shuddered, the floor shook, the windows shattered with jagged shards of glass flying everywhere. The force of the explosion hurled them both to the floor. Gavin crashed into the dressing table as the room seemed to heave around them. A blast of fiery air blew the curtains horizontally, revealing a snapshot of dark orangy-redness.

Gavin lay on the floor transfixed with fear. Was he still in one piece? He was. Could he feel his legs? Yes, they were sprawled over Claudine's shoulder. He twisted round. In the glow of the roaring redness he saw Claudine, face down on the carpet. He crawled over the broken glass to examine her. Thank God! She was alive! Her eyes flickered open and then shut again, her fists clenched in terror.

The flying glass had missed her too, though it was everywhere. 'You all right?' He paused for a moment, anxiously awaiting the response.

'You said I'd be safe! *Mon Dieu!* You said I'd be safe here!' Her tone was bitter, resentful, the words being sobbed into the thick pile of the carpet.

'I've got to see what's going on.' Even as he spoke Gavin was getting to his feet. He stooped to pick her up, gently lifting her slender body to the bed. 'You must stay here. You'll be perfectly safe. I'll lock you in but I've got to see what it's all about.'

'*No! No!*' Her head shook vigorously. '*Mais non!* Don't leave me! Don't leave me alone.' She was shouting, her face screwed up like a crumpled tissue. 'Don't leave me.' She clung to him with manic determination. Hatred, fear, resentment and confusion were written large. She writhed almost uncontrollably as he tried to hold her to the bed.

'I've got to.' He fought himself free, yearning to be able to comfort her. Instead he went to the remains of the window which was now devoid of glass, the framework shattered. The blackness of the Square was split by the intensity of the blaze. Wreckage was everywhere. An MGB and Gilbert Sedgeway's Audi Coupe were both on fire. Between them was the car which had exploded.

His car!

His Mercedes!

He wasn't surprised, couldn't be, not after the death threat. Nevertheless, the sight froze him in horror. My God! Where was Gilbert? Where was Alison?

On the bed, Claudine was still writhing hysterically, hands now across her face, the inferno outside flickering across her contorted features. Then she let out a scream, deep, long and agonizingly painful.

'Stop it!' He slapped her face, hoping that it was the right thing to do. She was silenced, her face sullen and resentful. The writhing stopped but it was more than she could take. Once again, he saw in her face the child refugee of the previous day.

'I'm sorry. Just lie here, perfectly still. I shan't be a moment.' He kissed her on the forehead, tasting the salty perspiration which was seeping from her hairline. Then he was gone.

Down in the street people were already gathering. All were in various stages of dress and undress. Despite the roaring fire, he was able to hear the confused shouts of people calling that they'd dialled 999, that the ambulance was on its way ... and the fire brigade and police too.

Ignoring everyone else, Gavin hurried by them towards his car. In the middle of that roaring crackling inferno must be Gilbert and Alison. He was reminded of a Belfast street scene on television. Except for one difference. Even the most advanced electronic news-gathering cameras can't capture the smell. It was a mix of burning oil, blistering paintwork, flaming seats and the pungent fumes of scorching tyres and roasting flesh. Gavin winced in disbelief at the searing heat and was forced to a painful standstill by the billowing, belching flames and black smoke. It burnt his throat, scalded his chest and singed his eyebrows. Behind him, someone yelled 'come back'.

He didn't. Not with Gilbert and Alison somewhere in there. He fell to the ground, finding the air cooler, the path towards the car clear from smoke. He started to crawl across the tarmac, arms and knees scraping along the hot surface. Without knowing it, he was shouting, 'Gilbert! Alison! Gilbert! Alison!' Vaguely, in the background, he was aware of people calling to him to come back. He ignored them, obsessively inching forward, determined to cross the last fifteen feet to the inferno from the three vehicles.

Suddenly he felt his ankles clasped, his progress checked. 'Come back, dumb-fucker,' shouted Art who was crouching, his eyes narrowed against the heat, his cheeks burning. He start pulling whilst Gavin's fingers frantically scrabbled at the tarmac, resisting the attempt to stop him. 'The gas tank on the MG's going up any minute.' Art's warning was shouted.

'Gilbert and Alison. They're in it. Don't you see? I loaned them my car.' Gavin's upturned face pleaded in the red and orange glow.

'Nothing you can do.' Art shouted to make himself heard.

'I must! I must!' Gavin's fingers clawed helplessly on the tarmac as Art pulled him away. 'Get a fire extinguisher. Anything. Water.' Art kept on pulling until he'd got Gavin out of the direct line of the flames and heat. Then he grabbed him under the armpits and pulled him up. 'Just do what you're told, dick-head! You're coming with me.'

The thirty-six-piece chandelier crashing onto the table beside Art a few moments before had been a rude awakening. Nevertheless, it had succeeded where iced water had failed. Now Art was in charge, hangover or no. He clasped Gavin's arm. Forcefully he steered him towards the darkness and the phone box at the far side of the Square. 'That bomb was meant for you. We've gotta tell Walt.'

'I know. But Gilbert and Alison! My God!'

They entered the kiosk and Art dialled rapidly. As they waited for the Director to answer, Art glared across at Gavin. In the small space the words had a special intensity. 'Claudine must have told someone you were here.'

'Bollocks!' Gavin was having none of it. 'She'd have blown herself up. And you.'

'Crap! She just had to send you out to the car first on a pretext.'

'I don't believe it. Isn't Walter answering?'

'No.' Art looked angrily at the handset. 'We're on our own.' He crashed the receiver back onto the cradle. For a moment the effects of the brandy hit him once again. 'No more *Frog* nights. Never!' The grin was wry, the bags under his eyes told their own tale of debauchery. 'Give me a moment to think.' He paused, running his hands through his tousled hair, then straightened up his shirt, tie and jacket. 'Here's what we do. No statements by you to the police. No mention of any death threat to you. No mention of any IRA connection. If asked, you've no idea why someone should have put a bomb in your car. Mistaken identity maybe. Better still, say nothing.'

'And Claudine?'

'We're gonna check out of the hotel now. She's coming with us. If she moves her ass one inch away from us, she's dead. Do you understand?'

Gavin's voice was anguished. 'Jesus! You've got it wrong. All wrong,' but Art wasn't listening, already hurrying back across the square. His bulky frame was bursting with alcohol-fired energy. As they drew near to the blaze, the first fire engine appeared, joining the police and ambulance. The crowd, noisy and fearful, had grown to several hundred. Gavin heard a man in a dark green tracksuit and trainers telling no one in particular, 'I saw it. I was over there. Two of them got in, posh they were, just before the thing exploded. The bonnet just missed my bleedin' head.'

'Have they found them?' Art queried.

The bystander gestured vaguely into the distance. 'Someone found an arm.' Gavin felt his stomach start to heave.

'Anyone know anything about the people or the car.' The voice beside Gavin was one of two policemen who had arrived in a white BMW, its blue lights flashing out a sense of urgency. A cordon was being set up, behind which lines of anxious faces peered and stared as the firemen rolled out their lengths of hose.

Gavin was about to reply when he felt his arm grabbed by Art and together they disappeared. 'Go and get packed. we're leaving.'

Together they hurried up the stairs. 'They found an arm! They found an arm.' Gavin kept repeating.

Art shrugged. 'It wasn't yours. It's your lucky day.' As Gavin entered his room Art wagged his finger firmly. 'And don't let that bitch out of your sight. I want you in the lobby in five minutes.'

Chapter 28

Corbin's Daimler pulled up outside the spruce semi-detached home of Detective Chief Superintendent Greenaway. It was in Merton, south west London. Called *Arcadia*, the house was like tens of thousands, all built between the Wars. At the front were regimented small fence-lined gardens with larger ones to the rear. The fallen leaves littering the street were the first warnings of an early winter. The recent gales had stripped the trees which lined Cheeseborough Drive. An occasional person was washing his new Fiesta or coming back from the corner shop with the Sunday papers. In most of the houses, mums would now be in the kitchen sorting out the roast beef and york-shires. In Cheeseborough Drive, a black Daimler stood out as expensively different. It was the type of car to cause the lace curtains to be pulled aside for a crafty peep.

Considering the career heights to which Freddie Greenaway had risen, he didn't seem to have much to show for it. Walter Corbin and Freddie Greenaway went back a long time and respect between them was mutually high. Corbin pressed the doorbell, looking round as he did so. 'Well, at least the press aren't door-stepping us here.' This was a reference to the journalists who were thronging Gavin's home and the Bureau in the hope of some news.

'Bloody jackals, some of these journalists,' commented Art as Greenaway opened the door, summoned by the ding-dong chime. Walter introduced Gavin and Art as the three of them were ushered into the G-Plan lounge. Its only claim to the 1990s was the expensive hi-fi and video recorder. Everything else seemed to have been lost in a 1960s time-warp.

'Tea, anyone?' enquired Greenaway. 'I'll get it. The wife's at church.' He went to the kitchen, a tall, lean man, so thin, so brittle, so gaunt, that he only looked to be held together by his grey flannels and blue cardigan. In contrast, Walter was in his hand-tailored three piece, the creases pressed to perfection, the shoes immaculate.

'We've got an hour,' said Walter. ' Then we must get to the Savoy. After that, the sooner we get you out of the country the better.' Corbin noticed the sullen look on Gavin's face.

'Can't I even explain why I'm not going to the funeral? They'll think me a right heel.'

'I'll make sure your note reaches them. But I'm not letting you risk everything. If the truth gets out, then the press will never let go.'

Walter stood elegantly by the window. He looked out of place in the small semi. In the back garden a clutch of gnomes overlooked the goldfish pond. 'One of the best police brains we've got,' he mused. 'Soon be up for retirement and this is all he's got to show for it.' Walter was pointing to the photo of Greenaway shaking hands with the Duke of Edinburgh.

'Paid all his bribes into a Swiss account', suggested Art, who was growling and irritable. The Friday night hangover had a long shelf life.

Gavin was not to be diverted either. His voice was flat. 'Can't I even go home? Pick up up some things for the States?'

'No. You'll do the radio interview here and then disappear. We've done well to hide you so far.' Though Walter looked calm, he was still shaken, any doubts about the death threat dispelled. Freddie Greenaway returned carrying a tray with the best china just dusted off. They helped themselves as the detective stooped to pull some papers from his battered attaché case. 'Take a look at this,' he said.

Gavin and Walter were quick to do so. Art merely eased himself slowly from the chair to get a better look. It was a photograph of Gavin which Walter had given to Greenaway the previous day. Only it wasn't. Someone had obviously spent half the night working on the negatives, blurring the image. Today and in the photo, Gavin was sporting a moustache, heavy sideburns and a pair of large black spectacles. The picture to be published was more like an Identikit of the wrong person.

'Splendid! We'll use that.'

'Now. The BBC don't realize this is my house?' Greenaway wanted further reassurance.

'No. They think Gavin's staying with his uncle. Their exclusive is on the basis of secrecy of whereabouts. Anyway, what's the news about the bomb?'

'I spoke to the Anti-Terrorist Squad this morning. The device was triggered by switching on the engine. It was on the driver's side, just behind the dashboard. Semtex, similar to that used on the Lockerbie jumbo.'

'Semtex? That doesn't help. All the main terrorist groups use that, including the IRA.'

Greenaway nodded. 'They can all get it. The best clues usually come from the timing device. This wasn't classical IRA. There was no phoned warning, no coded message. But don't rule them out. Not if you've got this hot tip for a connection. Who do *you* think it was?' Greenaway's small, grey eyes, which were narrow at the best of times, were even thinner as he stared at Gavin, the careworn forehead adding even more years. The benign look disappeared and Greenaway's features took on the shrewd, sharp intensity of a ferret.

Gavin's mind raced to come up with some instant solution. There was none. 'It's got to be connected with the death threat. It's got to be connected with *Ryme Lady*. Klodinsky's an obvious choice.' Gavin spread his hands helplessly, demonstrating his uncertainty. 'And he's in Cyprus, isn't he?'

Before Greenaway could respond Art did so for him. 'So what?' He slumped back into his chair and rested his bleary eyes. Even Art himself was aware that his drinking was getting out of hand. He knew the reason but not the cure. Or was it that he didn't want to be cured? His mind was working too slowly to care. He knew it. There was nothing more needed to put him in shape than a few work-outs and a little less bottle. Maybe he'd start ... tomorrow. Maybe.

Corbin looked away from Art, realizing that his contribution wasn't going to develop any further. Not yet. 'What about the money? What about the death threat note? Any progress on that?' Walter's questions to Greenaway were punctuated by the chimes of the clock which was next to a Spanish bull and a pair of castanets at the end of the tiled mantelpiece.

'The note was written with a cheap, felt-tip marker pen. Typical school notepad paper, available from thousands of shops across France. The writing was not Klodinsky's.'

'What about the bunch of shysters in Bristol?' Art growled again from under the shroud of his hangover.

'Ah yes!' Greenaway's mouth twitched slightly as he smiled at the intervention. 'Walter told me you'd wanted them checked out. No. There's nothing known against them, nothing to connect them with the money or the note.'

'And Sir Archie's wife?'

'I've checked with the Coroner. As far as he was concerned it was a clear case of suicide. The open verdict reflected a desire not to hurt the family. There was not the slightest evidence of murder.' Greenaway put a third spoonful of sugar into the dark brown tea and then turned to Art. 'Are you suspicious of Brads?'

'When you've got more bullets than guts in your body,

you trust nobody.' He was about to continue when the ding-dong doorbell chimed.

'Right on time.' Walter looked pleased as he turned to Gavin. 'Are you sure you're able to go through with this? Know what you're going to say?'

'I'll be fine.' The radio interview was Walter Corbin's idea, a chance to spread more disinformation. 'You'll leave me to it?'

For an answer, Walter led Art into the kitchen, taking their cups and the biscuits with them, whilst Greenaway answered the door. Moments later, the young woman appeared. She was casually dressed and clutching her tape-recorder. After a brief introduction by Greenaway 'to his nephew', she checked the levels and held out the microphone. 'Mr Blair,' prompted the interviewer, 'how do you feel about the murder of your friends, Gilbert and Alison.'

'They were dear friends. The answer must be obvious.'

'It was your car which contained the bomb?'

'Yes. Gilbert had borrowed it. His own wouldn't start.'

'But the police suggest that Gilbert Sedgeway's car *would* start. No flat battery. What do you say about that?' In the kitchen, Walter Corbin and Greenaway supressed smiles as they overheard the success of this little piece of propaganda.

'Nothing at all. After our dinner, Gilbert said it wouldn't start.' The inference from the questioning was clear. The media were now exploring whether Gavin had set them up. Sneaky. All part of the Corbin and Greenaway confusion scheme - a blind alley inconsistent with any plan to murder Gavin.

'Who put the bomb in your car?'

'I don't know.'

'You have ideas?'

'I can speculate as well as the next person.'

'What do you mean?'

'Mistaken identity, for a start. As you know, a Mercedes like mine but with CD plates had been seen parked just a few yards away. That's the most likely explanation.' More disinformation invented by Corbin slipped out easily.

'Any others?'

'It would be a longshot. When I was a barrister I rubbed up against some fairly rough people. Did a few prosecutions.'

'Any terrorist cases? Any particular examples which might have led to this?'

'No. No terrorist cases. I did a prosecution at Maidstone Crown Court when a bullion gang was jailed. One of the convicted men swore that he'd get me. I'm not saying it was him. Personally, I have no idea.'

'Have you told the police this?'

'Naturally. I don't think they took the threat seriously. It's the type of remark often shouted by convicted criminals as they're led to the cells.'

'You said you *were* a barrister. What's your present occupation, Mr Blair?'

Gavin paused whilst the recording continued. 'I advise the International Maritime Bureau on shipping law. I'm still a barrister. The difference now is that I don't practise from chambers in the Temple.

'Is your work dangerous?'

'Does it sound dangerous?' Gavin was pleased with the incredulity in his voice. It was sufficient to get the interviewer to change tack.

'And the funerals? You'll be there?'

'Why not?' The glib answer came easily and yet it was a lie. 'Gilbert and Alison were among my closest friends. I'm godfather to their first child, Sophie.'

'You're lucky to be alive. How does that feel?'

'I'm not concerned for me. I'm only concerned about the death of two innocent friends. I want the murderers caught.'

'Thank you Mr Blair.' She clicked off the recording. It had only taken three minutes. There was now ample time for her to get back to Broadcasting House for the slot which awaited the scoop on the One o'clock News. A minute later and the woman was gone and the men gathered again in the sitting room.

'From what I heard, you did well.' Walter looked pleased. 'We shall have to go in a moment. Always good to see you, Freddie. Thanks for your help. Let me know if you get any further leads.' They started moving towards the front door. 'And this Claudine woman.' Greenaway's voice was sharp. 'Where is she?'

'Still under sedation at a nursing home, run by my aunt - and that's a real aunt - down near Woking. The doctor says she's suffering from a nervous disorder, brought on by shock, but the prognosis is good. All she needs is some rest and lack of stress.' He paused. 'If she knew she had a twenty-four guard from your lot, it would set her back a bit.' The tone was bitter.

'You're right,' said Greenaway. 'The guard *is* to keep her there. I'm sorry, but we haven't cleared her yet. There are still blanks in our knowledge.'

'Blanks? Oh, for God's sake! What are you on about? Of course she's had a varied life. That doesn't mean she's out to destroy Brads .. that she's a plant.'

'That isn't what I was saying. Just that until our enquiries are completed ... we're not satisfied.' The awkward atmosphere prevailed, put a dampener on the departure.

'Too damned right,' said Art. The words had a menace which spoke of something deeper than Art's hangover. Walter was concerned. It was puzzling. Why was Art trying to destroy Gavin's relationship? Jealousy perhaps? He couldn't be sure. Art's meticulous search of Claudine's belongings at Wickham during dinner had proved negative. Yet he wouldn't let go.

212

'As far as I'm concerned,' Walter spoke decisively as he smoothed the hair round his temple,' everyone's not proven - until we find out who sank *Ryme Lady* ... and why. No one's picking on Claudine but what happened in Wickham is a warning. The closer you get to the truth, the bigger the danger. Maybe the USA trip will clinch it.'

'Scared, are you?' Art returned to the fray without prompting, as he glared at Gavin. The narrow hallway was scarcely big enough for the four men, let alone for the size of their personalities. Art's raised voice seemed to bounce from wall to wall. With his arms swinging loosely in front of him, his shoulders hunched forward, he looked aggressive.

'I'm not scared.' Gavin spoke with intensity. His face was defiant but his words were plucked from a dark cellar of self-doubt. 'Not fear. Just inadequacy.' Suddenly, the words started pouring out. 'One day, you're swanning about, playing the detective. It's a game. It's exciting. The good versus the bad. Enter the glamorous girl. Better still. Then ... suddenly you get a death threat. The adrenalin flows. The gauntlet is thrown down. You pick it up. You live life on the edge. You're scared but it's abstract. You don't believe it. It won't happen. You don't believe you're important enough to be eliminated. And then it happens! Christ!' His face twisted in anguish. 'There's more bits of The Hon. Gilbert Sedgeway lying round Wickham than they've found.' His eyes moved from man to man, ending up with Art. 'So no. I'm not scared. Not a coward. I'm not quitting. If I'm scared, it's of one thing only. Scared that I'm not good enough to succeed.'

'I understand,' said Greenaway gently. 'You saw the picture in there of me and the Duke of Edinburgh? You know what that was all about? I was thirty one then. I'd never faced danger. The odd pub brawl, the occasional scuffle at a football match. Then I got promoted to Detective

Constable.' He glanced at his listeners and noticed that Art, alone, was uninterested, apparently more concerned with the barometer on the wall. 'I was scared. Shared all your feelings. Thought I was inadequate. Wondered if I would be able to cope when the moment came. Well, it did come. A lunatic with a shotgun pressed against the head of his baby daughter. And he was mad enough to have done it. He had to be disarmed. I did it. When the moment came, I did it.' Greenaway's eyes had become damp with emotion at the recollection. Except for Art, who decided to tap the barometer with noisy indifference, there was silence. 'So you see, when your moment comes, you'll do it.' Slowly he extended his hand to shake Gavin's. 'One day you're going to prove me right.'

'Thanks for looking after us,' said Walter, anxious to change the mood and the place. 'We've got to be at the Savoy. The ...... shysters await us.'

Greenaway opened the door. 'Any more news on that possible sighting?'

'Maybe. A vessel similar to *Ryme Lady*, calling herself *Rio Massu* was reported near Sicily,' replied Walter. 'Nothing fits. Not yet.' Walter led them down to the swing-gate. The widow over the road let her imagination run riot about what that nice Mr Greenaway had been doing with three men and young woman. A young blonde come to that.

'Good idea, getting Claudine into your aunt's nursing home.' Corbin was looking across the low coffee table in the discreet comfort of the Savoy Hotel as they awaited the arrival of Brads. The aura of the five star hotel was everywhere. Even Corbin appreciated the history and romance of the surroundings. The venue had been Edward's choice and a table for six had been booked in the Terrace Restaurant for 1.00 pm.

'Claudine is not happy.' Gavin said with emphasis.

214

'Neither am I.' His face showed it. 'But as you want me to go to New York with Art and she needs care and cossetting - well Aunt Margaret's just the person.' It was said without enthusiasm. 'Especially with a squad car at the front gate to stop her running away.'

Walter put up his hands in protest. 'No, no, not that! To stop anyone getting at *her*.' Walter's smile was wolfish and Gavin was not fooled.

'And what do we say to Brads about the bomb?' Gavin thought he knew the answer, even as he asked the question.

'If the subject comes up,' it was obvious that Walter had no intention of raising it, 'then ... mistaken identity.' The flickering smile around the edge of Walter's lips told its own story. As he spoke, he looked at Art who had done a quick change. Not that he had volunteered. Corbin had forbidden him to appear at the Savoy in the frayed jeans and lime green sweatshirt which he'd been wearing at Greenaway's. He was looking uncomfortably smart . He'd even shaved better than usual so that his dissolute swarthiness was almost missing.

Art stubbed out his cigarette and glanced at Walter Corbin. 'Any more on the IRA?'

'I've been talking to someone, let's say, rather well placed in Whitehall. I'm told the IRA can't be discounted. In terrorist terms, they move in sophisticated circles. They've developed links throughout Europe, with Gadaffi and the PLO.'

'But?' Gavin had picked up the hesitancy.

'But personally I'm unimpressed. I'm only sending you because you've come up with nothing better.' There was a distinct edge in the voice and the eyes were flint-hard as they peered over the spectacles at the listener.

'Any updates on *Cerne View* and *Adber Arrow*?' Gavin's look overstated his vested interest in their safety.

'*Adber Arrow*'s OK. She's in the Indian Ocean with a full

load of crude. Steaming for Japan. As for *Cerne View* ... ' He hesitated. 'I was happy until I spoke to Whitehall. Now I'm not so sure. Lloyds' agents have confirmed she's heading for Dakalla and then Lagos. Our members have had big trouble in West Africa - more there than anywhere, except north from Singapore. Coincidence probably.' Corbin didn't sound as if he thought that at all.

Gavin remembered watching the television in Claudine's apartment. 'Dakalla's a bit unstable at the moment. Lumbola's merging with Sampopo but not everyone's happy about it.' He saw the interest in Walter's face but Art was more concerned with cleaning his finger-nails with a cocktail stick. 'All the top brass are going - the US President, our PM, the lot.' Gavin stopped, suddenly uncertain of what he positively knew. 'And of course Klodinsky. Guests of the Government.'

Walter raised an eyebrow. 'Sheer coincidence again I expect. *Cerne View* should be in and out of Dakalla before Independence Day.'

'Agreed!' Art brushed his hands dismissively and then wiped his mouth on the back of his hand. 'Hell! Dakalla's a big port. There must be twenty or more vessels like *Cerne View* passing through every day without a glitch. My dollar bill's on New York.' Art's dogmatic tone was a debate-killer but anyway both listeners understood his reasoning. 'Look - Klodinsky's in New York. New York is full of Irish sympathisers. Noraid, the Irish fund-raising body, is fiercely active in Brooklyn. Plus we have a tip-off. A positive lead.'

Walter needlessly adjusted his silk tie but said nothing. He'd said his piece, made his view of the New York tip-off as plain as he could. It was up to each of them to work out the solution. He looked at his watch and weighed up the possibilities. He wanted nine holes of golf. With the nights drawing in, eighteen would be out of the question. 'And remember ... no one must know you're going to be in New

York, Gavin, especially not Claudine.' His voice was brusque, not because of Claudine but because of Sir Archie's lateness. No doubt he would arrive, flustered and blaming the traffic.

'I went through every goddamned thing,' said Art ruefully. 'Nothing.' His face showed his disappointment that in among the packets of new stockings, suspender belts, blouses, skirts and jumpers there was not a whiff of anything electronic, nothing surprising at all. 'But I'm not convinced.' Art knew that this would annoy Gavin and to add to his irritation he noisily exhaled a stream of smoke from his Camel cigarette in Gavin's direction.

'I've told you.' Gavin looked angry. 'She's not a plant. The bomb wasn't her doing.'

'Well, sure as hell, I didn't see anyone following,' said Art. 'And if we weren't followed, then how did they know where we were?' Gavin had an idea but had no intention of playing devil's advocate. Neither did Walter.

'Ah ... ,' Walter exclaimed as he saw Sir Archie descending the broad, green carpeted steps towards them. Immediately behind him was Edward, both men expensively suited and similarly built to look like Chairman and Chief Executive.

'Sorry we're late,' panted Sir Archie. 'The traffic, y'know. Even on a Sunday too!'

'Yes. Cars. There are such a lot about these days.' said Walter with not a trace of irony in his voice. 'No Susannah? I was looking forward to meeting her.'

'Decided she had a better offer. Can't blame her.' Sir Archie dismissed her absence as irrelevant.

Walter's face didn't show his concern as he pointed towards the restaurant though he approved Gavin's quizzical look at the remark. 'Let's go straight to the table. Skip the cocktails. We've got an excellent view over the river.' Without waiting for any response, Walter led the

217

way into the elegant dining room. 'I've got an important meeting this afternoon,' he added by way of explanation for his obvious haste.

'Oh I say!' said Sir Archie. 'All this traffic nonsense threw me, d'ya see.' He turned to Gavin. 'Before I said anything else I should have explained how deeply upset we are that your friends were murdered. Terrible, terrible business. We do appreciate you being here today. It can't be easy.'

Gavin nodded his head in appreciation, the muscles round his jaw flexing, his lips tense. Walter saw the mounting distress and intervened quickly. 'I think we should order.'

During lunch Gavin sat quietly, saying little. He played with his food, half-listened to the conversation but his thoughts were of Claudine. Those shaking fits! That tortured face! He shuddered at the recollection and Edward noticed, giving him a curious glance. Suddenly Gavin was aware that everyone was looking at him. Unknowingly, he had sighed. 'Sorry. I was miles away.'

It was Sir Archie who spoke soothingly. 'We all quite understand, d'ya see, you've been through a lot.'

'So,' continued Walter, 'what happened at Wickham was nothing to do with Brads, nothing to do with the Bureau.'

'Yes ... they were saying 'mistaken identity', on the radio a few minutes ago,' murmured Sir Archie. He searched in vain for another morsel of crab meat on his empty plate. 'And what now?'

'Art's off to New York tomorrow. He's looking forward to going back to his spiritual home so much I'm not even paying him. As for Gavin, he's staying for the funeral.' It wasn't true but the old smoothie rolled off the deception without faltering. 'And *Cerne View* and *Adber Arrow*?'

'No trouble. Pinetto, as charterers, haven't caused us any grief so far. Just as well for the Bureau, isn't it?' said Edward. 'At least you got that right. But your brief ... if you don't mind being reminded,' he said pointedly and with a penetrating stare at Gavin, 'is to find out what happened to *Ryme Lady*. We need cash. The families need the truth.'

'Keep us posted on *Cerne View*, won't you?' The Director was thinking of Gavin's remarks. 'She's heading for Dakalla, isn't she?' The Director was fishing but there didn't seem to be any bites. 'Keep me posted.' The Director paused whilst the waiter topped up their glasses with the magnificent 1988 Fleurie. 'And *Adber Arrow*.' It was an afterthought, though none the less important.

'Anything new on the message from New York?' Art's tone was direct, knowing that he was to be in the front line tomorrow. He watched as both Sir Archie and Edward shook their heads.

'Nothing new. We'd have told you if we'd heard.' There was an edge to Edward's voice. 'Where are you staying?

'That's confidential.' Corbin intervened quickly. 'Any contact must be through the Bureau.'

Sir Archie cocked his head quizzically. 'You think it's that dangerous?'

'With the IRA?' Art's pause was deliberate. 'Would you care to swap places? Don't get me wrong. I could do with a bit of action, blood and guts - but at a time and place of my own choosing.'

Gavin looked across and could see that to Art, Wickham meant nothing. Suddenly he felt sick and, nodding apologetically, he slipped away from the table.

'Talking of blood and guts, that reminds me,' said Corbin, anxious to keep minds off Gavin. 'I've had a report from Malaysia. Apparently someone broke into the fishermen's boat. There was a bit of a dust-up. Nothing to do with you, was it?'

Art's fork stopped in mid journey, the piece of Chateaubriand suspended in the air. 'Me?,' he grinned. 'Come on Chief, give me a break.'

PART TWO

CERNE VIEW

Chapter 29

There had been a major international port at Dakalla since the mid-nineteenth century. Before that, the rocky promontory had provided a safe haven only for the local fishermen. The onset of European and other trade had led to its startling growth. Now, it was a major port on West Africa's Atlantic coast.

The giant horseshoe of the harbour could provide berths for over thirty cargo vessels at any time. The facilities for ship repairs, bunkering and refits were first class. Besides all this, the harbour housed the city's own modern fishing fleet, dominated by the tuna and shrimping industries but still with its flotilla of small craft for the in-shore fishermen.

In this harbour, beneath the relentless near-tropical sun, *Cerne View* had just berthed. The 20,000 ton vessel, with its mix of containers and bulk storage, was now moored at Berth 3, its deck stacked high with containers. On the quay, cranes were busily unloading cargo. Container lorries were winding their way towards the dock gates, through the noisy hordes on the quayside.

Beyond the gates, heavily guarded, lay the city of perhaps 600,000 people, the usual mixture of haves and have-nots endemic in any African culture. Modern tower blocks containing hotels, banks, insurance companies and shipping lines looked out imperiously over the low level tin shacks and hovels of the suburban township.

Immediately beyond the dock gates was Independence Square, largely concreted with a fountain in the middle and surrounded on two sides by commercial buildings and on the third by the gardens and grounds of the Presidential Palace.

Two articulated lorries passed between the stacked containers on the dockside. At the gates, the drivers showed their paperwork. Their containers were destined for the premises of Scrignac Lefebre whose warehouse lay in an industrial complex on the edge of the city. After the usual bureaucratic form-filling, signatures, debates, arguments, questions, pacing round the lorries, they were both waved through into the hooting, tooting traffic jams of the city centre.

Back aboard *Cerne View*, Captain Walker and his First Officer, Ian Baldock, were on the bridge watching the last formalities of loading and unloading. Everything had gone smoothly considering it was an African port. 'Make arrangements for weighing anchor this evening. Tell Bristol there have been no problems with Pinetto and that everything's just fine.'

'Better than being laid off,' agreed Baldock. 'But until they clear up the *Ryme Lady* mess, the company's always going to be in the shit.'

Similar thoughts were crossing the minds of the directors back in Bristol. No sooner had Sir Archie passed on the message that *Cerne View* would soon be moving on from Lumbola than Edward had dismissed it from the conversation. 'OK, the Pinetto charter's working but we're no further forward with *Ryme Lady*. Those wankers up at the IMB are getting nowhere. Susannah back from the bank yet?' The connection between the two lines of thought was not evident.

Sir Archie nodded affirmatively. 'Yes. Still alive too. Flesh wounds only, she said. Her report's being typed.'

'Well, isn't she attending our meeting?' Edward sounded irritable.

'No. She's had to go to London. We'll have her report, that's enough.' In Sir Archie's eyes Susannah could do nothing wrong.

224

Edward snorted his disapproval. Susannah had always been father's favourite. 'Right - item one on the agenda - Susannah's pay cut. Part time job, that's what she's got,' he grumbled, his features sour, his mouth downturned. 'Anyway, where does she go to? She's always slipping off.'

'She didn't say. If she wanted us to know, she'd tell us. Lover I suppose. Pretty girl. Let's hope he's rich. Do us all a favour.' Sir Archie sipped at his coffee. 'Time she settled down. Make someone a wonderful wife, d'ya see.' The door opened and Sir Archie's secretary appeared and handed over the report. 'Thank you,' said the Chairman. 'Right, Edward, we'd better go through these figures.'

'Well, I think she should be here. We've only two items on the agenda. The first is the financial report which is down to her and the second is *Ryme Lady* which concerns all of us. If she's got a lover, then she ought to suppress her pulses of desire until after office hours.'

'Jealous?' Sir Archie's raised eyebrow was designed to irritate. He was rewarded with a scowl.

Chapter 30

With a shudder and a farewell jolt, the British Airways 747 to New York left the runway, climbing steadily through the massed clouds. The dreary grey of a West London morning was obscured. Art had already downed a couple of glasses of scotch and was instantly calling the stewardess for a supply of miniatures to top him up for the flight.

Gavin was lost in an article about the Wickham bombing, his photo unrecognizable as he sat quietly sipping champagne, apparently at ease with himself. Art felt irritated, his feelings showing in the way in which he unscrewed the cap off the bottle. He eased the seat-belt and flipped the seat into recline.

For just a moment he hated himself, hated his increasing love of the fiery amnesia of the alcohol, wishing he didn't need its numbing effect. If only ... he glanced again at Gavin, made as if to say something but refrained as the stewardess reappeared. 'Just leave me four, would you. That'll do me till lunch,' he told her.

The pert, bright-eyed attendant handed over the bottles. 'Thank you sir. Will that be all?' Any sarcasm which she felt was carefully hidden.

Art helped himself to three bags of nuts from her tray. 'Sure ... for now.'

Outward appearances were deceptive. Gavin's feelings were in turmoil, though he felt safer now he was out of the UK. Above all was the fear but then there was the guilt ... about Claudine. And then there was Art. He hadn't always been like this. He seemed to be worse. He was even more boorish, more drunken. Only occasionally was there the passing flash of friendship. Mainly he was sullen, morose and snappily indifferent.

They travelled in silence until well after the arrival of the meal which Art accompanied with a generous quota of red wine. 'You're convinced Claudine led the bombers to us, aren't you?' Gavin decided he had to be blunt.

'Unless you know better, smart-ass.' There was an aggressive slur in the voice.

'We were followed. Must have been. We just didn't spot it.'

'Don't kid yourself.' Art inspected the rare steak with suspicion before chewing away with relish.

'So, maybe my car was bugged. Easy to attach a homing device and then follow from a distance.'

'The police haven't found one.'

'Are you surprised? It went up with the car. Could be hundreds of yards away. What's left of it.'

'More likely Claudine told Klodinsky - a quick phone call from Barking on Friday morning.' Art was in no mood to be convinced yet he sensed a hesitancy in Gavin's reaction. Wrongly he mistook it for vicarious guilt about Wickham. It wasn't - just a flashback in Gavin's mind to Claudine's mystery call from the Paris restaurant. That and the arrival of Denim Jacket shortly after. 'She may be hot in bed but don't let that fool you. That's if it interests you these days.' Art sniggered with a drunken leer as he sniffed his brandy.

Gavin's face puckered in puzzlement. 'What are you on about?' Gavin's eyes were burning with anger as he looked at the slob sitting next to him. 'Why don't you just fuck off and keep your drunken drivel to yourself.'

'One message from her to Klodinsky.' Art ignored the warning. 'That's all.' He saw that Gavin was on the defensive. 'But hey, big boy! Claudine's lingerie! Wow .. ee! The kid sure has erotic tastes! Did I enjoy going through those things or did I enjoy!' He rolled his eyes in lascivious recollection, knowing he would wound. 'Some turn-on that would have been for your big night in Wickham.' The words were slurred yet contemptuous. 'If you'd had a chance. If you could manage it.' Art laughed again, deep into his glass.

Gavin's body ached to retaliate. Not a physical man, nevertheless, he had the urge to smash his fist into Art's cheek, to kick him, to pummel him, to knock the sickly grin from the American's face. With difficulty he forced himself to look away, to let the feelings die. It was better that way.

They were a team.

In the silence which followed, Art's head slumped as he lapsed into a heavy stupor. Asleep, he felt no guilt, no contempt, no hatred, felt nothing at all. It was better that way. For both of them.

Six hours later, they were seated in a yellow cab crossing the Triborough Bridge which spans the vast width of the East River. Ahead was the Upper East Side, fashionable and sophisticated. Beyond that, the multi-shaped skyscrapers stretched into the sky, their lights almost turning night into day, making New York the city that never sleeps.

Art, in his check jacket and blue sweatshirt, was resting the heaviness of his head in a cupped hand, staring gloomily at a skyline which usually never failed to lift him. His brain told him he'd been in a fight and lost. His teeth were furred, his throat parched, his eyes bloodshot. He looked pole-axed and felt worse. If only Gavin wasn't so goddamned nice, so goddamned British, such a good loser.

'Hey!' Art banged on the partition separating the passengers from the driver. 'I'm no goddamned limey. You think this is the quickest way to the New York Hilton? Buddy ... just you go buy yourself a map. Better still ... sell up this heap of shit. Do something else. Sell candy.' Art nodded in satisfaction as the driver made a u-turn and cut

228

a swift left and right through to the Avenue of the Americas. 'Asshole,' muttered Art to himself in satisfaction.

In the hotel, their room on the 27th floor was comfortably furnished, twin-bedded and big enough for two good friends to live in tolerance. Just. 'I'm ringing Brads' agent. No time to lose.' Art, having showered away the flight, went to the phone between the beds and started to dial.

'You carry on.' Gavin flung his few things into drawers and hung a suit in the wardrobe. He was happy enough just to listen.

'Jesus Christ!' exclaimed Art, shouting down the phone. 'You're telling me you've just received this message. Look! I've just flown here to meet this sonovabitch tomorrow. Now you're saying he's putting the meeting back! Three days! Till Thursday, for Chrissake?' Art tapped his foot impatiently as he listened to the explanation. 'Ok. So you'll know the rendezvous before Thursday. Fine. You'll be getting a phone call? Ok. I'll call you.' Art lashed out at his case, kicking it across the room. 'Aw! Shit! The Irish informant's put it back. Three days! No reasons given. I don't like it.' He picked up the suitcase and threw it back on the bed with such force that it bounced off, spilling its shabby, crumpled contents onto the floor. As if it hadn't happened, Art continued his diatribe. 'I don't fucking like it!' He forgot that he'd previously backed the idea that *Ryme Lady's* sinking was centred on New York. 'This whole IRA thing stinks. And remember ... ' he jabbed a finger into Gavin's chest, 'don't go telling no one you're here. Got it?'

'Don't you think it's time you stopped treating me like a kid. We're here as a *team*, in this together.' The words carried a disparaging sneer. The pounding blood vessel on Gavin's temple, the clenched fists, the sharp delivery, showed Art a side of Gavin which was rarely seen. 'You won't make me back off. You may think you're smart, but to me you're just a bum. A drunken bum. A has-been professional. More dangerous than an amateur. So don't play the preacher-boy from some high moral ground.'

Art was stopped in his tracks. Till now, he had always assumed that Gavin respected him, regarded him as the senior partner, the professional of the team. He was taken aback, wondering how to reply. He started to open his mouth but there was nothing to say, no flash of inspiration. The booze had seen to that. He said nothing. Instead he sought comfort in the shape of the mini-bar and a can of Bud. 'I'm gonna call up Klodinsky. Corbin told me he passed through London last night from Cyprus. Took the breakfast Concorde. I'll go pay him a visit. We've time to kill.'

'Or be killed. Do you really want Klodinsky to know you're here?' Gavin was sceptical.

'Calculated risk.'

'Buy a better calculator then. Look Art,' he almost pleaded. 'It doesn't make sense. Not him knowing.'

Gavin had been planning to put a tail on Klodinsky but Art's impetuosity would torpedo that one. Quickly Gavin explained his plan but it was dismissed as irrelevant.

'I'm telling you - Big K knows I'm here already. Think Claudine will have kept her big mouth shut? He'll know you're here too.' Art kept dialling. 'Nice thought, eh?'

Chapter 31

Cerne View's design was a compromise between the old break-bulk carrier and its Maclean inspired successor, the all-container vessel. Container vessels operated on the principle of small crews, less handling of goods, less pilfering and speed of port turn-round. As such, they had represented a great advance in transit of goods by sea. *Cerne View* was one of the early multi-purpose ships, and at 170 metres long and 20,000 tons dead weight, smaller than the giant carriers.

Sir Archie still took the credit for his shrewd purchase. Even Edward acknowledged that his father had been right. Probably his last *good decision* had been Edward's expressed view on more than one occasion. The flexibility of choice of cargo was a major plus. Sometimes the vessel would carry motor cars, technical equipment, mobile cranes, bulk grain. On other voyages she might be full of timber or rice. Such was the beauty of the multi-purpose ship.

On the bridge, Captain Walker and First Officer Baldock were studying the weather reports in readiness for the 1,200 mile voyage down the coast to Nigeria. Unloading had finished. Fresh supplies had been taken aboard. Down on the quay they could hear and see the usual bustle and confused shouting.

The air conditioning kept the bridge cool but outside the late afternoon temperature was 32 degrees. Around the vessel, the crew were busying themselves in readiness for sailing, the Radio Officer was playing with the dials on the Ship-to-Shore. Down in the galley as the cook was boiling up fish and rice for the deck-hands, a noise from the quay

231

attracted Walker's interest. Forcing their way between the lorries, cranes and crates were two 3 ton army trucks and a scout-car. 'What the devil's going on?' he said as much to himself as to Baldock. They peered down - unconcerned but fascinated by this show of military force.

'Must be some army bigwig being met from a ship further along the quay.' Baldock leaned forward to watch progress.

He was wrong.

No sooner had the lorries reached *Cerne View* than they stopped. Soldiers armed with machine guns spilled from the vehicles, ran up the gangplank, reached the deck and dispersed at the double in every direction.

From the scout-car an impressive-looking officer appeared. His red peaked cap was laden with golden trimmings, his jacket dripping with medals and braid.

'For Christ's sake get Jack to send out a call.' Walker barked out the order. This was a reference to the Radio Officer, blissfully unaware of what was happening. 'Bloody West African ports. No doubt they'll commandeer the ship and steal the cargo. It's bloody bandit country.'

As Walker strode across the bridgehouse to lock the door, Baldock spoke to Radio Officer Jack Longworth who extinguished his cigarette. 'I'll get a message off immediately,' said Longworth. With skilled fingers, he was quick to tune the radio and was about to speak when his cabin door burst open. The force threw it back on its hinges with a heavy metallic crash. The room shook. There, beside him, were two soldiers, dressed in sweat-stained combat jackets, each of them pointing a machine gun at him from a range of five feet.

The leading soldier, who appeared to be a corporal in the local army, spoke English with a heavy French-African accent. 'Stop zat! Ze 'ands - oop!' He motioned with the gun.

Longworth knew when he was beaten. He nodded his head and moved to switch off the set. Corporal Ngoa, anxious to make his presence felt, or possibly misinterpreting Longworth's intention, opened fire. A hail of bullets smashed the equipment and cut a horizontal line across Longworth's chest.

The Radio Officer slumped over the transmitter, streams of blood pumping from the fatal wounds. Not to be outdone, the young private also let rip. Gleefully he unleashed a second burst into the body, which twitched and shuddered under the impact.

Up on deck, Captain Walker could hear the shooting as he pushed the door shut but before he could bolt it, four soldiers hurled themselves through the entrance. A volley of bullets split the ceiling as Walker and Baldock were hustled back, their faces contorted with terror and apprehension. At gunpoint they were made to stand facing the far window, arms above their heads. Not a word had been uttered. One soldier stepped forward. Rapidly he frisked the officers but found nothing. Walker could sense but not see that someone else had entered his bridge.

'Turn round.' The voice was deep, the accent strong, the tone intimidating. The Englishmen did so, leaning against the starboard window, hands held high, the sweat stains spreading down their crisp white shirts. Baldock licked his lips nervously, Walker clenched and unclenched his fingers as he glared at the man in front of them. They were staring at General Ojwaki, the medal-bedecked figure they'd seen on the quayside. 'On ze orders of ze Minister of ze Interior, zis ship is under arrest.' The General waved his swagger-stick in an accusatory manner. His small eyes were angry, the whites large in the heavy blackness of the man's face.

'Would you mind telling me what's going on. Who the devil are you?' Walker tried to sound in control when it was obvious that he was not.

'Ze ship, ze officers and ze crew, zey is all under arrest. For de fraud.'

'I'm sorry. Would you please explain. You're talking nonsense.'

'You treat me wiz respect.' The General advanced with short, aggressively-brisk strides to close the gap between them. He lunged forward and rammed the end of his stick into Walker's testicles. The officer involuntary doubled up, only to be struck a sharp downward blow across the back of the head, causing him to wince and almost forget the pain in his testicles.

'Bastard,' he muttered to himself, scarcely able to say anything coherent in his agony.

'Ze containers from zis ship for Scrignac Lefebre - zey were empty. Under ze law *you* take ze blame. You is a common thief. You go to ze jail. Ze ship is impounded.' Walker could see that the General liked that word. 'We keep it. Over zare.' The General pointed the swagger-stick right across the harbour to the Military Headquarters. 'Ze pilot will take charge.' Looking more than faintly embarrassed, the pilot, who had been hovering behind the General, stepped forward. 'Move zis ship at once,' he was commanded.

Walker knew it was hopeless. 'This is an outrage. If the containers were empty, then someone emptied them *after* they were offloaded. I demand to see the British Consul.'

The General laughed, a loud, deep, mocking, guttural laugh. It was not funny, distinctly not. 'You? You demand nothing. Under de law of Lumbola, we shoot de thieves.' The accompanying smile split his face from ear to ear.

Chapter 32

The express elevator slowed on approaching the 79th floor. Art emerged, looked round the lobby, took in the fifteen other elevator shafts and then saw the silver board with the confirmation that the Mentocca Group was in Suite 7979B. Even in the corridor there was a sense of opulence. He looked out of the window and saw New Jersey where he'd spent his childhood. It lay across the Hudson, a hotch-potch of buildings, almost lost in the hazy pollution. In-between, rose the masterful twin towers of the World Trade Center, like so many of the skyscrapers, non-existent when he'd been a street kid. In contrast, from this height, New Jersey and Hoboken looked much the same. No doubt they'd changed too. Chrissake, it'd been mean as a kid, twenty years ago. Even then, the drug scene had arrived. It had been the lingering death of his best buddy from heroin which had led him to join the Drug Enforcement Agency.

And now he was here, peering out across the skyline, about to meet one of New York's richest sons. As a kid he'd dreamed of going up the Empire State Building. But that cost money. Promises of a special treat by his parents had never materialized. Until he was fourteen, he'd never crossed the Hudson into Manhattan at all. He shook his head quietly to himself as he thought about what had been and what he now was. His mouth tasted sour from the alcohol, his eyes heavy, his eyelids droopy. He'd have to shake himself out of it. He spat into a trash can.

Somehow.

Soon.

Down the corridor he used the entryphone outside the

heavy wooden door and was admitted to the ostentatious elegance of Mentocca's worldwide headquarters. From the carpet with the Mentocca monogram, through to the subtle lighting and finest blue leather easy chairs, the atmosphere exuded wealth and integrity. Art was not fooled. He'd seen it all before - in Pei Fau Pang's office in Singapore for a start. Much the same, Art told himself. Ignore the image. Seek out the substance.

The black receptionist was immaculately coiffured, her eyes sparkling and alert, her smile warm. Her simple red dress was so expensively cut that Art judged it had not been bought on her salary. 'Good morning.' The woman's voice was smokey-brown, reassuring.

'Hi! Art Lemman. I'm here to see Carl Klodinsky. I telephoned.'

'Mr Lemman. Sure. Won't you take a seat? Can I fix you some coffee? Mr Klodinsky's taking a call right now. He won't be long.' Even as she spoke, the receptionist was rising from her chair, revealing just how tall and elegant she was. She left her grey desk and walked with poise, stockings rustling as she crossed the room to the bubbling coffee pot. As Art waited for her to bring the coffee, he took in the map which filled half of one wall. On it, different coloured lights were flashing.

'What's this mean?' he asked as he pointed to the map as she returned. She stood beside him so that he was able to savour her delicate perfume and the aroma of the strong black coffee.

'Cookie?' She opened a red tin with the Mentocca logo on the lid. He took two. 'That's the Mentocca fleet. Every flashing light represents the last reported position of one of our ships. They're most everywhere, as you can see. Black flashing lights are tankers, green represents bulk carriers, red are containers.'

'I see you've got a few in the Med. What are they?'

'You'll have to ask Mr Klodinsky.' The receptionist glanced at the switchboard on her work-station. 'Ah! He's cleared now. I'll take you in.' Head held high, black hair shining under the diffused lighting, she led him with a wiggle and a haughty stride down a short corridor and into the generous expanse of Klodinsky's office. The far wall was all glass, providing a panoramic view from Staten Island to New Jersey. Carl Klodinsky rose from his swivel chair and stepped forward to greet the visitor. In shape and pugnacity they had a great deal in common though Art was taller and his girth could not match Klodinsky's.

Art was ushered to a chair by the desk. Klodinsky moved his own so that they could both look out of the window with no intervening table. In contrast to the reception, Klodinsky's office was traditional in concept. The room was full of genuine eighteenth-century antiques culled at vast expense from the great stately homes of England. A twelve-piece chandelier dominated the room and everywhere there was gilt - mirrors, torchères, touches of ormulu, objets d'art. On two of the walls, were seascapes by Turner.

'My painting of *Port Marly*, by Sisley, is on loan to an exhibition in London. Leaves a big hole on that wall. Anyway, make yourself comfortable.' The flourish of Klodinsky's shirtsleeved arm directed Art to the easy chair. His tie was power-red with the Mentocca motif running through it in black. The depth of Klodinsky's voice with its rasp of gravel made the invitation more like a command. 'Some view, huh? I never tire of it,' he said. 'Even on a polluted day like this. Whatever shit people are giving me, I just take a look out there. It kinda relaxes me. Drops the blood pressure ten points. I just say to myself ... forget it Carl ... that view'll be here long after you.'

'And we're facing the window because you're expecting some aggravation?' asked Art. He was disarmed by the man's charm and his comment was said with something approaching a chuckle.

'If your questioning's like that guy, what's his name?' He look at the ceiling for inspiration ...'Blair, then sure, I'll be staring real hard at the Staten Island ferry.' Klodinsky flipped open a packet of cigarettes. Art accepted and Klodinsky lit up. 'Did Corbin tell you? When your Bureau was formed, I was approached to join. I said then - and I just know I'm right - that it would be a heap of shit. Ineffective. Shipping doesn't need folks like you playing at cops. It's all talk, no achievement.' He grinned wickedly at the listener. 'Art, I'm telling you ... there's more hot air in your Bureau than in the New York Subway on a July afternoon.'

'You're wrong! Take the *Lucona*. The loss of that ship has now led to Udo Proksch getting twenty years. Took a long time for the authorities to get the evidence. But they did.' Art said it with a clear warning in his voice.

'Huh!' Klodinsky wasn't going to admit he was impressed though, like everyone in shipping, he knew the amazing story of the *Lucona* fraud. Besides the death of the crew when the ship had been blown up in the Indian Ocean, the drama had unfolded with other deaths and suicides and the near collapse of the Austrian Government, some of whose members may have been implicated..

'Anyway,' retorted Art, 'I'm not here selling membership like a Jehovah's Witness selling *Watchtower*. I'm here for answers.' Art leaned forward, picked up his coffee and sipped appreciatively. He was enjoying himself. He could admire Klodinsky - a criminal but nonetheless impressive. The strength of character was impressive. There was a shrewd brain behind the bombastic bluster. 'That wall-chart out there? Are all your vessels on that?'

'Sure.'

'You've nothing round West Africa?'

'No.' The tone was definitive.

"And I mean not just under the name Mentocca. I mean under any other name which you might use.' Art wanted to know whether Pinetto was just another Klodinsky company is disguise. His question was greeted with a vigorous shake of the head and a slight curling of the man's heavy lips. Klodinsky patted down an unruly tuft of hair and ran his fingers slowly down his cheek. Art took in the jaw-line and the heavy jowls which sagged towards his chin. From the broad expanse of the nostrils, a cluster of black hairs protruded - just as they did from his ears. It was only the top of Klodinsky's head, browned by the Mediterranean sun, which was devoid of hair.

'No, we've nothing round West Africa. Funny you should mention it though. I'm going there soon. To Lumbola.' He nodded in the direction of a heavy, gold-embossed invitation which was propped on top of a Regency escritoire. 'It's just got to be the hottest ticket. You know why? It's the rhodium. It's a real precious metal. Hell, no time ago it was $1,500 an ounce. Now, it's about $6,000 an ounce. As a co-product of plutonium, any government, any big player wants to be there. You don't see the President of the United States over-much in Africa. Time was, the White House map never even had Africa on it. Suddenly they found it, dusted it down and they're going apeshit to get on best-friend status with the new Government. Rhodium's the answer. Whatever the official diplomatic jargon might pretend.'

'Sure.' Art was not really interested. His mind was moving on to his next question. 'I guess I don't know the right folk to get an invite. You obviously do.' It was not really a question at all but it brought a response.

'We've traded with Lumbola for many years. I ran a liner service with a Dakalla headquarters - container ships mainly, up and down the West African coast. That's how I know half the government.' He paused to watch a helicopter whirr past the building, almost within spitting distance. 'Things out in Dakalla are pretty rough right now. I mean, economically it makes sense forming a federation ... a time and motion man's dream. One plus one equals more than two - maybe more than three.'

'But?' Art really wanted to get back to ships but he could see that Klodinsky wanted to talk on.

'Why? You don't know? There's none more racist than African blacks. Look at South Africa. It's becoming a bloodbath. If it works, then Lupopo's economy is going to be second to none in West Africa. Maybe even pushing South Africa.' He adjusted the heavy gold clip on his tie. 'Lumbola and Sampopa are not two separate nations by coincidence. They've developed apart because of their tribes, centuries of bloodshed. Some of the hatred goes back generations just like the Brits in Ireland.' He shrugged helplessly. 'Well ... Lumbola's the same. Maybe three million out of 3.5 million want it to work. Or don't understand. Or don't care. But that minority, hell, they can cause a heap of trouble. Especially if ... an outsider stirs them up.'

Art listened attentively, not so much because the topic interested him but because he was trying to judge the speaker. He spoke with confidence on matters of which Art knew little and cared less. Dakalla to him was a dot on the map which had never impinged itself on his brain. He tried to look interested as he stared at some notes on the desk. Despite Forensic's initial view, he was trying to compare Klodinsky's writing with the death threat. It looked different. Maybe Forensic had been right but you couldn't always trust them. Anyway ... what the hell! Klodinsky would never have written the note himself. Crazy notion that.

'Ever heard of *Rio Massu*?' Art threw in the question fast and low. How would Klodinsky react to Corbin's hunch that *Ryme Lady* and the ship seen in the Med were one and the same? It was worth bouncing it off the tycoon's suit of armour.

'No.' The tone was dismissive, uninterested. 'Can't say I have.' Art waited in vain for Klodinsky to ask why. OK Carl, he told himself. I've got your measure. You're a cool one, talk freely about irrelevancies but volunteer nothing about the issues. Just wait.I'll get you. Right up.

'Anything of yours in the Med?'

The reaction was immediate. Klodinsky again turned his eyes towards the ceiling and closed them for a moment, as if reading from an internal computer screen. '*Mentocca Moon, Mentocca Saturn, Mentocca Jupiter* and maybe a charter. Yes. The Lady Mayler. Just the four of them. Why do you ask?' This time Klodinsky had been interested as Art was quick to notice. Perhaps Klodinsky had wanted to change the subject from *Rio Massu*.

'No matter.' It was Art's turn to be non-committal. He'd check out their itineraries and cargo later. Meantime let's give it to him. 'What about Claudine Flubert?'

'Claudine? Why?' Klodinsky's brow corrugated. Then his face changed to express interest. The large balding head turned in his direction. When their eyes met, there was a cold emptiness in the look.

'Because she disappeared. You never reported her missing.'

'Disappeared? Missing?' Carl stubbed out his cigarette and scratched the dwindling thicket of hair above his left ear. It was a theatrical gesture, designed to demonstrate the depth of his bewilderment. 'Are you kidding? Claudine's been on vacation. Left a message on the office answerphone.'

'Don't give me that crap.' Art was disbelieving. The time for polite decorum had gone.

'Sure. I phoned Paris from Athens. The messages play back anywhere I am.'

'Anyone else hear it?'

'I guess not. Why should they? It was no big deal. I erased it.'

'It was her? You're sure?'

Art received a withering stare. 'Sure I'm sure. Said she needed a break - wanted to vacation in St Tropez.' Klodinsky used his arms to lever himself out of his chair. He walked to the escritoire. Even those paces seemed to leave him breathless. 'I can see you don't believe me.' He opened a drawer and produced a card. 'Here. Take a look.' He slid the postcard from St Tropez across the desk. Art swallowed hard. This was not going according to plan at all. He tried not to reveal his thoughts as he looked at the evidence. It was a picture of the café-lined port. Art turned it over and saw that the card was addressed to Klodinsky at his New York headquarters. The postmark was indecipherable and the scrawl merely said, see you next month. It was signed with a letter C and a kiss.

'She wrote this?'

'Sure. Why not?' He looked puzzled. 'What is all this? What are you telling me? When was all this?' He rose from his desk. 'Claudine's a grown-up girl. She was due some vacation. Matter of fact she was due four weeks. She hadn't settled in Paris that much. Heck ... why should I be surprised?'

'Can I keep it?'

'If you think it important.'

'It may be.' Art slipped it into the pocket of his leather jacket, wondering why Klodinsky had kept the card. Wasn't that just a little too neat? Or maybe Claudine had sent the card but not this year? He'd have to find out. 'I suggest you look out of the window. I'm gonna give you some real aggravation.' Art paused to finger the skin above his upper lip. All the time his eyes were watchful but Klodinsky gave no sign of caring nor concern. 'Claudine says that she was kidnapped. By you.' It was not strictly true.

'By me? Quit horsing about. See here ... Mr Lemman ... take a look round.' He flourished a stocky arm in a gesture which embraced the wall to wall luxury. 'I'm not short of a few bucks. I need sinking ships and disappearing women like a miser needs a trip to Vegas. Kidnapping!' Behind the heavy black-framed glasses, Klodinsky rolled his eyes in despairing wonderment. 'Jeee-sus! Claudine's been sunning herself in St Tropez. Probably with a lover. Period. Anyway, how do you know different? Where is she?'

'Maybe she'll send you a card.' He saw Klodinsky bristle at the taunt but he said nothing.

'You see, er, Carl, despite all your tinsel and executive toys, you're a greedy bastard. Greedy for power. Let me tell you something else.' He looked Klodinsky full in the eye. 'You fucked Sir Archie's wife. Now you want to fuck his company.'

Klodinsky pushed his glasses up his nose, blinked behind them and then shrugged his shoulders as he gazed across the river. 'Ingrid? You've been busy. But it was nothing. Years ago - a nooner in Manilla. A one-off thing. Two lonely people with the hots. And Brads? Why should I want to screw them? You kidding? Boy! You're as crazy as that kid ... ' he struggled for the name, 'from the Bureau.'

'Gavin Blair.' It was Art's turn to smile. His preferred form of confrontation was physical. Even so this bear-baiting excited him and come to think of it, Carl with his growling voice and hairy body, gave a fair impression of a brown bear being poked with a stick. 'Uh-uh! I don't think so Carl. Not quite a nooner. It was an *affair*. Hot. Passionate. Primitive.' Art was making it up as he went along. 'Pillow talk. Ingrid told you more than she should have, in-between playing games with your pecker. She blabbed all about Brads' option.' He offered Carl a Camel which was rejected with impolite alacrity. 'There's your incentive to destroy Brads. You wanted the insurance market at Lloyds to distrust Brads. Wanted Brads' name kicked like a pup round the Baltic Exchange. I guess it was you who hyped up the journalists to give a bad press so that you could move in to pick up the pieces cheap.'

Klodinsky had looked away now and was fingering the knot in his tie as he stared through the huge plate glass window. He was about to respond when he realized that Art hadn't finished. 'When *Ryme Lady* left Singapore with the clean bill of lading, signed by Captain Scutar, the bankers for the Kuwaiti cargo buyers had to hand over the money for the goods they were buying. All those electronics. Even if they never went aboard. It was an easy story to peddle, wasn't it Carl? Blame Brads for the scam, paint them as the beggars of Bristol.' Art was in full stride now. 'I'm gonna prove it Carl. You're out to break them.'

'I've seen your lips move. If I hadn't, I'd have said you were talking through your ass.' It was a rare profanity but the provocation had cut deep.

Art was enjoying himself. 'You hated Sir Archie. Why? Because Ingrid wouldn't leave him for you.' Art pointed towards a photograph he'd noticed on the mahogany secretaire. It was of Klodinsky, looking slightly less corpulent, standing in a group of people including a Swedish-style blonde.

'Ok.' Klodinsky put up both hands to stop the flood of accusations. 'That's Ingrid. But the rest? Dream on! I don't need Brads. I wish to hell I'd never chartered *Ryme Lady*.'

Art was thoughtful. 'I don't believe you.' He was less certain than he sounded. Klodinsky was just too cool, a glib liar, measured in his responses. 'Meantime, I've plenty to do in New York.'

'Then you'll be leaving.' It was a command. Art rose to his feet. The two protagonists stood for a moment, eyeing each other with more respect than when the meeting had started. Klodinsky picked up the photograph. 'Take a look.' Art saw that Sir Archie was in the group though it was Lady Ingrid whose serene beauty caught the lens. 'Sir Archie never knew. Least, I don't think he did. But you're right about one thing.' For a moment Klodinsky's brown eyes softened behind the glasses. His facial muscles relaxed, the tension eased. His jaw sagged as he remembered the day the photo was taken, recalled the setting sun, fiery red across the Pacific, when they'd stayed in Hawaii. 'I loved her.' He stared at the photograph for a few seconds before slowly putting it down.

Art was surprised at the man's sentimentality but was it believable? Was he out to screw Brads because of Ingrid? Revenge? Was that the explanation? No ... it had to be a take-over, a corporate rape. 'Why did she kill herself? Or perhaps I should say ... why did she die?'

'I don't know.' Klodinsky's face showed his anguish. He pulled out a dark red handkerchief, littered with Mentocca motifs and blew his nose in a gesture which Art judged just a touch too theatrical. 'I really don't. I didn't go to the inquest. I couldn't. You can see why? I guess ... she was depressed.'

Art felt like saying that Ingrid could have left Sir Archie any time. If she'd wanted to. 'And Claudine? Do you still love her? Or do you just brand your women on their rumps like steers before moving on?'

'You're nothing but one dirty mouth!' Klodinsky's eyebrows almost joined as his face blackened, teeth bared as his thoughts changed from remorse to anger. 'I loved Ingrid. I told you and hell ... Claudine's a great kid. Got everything. Even a job ... if she starts back to work soon.'

Art was about to comment but refrained. Any sentimentality in Klodinsky's face had gone. The muscles were tight. Once again he was the tycoon, preening himself as he walked, chest out. 'Sure as hell, you ain't over here just to see me. Mind, that would be some compliment. So what are you doing?'

Art thought for a moment, wondering whether to let Klodinsky think he was centre stage or not. 'You think I'd tell you? Just one thing. When you lost the charters,' he continued, 'it was to Pinetto. Know anything about this group?'

Klodinsky's laugh was mocking. 'No. But you should. That's *your* job, isn't it.' The tone was convincing but Art remained unconvinced. There would be little that Klodinsky didn't know in the world of ship chartering. Klodinsky slid open the door. The interview was over. 'If I hear anything, then I'll get in touch. Where are you staying?'

Art ignored the specifics. 'I'll ring you. You can always get me through the Bureau.'

Klodinsky shrugged non-committally at the brush-off. 'Suit yourself but I'd say you guys are in a heap of trouble.' From off his desk, with slow deliberation, Klodinsky handed over a ticker-tape printout. 'Interesting huh?' It was timed at 9.30 am, East Coast time. Art read it quickly and then re- read it. "*Cerne View*, 20,000 tons, registered Cyprus, owned by British and Dominion Shipping and chartered to the Pinetto Group, has been arrested in Dakalla, Lumbola. Believed casualties. Captain and crew jailed for alleged discrepancies in cargo." Art put down the piece of paper and whistled softly.

'Game, set and match to me?' Carl's laugh was distinctly unfunny. The edge in his voice remained. 'I'd say you're sniffing the wrong dog's ass.'

Chapter 33

A few moments later when Art was standing in Liberty Plaza close to the Stock Exchange, he was not happy. Even in a streetful of disgruntled, hot, bitter and angst-ridden New Yorkers, Art stood out as one unhappy man. The arrest of *Cerne View* was disturbing. Odd too. Sounded more like a commandeering than an arrest. And what had he meant by *you guys*? Did he know that Gavin was with him? Or was it just a figure of speech?

Art mopped his brow with his handkerchief. He'd been outflanked. Hadn't asked all his questions. Hadn't learned as much as he'd wanted. Admit it Art. Klodinsky was pretty smart, too smart for you. His timing of the ticker-tape bombshell had been impeccable. He'd sat on that the whole meeting, to use it just when it suited him.

Art stopped off for a beer in a yuppy joint, all Art-Deco pinks and greens and waiting for the lunchtime blitz. There was plenty of time before he was due to meet Gavin and, as he took a seat by the sidewalk, memories of his time with the DEA flooded back as he looked at the shabbiness of the Lower West Side. Roller skaters, junkies, weirdos and the cutest of secretarial staff passed him by. The smell of trash, the rumble of the Subway, the constant horn-blowing, the angry shouts, the pall of diesel fumes and the wail of sirens made him feel good. Or made him feel better.

At 11.45 he took a cab and right on time was dropped off at Rockefeller Plaza. He paid off the driver and as usual gave no tip. Hands in pockets, he sauntered down the steps to the outside café with its bright coloured sunshades and the cool splashing of water. Gavin was sitting at a table away from the central bar, supping a glass of beer. In front of him lay a copy of Lloyds' List. 'Hi!' Art wiped his brow and draped his jacket round the back of his chair. 'Kinda humid.'

They ordered pasta and beers before Art updated Gavin on his meeting. The paraphrase was scarcely objective. Gavin received the sanitized, Art-is-a-hero version. When he'd finished he produced Claudine's postcard and watched Gavin's face. Interest changed to puzzlement, puzzlement changed to concern.

'Who said Claudine wrote it?' There was a touch of petulance in Gavin's voice which Art found amusing. The postmark was convincing enough.

'No one. If it's real, count Klodinsky out. If it's a fake, don't necessarily count him *in*.' Art grasped the frosted glass and downed the beer without stopping. He then asked the waitress to bring another four. 'And that's just for me.' He smiled mockingly at Gavin who's disdain was obvious. 'So what's your girlfriend going to say now, Romeo?'

'We'll get Forensic onto it. There's no way Claudine was in the South of France.' Gavin paused for a moment. 'Did you ask Klodinsky if she usually sent a card? Did you ask whether she often took off like this, without warning? Was he interested in where she was now? Why did he keep the card?' Gavin waited for a response but was met with studied indifference.

Art's beers arrived, filling the small, circular table which was already crowded with the stockpile of pasta and a mountain of Caesar's salad. 'Did *you* make any progress?' Art was on the attack. The hot sun and the beer added just a touch of aggression as Art posed the question. He knew that he'd lost his ten rounds with Klodinsky by an uncomfortable margin.

'I've got the tip-off meeting brought forward. It's now

tomorrow night instead of Thursday. Nine o'clock. And ...
wait for it ...I've got the address, down in the Bronx.'

If Gavin had been expecting a compliment for some
good work, then he was to be disappointed. 'Hot-damn!
Another thirty hours here! Just killing time! He jabbed
fiercely at his pasta.

'Maybe one of us should get to Dakalla.'

'Our brief wasn't to sort out *Cerne View*.' Art snatched
the note from Gavin's side of the table. 'The Bronx you
said?' He read the address. 'Hey! Now this is for real. Not
just the Bronx ... it's the South Bronx. Haven't been over
there these few years. Last time I busted a whole Puerto
Rican gang.'

'Dangerous?'

'In this crazy city, it's the worst. Like you just don't go
there. Not if you want to enjoy your pension.'

'You'd expect to meet an informant in a shady place.'
Gavin was trying to say the right thing.

'Bullshit!' Art shook his head as he scooped up the last
mouthful of penne. The fork was flourished with emphatic vigour as he developed the point. 'No way. You got
someone who really knows something. Ok they're going to
meet you secretly ... but the South Bronx? It's got to be a set-
up.' The last of the four beers were downed and he ordered
another two.

'So we don't go?'

'Sure as hell we're going. At least ... I am. But you?' He
shook his head. 'It's a man's job down there. I'll go alone.
You stay in the hotel and play with your Ninja Turtles. I'll
be just fine. Just fine.'

The combination of jet-lag, hot sun and the steady influx
of Budweiser was taking its toll. First Gavin had noticed the
increased bravado and now came the exaggerated movements, the arm waving, the roll of the eyes. Gavin pushed
aside the remains of his spaghetti carbonara and shifted his

chair to avoid the worst of the sun's power as it beat down into the cauldron at the foot of the skyscraper complex. 'If it's a set-up, then let's check the place out today. See the geography.'

'Don't be a jerk. There's no need. Like I say, this job's for men.' Art had other plans in mind.

'Don't treat me like a kid! I vote we check it out now.'

'I've got something better lined up. What the PR men would call a window of opportunity and I'm climbing right through it. She's quite something. Haven't seen her for a while.' Art looked at his watch. 'Still there's time for another drink.' He summoned the waitress and ordered a large bourbon on the rocks. An uncomfortable silence developed, Art not saying anything and Gavin seething at Art's lack of professionalism.

At last he could stand it no longer. Gavin pushed back his chair and stood up. The couple at the next table stopped gazing into each other's eyes as the suddenness of Gavin's move attracted their attention. 'You're supposed to be the pro. You're here because there's a job to do. You tell me it's dangerous. So what do you do? Get drunk and decide to go off whoring. Well, let me tell you.' He pointed his finger in short, aggressive jabs of accusation which Art feigned not to notice as he reclined, head lolling back to catch the sun on his forehead. 'You're not a pro. You're just a prick.' Gavin laughed in contempt, all his pent-up feelings surfacing at the sight of the casual conceit which Art now represented. 'Fine! You just go off and use it.' Gavin gave a withering look at Art who closed his eyes now as if to say that his ears were shut too. Then, with a flourish, Gavin draped his jacket over his shoulder, threw down a $20 bill and hurried towards the steps.

For a moment Art said nothing. He sat at the table swirling the tinkling glass of bourbon. 'Hey! Gavin!' He'd waited till Gavin was on the steps. The New Jersey rasp in the shout penetrated and stopped the noisy chatter. 'At least I can get it up.' He laughed into his glass and shared the moment with the couple at the next table who chuckled uncomfortably.

Gavin frowned as heads turned to look at him before he quickened his pace and disappeared from view. Even when he'd reached Central Park, he was still angry. God! Art was an ignorant bastard! Not an ounce of reason in him. No logic, no subtlety. Nothing but a chancer. He selected a sunny bench, well away from the noisy traffic and wished there was someone to share his burden. There was only Claudine and she was off-limits. Thinking of her, worrying about her, he nodded off and he was still thinking of her as he awoke. It was nearly 2.30 pm local time. He'd need to hurry to catch anyone at Brads now.

The nap had done him good. By the time he'd put through the call to England, his tone was crisp, businesslike. 'Sir Archie please. It's Gavin Blair.'

'Ah! Mr Blair,' said the night-duty telephonist. 'I'm afraid both Sir Archie and Edward are away. Susannah's just popped in. Shall I put you through?' Gavin agreed.

'Susannah here. It was about time we heard from you.' There was an edge in her voice which Gavin had never noticed before.

He shifted uncomfortably. 'I gather you're running the place.'

'Yes. Just when we've got this crisis with *Cerne View*, Edward's in Athens at a shipping conference. Father's in Paris. Flew off saying he was following up something interesting.' The line went quiet. Gavin was wondering if Sir Archie had heard something about Klodinsky's Paris office. 'Who knows what he's doing. Probably something in a skirt,' she said bitterly. The resentment was obvious. 'I suppose you do know about *Cerne View*?'

'That's why I'm calling.'

'You're not phoning from Dakalla, then?' There was a cynical bite in the question.

'No. The Bureau hasn't been retained.'

'Well, consider yourself retained as of now. *Cerne View* picked up a mixed cargo in Marseille. Her voyage to Dakalla was uneventful.'

'And?' Gavin had visions of writs flying against the Bureau for his advice that Brads should avoid Klodinsky.

'After docking, some of her containers were off-loaded. Two were picked up by the consignees called Scrignac Lefebre. That company's French associate, trading from Toulon, had despatched them via Marseille. Lorries took them to their destination.'

Gavin's guess completed the story. 'And like Old Mother Hubbard - the cupboard was bare. So what should have been in them? If not a bone?'

Susannah laughed. 'Sophisticated computer equipment, required for a government hydro-electric scheme. The goods may have been stolen after the containers left the quay. Who knows?'

'So?' Curiosity was etched in the lines on Gavin's face. 'Pinetto got the ship to the right destination and dropped off the containers. Nothing to do with Brads at all.'

'Tell that to the Chief Justice of Lumbola! Or to the Minister of the Interior!' Susannah's tone showed her views of them. 'I've been trying. No one over there'll speak to us.' Gavin heard the sharp intake of breath. He could imagine her in Bristol - the delicate beauty of her face now hard set, the chin pointed and determined. No doubt she'd been tossing her head dismissively as she'd spoken. There was much of her father in her, more than Gavin had thought. 'They've flung the Harbour Master into prison along with our crew. Everyone's guilty till they're convicted. Even the innocent are convicted there. Our Radio Officer was shot dead. Lloyds' agent in Dakalla can't get any sensible explanations either.'

Gavin whistled. 'That's Dakalla! One or two ships have been under arrest there for years. One English lawyer who went out there to argue for their release got himself arrested for conspiracy against the State.'

Susannah listened impatiently. 'Meantime, our crew rot in a stinking jail. Something's got to be done about it. So get on with it! Sort out *Cerne View*! You realize she's still full of cargo?'

'What about the charter? Have Pinetto been paying?'

'Yes. Fifteen days in advance. Now that the ship's under arrest and not earning any income, I doubt they'll continue. Can you imagine what this does to our credibility ... ?' Her voice trailed away. 'Once is unlucky. Twice looks careless.' She stared moodily at the slimline tonic but her face brightened as she glanced at the Piaget watch on her wrist. It too was slimline, a gift from Charles de Penichet. 'What happens if number three goes? *Adber Arrow?*'

Gavin felt defensive and decided to say nothing, judging the remark to be sheer rhetoric. 'Pilfering's so rife all the way down the West African coast. Bribe the men on the dock-gate and you could drive away with an entire convoy of Sherman tanks!' Gavin scribbled an uncomfortable note on his pad. The Klodinsky scenario, chartering and then finding a pretext not to pay, was developing. Yet Pinetto were the charterers. But Klodinsky was well connected in Lumbola. Could he have fixed the arrest? Yet another coincidence? He was about to continue when Susannah interrupted.

'That reminds me. One of the shareholders in Scrignac Lefebre is a Government Minister - Michel Mboro.'

'Mboro!' He voiced his surprise loud and clear. ' No wonder you've got trouble. One word from him and he can have everyone shot. He'll be one angry man.'

'So what are you doing? What's the Bureau doing?'

Susannah's irritation had turned more to despair. It had been a long day. She felt happier dealing with balance sheets. She wasn't looking forward to meeting the relatives of another crew in the morning. Her Touche Ross training meant she liked everything pigeon-holed, neat, double entries completed, the books balanced at the end of the day. Today hadn't been like that at all.

'I'll get enquiries moving on *Cerne View*. Art'll be back from New York on Friday. Then we'll know more about the IRA lead. You've heard nothing?' He paused and listened to her negative response. 'Let me know if you do then. What do you think about it?'

'It's not my job to have views on that,' she replied with cool equanimity. 'It's yours.'

Gavin was irritated. Didn't she want to help? 'Spoken like a true accountant. Keep your options open. Anyway, in the meantime, maybe you can get your MP to wake up the Foreign Office.'

'Haven't you done that? Doesn't the Bureau do anything?' Tiredness and frustration put a sharp, businesslike edge to her voice.

'Look, Susannah. Until just now, *Cerne View* wasn't our problem. Our advice was to avoid Klodinsky, not that that you *should* deal with Pinetto. That was your decision.' He fought to say the right thing. 'Were Pinetto's references OK? I thought they were.'

'Yes.' Susannah sounded doubtful. 'Unless its ownership had changed.'

'Unless the ownership has changed,' Gavin repeated each word thoughtfully. 'Don't say things like that. I thought we'd seen the back of chartering problems when we said goodbye to Klodinsky. Anyway, what was the value of the goods stolen?'

'4.5 million sterling. That's the insured value, paid for by letters of credit opened by Scrignac Lefebre in favour of the

254

French associates.'

'I'll keep in touch.' Gavin put down the phone. His boss Walter, that wily old buzzard, had warned them that New York was not going to be a happy experience. Was the action really in Africa? Meaning they were in the wrong place? Or was it the right place ... to pick up a bullet? Well ... whatever ... they'd still have to go through with it.

Despite the excellent dinner, Gavin awoke early the following morning, his time-clock still confused. Art's bed was empty and he could only imagine the type of bender the American had been having. He flicked on the television and watched a torrent of adverts, cartoons and news and switched off in irritation. Then he thought about Scrignac Lefebre. As he often did, he scribbled down the facts. Afterwards, as he reviewed them, line by line, a picture emerged.

Because of exchange control, getting money out of Lumbola was difficult. One way round the law was to order goods. Pay the supplier, preferably an accomplice abroad but never expect to receive the goods. Then have the containers stolen to conceal they were empty. Next put in a bogus insurance claim for the stolen goods. Plus point one - exit money from Lumbola - ultimate destination a Swiss bank account. Plus point two - double your money by the insurance claim. Have cake and eat it.

He poured coffee and smiled in satisfaction. It made sense. But why arrest the ship? As a smoke-screen? Because Mboro had the power? Because he was an angry bee once provoked? Maybe. That made some sort of sense. If anything did.

He phoned Carl Klodinsky's office on impulse. 'I'm sorry, sir,' said the receptionist, 'but Mr Klodinsky flew to Europe. He may now be in Paris.'

So was Sir Archie. Or, as Walter would say, so is the

Moulin Rouge.

No sooner had he put down the telephone than it rang again. With a sigh he went to answer, pushing aside the remains of his breakfast tray as he did so. When he had finished the call, he sat thoughtfully on the bed, his face a picture of bewilderment. Then he checked his watch. There were still twelve hours till the rendezvous. Twelve hours for Art to appear, twelve hours for him to sober up.

Chapter 34

By day, the South Bronx is shabby and broken-down, alive only to the imminence of death. Drug addicts and pushers abound. The tenement buildings stand scarred by fires, started by tenants in the hope of being re-housed. Abandoned warehouses, multi-occupation slums, their walls zig-zagged with fire escapes, provide homes for immigrants. The only sign of new paint is the latest graffiti, scrawled everywhere in illiterate Spanish. Every rat-run of poverty is crammed with Puerto Ricans, hispanics and blacks, many of them unemployed and unemployable.

By night, the South Bronx, just across the East River from Manhattan, takes on new terrors. Muggings, murder, rape and intimidation menace the unwary. Though darkness may hide the filth of the day, nothing can hide the blast of reggae from behind glassless windows. The lock-up shops, their windows boarded up or fronted with metal grilles, give the precinct an atmosphere of a city under seige.

Into the midst of all this cruised a black Pontiac, its age indeterminate in the darkness. For a few brief seconds it stopped outside a corner building. Three figures emerged to climb the crumbling stonework of the few steps leading to the front door. On either side was trash and rubble, piled high and vermin-infested. From the outside, the building looked empty, derelict. The door closed behind them. The Pontiac cruised off and moments later a light appeared in an upstairs front room.

It was 8.30 pm - half an hour to go until the rendezvous. The building fell silent except for the scuttling cockroaches, feeding on the filth of past occupants. From outside came the faint smell of spice and boiling rice from the tenants next door.

Twenty-five minutes later a yellow cab, its wings dented and with only one rear light working, pulled up about fifty yards away, just round the corner, out of sight. 'Yo' sure you wanna be dropped here?' The black driver's voice was shrill with incredulity. He felt bad about even coming here, uneasy about stopping and even worse about leaving his passenger.

Art eased himself across the torn, leather seat and opened the door. 'Yeh.' Even the single word showed the tiredness in his voice.

'Well, be sure and take care.'

'I'm out of diapers.' Art's cocky agressiveness was obvious as he stood for a moment beside the cab. He patted his pocket, felt the gun which he'd picked up from an old pal in mid-town. From across the block came the wails of a child, mixed with the heated shouting of two adults, man and woman. The street was empty or its occupants hidden in the shadows of beaten-up cars whose wheels had long ago been stolen. 'Wait here, if you wanna be paid! I won't be long.' The driver started to shake his head ruefully. Then he saw the size of the fare on the clock. He shrugged his shoulders reluctantly and fingered the three foot truncheon which always lay next to him on the front seat. Art nodded curtly and strutted, full of confidence to the corner of the block.

To his right, on the corner, was the rendezvous building, five floors high. He saw the few steps up to the door. Either side had become a dumping ground for trash. Except for the single, gloomy light from an upstairs window, the place looked empty. He smiled to himself. A tip-off? A genuine IRA lead? No way Art! He breathed as he took in the incipient nastiness of the area. This was someone with a message for the Bureau. For Gavin. Well ... he'd show them.

Just for a moment Art regretted his lack of preparation. A bit more homework might have been worthwhile. But hell! Hadn't Shirley been good! Gee! Those twenty-four hours.

He looked the building up and down and again felt uneasy. He patted his pocket for reassurance. A trap? He'd take his chance. He pulled out the small Smith and Wesson. But maybe, just maybe, he should have quit earlier, told Shirley for Chrissake to lay off and then got here sooner. No, forget it. It'll be no sweat, he convinced himself as he eased back the safety catch.

He took another few paces round the corner and studied the entrance. It ain't the Waldorf, that's for sure. He moved to the foot of the steps. Something else? He studied the shabbiness which confronted him. The single light above his head could barely be seen through the grime of the window. He listened. Not a sound from within. Not even the scuttle of rats fighting over yesterday's scraps. Yet something was nagging him. Come on Art, flush out the bourbon. Think straight. What is it? Think real hard. Where's that instinct? And then he knew. Keep outside. When the door was answered he'd play it his way. Dictate the terms on the doorstep. Put the gun in the guy's stomach. Maybe get him back to the cab. Go for a little drive. Maybe even beat the shit out of him. Sure, that was it.

As he mounted the half dozen steps, his feet crunched on the broken concrete. A gangling youth with a ghetto-blaster playing Bob Marley ambled slowly past as Art banged on the grey door. The noise reverberated inside. He put his ear to the flaking paintwork, awaiting the sound of approaching footsteps but could hear nothing. He banged again, big, heavy blows with his clenched fist.

He was about to try the handle when there was a movement behind him. He started to turn. Too late! The man, his face hooded, had been hidden between the stacks of heaped-up trash. Now, he had his gun pressed against the nape of Art's neck, pinning him to the door. 'Drop your gun! Drop it! And then put your hands up. Right up.' The man's voice was New York, harsh, guttural and with not a trace of Irish.

Possibilities raced through Art's mind but each one was a no-no. Kick back? Duck and elbow jab on either side? Shout? He considered and dismissed each possibility. Fuck it! He'd blown it, was trapped - a victim of his own lack of preparation. 'I said drop it.' Although Art could not see the man, he sensed that he was tall, big as his voice and just as uncompromising. Art wanted to take a look but with his nose pressed against the peeling paintwork, it was impossible. He dropped the Smith and Wesson.

Never moving his gun from the back of Art's head, the man swung open the door. It hadn't even been locked. 'Move it. In there ... to the right ... and up the stairs. And keep your hands up.'

Art stumbled forward, towards the foot of the stairs. The man flicked on the light. A dusty single bulb lit the lobby, revealing a flight of stairs rising to a landing and then doubling back on itself. The ground floor was empty, except for an old bath, some bits of charred and rotting timber and a pile of rubble from the shattered ceiling.

'We talk here,' said Art, as if he were in command of the situation. 'I've brought the money. Just give me the information.'

The man's laugh in response was scarcely reassuring. 'Information? From us?' Again the laugh. 'Is that why you think you're here?' Art felt the gun pushed harder into the base of his neck. It was an unspoken direction to mount the stairs. Ahead he saw the landing and the window behind it. Maybe there was a chance there. It was big, glassless, the framework rotted and broken. The other side there'd be a twenty-feet drop. He could take that.

He mounted the stairs, one at a time. Keep it slow, Art. Come on. He'd said *us*. There were others. More upstairs. But how many?

His weary brain was unresponsive. The slugs of bourbon and the hungry mauling by Shirley were affecting him like jabbing lefts and rights from a champ. Gavin had been right. He should have prepared better. The rendezvous was a trap. It always had been. Hell, he'd even *expected* it to be a fix. Fuck it! He should have listened to Gavin rather than the throbbing urges of his dick.

Now he heard it - the sound of voices from an upstairs room. There must be two of them, maybe three. Step by step he continued until he reached the landing. He turned on the thick dusty surface in readiness for the double-back upwards to whatever lay ahead. All the time the gun never wavered. Beside him now and to his right was the window. Maybe it was his last chance. Even the stench drifting in from the garbage below smelled sweetly of freedom. Just give me a second, a split second, Art told himself.

But the gunman didn't. His concentration was absolute. His control of the situation total. The muzzle was kept firmly pressed, ready to fire at Art's slightest movement. So close yet so distant, the opportunity passed. A jab from the gun kept him moving across the landing as he shuffled slowly and with deliberation. Escape was impossible.

'Move! Keep moving. Up.' The barked command was close to his ears. Reluctantly Art turned again to his left to face the next flight. He was about to take the next step when, just behind him, there was a roar, a flash of movement. The situation had changed, the gun at his neck had gone.

From his perch on the fire escape outside the window, Gavin had watched everything. He'd crouched there, peeping into the building between the shards of broken glass. He'd seen Art coming up the stairs and as he'd drawn close, Gavin had seen the tired bloated features. Behind him was a man in a black hood. Then Art had been within three feet of him on the landing before moving on to face the next flight. Still Gavin had waited until the hooded man was on the landing, standing sideways right beside him at the top of the first flight.

It had been now or never.

Gavin had crashed through the rotten framework, roaring like a demented lion, crunching his head deep into the pit of the gunman's stomach, the heavy blow knocking him off balance. Arms waving wildly, he started to tumble down the stairs. Gavin's own momentum sent him falling too. Together they rolled, bumped and banged all the way to the bottom.

As they fell, the gunman fired, the bullet aimlessly striking the plastered wall. 'Come on Art!' Gavin managed to get the words out, a split second before he landed in the lobby beside the gunman. Behind them, Art twisted round and bounded down the stairs. Then with a flying leap, he landed his 198 lbs on the hooded man's stomach. With a gasp, the gun was released.

'The gun! Grab it,' Art called loudly in a command to Gavin. From upstairs came the sound of shouting and rapid movement, then footsteps bounding down towards the landing. 'Time to go!' Again the command came from Art, his senses once again alert. He grasped Gavin's arm, pulled him up and dragged him to the door which he flung open. Once outside, Art slammed it shut behind them. 'Move! Move! Quicker.' Art shoved Gavin down the steps and towards the corner. Together they ran, hard and fast to the waiting yellow cab. 'Ok, driver. Hit it. Hit it hard. The New York Hilton.' The words came out in gasps, punctuated between the sound of their breathless panting.

The events of the last sixty seconds had been so fast, so furious, that nothing had yet sunk in but already Art was debating whether to blame Gavin for fouling up his plan. Tell him that he didn't need rescuing by a jerk like Gavin, that he had it all sussed and wanted to find out what was going on upstairs. Ball him out for buggering up his plan.

But it wasn't true. None of it. And he just couldn't do it. He sat panting, his clothes sticking to him, his tousled hair wet and clinging to the nape of his neck. It glistened round his forehead as they passed the occasional pool of light. The bags under his eyes hung heavily with remorse and bourbon.

Gavin was sitting awkwardly in the other corner of the cab, a white handkerchief held tightly to his eye. His breath was coming unevenly, his body was trembling and yet, despite all this, he exuded a strength, a sense of determination which commanded a respect all of its own. Art was about to say something, about to acknowledge that the coward of Kuantan had just saved his life. But he couldn't do that. Not yet.

More than a mile passed before Gavin realized that he was still clutching the gun. Gently Art took it from him, slipped on the safety catch and then tucked it in his pocket. 'Makes up for mine. You Ok?' It was their first conversation.

Gavin thought about it, by no means convinced that he was. 'I did my neck in when I hit his gut but it's not serious. It feels like he's given me a black eye.' He held the handkerchief even tighter as he spoke, a rueful grin breaking across his face.

'We were lucky.' In the half-light of the back of the cab Art turned to Gavin, a new look of respect on his face. 'Don't explain what happened yet. We'll talk about that later. Meantime ... just ... thanks for being there. I've been an asshole.' They fell silent as the taxi sped along the Bruckner Expressway, watching the lights of Manhattan draw closer as the cab crossed the Harlem River and into

First Avenue. 'Like I said, we'll talk later but there's just one thing. You're the brains of this team. Who set us up?' This was the old Art, the Art with his self-confidence returning. Gavin could tell from the tone in the voice. Art wasn't expecting an answer, was merely re-asserting himself, seeking to prove that he was the big shot.

'Know who set us up?' Gavin spoke thoughtfully, his face serious. 'Well, I might know. I've been busy.' Though he didn't say so, Art knew that Gavin was mentally adding - whilst you've been whoring around.

'Well?' Art was aggressive again.

'That slum. Want to know who owns it?' He paused deliberately to get maximum effect. 'Only a property company controlled by Carl Klodinsky. He owns the entire block.'

'No shit!' Art's head shook in disbelief. He squinted sideways at Gavin, unable to conceal his respect.

Chapter 35

Two hours later, they were able to tilt back their seats in the London-bound British Airways 747. 'I'm going to break all my rules,' said Art. 'We'll both have champagne. No scotch for me. I guess I've got to drink your health. You saved my life. Sounds corny, huh? But it's true.'

Gavin, ever matter of fact, nodded in agreement. 'That's true.' The conversation stopped whilst champagne was poured and small plates of canapés put in front of them.

'I've said some hard things, given you a heap of shit,' said Art, ' ... about Kuantan, about most everything. What you did today was smart ... took real guts too. You gonna tell me what you were doing whilst I was ... er ... with Shirley, screwing out my brains?' Gavin could read the invitation, could see that the respect was genuine.

'A million years ago, like this morning, I had an idea. Remember where all this started? The IRA tip?' He helped himself to a savoury. 'I got to thinking.' He loosened his tie and undid his shirt button. Somehow Gavin could do that and still look presentable. It was something which Art would never manage. Even in a tuxedo, he could look like a scruff. 'The rendezvous? Who owned it? Was it an IRA Provo lair? Offices? Slums?' So I hired a private investigator from Fifth Avenue, Larry Goulden. Took him no time to discover that Klodinsky tax-shelters in beaten-up real estate.' He was interrupted by the steward handing out the menu. 'So I thought - seeing as how we know where Klodinsky can be found, why the South Bronx?'

'Goddammit! So that sonovabitch really is in it. I'd have said he was clean.'

'Who knows? Perhaps he is.' Gavin helped himself to a

lobster tail and left Art's thoughts swinging in the breeze.

'Meaning?'

'That it's neutral. It means Carl Klodinsky set up the meet in his own premises or someone else set up Carl Klodinsky.'

'You go to Harvard or something?' The jibe was playful, full of respect. 'Ok, so what then?'

'I had some great fettucini and half a bottle of Californian Burgundy. Then I took a cab to the South Bronx. The first driver wouldn't even go there. The second one did. I never got out - just cruised past the building a couple of times, back and front. Saw it was empty, realized it wasn't the United Nations headquarters. Got back to the hotel just after five.' He finished his champagne and peered round for the steward who topped up their glasses. 'I lay on the bed for a while, thinking about Kuantan. Thought about you going alone to protect me. Wanted to warn you about the Klodinsky link.' Even the black eye couldn't disguise the scorn on Gavin's face. 'I waited as long as I could. You didn't call. You didn't show up. So I went alone.'

'What then?'

'I realized the building was empty, no lights, not a sound. Meaning that someone had to arrive!' He looked at Art and saw he was listening intently, despite his consuming interest in the smoked salmon canapés. 'I don't mind telling you, it was dark, scarey. The taxi dropped me just down the block. I lingered, walked a little, leaned against a beaten-up Chevvy. Tried to look cool.' Art could see the haunted look on the speaker's face as Gavin re-lived his fear. 'I could see the building was still dark until, at 8.30, this black saloon arrived. Three men got out.'

'Go on,' Art encouraged Gavin with a flourish of yet another Camel.

'I couldn't see clearly. Maybe they all went in, maybe it was just two of them. I couldn't tell. A light appeared upstairs. I went round the back. Up the fire escape. Most of the glass in the window on the landing had gone. I could hear men talking. It wasn't easy but I caught the words, "then we'll dump him," and someone laughed. I was just about to hurry down to warn you but it was too late. The next second you were banging on the door something rotten. The rest you know.'

'Hey! I could get used to this fizzy crap.' Art pressed the call button and asked for a refill. 'Well, like I said, you saved my life. But as for *Ryme Lady*?' He shrugged in acceptance of defeat. Then he tipped back the champagne as if he were downing a double scotch and looked over his shoulder expectantly for the attendant. 'Anything else happened today? While I was giving my pecker the biggest treat of its life?'

'Yes.' Gavin's face turned thoughtful. He looked embarrassed. 'Yes. There was something else.' Gavin's eyes narrowed and he looked uneasily at the streams of bubbles rising in his glass. His face, always a touch serious when he wasn't smiling, looked downright solemn. His eyebrows met at the recollection. 'There was a phone call for *you*.' Gavin turned to his right to watch Art's reaction.

'Oh yeh? Who from?' Art was not really interested. The drift of the conversation had failed to permeate.

'From Janie!'

The words fell heavily between them. An acoustic wall could not have been more effective at creating a divide. Gavin scarcely dared to look at Art's face, yet he wanted to see the reaction, see the embarrassment. Even now, Gavin could still hear Janie's words: "Art, darling, I've been so worried. You haven't *called* and I'm missing you." That was before Gavin had been able to stop her. Just the recollection of those words jarred as he re-lived the shock of the moment. He'd been stretched out on the bed at the time and, after putting down the phone, he'd been uncertain whether to laugh or beat his fists against the wall. Janie, his Janie had left him ... for Art. Gavin lowered his eyes once again. 'She didn't realize we were sharing a room. Assumed she was talking to you. Called herself Honey.'

They sat silently, Art chasing a peanut round a plastic tray.

Eventually it was Art who spoke. 'Aw shit! Gee, I'm sorry! About hijacking Janie.'

'It was her choice as well.' Gavin's English *sang-froid* produced a measured response. But then the cool head melted. 'Frankly, you've behaved like a complete and utter shit! For God's sake, why didn't you tell me? I'd have understood - my relationship with Janie had grown tired, complacent. We were like a couple of old bedsocks.' He nodded in emphasis at his own unflattering image of life with Janie. 'Then I was flattened by life's steamroller when Theo was ...' He stopped as Art raised his hand. He'd heard enough.

'Ok, Ok!' Apologies were not his style. 'I can't say more than ... I'm sorry.' Silence fell again. Even the champagne seemed flat now. As the jumbo cruised high over Boston, it was Art who spoke, stretching out his hand and placing it on Gavin's arm. 'But hell, I mean ... you find out ... discover that Janie has been shacked up with me ... that I've behaved like a shit ... and then ... you fucking go out and risk your life for me.' Never had Gavin seen Art so emotional as he grasped both armrests. 'Knowing all that! Knowing what I'd done to you! Knowing what I'd done to Janie! You risked your own life ... you saved my fucking life! What can I say?'

Gavin nodded sheepishly, the pressure gone now that he'd said it all. 'Call me a good loser maybe?' He gave a slight shrug of his shoulders and then flicked some crumbs from his trousers.

'Well, I'm calling you a pro. A real pro.' His thick fingers clasped the sleeve of Gavin's denim shirt. '*We're* a great team...' Art, too busy with his own thoughts, never noticed the slight parting of Gavin's lips as he smiled to himself. Beneath them, the last tip of New England was disappearing, unseen, six miles below. Then the urgency returned to Art's voice. 'By the way, did you tell Janie where I was today? What I was doing?'

Gavin's look was withering.

'I'm sorry,' continued Art, 'it was a dumb question. Of course you didn't. Like I say, you're a real pro.'

Chapter 36

A sleek, black Rover Vitesse, with driver, awaited them at Heathrow's Terminal 4. The journey was short as they were whisked westwards to The Compleat Angler. The hotel, right on the banks of the Thames, by Marlow Bridge, had always been a favourite of Walter Corbin's. They had arranged to meet at 12 noon on the terrace for drinks and then an outside table for lunch.

Leaving their few bits in the car, the two men walked to the entrance. Gavin was limping and aching from the tumble down the stairs. A nasty black bruise was hugely obvious just above his right eye which was half-shut. Art was walking better, though his joints were stiff and, as usual, he looked as scrumpled as yesterday's newspaper.

In contrast, Walter was looking urbane, spruce and relaxed. Seated on the terrace, he seemed to be enjoying the mainly sunny skies, his face upturned, his eyes hidden behind a pair of expensive shades. He was wearing a single-pleat pin-stripe suit, made by his favourite tailor in Kowloon. The cream-coloured shirt had been made there too. The dark red tie bore the gold emblem of his fashionable golf club. His shoes had been made by a shoemaker on Hong Kong Island who kept his measurements in a neat file. Busy admiring a cabin cruiser which was gliding its way past some swans towards Henley, Corbin didn't see them at first. He only did so as they approached the table and sat down. Walter nodded friendly greetings to each of them in turn.

'Good flight?' he queried, typically ignoring the chance to comment on the bruise.

'We're here.' Art's tone said it all. Walter studied them both more carefully before summoning the waiter. For himself he ordered a dry sherry and bottled water for the two arrivals. As a joke it was in character and brought a scowl to Art's heavy features.

'You two been fighting again?' The Director looked at each of them in turn, his cool appraisal ending with the bruise on Gavin's brow. By way of response Art leaned across and rested a hand on Gavin's shoulder to show the converse was true. 'Gavin saved my life.' If Art had expected any reaction from Walter, he was to be disappointed. Other than the slightest of acknowledgements to make clear that he'd heard, Walter seemed uninterested. Instead, he threw a biscuit to a couple of mallards.

'Let me bounce this off you. I was just studying the Austrian case. Remember the one?' He paused to sip and enjoy his sherry. 'Remember we talked about *The Lucona*? I don't say it's the answer but don't overlook it. They say that was a time bomb. Udo Proksch and the rest still say they're innocent. Who knows?' Walter turned to his menu and them summoned the waiter to give them help with their selection.

Gavin was puzzled. Why was Walter throwing a Gibraltar-sized rock in the pool when there had been subsequent sightings. He was about to ask but, after ordering, Walter seemed more concerned to discuss the overnight scores in the golf from Augusta, Georgia, than the mere trivia of international fraud. Art's eyelids quickly drooped although Gavin, to whom pars, birdies and chips were a foreign language, somehow managed to keep the conversation running. Happily, the Maitre D' called them to their table without delay and before Corbin had the chance to explain how he could have outplayed Faldo on the 17th.

The table was a shady one, Corbin's favourite, tucked away from the others and ideal for confidential discussions. 'You both leave for Lumbola tomorrow morning. Direct flight to Dakalla. I've set up the visas.'

'Beside the obvious reason of *Cerne View*'s arrest, what else?' Gavin forced his tired brain to concentrate. The events of the past twelve hours had left him with a mind best left in neutral. So much had become clear with Janie's call. It made sense of Art's hostility, his drinking to forget or numb, his throw-away jibes. He'd agonized over *them*. They'd haunted him. 'Can't even get it up' and, on the other occasion, the disparaging 'if you could manage it'. Now it was clear. Janie must have justified leaving him by being less than flattering about his prowess. Nice one Janie! Thanks a bundle for that! The affair, so Art had explained over brandy at 34,000 feet, had started when Gavin had been out in Malaysia on the boat people job. Born out of alcohol, opportunity and lust, they'd just drifted into it. Other than that, Gavin had declined Art's offer to describe the first encounter in the Barons Court apartment.

During the flight, whilst Art slumbered, Gavin had re-lived the last row with Janie. *Some sweets*, he'd said to her, *are hard-boiled outside but are actually soft. You however are sugar-coated with a hard-boiled centre.* She'd thrown an orange at him for that one. His face had brightened as he'd re-lived the sight of it smashing the unsightly vase which her mother had given her.

Peering over his Serengeti shades gave Walter a fatherly air as he glanced at Gavin. He'd noticed the tortured look but had said nothing. Now there was just a hint of a smile as he brought Gavin back to the present. 'Gavin, forgive me. You asked about Dakalla.' There was no reproach in the voice. 'I don't believe you heard my reply.' Walter knew damn well that Gavin had heard nothing. 'Do you think it's coincidence that *Cerne View* is in trouble?'

'Klodinsky's got nothing to do with Pinetto or *Cerne View*,' countered Gavin. Art's glazed eyes looked as if he agreed.

'No,' agreed Walter. 'Not unless ownership of Pinetto

has changed. It *was* managed by Alberto Forensi. Getting quick information out of Italy is never easy. Not unless you bribe the right person.'

'But ... ' Gavin was about to intervene but was cut dead with a friendly wagged finger.

'Before you say anything, let me tell you something else. Do you think it coincidental that Sir Archie has flown to Dakalla? Got a visa three days ago? Do you think it's odd that he didn't tell Edward and Susannah where he was going? Edward's in Athens and obviously has no plans to go to Lumbola. He *can't* be going to Lumbola because he hasn't got a visa. I checked. Neither has Susannah.' He helped himself to a Hovis mini-roll and broke it open before continuing. 'Alberto Forensi is also out there.' Walter was enjoying himself. He'd been picking up hard facts whilst his team had been kicking their heels in New York.

'As Chairman of Pinetto, so he should be,' responded Gavin. 'It's his charter. Ok, it is odd that he's gone there but .... not that odd. And I'd expect Sir Archie, as the owner, to be there.'

Art interrupted with almost his last contribution of the lunch. 'So why go without telling Edward and Susannah?'

Gavin had to agree it was odd but it was Walter who spoke. 'The Independence Day celebrations are on Saturday night. Just over forty-eight hours to go. If you'd been kept waiting any longer in New York, you'd have reached Dakalla in time to sweep up the champagne corks. As it is, you'll be there to see everything happen.'

Gavin worked it out. It was now Thursday. They'd reach Dakalla on Friday. Celebration day was Saturday. Was that relevant? Should it be? Could it be? 'We had a bit of trouble in the South Bronx.' Gavin glanced at Art for support but he was busy lighting his Camel. 'The place where it happened was owned by Klodinsky. He's going to Dakalla as well. Knows half the government.' Gavin was rewarded with a frown, a rare sight in Walter Corbin. It was quickly gone as the new facts were stored in his well-organized system.

Corbin raised and lowered his hands like a see-saw. 'It could be important, it could be irrelevant. That'll be for you to find out. Anyway, back to Dakalla. I want the crew released from jail. I want a complete rundown on Michel Mboro. What are his political links? What are his ambitions? I'm trying to set up an interview with him for you. He and his family are connected with Scrignac Lefebre.' He paused, expecting that he had taken Gavin by surprise but was disappointed. 'Mboro, as a government minister, should be supportive of the link with Sampopo. After the merger, he'll be second only to the President, higher than the poor sod who's President of Sampopo now. He's to be number three.'

'Perhaps Mboro doesn't want to be second best,' suggested Gavin.

'Maybe. But if you were President of Sampopo, how would you like to be number three. Lino instead of carpet, clapped-out Ford instead of Rolls.' There was something in Walter's look which left it open. Was his smile related to the conversation? It was never entirely clear with him. 'My lamb is delicious. Just perfect. Anyway, as to Mboro, that as they say is a matter for you. You know there's unrest. Don't expect me to complete the jigsaw for you. I've found the corners and straight edges.'

'I don't know much about Africa.' Gavin's knowledge of Africa came from an uncle who'd spent half his life fornicating there and the other half in England, seeking refuge from irate husbands. 'If he's an economist, Mboro ought to see the financial advantages. If he's against, then it must be personal ambition, political or tribal. Sounds crazy to me - asking different tribes to live as one.'

'Oil and water,' grunted Art, pretending to be alert, his chin resting on his chest.

Walter ignored him and fixed Gavin with a penetrating look, the eyebrows knitted, the deep blue eyes unblinking. To emphasize the point which he was about to make, a delicately manicured finger was wagged across the circular table. 'Just remember this. You've cheated death again. No one ... and I mean no one ... is to know you're going to Dakalla.' The finger stopped wagging. 'Is that understood?'

Gavin sat like a chastened schoolboy. 'Yes. I understand.' He concentrated his mind on the turbot or tried to. He couldn't help smiling at the irony. Here he was getting stick from the Director about confidentiality when it had been Art who'd given Janie their number in New York. He looked across at Walter and then at Art who was now snoring gently.

'Art certainly must have been putting in the hours out there.' Walter's eyes were twinkling in sardonic amusement. Gavin wasn't sure just what Walter knew. With him, one never did.

'He certainly extended himself.' Gavin surprised himself that he was able to cover for Art without a hint of sarcasm.

'Ah yes, I've got something for you.' The Director leant down and produced a video cassette. 'The funeral. I thought you'd want to see it. Your absence was noted by the media but we covered that. Greenaway worked wonders. Put it about that the sedatives that you'd taken had produced severe side effects. That you were under medical care.' Walter looked satisfied as he served himself with further petits pois. 'It helped with the *media*. As for your friends and the two orphans ... you'll have to make your peace with them when this is all over. I can't help with that.'

Gavin nodded and pushed his plate to one side. As he

held the cassette he noticed his hand shaking. He wasn't sure whether he really wanted to watch it after all.

Walter noticed the whiteness of his knuckles. 'Come on, put it down. I know it can't be easy. Just cover yourself in your professionalism. Tell me about New York. Anything new.'

'Not much to add to what we've told you.'

'The IRA? Your feelings on that one?'

'A distraction. Brads' agents couldn't identify who'd called them. Just said it was an American voice. Not Irish. I put a hot-shot New York private eye on it. Nothing. Mind you, he did uncover Klodinsky's ownership of the rendezvous.'

'Impressive.' The Director studied the health warning on his cigarette packet. 'And Art?' He nodded his head at the sleeping figure. 'In this tenement? Did he panic?'

Gavin's answer was decisive. 'No,' he said firmly. 'I'm sure it was a trap. It was a clever game. Get the Bureau chasing shadows round New York for as long as possible. Then would come the bullet. Classic intimidation to warn us off. Meantime, the real game's going on somewhere else.'

'Dakalla,' said Walter as he at last helped himself to a cigarette. 'I can't see why.'

'And *Ryme Lady*? Any more sightings?'

'*Rio Massu*? We've got an eye on her. That's if it is her.' He leaned across, peered over his glasses and then slowly extended a hand which he placed on Gavin's arm. 'Did well for someone who'd never faced a gun.' For Corbin this was as close as he'd ever get to a bear-hug of appreciation.

Despite the throbbing head, Gavin's face lit up in appreciation. Yet he was not one to dwell on the compliment. 'And what do you reckon about Klodinsky and Lady Ingrid?'

Corbin looked away, gazing across at the traffic on the bridge. 'Interesting. Was it serious?'

'He told Art it was a pretty heavy number. Denied it at first. But before we go into all that, what about ...'

'Yes?' Walter knew what was coming.

'Tell me about Claudine. How is she?' Somehow they both seemed to be talking in ever softer whispers.

'Claudine?' The Director managed to sound surprised that Gavin seemed even the slightest bit interested. 'Claudine,' he mused. 'I'm told she's doing well. Behaving herself. Not that there's much chance to misbehave in that place. I spoke with the doctor this morning. Claudine thinks she's better but the doctor's not so sure. Says it'll take another week or two yet. She's been through a great deal.' Gavin watched the Director as closely as was polite during his remarks. Corbin seemed to believe what he was saying. With him though, you could never be sure. 'Poor kid,' he concluded.

'I didn't know what shock, real shock, meant until I had to take Claudine to Aunt Margaret's. It was as if she were in a trance, abstract. I can't believe she's getting better so quickly.' He frowned and then stared hard at Walter. 'Perhaps you still think she was never kidnapped anyway. So you don't believe she's suffered this time either.'

Corbin did not answer. The muscles round his mouth flickered almost imperceptibly. Then he turned away.

Chapter 37

A few hours later, Art was still asleep although now he'd been shipped back to his Marble Arch apartment, where he was lying naked across the king-size bed. Beside him, staring at the ceiling, was Janie. Half an hour before, she'd given up any hope of sexual satisfaction. She was still wearing black underwear and the pale pink lipstick which he professed to prefer. Despite this, she had failed to raise even a flicker of interest. Now, as he lay beside her, he was grunting in deep sleep.

She wondered why she had flung Gavin aside for Art. Had she really thought that he had the hidden something which she'd been seeking? Fine, he'd been attractive, rampant in bed, tactile to the nth degree but now, as she looked at him, his sozzled face, his eyebrows dishevelled, the remains of his hair tousled and his bloated stomach rising and falling in rhythmic slumber, she felt only contempt. God! What a fool she'd been!

She thought of Gavin. If only she could turn the clock back. What a contrast! Tall and lean with an easy smile, he was neat and well-organized. Yes, he was cautious, maybe too kind and as old-fashioned as hell. So what! Touch him in the right spot and he could be fun. In or out of bed. Despite what she'd told Art. And the Theo thing ... according to Art, Gavin had scarcely laughed ever since. Perhaps he needed *her*. With angry strokes, she painted her nails, each of which was a pointed talon. The way she felt, she could have cheerfully scraped them down Art's face.

Yes! Admit it, she told herself. You were impetuous, too ready to walk out. But then Art's fast talk and earthy lust had been intoxicating and she had drunk the erotic nectar.

And now? A woman had needs, hadn't she? Her aching desire to be touched, stroked and ultimately dominated played between her thighs. She looked at Art again. As she watched the open mouth, the flared nostrils, the puffy blackness under the eyes, she could see only a seedy raffishness to which she'd been blind.

She pulled herself up to a sitting position and clasped her knees with her arms. Her stockings rubbed together and her nipples brushed her kneecaps, filling her with desires. Sod it! Was it just remorse? Remorse that Gavin had found out? She strokes her inner thigh thoughtfully. No. It was more than that. Oh hell! Admit it! She was missing him. Ok, Art had been great company. Big, noisy, selfish, funny and rough as hell. But if he wasn't bothered about getting it up any more ... what was a woman supposed to do? She brushed her nipples against her knees more strongly now, pushing them back and forth until they were firmly erect behind the lace of her bra.

Had it hurt Gavin? Her leaving? No goodbyes. Maybe she should say sorry. She poured more vodka into her empty glass. What about Art? He'd returned, promising to screw her till her ass dropped off but had promptly fallen asleep. Not for the first time either. She wondered just what he had been up to in New York.

Janie tossed her shiny black hair in irritation. Something else was bugging her. What was it? That's right. Art saying that Gavin had fallen for some French girl, Claudine something or another. Was it serious? Maybe it would become serious. Had Gavin made love to her? Had he sent electric pulses of slow-burning ecstasy through her? She drained her glass and poured another. Now that he doesn't want me, doesn't need me ... that's when I want him back. The ache between her legs was becoming unbearable. But maybe he does need me. And Claudine? No problem. Well out of the way. Nursing home somewhere. She stubbed out the rest of the cigarette and looked again at Art. Her mind was a see-saw of lust and common sense. She stroked his back, hoping for some loving smile.

'Leave me alone, honey. I need some sleep.' Art's voice was drowsy but the anger in his face was a warning - touch at your peril! She was about to respond but changed her mind. Instead, she swung her long, Nassau-brown legs off the bed and made her way across the bedroom towards the bathroom. Then she paused as something caught her eye beside his fallen trousers. A single condom in a packet of three.

So that was the story of New York.

Well ... thank you ... bastard! Her mind made up, she stormed into the bathroom. There she showered, her sharp features emphasized by her wet hair which clung round her face. Quickly she dressed, putting on a blue silk shirt and skin-tight jeans. After putting the finishing touches to her make-up, she swept her things into suitcases and, twenty minutes later, to the steady background noise of Art's snoring, she walked out.

It was time to move on. Art wouldn't miss her.

The taxi headed for Barons Court, crawling its way through Notting Hill Gate and down Kensington High Street. Gavin would be home by now. Anyway, she still had a key if he wasn't. Yet it was only when the cab pulled up outside the dull sameness of her old home that she paused to wonder. Wasn't she just being foolish and impulsive all over again? Could she really turn the clock back just by saying sorry? Make believe that it had never happened? She stood on the pavement, looking at the familiar entrance, with its grimy paint and crumbling brickwork. She looked up at the windows of Gavin's apartment. There was a light on! That decided her.

The cabbie who had waited, wondering whether she was going to change her mind, drove off as she stooped, picked up the bags and entered the building. It was then that she knew that she hadn't made a mistake. The same old smells: the French couple cooking with garlic on the third floor: the lavander polish on the lino. Even the pervading atmosphere of rising damp was welcome. The patch on the ceiling showed where the rain had penetrated in the great storm of 1987.

Yes. It was good to be back. And she'd be sorry. Very contrite. Ready to be dominated. Yes ... and she'd see off that bitch, Claudine. Huh! No competition there. From what Art said, she was just a screwball, laid up in some mental hospital somewhere. A head-case.

She paused outside Flat No. 8. Should she knock? No, she'd surprise him. He'd be catching up on some sleep, jet-lagged. She'd climb in beside him, smother him in kisses from head to toe, just like the old days. The key turned easily. The interior of the flat was as cool as ever, the lamp on the hall table was lit, still highlighting the cobwebs in the corner. A radio was playing in the sitting-room.

She pushed the front door gently shut and walked along the corridor. She peered into the sitting room but found it empty though the wall lamps were all lit. She went on to the kitchen. It too was empty. Good! He *had* gone to bed. She went back to the bathroom and stood in front of the mirror, preening her hair and sprayed some *White Linen* behind her ears. Then she played again with her nipples until they stood out beneath the flimsy blue silk of her blouse. Only then did she go down the corridor to the bedroom and push open the door. Her eyes were fixed expectantly on the bed as she entered.

It was one step too many.

The trigger mechanism for the bomb worked perfectly. The Semtex, concealed in the bookcase by the bed, was ample for its task. The floor exploded with a deafening roar beneath her, the room seemed to disintegrate and her body was thrown first up and then down, crashing among the furniture which was smashed and distorted. The bed, the bedside table, the lights, the cupboards all tumbled into the rooms below ... and on into the rooms below that.

So too did Janie. Or what was left of her.

Chapter 38

The Director had allowed Art to go home. For whatever reason, Corbin didn't seem over-concerned that someone might want to kill him. Home for Gavin, however, was the anonymity of the Penta Hotel at Heathrow. Once there it had been the usual routine - check-in, elevator, hotel corridor, unpack ready to re-pack, a pattern which was becoming all too familiar. From his bedroom window he could watch the take-offs and landings. At least he was well placed for the early flight to Dakalla.

The sky was darkening, the sun had dropped behind the clouds banked up to the west. The humidity outside seemed to get to him. He felt drained, run-down, ready to run anywhere that was *away*. Lonely too. Even the can of beer didn't help. The Penta, comfortable and warm, still left him with the rattle of death uncomfortably close. *Someone* out there wanted him dead. Not just a threat now either. Twice within a week, he'd been lucky. Someone was serious, deadly serious. He looked at his watch again. It was only 6.00 pm. With difficulty he forced himself not to call Claudine. For God's sake, she needed him. They needed each other, needed to talk, to whisper, to nuzzle and cuddle. But he wasn't allowed to.

Hell! He'd ring Brads instead. Susannah wasn't in but to his surprise the receptionist offered him the chance to speak to Edward.

'You're lucky,' said Edward breezily. 'I've just walked in. Been back ten minutes. Flew in from Athens. Looking at my desk, I wish I hadn't. Such a pile of bumph here. None of it good news either. *Cerne View's* still under arrest. The crew are still in jail. Lloyds are asking questions. The bank want a crisis meeting next Monday. The old bastard's gone to Paris. Seeing his kinky whipper, no doubt. Give me some good news, Gavin. Good news I can do with. Tell me you know what happened to *Ryme Lady*. Tell me the New York informant came good.'

'It's not your day,' chuckled Gavin. 'May have something by Monday to help you with the bank. Don't hold your breath though.' So Sir Archie still hadn't told Edward he was in Dakalla. Sir Archie needed watching. 'We're following up one or two things on Klodinsky. As for the IRA, it's too soon to be sure. We're still digging.'

'Well - just bring me good news.' Edward was about to put the phone down when Gavin heard a muttered exclamation from the other end of the line. 'Hold on. What's this?' There was a rustle of paper. 'My God! It's a note from the Gaffer. Says he's left Paris and gone on to Singapore. Says he thinks he can open up something on *Ryme Lady*. So now you know.'

'Good for him,' said Gavin, giving nothing away but wondering why Sir Archie was pretending to be in Singapore. 'I'll ring again to see if he's unearthed anything. Where's he staying?'

'Doesn't say. But he usually stays in the Valley Wing of the Shangri-La. You could try there.'

'Thanks.'

Gavin stirred his cup of espresso in the Coffee Shop at the Heathrow Penta. In front of him was the remains of his Salade Nicoise but, as he stirred, his mind was on the papers which he'd been reading. These were the company searches regarding Pinetto. Had he missed something? Alberto Forensi was still the Chairman. Had been since 1963. The registered office was still a law firm in Panama, no doubt just a name-plate on a door, littered with dozens of others. Anonymous. Impenetrable.

This wasn't a one-off charter by a just-created shelf company. The faxed papers from Rome had shown that Pinetto was a long-established business with proper management. Forensi was a familiar name to the Baltic Exchange, although based in Naples. So what was the worry? Well ... for a start, hadn't *Ryme Lady* been seen in Italy? Maybe even Naples? He drained the last of his coffee and re-read the bundle. Who owned the shares? Well, he knew the answer to that. Or rather he didn't. He flipped over another page. As a Panamanian registered company, the true owners of the shares were hidden. Bearer shares belong literally to the bearer, whose name and address are unrecorded. Anonymous. Totally. So who was the bearer? The same person since the company was first registered in 1963? Or somebody different? Presumably the bearer was Forensi or his family in some disguise. The registered office was unchanged but that meant nothing. The officers of the company would no doubt be faceless lawyers, their discretion assured.

He pushed back his chair and went straight to the bank of telephones. Then he called Mark Worthington QC, who had been a good friend at the Chancery Bar. As usual, he was still working, rarely leaving his dusty chambers, in London's Lincoln's Inn, before 10.00 pm. As a specialist in company law, Worthington was just the man to approach. Quickly Gavin explained the situation.

'Think you've got a problem, Gavin,' was Worthington's immediate reaction. 'Bearer shares preserve secrecy. From what you've told me, the reality is that Pinetto is a Panamanian company. It's shareholder is another company whose shares are owned by bearers. The wall is immovable. Just because the official records show no change in ownership means nothing. Not in Panama.'

'Oh Christ!' exclaimed Gavin. 'You'd better tell me more.'

'In Panama, there is no requirement to disclose the identity of the holder of the bearer shares. Ownership of the Panamanian company can change without you being aware of it. Have the directors of the Panamanian company changed? That could be a pointer.'

'I don't know.' Gavin sounded lame.

'Better check on that.' Mark Worthington had spent a long day in Court but his mind was still razor-sharp and, at fifty three, he was tipped to become a High Court Judge. 'Gavin, I'm sorry to pin you even harder to the ropes. But company law was always like Serbo-Croat to you.'

'Worse even that that. Thanks for your help. Is there any good news?'

'No.' The Queen's Counsel gave him the advice straight between the eyes. 'Give me a ring when you know some more.'

Thinking of Forensi as he went, he headed to the shop to pick up the evening paper. God! He'd been stupid! Forensi could just be a mere puppet chairman. The man was old, very old to be running a company. Then, *Evening Standard* in hand, he went to the elevator to go to his room. He'd scarcely sat down before a small feature in the paper caught his eye. 'Bloody Hell!' he exclaimed out loud. There had been no flights in or out of Athens all day. A strike by air traffic controllers. 'My God,' he muttered more quietly this time. So if Edward hadn't been in Athens, where had he been? Was anyone where they were supposed to be? Including himself? Edward thought Sir Archie was in Singapore, or that's what he was saying. Where was Susannah? Where was Klodinsky? Should he challenge Edward? He recalled his father's advice on how to deal with witnesses. Keep'em guessing. Don't reveal how little or how much you know.

He decided to ring Lotte, down at the Bureau and set her working on anything, personnel changes or whatever which might indicate something wrong at Pinetto. Although it was after six, she promised to ring him back.

Then he decided to ring Edward, adopting a policy of playing both ends off against the middle. 'Glad I caught you, Edward. I'm just trying to re-cap.' He remembered that he was now supposed to be in New York. 'I shan't be long. This call's costing a fortune. Yes. New York. Klodinsky? Do you think he's having an affair with Susannah?'

'Not that I know of,' scoffed Edward. 'As far as I've heard, Susannah's got something going with an advertising executive from Newbury. She's a bit quiet about it but I think that's because he's married. Whatever gave you that idea? But did you know he'd had an affair with my mother? The Gaffer told me that Klodinsky had admitted that. To Art. Anyway, why not ask her?'

'I will. Stranger things have happened. Ok. Let's try something else. Klodinsky used to live in Bristol, was once a student at the Brunel Marine Department. Could he have discovered something about Sir Archie or the company which was a soft point? Something he could use for blackmail?'

'You mean my father's whoring in Paris?' Edward sounded disdainful. He swivelled in his leather chair, rested an arm on his stomach and put his legs on the desk.

'I wasn't thinking about that sort of thing.' Actually, Gavin was thinking of everything and anything. 'We know he was stalking the company, or at least had the material to stalk the company. He's denying any intent. Are you sure you are telling me everything relating to Klodinsky and the company?' Gavin waited for a response. Face to face would have been more effective, watching for telltales in eye and lip movements.

'I can't think of anything.'

'I know you flew in from Athens today from what you said earlier,' Gavin re-baited the trap. 'But I was wondering whether you were there for anything significant to my enquiries?'

'No. Not all. A shipping conference, followed by a routine meeting with our agents there.'

'You didn't happen to see Alberto Forensi?'

'No. No reason to. I think you'll find he's in Dakalla. That's what he told Susannah.'

Gavin debated whether to ask the next question and decided that he would. 'Ever been to Dakalla?'

'No. I was just debating whether to fly out. Frankly, I don't think there's much I can do. Our P and I Club, your lot and Forensi seem to be working on it. I'd be superfluous.'

'The Director's got our side under control.' Gavin was evasive.

'I'm glad to hear it.' Edward's tone was sharp. 'As far as I can see, you've achieved nothing. By the way, there's something I've been meaning to ask you. That bomb in Wickham. I was talking to the Gaffer about it. It *was* meant for you, wasn't it?'

'Who knows. There's no evidence.'

'Pull the other one. Anyway, I won't press you on it. Anything else? No? All right. Keep in touch.'

Gavin put down the receiver thoughtfully and then flicked on the TV. The news was almost over. There was a brief report about the Prime Minister's forthcoming visit to Dakalla and then, just before the newsreader was about to sign off, he added a postscript.

'Reports are just coming in of an explosion in a block of flats in West London. First indications suggest at least five fatalities and several injured. Emergency services have gone to the scene. The cause of the explosion is not known.'

Gavin thought nothing of it, switched off the television and stood by the window, waiting for Lotte to telephone. She did, shortly after 7.00 pm. Her conversation was typically sprinkled with the type of English learned out of phrase books and spoken with a gutsy German accent. 'I am so glad to have caught up with you. Pinetto is like a can of worms. So you are right. Alberto Forensi is still Chairman but the power has passed to a new generation. The new young turk hails from Marseille. His name is Hugo Gonfleur. Forensi is only the front man.'

'How did you find out?' Gavin was impressed.

'I flipped through the Director's list of contacts for Naples and Marseille. A couple of phone calls was enough.'

'Lotte! You're a brick!' Gavin felt the need to join in the clichés. 'Tomorrow, I want you to get a rundown on Gonfleur.'He replaced the receiver with absent-minded precision. Gonfleur? Marseille? City of big crime and big criminals. Oh God, he thought. Things really could not be worse.

Meantime, over at Marble Arch, Art had quickly concluded that Janie had quit. The empty dressing table, wardrobe and the missing suitcases said it all. He wasn't sure what he felt. Relief? Regrets? Anger? Where had she gone? Did he care? No ... not a lot. Life would go on. He poured himself some orange, appreciating the tangy coldness against his parched throat. He looked at his watch. It was 7.10 pm, a whole evening ahead of him. No sweat, so long as the bitch hadn't taken his whisky. He padded across to the drinks cabinet. Good! The Wild Turkey bourbon was still there. Fine. So he'd have a pizza delivered, maybe watch a video.

It was about 8.20 pm when the phone rang. The pizza had not yet arrived as Art lifted himself off the sofa. He hadn't realized how irritable he was until he heard his own voice answering. 'Yes.'

'Walter here. Did I wake you or something?'

'Not exactly. Just relaxing.'

'Not for much longer you're not. Do you know where Gavin is? He's not at his hotel. The Penta have no idea.'

'Why?' Art was alert now, realizing that there was something in the timbre of the Director's voice suggesting concern.

'His flat was wrecked two hours ago by a bomb. There are at least five dead. Greenaway tipped me off.'

'Five, in his flat?' Art sounded disbelieving.

'No. One side of the building collapsed. It's a hell of a mess. No one knows who's who or what's what. Greenaway's at the scene. He's got a watching brief for us. I want you there as well. Pretend to be a journalist. Better still, get close to Greenaway, he'll keep you up to date.'

'Shit! I just don't know. I just can't ...' Art's voice was as near to breaking as it had ever come. 'I can't believe it.'

'We don't know how the bomb was triggered off. We don't even know when it was placed there. It appears to have been in the bedroom.

'To prevent him going to Dakalla?'

Art shared the silence as the Director paused. Then came the sharp intake of breath.

'I doubt it. No one knows he's in London. It may have been there since before Wickham. Anyway, take no chances. I want you out of your place. Check into the Novotel at Hammersmith. That's near Gavin's. Handy for a quick journey to the airport in the morning. Whatever has happened to Gavin, you leave for Dakalla. Understood?'

'Sure. My last dime's on Klodinsky now.'

'Maybe.' The Director was non-committal. 'Glib assumptions that we're after Klodinsky or Brads may be leading us astray. There may be others. Let's not forget that.'

'Sure!'

Hastily, Art shuffled clean and dirty clothes in and out of his case, took a rain-check on the pizza and was gone.

After speaking to Lotte, time hung heavily. There was nothing to do, nothing Gavin wanted to watch on the television. Worse still, there were too many uncomfortable thoughts, a vicious circle of *Cerne View*, Forensi and Gonfleur. If only he could talk to Claudine. Damn and blast Corbin. He'd got it all wrong. She *could* be trusted.

He padded round the room, picked up a book, put it down again, looked out of the window at the incoming planes, checked his watch, packed his things for the flight and got round to looking at his book again.

Suddenly, almost without realizing it, he decided. Claudine was so close. The Director would never find out. Having taken the decision to defy instructions, everything slipped neatly into place. He phoned Claudine who quickly explained that her room was on the ground floor, in the new extension, with a window off the south lawn.

He hired a car at the airport and the drive round the M25 and then out along the M3 only took thirty-five minutes. In less than an hour since taking the decision, he'd parked the Cavalier well away from the main entrance to the nursing home. He guessed the discreet police guard would still be on duty there. His car, hidden under some pine trees where he'd played as a child while staying with his aunt, was well out of sight at the bottom of the grounds.

The night was dark with scarcely any moon at all. The air was full of the heady smells of tangled undergrowth as he climbed the fence. It was a still evening and his progress was quick in the ample cover as he skirted the freshly-cut lawn towards the annexe. That had only been built in the last three years but it was just as Claudine had described. Contrasting with the Victorian austerity of the old vicarage, the additional two storeys of red brick were built like a school dormitory, with the garden door at one end. Claudine's window, with the curtains open, shone out in splendid isolation. The other windows were either in darkness or heavily draped.

It was scarcely 9.00 pm. Someone was playing a chorale

on a hi-fi but otherwise there was silence. From behind heavy curtains around the main house, he could see the occasional flicker of a TV screen.

Claudine was standing at the window. She watched as he climbed through and stood in front of her. They looked at each other, more in disbelief than pleasure. Could they actually be together? Was it real? Then he clung to her and she to him, their heads touching, her trembling body vibrating right through him. He gripped her harder as if trying to squeeze the sobbing tension into relaxation. Surges of emotion rippled up and down her back until, at last, she pulled away so that he could see her face and he looked deeply into the pale green eyes.

Nice Airport, where he'd first seen them, seemed a lifetime ago. Now, her eyes were full of tears but her stay at Aunt Margaret's private nursing home had restored the model girl features. She was unrecognizable from the mindless automaton he had left there just days before. From the glow of the bedside light, he saw that her face was once again delicately pink, her cheeks fuller, her hair lustrous, her make-up subtle. She'd been busy in the last sixty minutes.

He kissed her, just a gentle brushing of the lips, then wiped back a rolling teardrop from her cheek. 'Don't cry. There's nothing to cry about now. Everything's going to be all right.' Gavin recalled that he'd said that before. When she'd arrived from Paris. Empty words then and now - yet they worked. A watery smile creased her cheeks as she wiped back another tear.

'I know. That's why I'm crying.' Her eyes seemed enormous, elf-like, as she gazed up at him. Then she noticed the deep purple bruising above his eye. 'And you? Are you all right. What happened here?' She touched the bruise with a cool, gentle finger.

'A minor skirmish. Nothing serious.'

'I don't believe you.' She tapped him on the nose. ' Tell me later.'

'You're looking wonderful.'

'That's your aunt's loving care. Flaps around like a Rhode Island Red.' Gavin was delighted to see the twinkle in her eye. 'I'm better. Really I am.' She placed her hands on his shoulders. 'Take me away from here. Please.'

'Is that what the doctors say?'

'You know it isn't.'

'You've got to do what the doctors tell you.' He tried to make the blunt message sound caring. 'Being with me is just too dangerous.' He laughed. 'I seem to be a bit accident-prone these days.'

She wavered. 'But you'll come and see me tomorrow? And the next day?' Her tone was childlike, pleading and yet forceful. As she spoke she clung to him more fiercely. Gavin found it hard to refuse but impossible to accept. He kissed her, more fully this time, parting her lips and pushing her head backwards, cradling the back of her head in his hands. 'No more talk now. We'll sort things out later.'

He led her across the simply-furnished room. The carpets were rose pink, the wallpaper had a flowery motif with bedspread to match. It was warm, comfortable and, with the window and curtains closed, surprisingly intimate for a house ruled on calvinist principles. By the bed was a bottle of champagne and two bouquets of flowers.

'Champagne? Where did you get that from?'

'A present from Walter Corbin. And the tulips with a card. He's really a very thoughtful man. The roses were from you. My favourite.' She kissed him.

'Walter's certainly chivalrous.' As he was talking, he had opened the Bollinger and filled some glasses whilst she had slipped off her white blouse, short black skirt and the precious little she'd had on underneath. By the time the champagne was poured, she was reclining seductively naked beneath the pink sheets. He hastily discarded his navy sweatshirt, chinos and the rest before joining her. There was an urgency in his movements, for he had memories to lay to rest - the lost day in Paris, the fierce arousal at his flat, and the warm expectancy at Wickham. The bomb had changed all that.

Now, as he saw her lying on the bed, her mouth slightly open, her eyes watching him hungrily, he knew that nothing would come between them this time. The urge to lie beside her, to caress and cosset her, was overwhelmed by lust as his body dictated an irresistible pace. He slipped his arm round her shoulders and gently caressed her while they sipped at the champagne.

'You'll stay? The whole night I mean?' She knew it was impossible from what he'd said on the phone.

'No, sweetheart. I'm sorry. Not even you, looking like you do, could get me to change my mind. I must get back tonight.' He kissed her right ear. 'Please understand. I shouldn't be here at all. I'm supposed to be in New York.' He looked at her intently. 'No one must know where I am.' He ran a finger round her nipples. 'I'm taking a real chance being here. I'm putting all my trust in you.' He wondered if she was aware of the police guard arranged by Corbin. Better not to mention it.

'I know.' Her eyes made it clear that she understood and did not approve. 'Promise me - when this is over - you'll take me somewhere warm with sandy beaches and crimson sunsets.'

'Mmm - sounds wonderful! But before that ... I fly to Dakalla in the morning. ' Even as he spoke, he realized what he'd done. It had slipped out. 'Forget I said that.' He squeezed her more tightly. 'Please.'

'How can I?' She shook her head and wrinkled her aquiline nose. 'And Dakalla. I've told you before. I've been there with Carl. I could help you. I've still got a visa.'

294

'No. Absolutely not. It's far too dangerous. And you're a security risk. That's what Walter says.'

'*Quoi*?' Claudine's irritation showed by the way she had reacted in her native tongue. 'Me? I thought he liked me.' She looked for a moment as if she was going to spit out the champagne. 'I thought he wanted me here to get better, not to keep me out of the way.'

Gavin tapped her on the nose. 'A bit of both I think, so just relax.' Clearly, she didn't know about the police outside.

'But you trust me, don't you?' As she was speaking, she was turning in front of him, so that she could face him. The low light from the table lamp by the bed emphasized the pleading look on her face. 'You trust me, don't you, Gavin? You're not like Walter?' Her eyes searched questioningly, her mouth teasingly close to his, her breasts brushing against the hairs on his chest.

'Of course. But above all I trust you to stay here and tell no one. I'll be back in a few days.' As if by unspoken consent, each put down their glass. He rested his hands on her shoulders, easing her backwards till her head was on the pink pillow. Her body lying next to him was soft, smooth and desirable. He noticed her breath was coming quicker as he started running his hands over her warm skin. This time, as they grasped and explored each other to fulfillment, their passion was intense, meaningful and leading to a crescendo of shared happiness.

'*Incroyable*! Ah Gavin! That was wonderful,' Claudine murmured as she snuggled deeper into the bed. 'I told you it was in our stars.'

'Whatever it was, I'm not complaining.' Gavin eased himself into a more comfortable position, arms clasping her and smiling at her across the pillow. 'The stars, eh? That beautiful lovemaking was certainly the most convincing evidence you've produced.'

'I told you. Aquarius and Taurus. It's even better than that. I've been looking at our Chinese horoscopes. You know the Chinese have a name for every lunar year. There are twelve Animal Signs, such as the Monkey, the Pig and the Buffalo. You were born in the year of the Tiger. I'm a Dragon.'

'Is that good?' A Tiger and a Dragon?'

Claudine nodded her head and grinned hugely. 'It's a plus-plus rating. Five Star. The best there is. A male Tiger and a female Dragon. Look.' She eased herself up to open a bedside drawer. 'Here,' she said proudly, as she produced two pieces of paper, each with a circle drawn on it and, within the circle, two further circles and, within the innermost circle, a series of triangular shapes, criss-crossing each other like a geometric puzzle. 'That's you. Born at 10.15 pm on the 16th May 1962. It's called a Natal Chart. It's like a snapshot of all the planetary positions at the moment of your birth.'

'You really do believe all this, don't you? Did it predict that I would meet you? Did yours predict that you would meet me?'

Claudine pushed him playfully. 'This isn't a game. I've told you before. I'm not a gipsy in a tent, looking at a crystal ball, talking of tall dark strangers.'

'So all these signs and symbols can explain my personality, how I would react?'

'Exactly. If interpreted properly that is.'

Gavin looked thoughtful. 'Then, while I'm ... away ... run through Sir Archie, Klodinsky, Edward, Forensi and Susannah.'

'If you know the dates, that's easy. Really though I need to know their times of birth.'

'I can scarcely ask them that,' he laughed in response. 'I checked out the dates from Companies' House, Lloyds and *Who's Who*.'

'Seems you're starting to take astrology seriously after all,' she chided.

His grin was broad. 'Are the times really important?'

'To do a real chart, yes, but I'll do what I can.' He handed her the scribbled dates. 'Forensi you won't know about.'

'*Au contraire*,' she said quickly. 'I have heard of him. I think I've met him. Alberto. Born, 5th October, 1917. A Libra. I guess that would figure.' She didn't expand as she scanned the dates. It was evident from the excited look in her eyes that she was looking forward to the task. 'I'll check out the Chinese Year Signs as well. One difficulty, without knowing the time of birth is that the moon may be changing. Secondly, the position of the planets is always on the move. Each of them plays their part.'

The look on Gavin's face was cynical but he nodded his head enthusiastically. 'I'm not interested in whether they're any good in bed. I want to know whether *Ryme Lady* was sunk by Brads or Klodinsky, or Forensi, or none of them. Simple as that.' He kissed her on the lips. 'Now tell me some more about male Tigers and female Dragons. I like that.'

'I'll do better than that. I'll show you.'

Chapter 39

Back at the Penta Hotel, the receptionist shook her head. 'I'm sorry. Mr Blair isn't answering.' She put down the receiver. 'He hasn't checked out. He took his key with him.'

'I'll wait.' The visitor removed his black leather gloves. For a few minutes he sat on an easy chair looking uncomfortable. Then he slipped on his gloves, walked round the corner and into the elevator. The receptionist never noticed. She had her hands full with a woman who wanted her to ring Olympic Airways to check about flights to Athens. Again.

Claudine nibbled Gavin's ear. 'You see. We've proved it again. Dragons and Tigers.' Her voice was dreamy. 'Lovemaking for me has never been like that.'

'Nor for me either.' Gavin felt so content he'd have agreed to anything.

'So you see, there is something in it. You should take it seriously.'

'You're persuading me.' She wriggled appreciatively as he ran his finger down her spine.

'*Attention*! Stop it,' she said playfully as his hand cupped itself round her firm buttock. 'I'm trying to concentrate on Sir Archie. Sagittarius. I'd say he's a smooth, apparently even-natured type concealing a smouldering fiery temperament. A tendency to, how do you say it in England, to bully. Does that fit in?'

'Possibly. What about Klodinsky?'

'Carl? He's Taurus. I've told you before - his interest is in deals, not people. He's single minded but for material gain - that's the true Taurus.'

'Do Sagittarian men murder their wives?'

'It would depend on the wife's sign. But a large number of murderers are Sagittarians. When they erupt, it can be violent.'

'Hugo Gonfleur? What do you know about him?'

'Carl would know him. He's big down in Marseille. Do you know his details? Where does he fit in?' The brightness in her eyes showed her interest. On seeing this, Gavin thought carefully before answering, whilst topping up their glasses with more champagne.

'I just don't know.' He was about to tell her more but something made him hold back. 'Tell me about Edward,' he asked, changing the subject.

Claudine looked reproachful. 'You still don't trust me, do you? Not telling me everything about Gonfleur.'

'I don't know much. Tell me about Edward.'

'Another Sagittarian. Should be just like his father but you say he isn't.' She frowned. 'I'll have to do more work on him.'

'And Susannah?'

She looked at the dates in front of her. 'Ah yes. January. Capricorn. Cool, well organized. Capricorns are often cut out to be professionals. Likely to be ambitious and not to be under-estimated.'

Gavin smiled. 'You've certainly got the family right. Superficially that is. Now I need the full works. Moons, Planets, Chinese Animals ... the lot!' He put down his glass, adjusted the pillows, enabling him to play with the simple gold chain which hung round her slender neck. 'Let's go back to Klodinsky. You say he was never interested in women? I happen to know that isn't true.' He looked deep into her eyes. 'And so do you.'

Her face looked puzzled rather than concerned as she looked at him. For a moment her brow furrowed and she appeared ready to say something but then didn't, not until there had been an indecently long pause. 'Oh ... if you mean has he been to bed with women rather than rent-boys, then the answer is yes. But he's not interested in them as people. Just as conquests. That's my view. He did get involved with a woman once, a while back. Don't ask me who. He was a bit secretive. I bet there was a motive though. Money or a deal.'

'So, if I told you that Carl had an affair with Lady Ingrid, Sir Archie's wife?' He watched carefully for her reaction, sensing a moment of hesitation. He'd have sworn that a shiver ran through her. 'Did Carl kill her? Have her thrown over Clifton Bridge when she was of no further use? Once she'd told him that the key to Brads' treasure chest was in the land options?' Again he felt her body tremble but when she spoke, her voice was neutral, her tone matter-of-fact.

'Out of character.' She shook her head. 'A true Taurus like Carl would not behave like that. Any more than you would. ' She rubbed the side of her nose, screwed up one eye and shrugged. 'Maybe he was using her. Wanted information.' She nodded as she developed her theme. 'Then he finished with her. But then she was in love with him. So she took her own life. That could explain what happened. Get me her birth sign. That would help.'

'In deciding whether she would commit suicide?'

'Precisely.'

'I'll check.' He poured the last drops of champagne from the glass. 'You don't think I'm using you, do you?' He turned so that he could look at her squarely, anxious to emphasize his sincerity.

'Not now, I don't think so. In Paris? I was not so sure.'

'I'm glad you understand.' His voice was low, husky. 'We're a team, with a purpose, with a goal.'

She laughed. 'And in your team, I'm left back - left back at home.' The gentle brushing of his lips with hers softened the acidity of the remark. 'And our goal?'

'To crack the mystery of *Ryme Lady*. And then? To share

our time. I want to get to know you even better, to play more Lions and Tigers.'

'Tigers and Dragons, *mon petit*', she laughed.

Though he didn't say it, there was another goal.

To come back from Dakalla alive.

Chapter 40

It was late afternoon in Washington. The early morning blue skies had given way to a grey overcast atmosphere. The temperature was lipping twenty-six degrees, the humidity sapping every ounce of energy from the people on the White House Lawn. It was a relief to those in military uniform and the other staffers when the helicopter pilot revved the engine. Moments later, it left the ground, it's nose tipping towards the Washington Monument, before soaring away.

The TV camera cut from the chopper, turning instead to the commentator. He spoke with the freshly re-painted White House as the perfect backdrop. 'That was the President speaking live from the White House before making the short flight to Andrews Air Base. There, Air Force One awaits him for the transatlantic overnight flight to Dakalla. Tomorrow, he will meet with other leaders who will visit the US Embassy. On Saturday, the President and the First Lady will attend the banquet celebrating the birth of the new state of Lupopo. There will be maximum security. Reports continue to indicate some unrest in the community but any demonstrations will be kept well away from the Presidential Palace. Although a White House spokesman has denied that any assassination threats have been received, no chances are being taken. *Security around the President is always vigilant*, was today's official comment from the White House. This is Smith Adamson, for NBC, at the White House.'

The mikes were switched off. The camera team put down their equipment. Adamson removed his jacket and tie and decided to wander down Pennsylvania Avenue to pick up a cool beer. Maureen Hennessy, a reporter from the *Washington Post* approached him. 'Got an angle on the assassination story?' She was an old friend. They'd both been cub reporters on the *Chicago Tribune*.

'Nope. Even off the record, the White House press spokesman was tight-lipped. All he'd say was that the President was in no more danger in Dakalla than Kennedy had been when he went to Dallas. And look what happened to him!'

'I heard him say that too. I guess he meant that the President is at risk anywhere, anytime.'

'I'm going for a beer. Fancy one?' Adamson saw her nod in agreement and together they headed towards the black gates. Outside, the usual throng of tourists and bystanders were gathered. 'My own deep throat contact at the State Department has confirmed real fears. Is your paper taking it seriously?'

'We've sent a top team to Dakalla. We'd heard too.'

'Our editor says it's all to do with religion and tribes. Or rather - exploitation of religion. I'd say he's talking through his ass, not uncommon. I'd say it was all about power. Lupopo will be the richest country in West Africa.' They paused to cross the road by the Old Executive Building. 'What did you hear about people like Gaddafi?' He went on to answer his own comment. 'Off the record, some people say that stability in Lupopo will be inconvenient for anyone pushing for fundamentalism.'

'Oh sure,' she nodded. 'We picked up reports that Gaddafi spent time in the '80s stirring it right through from Gabon in the south to Senegal in the north. Lumbola and Sampopo apart would have been easier for him to pick off.' She looked at him curiously and liked what she saw. The extra few years had seen off the puppy-fat and had added some strikingly rough edges to his appearance. It had been a while since their paths had crossed. 'So, what are you trying to tell me? That Gaddafi may be involved?'

'No. Not at all. Forget Gaddafi. Most anyone looking to make trouble could do worse that start in West Africa. Pick off the little countries one by one. Join the troubles in the south with the troubles in the north.

'But hell, Gaddafi's scarcely a friend of the United States since Ronnie Reagan sent our air force in to bomb him.'

'But where the hell is Dakalla?' They both laughed. 'Tell you what. Like I mean it's been a while. After the beer. I mean, would you like to go down to the River Club? If you haven't been there, it's great.'

'Sounds better than Dakalla. Sure. Let's do that.'

Chapter 41

Gavin parked the Cavalier in the sprawling Penta car park. It was gone 1.00 am and there would be ample time to return it before the flight. He entered the lobby and was about to pick up his key when a familiar voice spoke from behind him. 'Mr Blair I believe.' Gavin spun round in horror and saw the Director easing himself out of a chair. He was wearing an expensive overcoat, pale yellow scarf, one of his finely-cut suits and a pair of hand-stitched shoes. This was certainly no casual occasion. There was a determined look on his face. 'And just where have you been?' The two men were now facing up to each other, alone in the middle of the lobby. 'And I don't want any bullshit.'

'I've been to see Claudine.'

'I thought as much! We'll continue this conversation in private.' Gavin tried to look unconcerned as they made their way to his room, the journey seeming to take an age as they walked in silence. Gavin could sense the wrath of the man beside him, as he fumbled with the key, his hands shaking. Walter Corbin was not slow to notice.

They entered the room, switched on the lights and closed the curtains. 'Sit down,' barked Walter. 'No. Not on the bed. There.' Gavin was made to sit on an upright chair, dunce-like, in the corner whilst the Director stood in front of him. Walter's eyes were cold and Gavin noticed the jaw muscles twitch with anger. 'I suppose I should say I'm glad to see you. Under the circumstances, I'm not so sure.' He saw Gavin's look of puzzlement and decided to explain about the bomb. The only fact he omitted was that Janie had been the trigger. Gavin started to ask what had caused the blast but was waved silent.

'There's been a serious breach of security,' continued Walter. 'Your safety is vital to the Bureau, to the whole integrity of our operations. I cannot afford another death. My instructions were plain. Tell no one you were in England. Yes?' The raised eyebrows and the narrowed eyes were withering. 'Not least Claudine.'

'Yes.'

'Yet you risked everything because of your own futile little sex drive. Told Claudine where you were.' He paused as if expecting Gavin to volunteer something and was rewarded by a delayed almost imperceptible nod of the head. 'And you told Claudine where you're going!' It was not a question. This was a barked-out challenge. The Director stood a few feet away, quite motionless, his eyes relentlessly fixed on him.

Gavin did not dare to look up. His eyes stared at the carpet. His mind was swimming. He grasped for the right thing to say. Should he deny it? No. That would be pointless. 'But I trust her,' he faltered. 'And I thought she could help.'

'Trust her! You think that because she lets you play with her titties, you can trust her?' He made the word *trust* sound a matter for utter disdain. Walter spun round on his heels and crossed to the other side of the room. 'Even if she could be trusted, it's no excuse. My orders, remember?'

Gavin looked up for the first time. 'You're right. It was unforgivable. But she wouldn't let me down. She's on our side. Part of our team.'

'Baaagh! Let me tell you something. No. I'll tell you two things. Did you know she'd been to Dakalla before?'

Gavin brightened. 'Yes I did. She told me she'd been there with Klodinsky.'

'Did she tell you they shared a room? Did she tell you that later she'd had to have an abortion?' There was a prolonged silence. Walter knew that he'd struck deep. He'd wanted to. It wasn't true. Not entirely anyway but the deceit was essential if Gavin was to be brought to his senses.

Gavin leaned forward and placed his head in his hands. Then he looked up, his eyes showing his confusion. His tired features showed all the rigours of too much stress crammed into too little time. 'No. She didn't tell me that.' He could have added that she'd always denied anything of the kind. 'But that's in the past. Not relevant.'

'Not relevant!' Corbin's roar filled the room. 'Not relevant that you're playing four legs in a bed with the personal assistant, the mistress of the person you're investigating.'

'Is that all?' Fortunately for Gavin he did not make the question sound contemptuous. His face gaunt, he glanced up sheepishly. Above the thin line of his eyebrow, the purple bruise was throbbing painfully. The Director was by now standing in front of the mirror by the dressing-table, needlessly adjusting his tie. At the same time he could watch Gavin without appearing to stare. Walter had never had a son but had always wanted one. The moment of friction had gone. There was an almost paternalistic air as he walked over to where Gavin was still seated.

He put his hand on Gavin's shoulder. 'We're not playing games. Someone tried to kill you again tonight. I thought they had. So did Art.' He was speaking more slowly now, the cultured tone in his voice almost melodious. 'We need you.' He saw Gavin swallow hard as he listened. 'You see, I've heard from Art what you did in New York. He's told me everything. Not only was it brave, it was well-planned. As Art would say, it was more than his dumb behaviour deserved.'

Walter went over to the drinks cabinet and poured each of them a whisky from a miniature. 'You've proved yourself, not just to him but to us all. Better still - you've proved yourself ... to yourself.' He raised his glass to Gavin and they both drank. 'Now you've spoiled it. Tonight, you've let yourself down. And the Bureau.'

'I'm sorry. I don't think you understand just how badly I feel about Claudine. It's down to me that she's in this mess.'

'Maybe.' Walter did not sound convinced. 'Anyway, for your own safety I'm getting Claudine collected in the morning and taken to somewhere ... secure.' He raised his hand to show that he wouldn't listen to any objection. 'She'll be safe and comfortable, that I promise. I just can't take any risks with her.' He cleared his throat which was showing his emotion and the lateness of the hour. 'I'm not sorry I was so angry. You deserved it. I am sorry about what I'm going to tell you now. You'd better sit down.' He waited whilst Gavin retreated once again to the corner. 'The blast at your flat was so bad that at first they couldn't recognise the bodies. It wasn't until after eleven that Freddie Greenaway confirmed that all five fatalities were female.'

'Females?'

'Unofficially, Greenaway tells me that the person who triggered the bomb was ... Janie.'

'Janie? I don't understand. What was she doing there? She was living with Art. My God! Is she dead? Blown up? Oh Christ! Poor Janie.' His voice faltered. 'And her father too. Dear old boy. Blind and a widower. He'll never cope. And what about Art? Does he know?'

Walter was quick to notice how Gavin's concern was for everyone but himself, though his own distress was obvious. 'I didn't even know that she'd moved in with Art,' confessed Corbin. 'He explained that to me tonight. Today, she just walked out on him. The remains of her suitcases were found in the debris. It looks as though she had come to make it up with you.'

So many questions flitted through Gavin's mind that he

wasn't sure which was the most urgent. He stared mind-lessly at the wall. 'Poor Janie,' he repeated. 'She deserved better. But coming back to me? I don't understand it.' He turned to face Walter again. 'So, how's Art?' he repeated. 'And have they caught anyone?'

'Art's fine. He's more concerned about you. As for Janie's death, you should know him. He doesn't give a toss about women. To him they're just fleas on a dog's back.' He drained the last of the Glenfiddich. 'He's been standing outside your flat at Barons Court all evening, thinking you were dead. When it turned out to be Janie he nearly laughed with relief. Seems he's really quite fond of you.' It was evident from Walter's tone that he shared similar feel-ings. 'And no. We've no idea who planted the bomb. It could have been there for minutes or days. Anytime since you were last there.'

PART THREE

RIO MASSU

Chapter 42

Art greeted Gavin with a sardonic grin at Heathrow. 'You're just one lucky sonovabitch. You've cheated those bastards again.'

There was not much that Gavin could say, not without bringing up the subject of Janie. He decided to leave it but during the flight, after their breakfast had been cleared away, Gavin veered back to the subject. 'I'm sorry about Janie.' Gavin had picked his words with care. Art could take them whichever way he liked.

'So am I.' Art had seen the two sides to the comment and had avoided committing himself to either route. 'I guess we meant nothing to each other ... just I was there ... giving her what she thought she needed at the time.' In a series of reflex movements he pulled his cigarettes from the breast pocket of his shirt, found his blue disposable lighter and lit up with contentment. 'She'd never hinted she'd leave me, especially for you. The way I see it ... I guess she was jealous of Claudine. I'd explained about her. I'd say Janie wanted to get back to you before it was too late.'

Gavin blew his nose firmly into a handkerchief. 'Forgive me. You can't live with someone for years and then ... just switch off. Can't hate, least, I can't. Whatever she's done. Especially when the bomb wasn't meant for her.' He tried to conceal the watery look round his eyes. 'So I'm not sure what I think. It's just so bizarre. You know. Her wanting to come back to me.'

'Would you have had her?' It was a blunt question typical of Art.

Gavin sucked in his teeth thoughtfully. His eyes were downcast. Then came the emphatic shake of the head. 'No.

313

I wouldn't have taken her back. Not because she walked out on me - though that hurt. No, I wouldn't take her back because she left knowing it wasn't going to work.' Art noticed the rueful shake of the head. He could see that Janie had meant more to Gavin than he'd ever understood. 'She was right too,' Gavin added. 'I couldn't see it then. Now ... it's so obvious. Anyway, there's Claudine.'

They fell silent as Art contemplated the controls built into the side of his seat. 'I guess she'd had enough of me too,' he said at last. 'The booze ... that was pretty heavy.' If he'd seen the look on Gavin's face, he'd have known that was an understatement. 'That ... and finding the pack of condoms, strawberry flavoured too. Guess that didn't go down too well.' He sipped his coffee thoughtfully. 'If she hadn't schlepped out, maybe been a little patient, she'd have understood. The boozing was just about over, now that...' He didn't need to add that it was over because his guilty secret had ended.

Gavin's nod cut off the rest of the sentence as he stirred his coffee, lost in a sea of if-onlys and what-might-have-beens. Not that they mattered. Not since Claudine. 'Oh, to hell with it. Let's concentrate on the job in hand. Better still, let's have a brandy. I could do with one.'

'Agreed. Make it two,' Art told the flight attendant.

Moments later however, Art decided to watch the film rather than talk about *Cerne View* so that inevitably Gavin's thoughts drifted back to his conversation with Walter. He'd been too tired, too disadvantaged, to make his point. Yet he was convinced that the Director was wrong about Claudine.

Then, like a kick in the stomach, came the recollection that she'd been pregnant by Klodinsky. Was that true? Invariably Walter gave the impression of knowing so much, yet surely it had been just a scare-tactic? But, if true, what did it mean? What were the implications? Did it

314

change his views? Did he still want to see her? Make love to her? Trust her? Well ... she was entitled to her past. She was even entitled to deny it. Well ... in most situations ... that would be true. But not when she knew he was investigating Klodinsky.

He put on a set of headphones and switched on the Jazz Channel. It helped him relax. Within moments he knew that nothing had changed. He still wanted her, still trusted her. Yes, he'd confront her ... but in a nice way. To the powerful lament of Billie Holliday singing a 1936 blues number, he fell asleep. It was only when they were on their final approach that Gavin stirred and re-orientated himself.

The clock on the terminal at Dakalla showed the local time as 3.30 pm when their aircraft taxied to a halt. Well away from the main buildings an area big enough for at least fifteen jets had been cordonned-off. It was bristling with military personnel and armoured vehicles. 'A parking lot for the top brass,' commented Art as the *cordon sanitaire* disappeared from view. 'You know what?' Art's voice was conspiratorial. It was obvious that he was going to make what he thought was a profound comment. 'We think we're here to sort out *Ryme Lady* ... or *Cerne View*. Maybe both of them. I think we're here because my President is here. See that,' he pointed through the window. 'That's his little freebie parked up over there.' Air Force One, with its presidential symbol clearly visible, stood all alone, surrounded by a formidable ring of protection.

'President O'Brien? Why him? Why not our Prime Minister. Or the French President.'

'Ok.' Art raised his hands momentarily. 'I didn't quite mean that. I mean we're here because all roads lead to Dakalla. It's all just too neat', he grinned cheerfully. 'But hell, you're the brains. You work out why we're here.'

'The creation of Lupopo? You think that's what it's all

about?' Gavin slung his cabin bag over his shoulder. Moments later he was following Art down the steps to the shimmering heat of the tarmac. 'Original thought, or did Walter prompt you?'

'All my own work.' Art looked back and laughed. The impressive front teeth were all replacements after a fist fight in Orlando. 'I am allowed the occasional original thought. Even though you are the brains.' He slapped Gavin on the back. They both sensed that events were moving to a climax and that teamwork would be essential. 'If I'm right, things out here are gonna be rough.'

Progress was slow as the snake of travellers wound its way into the terminal. The roof was bedecked with 'welcome' signs in every language. Flags of all nations hung limply in the sultry stillness of the afternoon. The deep rhythmic beat of jungle drums, accompanied by tribal chanting, played over the sound system as they waited on the hot tarmac. The dank water on either side of the main runway was rife with sewage and the stench mixed with the fumes from the aviation fuel made the stop-go trudge to the airport building seem interminable.

Inside, conditions were no more pleasant. The facilities were ill-equipped to cope with a nine-seater plane, let alone a packed Boeing 747. With no air-conditioning and the nervous energy of the waiting passengers, the heat was unbearable. Frustration turned to mutterings of anger at the slow pace of the bureaucrats checking the papers and bags.

'When and if we ever get out of here,' suggested Gavin, 'shall we go straight to the prison to see the crew?'

Art, whose face was covered with perspiration and whose shirt needed a spin dry, thought for a moment. 'Sounds more comfortable than this heap of shit.' Art pointed round the Arrivals Hall. 'Why not? I guess so. The big shots don't get to put their trotters in the trough till tomorrow night. If I'm right, that gives us over twenty-four hours.' Art made it sound like a long time, a sentiment which Gavin certainly did not share.

'We'll have to find out when *Ryme Lady*'s expected. Corbin's last info suggested she was still calling herself *Rio Massu*. Could be here tomorrow - if she's coming at all.'

Art nodded. 'The description fitted. All roads certainly don't lead to New York. Nor to the IRA. Yet only Corbin could smell the red herrings. The question is, who baited the hook?"

'As a lawyer I'm not guessing. I want facts. Maybe I'll get some in the morning. Corbin's fixed for me to meet Michel Mboro.'

'He agreed to see you? To talk about missing cargo?' Art's laugh was derisory. 'You won't see him. I'll bet you a bottle of bourbon to a coke.' They shook hands on the bet. 'Anyway, let's take a taxi straight to the prison.' He broke off as a beautiful young black woman in tribal costume walked past. Her back was straight, her cheek bones high-set, her eyes brown and sparkling. 'We may even have time for a bit of ... local pleasure.' The sap was rising.

'Forgotten your vow after New York already?' The chide brought a wink and a grin from Art but, before he could respond, they had reached the front of the queue. The official cursorily checked their passports but studied the visas with more care. No visa, no entry was the rule. Usually it took days, if not weeks, to satisfy the authorities but a call to the Foreign Office had enabled Corbin to get their passports stamped at the London Embassy within hours of their touchdown from New York.

After cursory customs formalities, they loaded their bags into a battered Citroen Pallas taxi. Once, it had been silver but over the years it had been patched and daubed with any colour which had been handy. One end of the bumper hung low and the exhaust pipe was held precariously by string and the ultimate wish to defy Newton's law of gravity. To Art's barked command 'Take me to the jail, buster', the driver merely shrugged in confusion. Gavin's french however soon had them heading away from the city.

At first the road was broad and made-up but after a mile it deteriorated to a pitted, rutted surface over which the car bumped and lurched its way. The outskirts of Dakalla were a shanty town, an endless horizon of corrugated iron, old packing cases and a generous dose of polythene. By the roadside there were children playing, chasing hoops made from old bicycle wheels, kicking plastic bottles, dodging the excreta left by roaming dogs, goats and sheep. The wrecks of abandoned cars lay rusting, homes to the homeless, playgrounds for the kids.

Typical of West Africa, their driver believed that he could steer without using his hands except for emergencies. Of these, there were plenty as he swerved and gesticulated through a succession of wandering goats, chickens and children.

'I hope he understood your french,' Art suggested doubtfully, pointing at the corrugated iron-clad shacks. 'You didn't say Timbuktoo, did you?'

'Just wait and see.' They did so in silence, clinging to the grab handles as the Citroen lurched its way through the corrugated jungle. When they'd gone about four miles from the airport, the slums ended and they were into real jungle, dank luxurious undergrowth prevailing. From the giant trees, thick with hanging creepers and foliage, came the screeches, shrieks and screams of all manner of animals, birds and insects. A monkey, sitting in the track, narrowly escaped death with a flying leap onto the verge.

'Jesus!' exclaimed Art as they rounded a particularly acute bend, passing through a deep rut as they did so. The taxi rocked as its chassis scraped the surface. 'I'm giving this two minutes. After that, we turn back.'

Both their unspoken thoughts were the same. Could the driver have misunderstood or was this some kind of set-up? 'How far?' queried Gavin in french.

'*Pas loin*,' came the reply and within a few seconds, Dakalla jail appeared. All the trees had been cleared from a huge area. The bounds of the prison were marked by a high fence made of tree trunks, their tips, sharpened to a point. Escape, if not impossible, was unlikely. The density of the jungle beyond the boundary was in itself a deterrent.

'Looks just like some old fort out in El Paso,' suggested Art. He was looking at the well-guarded gateway beside which the taxi had stopped.

Gavin nodded. 'Not the best place to stay too long.' They were standing by the taxi now and the stench of rotting undergrowth and the open sewage ditches filled the evening air. 'Leave the guards to me,' said Gavin as he went forward and rapidly explained their purpose. Under close escort they were permitted to enter but on foot only, the taxi driver being commanded to wait outside. From the prison gates to the Governor's block they were escorted by four guards, each of them armed and with a disdainful look which suggested that at the slightest sign of trouble their fingers would be only too ready to fire. The walk across the wide open space gave the visitors time to judge the area. It must have been four hundred yards at least in each direction, with single storey cell blocks running in lines behind the administrative headquarters. From some of the blocks came the noise of angry men, locked up for the night. The air was filled with the endless clatter of metal banging on metal and shouts of pent-up frustration.

'Reckon there's room for at least 3,000 prisoners here,' said Art. Judging by the noise in the background, there probably were. As they waited for the Prison Governor to appear, Gavin pointed out of the pre-fab window. There was a single stake, obviously recently used as the execution point for the firing squad. Just beyond it, four guards threw a corpse onto a lorry as if it were a sack of grain. Another man was sprinkling fresh sand over the blood at the foot of the stake. Gavin pursed his lips. 'Glad we weren't here when they did that.'

Art nodded. 'I've watched the electric chair at work. And the gas chamber.' He seemed unconcerned at the recollection as he looked out of the window again. 'Just so long as it wasn't one of the crew.'

The door at the back of the room opened and they were ushered in to see the Governor. An electric fan was doing its best to keep the temperature down. The official, covered in more gold braid than Harrods could sell in a year, sat behind his desk, playing with a sharply-pointed paper-knife. He made no attempt to stand up to greet them. On the wall behind him was a picture of the President of Lumbola and next to that a picture of the Minister of the Interior, Michel Mboro, the man in charge of the prison service.

'Speak english?' enquired Art in his nasal New York accent. Gavin suppressed a desire to chuckle.

'Yes,' the man beamed at them. 'That is my third language.' He spoke with precision in english, learned at Sandhurst Military Academy. His voice was deep and booming in the small room. 'And how can I help you?' The smile was disarmingly friendly yet the atmosphere somehow was not. On either side of him, his two muscular guards were each armed with a machine-gun. The Governor, who was aged about fifty-three, was wearing a military uniform, sandy in colour with gold epaulettes and cuffs, the image completed by a black belt over his highly charged stomach. 'You want to ask about the prisoners from *Cerne View*? Yes ... they are here.' He smiled. 'And alive ... at the moment.' The Governor mopped his brow in a Satchmo-type gesture whilst beads of perspiration continued to drip and gather in his incongruous goatee beard.

'They've done nothing wrong. They should be released,' said Art.

Gavin joined in. 'With Independence Day tomorrow, surely you can release innocent men. It's a bad start for the new State of Lupopo to have an outcry about injustice.' Gavin wondered if he had gone too far. He had no wish to join the crew in one of the stinking, hot cell blocks round the back.

'*You* say they are innocent. I have orders from the Minister. They will go to Court. Theft of cargo. Fraud. Etcetera. Etcetera. ' The Governor obviously enjoyed the latter word. 'Much paperwork.' As if to demonstrate the point the Governor waved a hand towards the files on his desk. 'Many, many statements etcetera.'

'Are you talking about the officers or the crew?'

'The Minister says all guilty till innocence proved. Of course,' he spread his hands in a gesture of open explanation, 'if the Captain confesses, then the others can go free. Often,' he smiled too cheerfully under the circumstances, 'my prisoners do confess. After a few weeks here. The flies and the dirt etcetera.'

'I've no doubt,' said Art with a singular lack of diplomacy. 'Well let me tell you. Mr Blair here is seeing the Minister, Mr Mboro, tomorrow morning.' The listener did not seem impressed, his smile just widening a fraction further, his big brown eyes still staring without blinking.

'If you have nothing further to add?' The Governor made it plain the interview was over. 'I have listened to your comments. I shall pass them on to the highest authority etcetera.'

'We would like to see the crew. Speak to them, etcetera.' Gavin couldn't resist the dig. The Governor failed to notice.

'No visitors. Not allowed.' The shrug of the shoulders

warned it was impossible. Art, for a moment, contemplated a bribe. His hand reached into his pocket but he decided
against it. The smiling bastard could use any pretext for
jailing them. Attempted bribery would give him the
excuse.

The Governor rose from behind his desk. He stretched to
his full height of 6', 7", towering over his two uniformed
guards. 'Thank you for visiting me,' he boomed. The smile
never wavered and the proferred handshake was full of
old fashioned courtesy. 'You are not the first to visit about
this crew.'

'Oh, who else was there?' enquired Gavin.

'Names ... I never remember.' It was obvious he had no
intention of telling them.

Seconds later the visitors were being all but frogmarched back to their taxi. 'Y'know that guy, he'd smile
even when he was telling you that your firing squad was
ready,' said Art

'Etcetera, etcetera.'

Their journey back through the densely-populated
slums was more sinister. Darkness had now fallen.
Makeshift lighting, gas lamps and the flicker from an occasional fire cast shadows between the bamboo fences and
corrugated iron huts. Through the car windows came the
smell of woodsmoke and hot rotting vegetation, mixed
with the cries of children in grubby T-shirts. Then they
were through all that, not a square inch of corrugated iron
in sight. Luxurious villas lined the streets, deep-set in high-
walled gardens with guards outside to keep the have-nots
at bay.

Moments later the Citroen stopped, more by willpower
than by its faded brakes, outside the Independence Hotel.
Twenty-one storeys tall, it dominated Independence
Square in the middle of which stood a statue of the
President on a patch of dying grass. Around the sides of the

square were illuminated advertisements and buildings evoking an atmosphere of a prosperous part of Paris, built in the late nineteenth century. The influence of the French architects and of the French colonisation was everywhere. Mainly the fine buildings were occupied by airlines, banks and designer shops. At the top end of the square stood the President's Palace, three floors of luxury, modelled on a French chateau, its gardens floodlit. By the wrought-iron gates were soldiers wearing bright yellow uniforms with black three cornered caps. Above the main portico flew the flag of the Republic.

'I'd rather drive blindfold round the Daytona Circuit than take another lift with that crazy asshole,' commented Art. They paid off the man and stood outside the hotel, taking in the scene.

'No worse than the rest.' Gavin was pointing at the tooting, zig-zagging throng swerving their way through the jams. Rush hour in Naples had nothing on this; Times Square was like the dark side of the moon in comparison. They stood absorbing their bearings in the sickly sweetness of the dusty air. Within seconds the first peddlar approached them offering watches, ivory pendants or Marlboro cigarettes.

'Heh man! Give me a break!' Art pushed the seller away. 'Time to go in.' They mounted the wide sweep of white steps and entered the cool, slightly scented foyer of the tower block. Everywhere was marble - even the walls from which hung tribal shields and spears. In a corner was the reception desk, lit by subdued and hidden lighting. The receptionist was a stunner, with doe-like eyes and a pale black skin. She was wearing a crisply-starched gown and a dark red scarf on her head. It was tied to make a form of head-dress. 'That's a mousor,' Gavin nodded at it as she checked them in. His knowledge had been picked up from the In-Flight Magazine.

Art nodded. 'Sure. I had a cat once. We called him Mousor.' Art cackled mightily and attracted a hostile glare from the cashier behind the desk.

Formalities completed, a young boy, all smiles, new uniform and curly black hair, took them to adjoining rooms on the 17th floor. The balconies had magnificent views across the square to the harbour and beyond that to the Atlantic Ocean.

Gavin flung his clothes into the fitted wardrobe before he joined Art next door. His suitcase was still untouched. Priorities, as Art would have said, as he sat reclining with his second beer. Gavin helped himself to a can from the fridge. Then, together they stood on the balcony, taking in the view. 'Interesting, not beautiful,' suggested Gavin.

'It ain't exactly San Francisco Bay.'

'Nor Sydney Harbour either,' agreed Gavin

Dakalla was a big city. Over 600,000 people owed their existence to the port. But for its calm waters, Dakalla would have remained a two-bit fishing village. Now the safe harbour and Independence Square with its Palace and ring of palm trees, was the centre of the modern city. Directly opposite and maybe three hundred yards away on the other side of the square, were the dock gates. Without comment, they watched the headlights of the disjointed line of vehicles filing out of the docks through Security where the simple task of raising and lowering the blue and white barrier kept at least a dozen officials apparently fully engaged. Within the perimeter fence, dockers, layabouts and would-be pilferers abounded. 'See all the containers stacked in there.' Art was pointing to an area inside the dock gates. 'Total confusion. Anything could happen.'

'Anything if there's a bribe.' Gavin was gazing at the bay. 'Which one's *Cerne View*?' They looked round the huge horseshoe of the harbour, the open sea at the far westerly end. On the southern side were the Palace grounds, the military compound and beyond that some shanties and stacks of kaolin. Most of the quays were to their right, on the northern side, with lines of jetties, all floodlit, some with cranes still working, all with trucks manoeuvring in and out of the fifteen or so ships.

'I'd say that's her,' said Art, pointing now to the nearest ship to them. The vessel, its outline clear in the darkness, matched the approximate shape and size but it wasn't that which had convinced him. 'We know she was shifted after arrest. I'd say that's her there. On her own. Right by the military compound.'

Gavin peered across the square to the Presidential Palace on his left. The magnificent white building, set in a luxurious garden, was well guarded. Beside it were the military headquarters, barracks and army vehicles filling the area between the Palace and the dockside. Close to the barracks were the fuel storage tanks, each of them standing twenty feet high. 'I think you're right,' replied Gavin. 'The silhouette looks just like *Cerne View*. Just beyond the fuel tanks. Let's take a look in the morning.' He turned to go inside. 'Another beer?'

Art declined. It was out of character but Gavin said nothing. 'We ought to be doing something, whaddya think?' Art waited expectantly.

Gavin raised his finger. 'Idea!' He nodded as he left the balcony to call Reception. When he returned, Art looked at him quizzically. 'Sir Archibald Crawford is in Room 1312. Alberto Forensi is not staying here. Klodinsky is due in about two hours. The only other international class hotel is the Tricoleur. Forensi must be there. Maybe we should check that out later.'

'Do we tell Sir Archie we're here?' enquired Art.

'We volunteer nothing. After all, officially we don't know he's here. He's supposed to be in Singapore. Keep'em all guessing.' Down below a police car appeared.

Its lights flashed and its sirens split the night as it forced its way through the traffic and stopped outside their hotel. Two policemen emerged and walked up the hotel steps. They came out less than a minute later, clutching the passports of all the guests who had registered that day. It was a new system introduced by Michel Mboro ten days before.

By 8.00 pm the Minister of the Interior knew not only that Art and Gavin had been to Dakalla jail but that they'd checked in at the Independence. The ice in Mboro's glass of brandy clinked as he swirled it round. In his hand was the report from the Prison Governor which he'd read through twice. He had to admit it. The Englishman's arguments were telling. The *image* of Lupopo. The crew locked in jail. TV cameras and journalists everywhere just waiting for a story, any story. Yes. Perhaps it was time for a gesture. He rang the Governor. 'No. The officers will not be released. Only the crew. Phone me in the morning for final details.'

He put down the phone, flipped open the passports of Blair and Lemman and had photocopies made. They'd be returned to the hotel later. 'They may be subversives,' he told his deputy.

'Shall we arrest them? Invent something?'

'No. Not yet. Circulate their photos. If there is any trouble with them, then I want to be told at once. Understood?'

'Of course. And your meeting tomorrow with Mr Blair?'

'Let's say I shall see how I feel in the morning.' Mboro grinned at his deputy.

Chapter 43

'I'll tell you what,' said Art. 'I'll go see Scrignac Lefebre's depot. We know the address.'

'Want me to come?' Gavin kicked himself for not thinking of this. His brain seemed to be paralysed with exhaustion.

Art shook his head. 'You go to Lloyds' agent. Could be an interesting evening. If he's still working. Ok?'

The road was good all the way. In the hired car, Art took no more than twenty minutes to reach the industrial zone. The estate was ridiculously huge, sprawling, designed to bring wealth to Lumbola. Plainly this was yet another of those schemes which had brought wealth to someone and bankruptcy to many. For the moment the place was almost derelict with most units still unlet. Those which were let seemed to be distribution warehouses. Almost all were shut for the night. The zone seemed deserted, black Africa's white elephant.

Slowly, seeking out the name of Scrignac Lefebre, Art drove up and down the criss-cross of streets. The whole area covered several hundred acres. Then at last he saw it. Tucked down a cul-de-sac was a white board bearing the name 'Scrignac Lefebre'. Fixed to a gate in a high security fence, the sign looked as if it had only been erected quite recently.

A single floodlight showed the solitary door to what looked like a warehouse. It was single storey, about twenty yards wide by about fifty, with no windows. There was no sign of a guard, but access was not easy. He parked and crossed the road to the gate. It was heavily padlocked and there was no sign of a bell. He rattled the gate. Maybe there was a night-watchman snoozing somewhere in the complex.

The result was immediate. A pair of alsatians, previously unseen in the shadows, crashed against the gates, barking furiously. He leapt back in fright as the animals continued to snarl, teeth bared, jaws slavering. Without hesitation and with hasty strides, he retreated to the car, ready for a swift escape. Surely someone must have heard the commotion? He sat in the car, waiting for someone to appear. He looked across at the building. Nothing. He got out of the car again and, walking silently, approached the gates. The dogs paced backwards and forwards, just the other side, snarling viciously. He shone his torch across at the warehouse door and saw the lock. First grade stuff. No problem.

With just a tinge of regret, he removed his cap with the Budweiser logo. It would be a sad but worthy end. Then, after rummaging in his pocket, he found what he was looking for. The gun was his prized possession. It was not IMB issue. Indeed, Corbin would have gone apeshit if he had known about it. It was no ordinary gun either. Purchased from a dealer in Hamburg, it was designed to pass through airport security. It looked as innocuous as any expensive gold pen. Expensive it was, innocuous it was not. Placed close to the victim's brain it was lethal. At Heathrow's metal detector and frisking it was never queried. To fire it was as simple as pressing the cap.

He flicked off the safety catch. 'Sorry old pal,' he muttered to his cap rather than to the slavering dogs as he poked the cap through the fence. Immediately the dogs scrabbled at the fencing, growling from deep in their throats. Then the first one sunk his teeth deep into the material and as Art tugged from beyond the fence, he had the perfect position he needed. The small retort, sharp and lethal felled the dog and, seconds later, he'd re-loaded and repeated the exercise with equal success. He looked round. Had anyone heard? Surely someone would come running? But no. Nothing. No one came. Good. He went over to his car and drove it up to the fence and parked right beside it. Then, using the bonnet and roof as stepping stones, he clambered over and jumped down the eight feet inside, hurrying across the baked earth yard to the building. The lock looked as easy as he'd hoped. He was about to apply his skills when, from within, he heard a noise - a slight creaking, the sound of almost imperceptible movement. He paused for a moment before turning the door-handle. It moved at once. It wasn't locked.

If it were unlocked and there was a noise from inside, something ... or someone was in there.

Chapter 44

Gavin was seated in an ancient, canvas and metal stacking-chair, sipping a cup of coffee in the office of Amadou Cayor, Lloyds' local shipping agent. The role of Lloyds' agents around the ports of the world is to provide an information and support service. Collectively, through these reports, Lloyds has more know-how on ships and their movements than any other single organization. It is not only indispensable to the insurers of ships and cargo but invaluable to owners and charterers alike.

Except for the technical equipment, Cayor's office was shabby and sparse. There were telephones, telex, fax, computers positioned on and around chipped metal desks and old filing cabinets which were barely functional. Cayor, himself a local, aged forty-six, was sitting on his desk speaking passable English. His western-style suit hung loosely on his tall, lean body and his jaw was lantern shaped, emphasizing that his tribal background was very different from that of the prison governor. The office, in a building close to the main dock gates, had a view from the fourth floor across the entire port. From outside came the heavy clanking of a dredger at work in the bay.

'Here's a fax that came for you this evening.' Cayor handed the document to Gavin who read it quickly. It was from Walter Corbin. 'Your mother could reach Basingstoke by midnight tomorrow.' To Cayor, or anyone else, the message was meaningless. To Gavin it meant that *Rio Massu* was expected to be able to reach Dakalla next day.

'Trouble?' enquired Cayor out of politeness. His face had a mournful look. His voice was soft and unchallenging.

'Maybe. What's that noise?'

'The dredger. Come to the window and I'll show you. We have a silt problem from the Sampopo River.' He rose to reveal his full six feet, though he looked more because of his slender body. Before going to the window he showed Gavin an aerial photo. 'You see. That's Lumbola. There's Dakalla. That's Sampopo to the left. That's south. There's the harbour, facing east, where we are now. Dividing us from Sampopo is the river which runs into the sea just here.' He pointed to the harbour mouth. 'That's where it dumps all its silt. So the dredger has to work day and night.'

He pointed a long black finger to a point on the river, just behind the Presidential Palace. 'This photo was taken several years ago. Then, the only way between our two countries was by this ferry. Now, at this point, there's a new bridge. The official opening is on Sunday.'

'And Lupopo? The combined country? Will it work?'

'Mainly we are the same tribe. That will be important.' He faltered, wondering whether to comment further. 'Not everyone is happy. Here, we have been tolerant in religion. As a French colony for so long, there are many Roman Catholics but there are also Moslems. Now, just like in Iran and North Africa, we have troubles here with fundamentalism.'

'If you don't mind me saying so, you speak amazing English.'

'I spent time in England, at Lloyds' office in Colchester. I was educated in Paris ... and now ... this.' Plainly he wasn't enamoured with the power, the glory and the trappings of being Lloyds' man in Dakalla. His laugh was sardonic.

'So what happened to the cargo from *Cerne View*?'

'I don't know.' He spoke cautiously. ' Most likely, the containers were emptied after leaving the docks and before reaching their destination. That's assuming the goods really were pilfered somewhere.' His restless eyes suggested uncertainty. It was as if he were scared of being overheard.

'Not from the ship?'

'No.' He was emphatic. 'Not on the voyage.' He shook his head. 'Unlikely to lose two containers, even from these docks.' He wagged his finger forcefully. 'Unlikely they were stripped out either.' He paused. 'Don't say I said that,' he added quickly with a furtive glance over his shoulder. The reasons for his unease were evident to him more than to Gavin.

'And Mboro? Where does he fit in? Isn't he involved with Scrignac Lefebre?' Gavin watched the African for his reaction and wasn't disappointed. Cayor became agitated, his hands and arms seemed more gangling, his eyes furtive and watchful. He started to pick his words even more carefully.

'Mboro is a politician. Who knows what he thinks or what he does. Who knows whether what he thinks, what he says and what he does are the same?' As Gavin was thinking just what a philosopher Cayor was, the agent continued. 'Yes. He is powerful.' There was more than respect in his voice. There was fear too. 'Before Mboro was Minister, Scrignac Lefebre was his business. Now, officially it is run by his brother. The truth is,' he shrugged suggesting it was the way of the world, 'nothing has changed.'

Gavin laughed. 'What does it import usually?'

'Depends. With Mboro's influence, it supplied the Government with everything from office equipment to carpets and soft furnishings. But never computer equipment or anything valuable like what they *say* has been stolen.' Again there was a sardonic laugh, and a half-glance over the shoulder as if he expected to be jack-booted to oblivion..

'I understand. But *Cerne View*? Are ships normally arrested here? Bloodshed ... and then quarantined?'

'No. This was no ordinary arrest. Even here, bloodshed is not every day. Yes, it does happen as a rarity. Usually it's just an arrest and years of legal argument.' He scratched the tight curls on his head. 'I can't remember when an arrested vessel was treated quite like this.' Needlessly he adjusted the soft collar of his flannelette shirt.

'Does that surprise you?'

'No.' It was barely a whisper. 'Not if you screw Michel Mboro.' To Gavin it seemed strange to hear this black man with a French accent coming out with up-to-date international slang. 'He can act or over-react as he wants.'

'What about the cargo? What have you got on that?'

'Wait a moment.' He crossed the bare floor from the window and removed a slim folder from the filing cabinet. 'Scrignac Lefebre were due to receive computers. They were to be used on a government contract for controlling a hydro-electric scheme. Take a look.' He handed the papers to Gavin who flicked through them. There was nothing new. Just confirmation that they'd been put aboard at Marseille and that the ship's master had signed for the goods.

'*Cerne View* was due to go to Port Harcourt.' Gavin flipped over a page and read the details. 'A real mixed cargo.' He started to read out from the manifest. 'Bulk ammonium nitrate fertilizer, knocked down engines, tyres and paint. 250 drums of high viscosity engine oil. Steel tubing. General mixed cargo in the other containers.'

'Well it won't be reaching Port Harcourt. Not for a while. Not without this.' Cayor rubbed his fingers together, suggesting considerable quantities of cash having to change hands. 'You wanted to know about shipping movements?' He produced another sheet of paper and handed it to Gavin, who read the long list without comment. There it was. '*Rio Massu*. ETA Dakalla 11.00 pm. Saturday. 9,800 tonnes. Mixed cargo. Bunkering required. Ex Naples. Next destination Port Harcourt. Berth 17.' He nodded thoughtfully. The weight was similar to *Ryme Lady*.

'Thanks. By the way, do you recognise any of these people.' From his file, Gavin pulled out photos of Carl Klodinsky, Sir Archie and Alberto Forensi.

'No. Should I?'

'Just a thought. Thanks again.' Odd though, Gavin concluded, that neither Sir Archie nor Forensi had visited Lloyds' agent. Surely that was the obvious place to make enquiries.

Odd, but inconclusive.

An unlocked door. Art could not believe his luck. But was there someone inside? Since he turned the handle the slightest hint of movement had ceased. He pulled back one of the two sliding doors, either of which would have admitted a small pick-up, opening it just enough to slip through into the darkness. Then he closed the door behind him. Was someone in there? If so, they were keeping very still now. Not a sight, not a sound. The place felt cavernous, decidedly empty. Yet someone had been moving. He checked his gun again. Surely there was a light switch somewhere. He took a fumbling step and then a second one. The blackness was intense, the air stale.

'Ah!' He gasped as something struck his shoulder, causing him instinctively to duck. Startled, he jumped back only to be struck again, a heavy, solid impact. Who the hell? What the hell? The only sound was a general creaking from somewhere above him. He ran his hand along the wall. Thank God! He felt the familiar shape of a switch and flicked it on and turned round.

He gasped.

There, right beside him, his face blue and contorted, was the hanging body of Alberto Forensi, his Italian shoes

334

swaying just inches above the concrete floor. His tongue was lolling from between his lips, his eyes bulging. Still in his best suit, the body was swinging gently on a rope suspended from a steel girder.

Otherwise the warehouse was empty.

Chapter 45

Saturday morning was the start of Lumbola's official holiday. Crowds started building up in the square early, not long after the sun rose sharply to turn the African night into shimmering, dazzling daylight. After breakfasting on coffee and tropical fruit, Gavin and Art, both in casual lightweight clothing and sunglasses, joined the excited throng of locals. Art's first task was to replace his beloved cap. From a street-vendor he picked up a blue one advertising Labatt's. Adjusting it to a jaunty angle, high over his forehead, he walked through the crowd with a screw-you look on his face. Here and there were early tourists. 'So we just leave Alberto Forensi. Say nothing?' Gavin was debating the decision taken the night before.

'Why not,' Art chuckled. 'He's having a swinging time, way beyond the pain-barrier. There's no choice anyway. Hell! I shot two of Mboro's pet pooches, broke into Scrignac Lefebre's premises.' He turned to Gavin, arms outstretched, palms upturned in an exaggerated pose. 'So after that you want me to tell the cops what I saw?' He laughed at the absurdity. 'Look. Change the subject to this. Forensi was an old man. Don't you think he was kinda active if he no longer controlled Pinetto?'

Gavin was quick to agree. 'Obviously thought it worth coming out here. Maybe he was protective of Pinetto's *reputation*.'

'And this guy, Gonfleur?'

'He's not checked in at our hotel or the Tricoleur. If he's staying anywhere else, then he's fallen on hard times and doesn't mind sharing his bed with cockroaches. I don't think he's here.'

'If he's bent, then maybe he wants to keep well out of it.' Art pushed aside yet another beggar who had grasped his leg and was pointing hungrily to his mouth. 'Pity Mboro cancelled his meeting with you but I win my bet.'

'I should never have taken you on. His aide told me Mboro had a touch of flu. Diplomatic, no doubt.'

'He'll make it to the banquet tonight, you bet.' They were close to the Palace now. Entire families, with huge wicker baskets filled with provisions, were jostling for the best views, some sitting, some standing, all shouting and many chewing bamboo. The women had particularly fine features with high cheekbones, large, brown eyes and smooth skin. On their heads most wore multi-coloured scarves, from their ears hung extravagantly large rings and, round their necks, were beads in red, green, white, black and yellow. On their backs many carried the youngest child of the family. The noise was deafening, a blend of tears and laughter, of excited shouts of recognition amid a flurry of waving arms and flashing eyes.

As Gavin and Art stood close to the barricade they were able to look across the cleared area to the wrought-iron gates at either side of the drive which swept round in front of the Palace. At each gate were armed guards in sentry boxes and behind them the driveway was lined with trees and colourful shrubs. The main door into the Palace was set in a porch from which hung a large and elegant chandelier. All the streets to the left of the Palace had now been cordonned off and the diagram on the front page of the morning paper had shown that the guests in their limousines would pass through the main gate, be dropped off and the chauffeurs would then exit left into the parking lot. In the garden to the side and to the rear of the Palace by the military compound, was a magnificent marquee out of sight of the onlookers.

Art looked at his watch. 'OK. Let's split here. You go

round to Cayor. See if there's any update. I'll take a look at *Cerne View*.' So saying, Art left the square and strolled casually the few yards to the dock gates which he passed through without anyone checking his identity, despite the official notices declaring that entry was banned except for those on official business. No one seemed to care.

Other than his cap, he was dressed in only a blue short-sleeved shirt and slacks, yet every pace was an effort in the relentless pounding heat. Though it was not yet 10 am, he judged the temperature to be in the low thirties. Sweat was gathering round the back of his ears and trickling uncomfortably round his neck, soaking his shirt.

As he looked round the huge half-moon bay, the water was a mix of shimmering blue-green and oily waste-ridden brown. The ships, dimly seen the night before, had become personalities, each with its own colours, shape, styling and age. All around, the dockers were busy, crane jibs swinging, their loads rising or falling, containers being lifted or lowered, stacked and re-stacked. In the distance, at the phosphate dock, the air was thick white, rising to blend into the endless blue of the horizon.

Art turned along the quayside. Beside him, to his left, was the fifteen-foot wall of the Presidential Palace, guarded by remote-controlled TV cameras. Now he could see the top of the marquee, its pink and white stripes clearly visible above the wall, close to the end of the army HQ. The whirr of air-conditioning units, fighting a relentless battle, could be heard but not seen beyond the walls.

To his right and ahead of him was *Cerne View*, her black bow rising from the water. From the quay to the deck stretched the ropes and hawsers, mooring the ship in position. On the for'ard deck he could just see the tops of the hatches. Towards the stern, the containers were stacked three high from mid-ships to the fo'c'sle.

For a moment Art relived the moment when Lumbolan

soldiers had stormed the gangplank. He could imagine Captain Walker and his crew being frogmarched off to the stinking jail. Except for the radio officer. Just another death, a wasted life. And all for what? He lit a cigarette. If lives were cheap, then the stakes were high. It had to be money or power. Probably both.

Art looked down at the oily scum and litter on the surface and then at the twenty-foot chain-link fence which confronted him. Further progress round the quay was impossible. *Cerne View* was unreachable, moored within the perimeter of the military compound. At the foot of the gangplank, about 80 yards away and smoking a cigarette, was an armed guard. He gave a casual, dismissive glance at Art who continued his appraisal of Lumbola's military headquarters. Beside the fuel storage tanks were the army vehicles - three tonners, armoured cars, trailers, a couple of M.48 tanks and an M.60. There were some howitzers and mortars, relics of a bygone war. Beyond all that were about one hundred and fifty raw recruits being given drill on the tiny 'parade ground', their arms and legs swinging hopelessly out of time.

He looked the ship up and down. The water was lapping only just below the Plimsoll line, confirming that she was still heavily laden. Getting aboard *Cerne View* wasn't going to be easy. From on board he could hear noises but could see no activity. Hoping for inspiration, he leaned against the mesh-fence, looking at the vessel, thinking about its details recorded at Lloyds. 20,000 tons dead weight, made in Germany with cross bunker fuel storage and the remainder of the diesel and fuel oil in the double-bottomed tanks below the cargo hold. If the ship's papers were correct, then both holds and containers were carrying a mixed cargo which had required careful attention during loading at Marseilles, particularly in the storage of the ammonium nitrate.

A movement caught his attention. Coming across the compound were two soldiers in floppy khaki bush-hats, each armed with a machine-gun. Knowing that he was doing no wrong, he ignored them until they were standing two yards from him, separated only by the fencing. Only then did he give them a nod of acknowledgement. The response was a grunt and a swing of the guns, motioning him to clear off. Art shrugged his shoulders, eased his cap until the peak pointed to the heavens and was about to turn away when he saw two swarthy looking men descend the gangplank. Behind them was a soldier with a gun.

The men, both white with tousled dark hair, looked European. Ignoring the further jabbing motion of the machine guns, he carried on looking. As one of the men glanced in his direction, Art recognised the man's face. It was a crewman from *Cerne View*, whose photo was one of many in the Bureau's dossier. Odd. Very. Should've been in prison.

Gavin knew as soon as he entered Cayor's office that something was wrong. The man's smile was friendly enough but there was a furtiveness as he rose to greet him. The eyes seemed to avoid Gavin's, the lips were licked. Overhead the central fan swished relentlessly. From outside came all the noise of a major port.

'Good morning,' said Cayor. 'I hope you slept well.' Even as he muttered just these bland greetings, Gavin sensed that Cayor had something more significant to say ... or perhaps to conceal.

'Beautiful day, spoiled only by Mr Mboro getting flu and being unable to see me.'

Cayor shrugged non-committally. 'It happens. Are you meeting his deputy?'

'It wasn't offered and, even if it were, I wouldn't have accepted. I need to see Mboro himself. Anyway, I don't want to keep you long.' He accepted Cayor's pointed invitation to the same uncomfortable metal-backed chair. ' Thanks. I just want to confirm shipping movements today. Any change in what you told me yesterday?'

Cayor picked up a dog-eared sheet of paper. He glanced at it briefly and then shook his head. 'No. Just the same. Take a look.' Gavin glanced at the information and asked questions about several ships due to dock, including the one known as *Rio Massu*, for which Berth 17 had been earmarked. He wasn't going to tell Cayor of his interest in any particular vessel.

'Coffee?' enquired the agent. Gavin accepted and Cayor made him a cup of instant whilst Gavin moved to the window to gaze across the docks towards the harbour mouth. *Rio Massu* would come through there tonight, laden with ... goodness knows what. And for why? To his right, he could see Berth 17, empty and awaiting the ship. A shiver of nervous anticipation ran through him. Could it really be? Was he going to come face to face with *Ryme Lady*, see Scutar and crew? Cayor handed him a mug decorated with a chipped picture of General de Gaulle whilst Gavin helped himself to a savoury biscuit of evil appearance and even worse taste.

So why was Cayor so defensive? 'Is a pilot essential for docking here?'

Cayor shook his head. ' You can see that today we have eight ships leaving and fourteen arrivals. Of the arrivals, six will have dropped anchor in the outer-roads to wait for a pilot. We take vessels up to 40,000 tons here. The smaller vessels can dock on their own.'

Gavin nearly named *Rio Massu* but decided to avoid it. By Dakalla standards, it was small. 'So what about *Cerne View*?'

'Yes, that had a pilot. But anything less than 10,000 tons would normally make its own way to its berth.' Cayor rose from his chair. 'Let's drink our coffee on the balcony. Take a look at the harbour in daylight.' He led Gavin outside. The balcony was supported by rusting wrought-ironwork. It was so decayed that Gavin could feel the vibrations and could see the metal flakes falling below them as they moved. With a thirty foot drop, Gavin's face showed his apprehension. 'Is this safe?'

Cayor laughed. 'It'll last another hundred years. Well, five minutes anyway.' They looked across the roofs of warehouses and container stacks and took in the two chain and bucket dredgers which were noisily sifting the silt brought down by the surging torrent of the Sampopo River. 'You get used to this,' Cayor shouted. 'Without them, we'd never get ships like that into here.' He pointed to a supertanker which was nosing its way towards a distant berth.

Their vantage point was perfect for looking at *Cerne View*, moored to the left, splendidly isolated from the bustle of the harbour. Berth 17, to their right , was a mere 850 yards of stinking, scummy water away. The giant horseshoe of water was full of movement. Fishing boats, ferries, dredgers, a pilot cutter, an incoming passenger ferry and a large container vessel were all manoeuvring, to-ing and fro-ing about their routine business.

'You heard that the crew of *Cerne View* were released?' Cayor relished the chance to break the news. 'Not the officers though. It happened this morning.'

'Interesting. Even if it wasn't down to me, I'll take the credit.' They both laughed, the African's lantern jaw moving up and down rapidly as he did so. 'Do you know what's happened to them?' He seemed more relaxed than earlier, yet he still seemed brittle enough to fragment at any time.

'No.' Cayor was emphatic.

'Maybe they'll sign up with another ship.' Gavin felt they were just going through the motions of a conversation and that Cayor still had something else to say. 'Well, I must be moving on,' he prompted.

'Fine.' They turned in from the balcony and Cayor went over to his desk. 'Oh yes, I meant to give you this last night but forgot.' He thrust a fax in Gavin's direction. 'I gave you one but forgot the other. This one came in first. I hope it wasn't urgent. Sorry.'

Gavin's brow furrowed as he read the message from Walter Corbin. 'Bird flew this morning from Surrey nest. May sing like a canary. Beware.' Momentarily punch-drunk, Gavin folded the message and tucked it in his pocket. His eyes glazed over, his heart raced. In his pockets his palms were damp, indeed suddenly he felt clammy all over.

'I'm sorry. I just forgot.' Cayor's voice, penitent and velvet-soft, pulled Gavin out of the trance.

'No,' Gavin replied. 'It was important but not urgent. If there's anything else, be sure and tell me. Leave a message at the hotel. Not the details. Just ask me to get in touch.' They shook hands and Gavin descended the stone staircase, hands in the pockets of his chinos, head down. So what the hell was Claudine up to? Damn her! She must have left just after him. Slipped her police guard. Got away before Corbin had moved her to somewhere more secure. Had he really got her wrong? Where the hell had she gone? Why had she let him down? He angrily kicked a tin can and watched with satisfaction as it tumbled over the edge of the quay into the water.

He seated himself on a bollard. Had Cayor deliberately withheld the fax? Or had it been a genuine error? The man had seemed honest enough but then this was West Africa. Sometimes even the best of people had to do what they were told ... depending on who told them.

Chapter 46

L'Hotel Belle Marie at Dakalla was known to sex-starved
sailors from Hong Kong to Hamburg. Just a short walk
from the harbour, it was well-positioned down a narrow
back street where the dusty air was filled with the smell of
fish. The two-storey building dating back to the late nineteenth century had faded red shutters and what had once
been a white wall. Now it was grubby and covered in graffiti. The second 'l' in 'Belle' had dropped off, probably
countless years before.

Art was leaning against the bonnet of a dusty grey
Renault which was parked just opposite. It was to here that
the two sailors had led him, disappearing inside before he
had a chance to reach them in a breathless run from the military fence, through the docks and back to the main
entrance to the compound. There, he had been just in time
to see the men head for the town centre before turning
down a side street and into the brothel. Hot and panting,
Art had arrived just too late to catch them.

He'd decided to wait outside, expecting them to come
out within half an hour.

He looked at his watch yet again. It was more than an
hour. Hell, they must be having quite a party in there. A
movement caught his eye as the red door opened. His
hopes rose only to be dashed when he saw that it was a
black American Marine. Art wandered across. 'Hi pal!
Worth a few bucks in there?'

'Man, are they hot, or are they hot!' He punched his arm
in the air in triumph. 'Wow ... ee!'

'Is it busy?'

'No. There's plenty of ass. Big chicks, small ones and

man, they're just ready to fly.' He beckoned back towards
the door with his thumb. 'There's a bar. Go on in. See for
yourself. Man, it's some of the greatest pussy this side of
Thailand.'

There was a bar in there! Fine! Art had found out what he
wanted to know. 'Sounds great. Take care now.' Art
pushed his way through the door and into the dimly-lit bar
which was lined with grubby chairs and formica-topped
tables. Instantly he was approached by four gaudy young
women, each seductively dressed, each covering the smell
of stale sweat with cheap scent. Propped against the bar
was a customer who had fallen asleep from a surfeit of sex
or alcohol or perhaps both. Of the two sailors from *Cerne
View* there was not a sign. At the back of the bar was a staircase leading to the bedrooms. He'd just have to sit it out.

The first girl to reach him was wearing a flimsy red
blouse and slit skirt which revealed her ebony legs to the
top of her thigh. 'You American? My name Mu-Mu. You
like? 100 Kuru. For 100 Kuru I make very fee-eelthy
knocky-knocky.' She knew the international language of
her trade and spoke in broken English. Her lips pouted like
a carp's and she gyrated her hips in a lazy grind. Then she
pushed the other three girls away and hustled him onto a
vermin-infested bench-seat, quickly positioning herself
beside him, legs crossed and skirt falling away.

'I'm Art.' He turned to one of the other girls who was still
hovering expectantly. 'I want a beer.' He turned to Mu-Mu
and pointed at his watch. 'I'm meeting two friends here.
They arrived over an hour ago.'

Mu-Mu shook her head. 'Two men. Yes.' She raised her
eyes towards the ceiling where a single bare bulb was suspended and swaying. 'They having good knocky-knocky.
You want me? You like?' She turned to face him, placing
one arm round his neck whilst thrusting her ample breasts
against him. Then she pulled his hand into the slit of her

skirt so that he could feel the smooth skin, surprising cool, between her thighs. Hell! He looked at her more closely and felt the urge to take her upstairs. For 100 Kuru! It was a gift! Cheaper than Coca Cola. He smiled lecherously at her and gave her a wink. Wait one! Hold it Art! Not now! You'll miss the sailors. For a second he pushed his hands further between Mu-Mu's thighs and surprised himself to find his fingers entangled in a bush of hair. She smiled appreciatively but then frowned as he pulled back.

Art guessed that she was about seventeen but the hardness round her eyes made her look older. The smell of her cheap perfume was almost overwhelming and there was a sad gentleness in her face which he found appealing. From his pocket, he produced a 100 Kuru note. 'That's for you if you behave yourself,' he said very matter-of-fact.

She leaned forward and planted a heavy kiss four-square on his cheek and started to pull him towards the stairs. 'Big sucking,' she grinned. 'Fun time.'

'Sit down,' he commanded and was rewarded with a sulky frown. 'Do what you're told. My friends: will they be long now?' He tapped his watch and pointed to the flimsy ceiling which still seemed to be trembling to the movements upstairs.

'Soon. Now we go upstairs. You like my friend too? For 150 Kuru we both make fee-eelthy time. You like? Yes, you like.' She answered her own observation and looked disappointed as Art ignored her and stared at the bar.

'My beer. Where's my beer?' He shouted across the bar and saw the African version of a scurry of movement. A tart started to amble across with a glass and a bottle dripping with condensation. He resumed stroking the side of Mu-Mu's thigh. 'You know these men? The ones upstairs?'

She didn't respond but Art wasn't sure whether it was because she didn't understand or had just turned sullen.

The tart and beer arrived. Sloppily, she poured, some into the glass, much onto the table.

Such was his thirst that he drank half without stopping. Mu-Mu chatted, babbling away in broken English. He ignored her because from upstairs came the sound of footsteps. The two men appeared, both aged around thirty, walking slowly down the stairs. Each of them looked knackered and shabby, hair glistening with sweat but judging by their sickly grins, they were both well-satisfied. One was wearing a dirty pink shirt, faded jeans and sneakers whilst the other was in a singlet and linen shorts. Neither was tall and both were chubby, bloated with laziness, their eyes nearly lost behind tired lids, their faces unshaven. As they approached him, he could smell their odour of spent passion.

They seated themselves at the next table. Art leant across at once. 'You'd like beers?' Though the men looked surprised, they both accepted and Art slid himself off his seat and sat himself on a plain wooden chair at their scuffed and dirty table with its battered tin ashtray. 'I'm Art.' He produced his IMB card. 'I've been sent here by the owners of *Cerne View* to get you released. Last night I spoke to the Governor. Obviously it worked.'

Of the two men, Kazim and Spiro, Spiro was the spokesman. 'We hear this morning. Big surprise.' Spiro's English was thick with his Greek accent making the word *big* sound very 'beeg' indeed. His face was a picture of contentment. After days of imprisonment, suddenly there was freedom, a few beers and some relaxation at the Belle Marie.

'Who are you?' Kazim joined Spiro in nodding questioningly. The IMB appeared to have meant nothing to either of them.

Patiently, and picking his words slowly, Art told them about the disappearance of *Ryme Lady* and the owners' con-

cern about the arrest of *Cerne View.* 'More beer.' He shouted the order across to a girl who was filing her nails by the
bar. 'Now I want a few questions answered. Was there anything unusual about the voyage to Dakalla? Any kind of
trouble?'

'No. Work in engine room. Ok. Both of us. Then in port.
Ok. Then soldiers everywhere. Guns. Beeg truck. Then jail.
Then free.' Spiro spread his hands indicating the moment
of release. As he did so, Art noticed that the hands, dark-
skinned and rough from years toiling with engines, had a
yellowish fluorescent tinge. Art glanced at Kazim's hands
which were clenched round his glass of beer. They were the
same.

'Hold it! Hold it! Not so fast. What were you doing on the
ship?'

'Thees morning. At seex,' he tapped his watch, 'guard,
he tell us, go to shee-eep. Do work. Puneeshment. Then
free.'

'All of you?' Art could feel a mounting excitement, a
sense that he was making progress, even though the direction was uncertain.

Spiro shook his head. 'No ... me ... and heem.'

'So what were you doing?' Art's voice showed his impatience at the pedantic pace. Nothing was being volunteered, yet nothing was being held back. 'Mu-Mu, bring
some red wine.' He patted her on the firm left cheek of her
bottom as she wiggled her way across the bare wooden
floor, her flip-flop sandals stirring the dust as she went. At
a distance, the lines on her face mellowed and she looked
like a waif.

'Painting.'

'Painting?' Art sounded puzzled but pointed at the yel-
lowy tinge of their hands and the two Greeks nodded.

'Paint containers. Hurry, hurry. Queek, queek.' Spiro
grinned as he relayed the instructions. His bushy eyebrows

arched and his face showed the stupidity of painting containers on an arrested ship. He shrugged, splayed his hands apart in a gesture at the futility. Kazim roared with laughter at all the nonsense.

Mu-Mu returned, brushing between them and placed the pitcher of red wine and three glasses on the table. 'Sounds crazy,' commented Art.'

'Crazy, yes.' Kazim's laugh was infectious. 'Fucking crazy!' Art could imagine this zany character back in Athens dancing wildly to the bouzuki and smashing a few plates on a Saturday night. Mu-Mu poured the wine whilst Art produced a paper and pen from his pocket and rapidly drew a picture of *Cerne View*, with its containers stacked on the deck.

'Did you paint all the containers?'

'No. ' Spiro took the pen and etched in a group of containers in the centre. 'These ones.'

'Do you know what was in them? Why those containers?'

'Not know. Capteen Walker. May-bee he know.'

Art frowned, debating what to do. Then he pulled 300 Kuru from his pocket, giving each of the men 100 and the last note to Mu-Mu. 'You come now,' she purred, pushing her breasts forward and standing, legs apart, between him and the door.

'Another time, sweetheart. Look after my friends.' He stood up, nodded goodbye and left. Outside, the temperature was still rising, the atmosphere full of hot dust and acrid blue diesel fumes from a passing bus with clapped-out piston rings. The smell of fish lingered. Even so, he took in gulps of air, welcome after the sleaze inside.

Gavin edged his way through the throng of shouting, chanting, hand-waving Africans - men, women and children gathering in the hope of a glimpse of the world leaders. The temperature was nudging thirty-five degrees and the crowd's mounting excitement had risen with it.

As he fought to make progress through Independence Square he wanted to shout: let me pass. I'm only trying to help! True. But over what? How? About what? Well about something ... er ... nasty ... er ... something to do with ships disappearing and re-appearing under new names; something to do with cargo vanishing and entire crews disappearing or being jailed. God! It was pretty woolly stuff. Only the death threat was real enough - just as stark as when he'd first read it back in Paris.

Hot and dishevelled, he felt a touch less irritable once the first blast of the air-conditioning reached him. It was a relief to be in the hushed atmosphere compared with the babble outside. The cleanliness of the lobby was almost indecent after the filth of old chicken bones, fast-food wrappers and discarded plastic bottles. From the overhead fan, the swish was the only sound in the marble-lined lobby. On all sides the luxurious tropical plants, some over twenty feet high, broke up the wide-open space, adding to the ambiance for those guests who were sprawling in armchairs or sitting at the bar enjoying a pre-lunch cocktail.

Looking forward to a shower and wondering how Art had got on, Gavin went up in the elevator and walked down the lime-green corridor towards his room. He was just about to insert a key when he heard a noise from inside. Puzzled, he checked the number. Yes. This was his. The cleaner? No. Not with the door shut. Not with no service trolley outside.

He pressed his ear to the door. Had he been mistaken? He hadn't. From inside came a noise, came the sound of movement. Someone was searching his room? Worse still, someone was planting an explosive device? Images of Barons Court filled his mind. He stood uncertainly, wishing that Art were here. God! Maybe there was more than one person in there. Ok. Go get some help! Go tell the police! The police! You must be joking! In Dakalla? If you distrust Mboro ... no way! Then ... wait for whoever it was to come out? Time was precious. How long could he wait? He was due to meet Art.

A brief smile crossed his face. His knife ... bought at Art's suggestion that morning. 'You might need this,' he'd said as they stood in the colourful market. Gavin pulled the knife from its sheath, appreciating the glint of its five inches as he clenched the carved wooden handle in a tight grip. Slowly, with great deliberation, his hand clammy, he turned the key until he was able to push open the door a fraction at a time. Then he looked into the short passage which led into the bedroom and, ultimately, to the bathroom. Straight ahead was the window looking out onto the harbour.

Not a sign. Empty. Ok. Full steam ahead. Except ... the noise was louder now but still hard to define. Knife at the ready, he took two paces into the room, his Reeboks silent on the thick carpeting. He stood for a moment, straining to hear, fighting to interpret the sound of movement. Though part of the bedroom was out of sight, he was sure that the intruder must be in the bathroom. That was also where the wall-safe was fitted. In there were his papers - at least those papers he hadn't left scattered round the room.

Another pace took him into the bedroom and a quick glance confirmed it was empty. Silently he took the few paces to the bathroom and with his knife at the ready he kicked open the door.

Claudine, naked and bent forward while drying her legs, straightened and screamed at the same time at the suddenness of the intrusion, her mouth wide open in terror, her eyes wild with fear. This was Wickham re-lived. Only different. Not till she realized who it was did the scream die as Gavin, looking equally startled, stood just a

351

few feet from her. The pumping blood vessels on his fore-head revealed his stress. The muscles in his face were taut, his adrenalin system on full power. Even after recognition, his voice gave away the jangled nerves. 'What the hell are you doing here?' Each word was punctuated by over-long pauses. He dropped the knife, took a step forward and grasped Claudine on each shoulder as she clasped a towel loosely by her side. He shook her angrily. 'Just what the hell are you doing here?' His tone was almost manic. 'How did you get in? Why did you come? God! Haven't you caused me enough trouble?' His tone changed to despair.

'Gavin!' Her eyes pleaded for release. 'Stop it! Stop.' Her french accent was pronounced as he continued to shake her. Her eyes were panic-stricken at his frenzy. 'Let me go! Let me go, please.'

Still fired up, it was a moment or two before Gavin released her. Then he took a pace back, standing rather sheepishly as the fury subsided. She smiled at him, a watery, imploring look. Gavin was immune to it, his face grim. He stepped round her open suitcase, went through to the bedroom and closed the door into the corridor.

She heard his deep long sigh and then a groan of resig-nation as, unseen by her, he slumped onto the bed, drained of energy, his adrenalin spent. As he sat, head in hands, he sensed rather than saw her approach. All he could think of was the dressing down by Corbin at the Penta. Memories of it flooded back, the blunt warning, his own bland assur-ances that Claudine would behave because he *trusted* her.

His instinct then had told him that the Director had got it wrong. Now ... he wasn't so sure. Had she been through his things? Had she been studying his papers? Passed on infor-mation to Klodinsky? Slowly he looked up and saw the imploring look in her eyes and he felt ashamed at his out-burst of anger, guilty at having doubts about her. Such was her power over him that she had only to smile, to lower her eyelids in a demure and crestfallen manner, for him to melt.

'Why, Claudine? Just explain why.' His tone was gentle, his voice soft, the words spoken with slow deliberation. 'Don't you realize what Walter Corbin must be saying?'

'I don't care. He doesn't own me. I wasn't a prisoner.' Her tone was resentful and the creasing round her mouth showed her petulance. She was still quivering as he put his arm round her. 'I wanted to be with you. Is that so bad?' She eased herself closer to him on the bed, the towel replaced now by a luxuriously thick bathrobe. 'Don't you see, Gavin, I think I can help.'

'You mean you've been holding something back?' Gavin eyed her suspiciously but saw the fierce denial.

'No. The star signs. Or have you forgotten all about what I was doing. I've been working on it. I thought you'd want to know.' She looked at him doubtfully. 'I thought it was important. I thought it was something we could share.'

He hesitated as a lump appeared in his throat. As she smiled he felt weak, hating himself for his distrust. He tightened his grip round her shoulder and pulled her even closer. 'You could have phoned the Bureau instead of doing a bunk. So what are you trying to tell me?'

'I've done the Sun, the Moon, the Planets, the Rising Signs, the Houses from First to Twelfth. I'm still working on the Chinese horoscope.'

'If you hadn't finished, then why bother to come?' Gavin knew it sounded gruff and for a moment was tempted to add something softer but he refrained.

'Because I'm worried. Everyone is acting out their part just as they should according to their horoscope. Everyone, that is, except for Edward.'

'Is all this going to get us anywhere? Time's running out on me.'

'Just listen.' She twisted her slender body round to confront him, her face cross, her eyes narrowed. 'Just listen, will you. Tell me who this is. 'Jovial, outgoing, loves outdoors, sport, is spontaneous, warm and friendly and chases the opposite sex.' '

Gavin thought only briefly. 'Sir Archie.'

'Precisely. Sagittarius. 6th December.' She shook her head in puzzlement. 'That's what I don't understand. Edward is also Sagittarius. 27th November. Yet he's not a bit like a Sagittarian. Tell me who this is. 'A perfectionist, loves research, analysis, is hard working and is precise in attention to detail.'

For a moment Gavin wondered whether this was a reference to himself but it wasn't quite how he saw it. 'Susannah? The accountant? Keen on balancing the books to the last penny?'

'Yes!' Claudine's face lit up with pleasure and satisfaction. '11th January. Capricorn. And Art - he's a typical Aries. 7th April. Neither devious nor subtle. Just a blunt instrument who is quick to anger.'

'That's Art. And Carl?'

'We've discussed him before. As a Taurian, he's strongly goal-directed, methodical, full of determination, down to earth and persistent in achieving an end result.'

'For good or evil?'

'Maybe. Taurians have an instinct for what is right. Believe me, Carl is too determined for the success of his business to jeopardise it by crime. That's the Carl I know, that's the Carl consistent with his horoscope.'

'And Edward's the only enigma?'

'Yes. So unlike his father from your description. Far from sharing interests they seem to fight. They shouldn't. Edward shouldn't be a problem. Yet he is.'

'Which shows that astrology doesn't always work.' Gavin felt time was ticking away. How long was all this going to take? Where was it getting him anyway? She hadn't even started on the Chinese animals yet. 'Look. When I telephone Walter Corbin and tell him you've flown out to solve Brads' problems by comparing Rats, Goats and Monkeys, my arse is going to be kicked black and blue.' From beneath lowered eyelids and with his face down-turned, she looked at him, uncertain just how angry he was. He smiled, just a small playful smile and gently brushed his lips against her cheek. 'You do realize, don't you, that I'm probably out of a job when I get back. Because of you.'

'Because of me?' She looked chastened. 'Don't you want to hear as far as I've got on the Chinese part then?' She looked disappointed as he shook his head.

'There's no time.'

'You'll regret it.' She nodded her head to add emphasis. 'Beware of Edward and Sir Archie. Something doesn't work there.'

'I'll remember.' Was she leading him away from Klodinsky deliberately?

'You know that Carl's downstairs? Sitting in the bar?'

'No. I didn't see him when I came in.'

'You see - you do need me. He didn't notice me. He was in a corner, talking to that man ...... you know, the one we saw on the television in my apartment.'

'Michel Mboro? The Minister?'

'That's the one.'

'How interesting! He's supposed to have flu. Dammit! I don't like them being together - whatever your star-gazing might tell you.' He rose to look out of the window. 'Anyway,' he stopped in mid-track, 'how did you get in here?'

'*Pas de problème!*' The maid was cleaning the room. I just walked in.' She laughed at the simplicity of it all.

'Then you've got to stay in here. No one must know you're here. Keep the door locked. Promise me? I've got to meet Art down the road.'

'If I must,' she tossed her head in irritation. 'I want to finish the Chinese work on Edward.'

'He's in England. Sir Archie's here. He's the one I'm worried about.'

'Ah! Sir Archie's here. That's interesting,' she paused. 'Oh ... I almost forgot. Alberto Forensi. I've done him too.'

'I'm not too worried about him. He's up with the stars anyway. Did you predict that he'd end up hanging from a beam?' He saw that she looked hurt at the jibe. 'Only joking. Come here.' She joined him by the window and he kissed her, firmly this time. 'I'm glad you're here.' The smile was wry. 'I just wish you hadn't come.'

'Trust me. Just trust me.'

'I must shower. Then I'm meeting Art.' Ten minutes later, refreshed and more comfortable in a clean T-shirt and shorts, he kissed her goodbye.

'Take care, Gavin,' she said. 'And don't worry. Trust me.'

'I'll see you later. As soon as I can. But who knows when that'll be.'

Then he was gone, feeling ashamed that he had gathered together and locked away all his papers. Just in case.

She closed the door behind him, waited for a few moments and then went to the telephone.

Chapter 47

'Mboro's been at our Hotel.' Gavin's eyes twinkled, showing his pleasure at being able to produce such vital information.

Art tapped his packet of cigarettes on the table, lit one and then drew deeply, his head nodding all the time as he thought about it. 'And he kissed you? On the right cheek?' The nasal accent was deadpan. Gavin reacted by reddening slightly, then raised his hand to his cheek in guilty self-defence.

'Oh ... that.' There was a pause while he ruined his white handkerchief. 'I'll tell you about that ... later. Anyway, I didn't see Mboro. I was just told it was him. Talking to Klodinsky. How about that?'

Again Art drew heavily on his cigarette, his eyes now downturned, his cheeks drawn in as he sucked hard. His response came as he exhaled. 'Interesting. Maybe. We knew they were business friends anyway. Anything else?'

'Not much. I looked round Mboro's waiting-room. Couldn't move for pictures of him. Here with George Schultz, there with James Baker, here opening a university, there signing a contract for the new deep sea port. Besides that, there were photos of him as a student in London and Paris. Nothing new.'

'So it seems. And the lipstick? Been in a brothel?' Art's stare was penetrating as he fired the bullet of accusation across the small bowl of olives and nuts which lay on the table in the shady courtyard where they were having lunch.

'Not my scene. Anyway, I don't have time to waste in brothels.'

'I do.' Art enjoyed springing his trap. 'I've been in one ... most of the morning.' Art tapped his teeth, hoping that Gavin would blunder in. He needn't have bothered.

Gavin sidestepped the pitfall. 'And you've got a breakthrough?'

'Could have. Let's order and then I'll explain.' They browsed at the tatty menus. Art chose a burger, made from meat of unknown origin, whilst Gavin selected fish and a bottle of white wine. 'When did Claudine arrive?' Art's face was a mask.

'Claudine? Oh ... she arrived this morning. Flew in from London with some information. Feels sure she can help. Astrology.'

Art's laugh was raucous and dismissive. His head rocked back with merriment and he banged the table with his fist. 'Well I can tell you, without watching the influence of the lunar cycle on Jupiter, that once London gets to hear of this you'll be looking for a new job. Uranus will be kicked right out of orbit.' Art flicked an olive stone at a sparrow which flew off in panic. Art's eyes looked only at him piercingly. 'Just listen dick-head. Get that bitch on the next flight to London.' He leaned forward and waited till Gavin did the same, so that their heads were close together. 'She's a fucking menace.' Though said in a whisper, the impact of the words was sharp. Art's belligerent look was sufficient to intimidate all but the strongest.

Gavin listened but was in no mood to capitulate. 'She stays. Conversation closed. She's suffered enough. Point one - she wants to be with me. Point two - she says she can help. I believe her.' He tasted the Chardonnay and found it too warm, so put it back in the bucket. 'Besides which ... I need her too. That's the perspective. Things which have divided us have joined us, things that have joined us have divided us. So please - just lay off about her. I'll contain her.' He enjoyed seeing Art's quizzical raised eyebrow. He poured and then raised his glass to examine the pale green wine. 'This time,' he wanted to emphasize his conviction, 'this time, you've got to believe me. I'm not letting my feelings for Claudine rule my head.'

Art wrestled with his inner doubts. 'I hope you're right, pal.' As a warning of distrust, Art made sure that he'd left no room for misunderstanding. 'Just remember. My life depends on it. Your judgment, that is. And if you thought things were tough with Theo, just wait. We don't need no weak links today. If we're both alive tomorrow morning, we'll be lucky.' He stubbed out his Camel in a theatrical gesture. 'Don't ask me why I know. I just know.'

Art wiped some dust from a lens of his Polaroid glasses and put them back on with affectation. 'Why would anyone paint containers?' Art knew it was a conversation stopper. Gavin was flummoxed. Neither of them could make any sense of it. It dominated their debate until Art had finished his burger, professing it to be the best donkey he'd had since Cairo.

'More fries,' Art turned to call to the waiter, highlighting his profile. Then he remembered his new regime. 'No! Forget it. Just coffee.'

Gavin stopped what he was about to say. 'Heh! Now tell me *you've* been working all morning.' He watched as Art's hand rose instinctively to the correct cheek. Mu-Mu's lipstick was still apparent. Gavin had waited for the right moment.

'I was gonna to tell you about that,' Art grinned. 'That was Mu-Mu. Strictly business. That's how I found out about the containers.'

'Expect me to believe that! Mu Mu with the big red lips told you all this?'

'Hold it! Hold it! I'll explain.' As they sat under the sunshade, the temperature in the walled terrace was stifling as Art went on to recount the full story of Spiro and Kazim. 'So you see,' he concluded, 'Dakalla seems to be where it's at. Sir Archie, Klodinsky, Forensi ... well, he was ... *Cerne View* ... and what may be *Ryme Lady* in drag coming tonight.' He ran the points off against his fingers. 'Even Claudine is here.'

'To say nothing of the President of the United States, the British Prime Minister, the French President and so many African dignatories and other world leaders you'll hardly be able to speak for the noise of jangling medals.' Gavin paused. 'But we don't know about Hugo Gonfleur from Marseille.' Gavin pushed aside the remains of his fish. 'And Mboro's involved with Scrignac Lefebre ... and for some reason *Cerne View's* got painted containers. There's only one thing to do.'

'Get aboard *Cerne View*,' interjected Art.

Gavin over-reacted in jest. 'Don't spoil our beautiful new relationship. Remember. You're the beef-cake. I'm the brains. But yes. Get aboard *Cerne View*. Check out the cargo, see why those Greeks were painting.'

'OK, so how do we get aboard?'

'For a start. We'll go to the harbour.'

Art looked incredulous. 'Say that's good, professor. We go to the harbour. Sure I can live with that.' He grasped Gavin's arm across the table and his face creased again into a smile and then a laugh. 'How do you plan to get us aboard?'

Gavin shook his head. 'I know how to get *you* aboard. After all, you're the Clint Eastwood of our team. You get to do the heroics.' Gavin watched as Art paid the bill and carefully re-positioned his cap.

They pushed back their chairs and headed through the dusty streets towards the docks. 'Maybe we could disguise ourselves as soldiers. Go in the front gate,' suggested Art.

'Buy some black boot polish you mean? Get a tailor to knock up a couple of officer's uniforms? Strut round with a swagger-stick and say *etcetera* every other word?' Gavin patted Art on the back and laughed. 'Come off it pal. Just stick to being a slob. Otherwise I'll start to feel redundant.'

Art grinned as they approached the docks. 'I may be dumb but I don't have to be dumb all the time. Tell me your plans.'

Chapter 48

Sixty nautical miles north of Dakalla, *Rio Massu* was making steady progress through the relentless roll of the mighty Atlantic. At both bow and stern the name *Ryme Lady* had been crudely obliterated with black paint. If you could believe the new legend, she was *Rio Massu* and registered in Monrovia, although the vessel had undergone more than a lick of paint change.

A Greek Cypriot skipper and crew had been put aboard after Captain Scutar had abandoned ship in the Malacca Strait. After an instant name change, they'd steamed for Naples. En route, $60 million of valuable cargo had been sold in Tripoli for a cool $35 million. The money was paid into a numbered bank at Credit Suisse in Zurich. After paying off expenses, bribes, Captain Scutar and the crew, there was still a tidy sum left. Most of that had passed through the hands of a black marketeer operating from the 14th arrondissement in Paris. The shadowy figure, well-known in the world of international arms dealing had arranged the weaponry. Kitting out the ship had creamed off another couple of million but even now, with all expenses paid and the mercenaries well catered for, there was still $11 million now lodged in a further account, recently opened on Grand Cayman.

After leaving Tripoli, *Rio Massu* had made the short voyage across the Mediterranean to Naples where some of the up-front bribes had assured a swift transition from cargo ship to warship. The work had been discreetly done and had involved some well-placed and influential people. The bribes had been both substantial and indispensable.

In the Italian port, far from the usual exports of fruit,

wine or machine spares, 200 mercenaries recruited in Hamburg and London had slipped aboard in ones and twos under cover of darkness. The men were battle hardened, veterans of conflict in Central America, the Far East and Southern Africa. Each man had been personally selected by Colonel Sean O'Hara, a man who'd lived for violence and would be happy to die in the same way. Formerly a member of the crack British SAS, some of the men had been trained by him up in Hereford. Others were ex Special Boat Service and yet more were formerly members of the elite US Marine Corps. Of the remainder, many were the sort you'd see kicking hell out of each other after closing time in Glasgow's Sauchiehall Street. During the voyage the group had been trained, lectured, drilled, rehearsed, until every move of what they had to do was going to be second nature when the moment came.

On board, crates which had been certified at Marseille as being full of air-conditioning equipment and ducting, were filled rather differently. Weaponry and in particular rocket launchers, flame throwers, bazookas, mortars, machine guns, grenades and plenty enough explosives were the real manifest.

Now, in the relentless grey of the Atlantic, more than fifty of the men under O'Hara's watchful eye were doing keep-fit routines in shorts and singlets whilst the remainder were making last minute checks on the armaments.

There was an air of quiet expectancy. Ahead, and not too far ahead, lay the violent action for which the men lived and for which they were prepared to die. It was the only life they'd ever known, the only life which gave them the adrenalin punch. Without it, life would have been unbearable anyway. No job was easy, no assignment was to be underestimated and tonight's action would be tough. Yet each man knew that the team had the determination to succeed.

Moments later, Colonel O'Hara called the men to order.' I have our final briefing. The objective remains as I told you, namely the overthrow of the new Government of the State of Lupopo. The criteria are the same.' His face became as solemn as his voice. 'The implications are now even greater. Let me tell you why.' He proceeded to give them the latest information from Dakalla. 'So tonight,' he concluded, 'many of you will die. But we shall succeed. The mission will succeed. We shall succeed because death holds no terrors for us. We shall succeed because of our skills, the expertise which we have gathered together. We shall succeed because our plan is so simple. May your God be with you.'

Back in Dakalla harbour, Gavin and Art were seated in the bow of a small boat powered by an outboard motor and steered by an elderly African whose face was set in a permanent grin. His new pair of dentures, bought in a street market, had been designed to fit someone but certainly not him. The man, however, nodded his head happily enough as the little boat chug-chugged through the oily sheen of the harbour.

Old wooden fruit boxes, plastic bottles and the occasional dead rat brushed by the boat. Ahead of them was a dredger, continuing its endless battle to prevent the harbour mouth from silting up, the heavy metallic clanking a constant reminder of Dakalla's struggle against nature.

Behind them lay the curve of the harbour. Most of the berths were full and the bay, over one mile across at its widest, was busy with all manner of craft going about their daily routine. 'There .... Berth 17.' Art pointed to the empty quay. '*Ryme Lady's* berth.' He swivelled to face the other way. Now he could see *Cerne View*, towering above the quayside, blocking out the view of the military HQ and the Palace behind it.

They fell silent as the boat covered the last few yards towards the harbour mouth, the small craft starting to rock as it reached the heavy swell from the Atlantic. No more than 300 yards away, the surface was dangerously choppy, where the surge of the Sampopo river met the mass of the ocean. The African, well aware of the danger, steered them away from the foam-flecked surface.

'Some bridge,' said Gavin pointing up the river. 'Cayor says it's being officially opened on Sunday.' The structure, essential to the new State and a multi-million dollar project, carried a six lane highway. A massive tower at each end held the suspension cables for the bridge which was second only in size to the one over the River Humber. It was a credit to the engineers who had masterminded its creation over seven years, a memorial to the twenty three men who had died whilst the project had taken shape. 'There's more than this river divides these countries. Cayor was too frightened to say much but everything you read talks of the tribal feuding and clashing cultures.' Gavin wasn't sure whether he was talking to himself. Art seemed more interested in delving finger-deep into his right ear. 'I was looking at the local paper. The editor was calling the new bridge a giant handshake between the two nations. Yet even now they're exhorting that the traditional rivalry and amimosity should be relegated to history.'

'Bit late for that.'

'Not necessarily. Take someone like Mboro, who's had a nice little number in corruption over the years, stitching up government contracts by taking every bribe possible. Wouldn't suit him, would it? Wouldn't suit families whose ancestors were slaughtered in border clashes up-country. You could go on and on.'

'And sometimes you do, professor,' said Art. 'Maybe we'll take a drive up there tomorrow. Have a look at the opening. See the razz-matazz, the bands.'

Gavin was quick to agree. 'Could be fun. I'll tell you one thing. We'll watch all the crowds cheering as the ribbons are cut. Then they'll all go back to their hovels, wondering just what *has* changed and what they were really cheering about.'

'I guess you're right.' They stared at the huge suspension bridge, its girders glinting red from the setting sun and towering high over the thick brown water which surged beneath it. Gavin pointed to their right at the far bank. 'And that's Sampopo. Pretty, eh?' The irony was lost on Art who ignored the distant view of shabby squalor.

'You graduate in geography or something?' Art grunted before shouting to the local with the tombstone teeth. 'Back now.' He waved his arms and the message got through. The dinghy turned through 180 degrees and started to make for *Cerne View*. As they slapped and slopped across the bay, day became night. With amazing speed, the sun dipped below the horizon behind them. What seconds before had been a flaming red sunset was now blackness. What remained were the floodlights round the harbour and the colourful reds, greens and yellows from the cele-bratory street lighting now switched on.

'Gee! This sudden day-night scene. Takes some getting used to,' said Art.

'We're so close to the Equator. That's why. You see ...'

'Cool it, professor. Take a look at this.' Art pointed towards *Cerne View*, seen now only as a black silhouette, stark and silent, which rose from the water. It's wheel-house and officers' quarters were all in darkness. Yet one thing was apparent, something which in daylight was insignificant. Now, after dark, shining from the blackness like a religious symbol, was a giant cross, a big luminous X created by the painting handiwork of Kazim and Spiro. Even from 400 yards away it was visible, with the upstroke covering what must have been twenty-five feet. 'Reckon that's three containers up and two across they've painted. And for why?'

Was Art's question rhetorical? Gavin wasn't sure. 'You know the answer, don't you? X marks the spot.' Gavin was convinced.

'Well, sure as hell Kazim and Spiro weren't painting *The Last Supper*.' Art's voice was thoughtful. 'Reckon I can get aboard now?'

'Yes. It won't get any blacker. Got everything?' After lunch, they'd bought the items on Art's shopping list of odds and ends before going out on the boat. Gavin waited for the grunt of acknowledgement. 'Fine. Then I'm going back to the hotel. I'll wait for the signal.'

'And keep your hands off Claudine's ass. Stay on the balcony. Watch out for my signal. Five long flashes for yes. Two shorts for no. Ok?'

'Got it. Don't keep me waiting though. I might get a bit frisky,' Gavin said. 'I'll phone Corbin now. Then again when we know the answer.'

'Sure. And remember - four long flashes back to me when you've understood my message. Ok?' Art put his beefy arm across Gavin's shoulder. 'Practising counting to four will help keep your mind off your dick.' They climbed onto the rickety wooden jetty and then mounted the steps to the quayside. There they paused and their eyes met. Not a word was spoken yet the eye contact said it all. The look confirmed their growing closeness. It was silent recognition that what Art was now going to do was unspeakably dangerous.

Chapter 49

The docks were quiet, much quieter than usual. The excitement of the celebrations ahead had sent most people back home to dress up ready to shout, cheer, dance and feast the night away. Tonight the hatchet which had divided Lumbola and Sampopo would be buried forever. Beyond the docks, the noise of canned music and random trumpets blared from Independence Square. The hot rhythmic jungle sounds were designed to capture the hearts and minds of the people of Dakalla.

Art wasn't sure whether the empty docks by the compound would be to his advantage or not. He'd got past the joke-box known as Dock Security, without a problem. The solitary guard, who was reading a magazine and munching a banana, never even looked up. From then on, he was a lone figure slipping through the shadows in his black jeans and navy sweatshirt. Sometimes he was in the lee of wooden crates, sometimes in the protection of a gantry. Along the way he camouflaged his face and hands with mud from the tyres of a truck.

Would Gavin's plan work? The theory of the backroom boy? He was uncertain, even more so when he reached the heavy chain-link fencing. Beyond the fence there were bright security lights beaming down on all quarters of the parade ground. But to his right, *Cerne View* was in the shadows, her outline clear-cut as her bow curved away from the dockside to the sharp apex beyond the name.

He paused by the water's edge, in the last shadow available to him. Again he weighed up the chances. Eighty yards away, by the gangplank were two soldiers, machine-guns slung across their shoulders. Each looked as sloppily relaxed as only Africans can without being completely asleep. The dusty parade ground was empty, the soldiers either out on duty or in the barracks.

Art ran his fingers up and down the wire-mesh, all the time crouching low by the water's edge. The fence in front of him projected several feet over the water. At its extremity was a mass of tangled barbed wire. Gavin had been right. Climbing along the fence and back round the other side was impossible. He'd be torn to shreds. The only possibility was through the fence ... and that would be the easy bit. From his pocket he removed the wire cutters. Slowly and painstakingly, wincing at every noise and with one eye on the guards, he made cuts, wire by wire, until a sufficient hole had been created for him to wriggle through. There he paused, crouched low behind the bollard to which the hawser from *Cerne View* was attached. The guards hadn't noticed anything.

Ok Gavin. So far, so good. You said it was possible. Let's try now. Without a further thought, he grasped the thick roughened rope and swung away from the quay. For a second he was dangling suspended from it, immediately above the water. Panting with exertion, he pulled up his legs, cursing the way he'd let his body run to seed these last few weeks. At the second attempt, he made it, his legs locking themselves round the rope, so that he hung from underneath it by his arms and legs, ready now to make the treacherously steep climb, inching up the rope to the deck.

As Gavin had said ... if rats can do it ... you should have no trouble. The thought amused him as he fought to work his aching arms and legs up the steep incline. Somewhere unseen beneath him was the faint sound of water slapping against the hull. The rising stench was a reminder of the filthy, floating debris, of the stinking effluent from the city's drains.

'Don't move now,' Art muttered to himself, referring to

the guards. 'Just you stay there, boys, relax and enjoy your smoke.' Only another twelve feet, twelve feet on and upward, every movement painful. Hand over hand, foot by foot he advanced until he reached the top of the bow. The name *Cerne View*, in big letters, loomed right beside him in white paint on the rusty black of the hull.

He glanced above and then looked below. Now he could see nothing of the water, could barely hear it slap-slapping its scum round the Plimsoll line. Above and ahead of him was the supreme effort, the twisting, the turning, the gripping, the pulling and yet more twisting. With a final effort, he grasped the ship's side and swung his punished body over to tumble onto the deck.

He landed on a coil of sun-dried rope, where he lay gasping, opening and closing his hands to restore circulation. He wiped the sweat from his face and wished he could do the same to every nook and cranny, yearning for a shower and a cool beer. Instead of that, there was just 100% discomfort - that and a big job still to do. As his pulse dropped to around 130 and his breath started to come more evenly, he inched himself up to peer over the ship's side. The two guards were still there and despite the clank-clank of the dredger, he overheard a snatch of conversation, a dirty laugh. Good. They were unconcerned. The sirens on the poles round the parade ground had remained silent. He looked about him and saw the stack of containers lining the deck through to the fo'c'sle. It was time to move.

He crossed to the port side and then scuttled, rat-like, along the deck, with no chance now of being seen from the compound, any view being obscured by the containers. The smell of fresh paint brought Art to a standstill. There they were. The painted containers which formed the strange luminous cross. As he studied the sides, tapping them gently, the air was filled with a new sound. Strangely incongruous and muffled by the containers, it wafted through the night air. It was an orchestra - the string section tuning up, putting the finishing touches to their routine. It was a sharp reminder that the festivities at the Palace, just beyond the compound, would soon be starting. From somewhere in the city came the sound of sirens rising above the noise from the throng in Independence Square.

Goddammit! Spiro and Kazim must have used ladders. Where in hell's name had they put them? Art moved down the line of containers. Surely they'd have abandoned them about here. He was right. His ankle found a ladder, a nasty jabbing impact in the darkness and he had to fight to suppress a shout of pain. It was lying along the deck, leaning against the ship's side but within seconds he had it swung round and had placed it against the stack.

The noise from the dredger stopped. The ship itself was just as silent and the container stack muffled the strains of a Mantovani number from the landward side. Art looked the stack up and down. Gavin had been right. He'd explained that the weakest part of a container was its roof. For reasons of lightness, the steel framework often had a roof of flimsy plywood, plastic or aluminium. The sides, floors and doors were strong, designed to be unassailable to thieves. Art looked at it carefully. There was no choice. Up to the top then.

His face screwed up with tension, his hands blistered and painful, he climbed the ladder. What secrets were concealed by the containers? It depends how you said it. *Just routine cargo really. Building equipment, ball-bearings, ammonium nitrate, some paint, some knocked-down engines. Nothing much.*

Harmless really.

Harmless that is unless you had Gavin's brain. Chemistry, he'd said. Schoolboy knowledge, he'd added. Art looked at the freshly-painted containers in front of him. Did they contain the most lethal of cocktails as Gavin had suggested? Did the harmless cargo suddenly become sinister? Say it slowly, the way Gavin had said it. *Drums of cellulose paint, high-viscosity oil, steel tubing, six inch nails, ball-bearings, knocked-down engines, 500 tons of the ship's fuel, several thousand tons of bulk ammomium nitrate. Harmless really ... unless you had a trigger, a flashpoint. Then ... Cerne View was no longer a ship ... then Cerne View became a floating bomb. 20,000 tons of mass destruction.* The blast, the flames, the flying ball-bearings, the six inch nails and the exploding ship's debris would flatten the Palace and a great deal more beyond.

Just a detonator. That's all it needed, if Gavin's chemistry was up to Grade A. Art gritted his teeth as he swung himself over the top of the ladder and lay panting twenty-five feet above the deck. He was at the highest point of the luminous cross. He was also just above the guards, fifty yards from the nearest barracks and a stone's throw from the Palace grounds. The brightly-coloured marquee was uncomfortably close, rising from beyond the Palace walls.

With a snake-like motion he wriggled to a corner of the container, convinced now as he lay on the cold metal that Gavin had been right. The Palace was just so near, such an easy target. Then his thoughts turned again to the container. Plywood might have been flimsier but aluminium was going to be quieter. With probing fingers he played with the rivets fixing the thin metal to the sturdiness of the steel frame.

Using the sharp point of his sheath-knife, he jabbed a hole through the casing. Then with the wire cutters, he slit two sides of a square in the metal until he could push the aluminium triangle inwards, down into the darkness. Gingerly, he inserted his arm, deeper until it was in, right up to his shoulder. At first he felt nothing but empty space. Then his fingers touched something. It was cold, deathly cold to the touch, smooth and well-rounded. He ran his hand along its length. It was cylindrical with a diameter of perhaps ten inches or more. Steel piping perhaps? Sure. In theory.

He rummaged for the last of his purchases and found the torch. Silently he lowered his arm back into the hole and flicked on the torch. Instantly the secrets of the container were revealed. He was lying on row upon row of torpedo-like cylinders, a mix of oxy-acetylene and Calor gas.

Neither had been part of the ship's cargo. If the rest of the cross were the same ... Christ, when that little lot ignited, it would be put-your-fingers-in-your-ears time.

Art had seen enough. The other containers would be no different. Maybe worse. A shiver ran through him. His jaw tightened and his mouth felt dry. His hands which had never trembled when holding a gun now shook at the awesome audacity of the revelation.

He was sitting on the bomb's trigger.

'Holy shit! Art my boy - it's time to get the fuck out of here', he muttered as he edged back along the container to the seaward side. 'You've done well so far. Just keep it quiet now. And get that signal off to Gavin.' As he turned to face the bow, he saw the lights of the Independence Hotel rising high above the square, no more than 400 yards away. As arranged, he flashed five times with the torch, five long flashes, and then repeated it, both times aiming the light at where he judged Gavin must be watching. He was.

'See that! See that!' said Gavin excitedly as he stood on the balcony, side by side with Claudine. 'Five long flashes. *Cerne View's* a bomb. Christ! We're going to have to act fast now.' He flashed back the message received signal.

'So what do you do?' Claudine's lips were pursed, her elegantly manicured finger resting delicately on them.

'With the biggest bomb since Hiroshima right by the Palace? Christ! This is too big for us. I'll try ringing London again. That's if the operator can get their bloody system to work.'

'Won't you tell somebody here?' Claudine's voice was tense, contrasting with the relaxed yellow sun-top and jeans which she was wearing. Her feet were bare, her toes without varnish. She'd spent most of the day working on the horoscopes but since Gavin's return, had been leaning anxiously on the balcony rails, her arm clasping him for togetherness rather than security.

'Maybe. Don't know who to trust. I'll see what Art thinks. For God's sake, I don't know which side anybody's on.' He patted her well-rounded backside. 'Art would include you in that.'

Claudine's smile was thin as she patted his arm in reassurance. 'You know, don't you Gavin? You know that I'm with you?'

'Yes, yes. Of course I do.' The tone sounded gruff, dismissive. His mind was already elsewhere. As he clutched the phone by the bed, waiting for the front desk to answer, he could imagine Art perched on the containers. What had he found? What did it all mean? Could they do anything?

'Ah! Thank you. I want to ring London. Yes ... I know you had trouble. Try again.' Claudine was watching his face. She saw it pucker into a frown and then watched him bite his lip in frustration. 'A fire? So how long? You don't know?' He replaced the receiver and turned to Claudine. 'There's been a major fire in the Dakalla telecommunications centre. There are no international calls going in or out. That's what all those sirens must have been.' He ran his hands through his hair. 'Just my bloody luck.'

'Luck?' Claudine prompted.

'Now you mention it ... maybe it just could be more sinister.' He nodded his head, at first thoughtfully and then more enthusiastically. 'Yes. Sinister.'

Chapter 50

Once his leg had made contact with the top rung, getting down the ladder had been easier than Art had expected. At the foot, he debated. Leave the ladder or not? He decided it was a dead giveaway if the guards patrolled the ship. He swung the ladder away from the stack and tilted it over, walking backwards as he did so in the time-honoured manner of all window-cleaners. They, however, didn't have to work in the darkness, didn't have to contend with Spiro and Kazim's paint buckets lurking on the deck. Art stumbled and cursed as his foot caught a bucket. He fell with a noisy clang, dropping the ladder as he did so. Twenty feet of ladder crashed noisily to the deck, momentarily pinning his right arm.

The two guards, just the other side of the stack at the foot of the gangplank, heard the noise with alarm. As Art tried to ignore the pain and force himself to his feet, they looked at each other in startled fear. Who was on board? The ship was empty. Or supposed to be. After momentary hesitation, they climbed up the gangplank, machine-guns at the ready. Each was dressed in dark green uniform, their heads bare, their jungle boots rubber soled. On the deck, they separated, one passing between the stacks and the fo'c'sle to get to the seaward side, the other running along the starboard side towards the bow.

Art too ran along the deck beside the containers and into the open space leading towards the rise of the bow. He could hear the shouts of the men behind him as one of them spotted him.

He had two choices. Jump overboard or go back the way he came. No. The same route would be far too slow. They'd pick him off easily with a volley of bullets. Overboard it would have to be. He changed tack and had almost reached the seaward rail, when a chain, lying across the deck, tripped him. He fell full tilt, striking his head a hefty blow against a winch. Though he was disorientated for barely a second, it was a second too long, a second which he hadn't got to spare. As he started to pick himself up he felt a kick in the back and was pinned to the deck. Seconds later, he had been stripped of his knife and, more importantly, of his beloved pen-gun. The two soldiers babbled excitedly as he lay face down with a heavy boot crushing his spine.

The talking stopped.

It was then that he felt a gun placed firmly against the back of his head.

'Where in hell has Art got to?' It was not the first time that Gavin had said this as he paced up and down. He was peering over the balcony at the thousands of people jostling shoulder to shoulder in the square below. 'It's 7.45. Nearly three-quarters of an hour since Art's message.' He paused to look across at *Cerne View*, her profile clear. Aboard, there was no sign of light or movement.

'Maybe he's been held up in the crowd,' suggested Claudine though her voice echoed her concern.

'Maybe.' The response was mechanical. Gavin doubted she was right. He left the balcony and entered the cool of the bedroom. 'Time's running out. I'll try the phone again.' He guessed it would be hopeless but it was better than doing nothing as he sat on the bed and spoke to Reception.

'I'm sorry sir.' The woman's soft African lilt was soothing but her message was not. 'It's still impossible to ring in or out of Lumbola.'

'Dakalla, to put it bluntly, is cut off,' Gavin summarized as he put down the phone.

'What about Sampopo then?' Claudine's response was instant. As he looked at her in profile, Gavin was caught for a moment by her beauty whilst appreciating the sharpness of her intellect. 'Sampopo?' His boyish face became lined. He ran his hand through his hair yet again and rubbed the side of his cheek. The stress signals were obvious.

'Yes, there's a chance,' he murmured. Then his voice became urgent. 'Put on your best things. The British High Commissioner from Sampopo's due at the Palace with the other guests within half an hour. We'll catch him there. He might believe us. Most wouldn't. It's all too vague.'

'Without Art ... and what Art knows ... I agree. And if we miss him?'

'Then we'll cross over to Sampopo.' Even as he was speaking, Gavin was tearing off his clothes and throwing them onto the bed. In a series of rapid movements he put on a clean blue shirt, navy tie and a pale grey suit. Claudine smartened herself up with a blouse, white slacks and a pair of flat-soled shoes. It was the best she had. Three minutes later they looked credible, if scarcely dressed for the banquet.

Gavin slipped the sheath-knife into his pocket and was ready to go. 'Do you need that?' enquired Claudine who had been watching, one hand on the bedroom door.

'Who knows?'

Moments later, they passed through the crowded lobby. It was busy with diplomats and that blend of the great and the good who held gold-embossed invitations to the Palace. At the corner of the bar was Mboro, talking earnestly but in the melée Gavin never saw him and he never saw Gavin.

Clutching Claudine's arm, they left the comfort of the air-conditioning and entered the rich tapestry of colour in the square. There was a blast of hot air, the smell of chicken roasting on an open fire, the blare of reggae, fathers carrying small children, mothers holding babies and everyone milling about. 'It's going to be hell getting through this rabble. Stay close.'

The police had prepared two routes to the Palace - one for the world leaders in their high-security motorcades and another for the lesser dignatories. Those arriving on foot had their own cleared path. Already, lines of chauffeur-driven cars were edging forward to file through the Palace gates. Although their progress was slow, it was quick compared to Gavin and Claudine. Behind the ropes the throng was pressing forward, anxious to glimpse President O'Brien with his First Lady whose arrival was now imminent. In the distance, the wail of sirens heralded someone important.

The nearer they got, the worse the crush, the worse the hostility at their pushing. Hot and dishevelled by the time they neared the Palace gates, it was 8.11. The countdown was on. If *Cerne View* were a bomb and *Rio Massu* slipped into Dakalla during the evening, the climax could be only hours away, before midnight at the latest. Even before they'd pushed their way to within twenty yards of the Palace, there was the roar of motorcycles, all blue flashing lights and sirens, heralding the approach of the President's bullet-proof car. All that Gavin and Claudine saw was a sea of waving arms and flags as the crowd cheered its welcome.

'We're too late,' shouted Gavin. 'That big cheer must have been for the President. Lesser mortals like the British High Commissioner must already be there.' He caught Claudine's eye for a moment and she gave him a nod of encouragement.

'Don't give up,' she shouted. 'You've got to do something.'

It was what he needed. 'Come on. We'll never get any nearer the entrance than this. Stay close.' She clutched his hand as he battered a route away from the Palace towards the car park. He knew exactly where he was heading, pleased that he'd done his homework that morning with Art. No doubt the security around the Presidential motorcade and for the other leaders had been tight but for the parked cars of lesser diplomats there was no security. Gavin was able to lead Claudine though the lines of vehicles, many of them displaying their national flag on the bonnets. In most of them were chauffeurs, some eating, some reading, some snoozing.

From the marquee, Gavin could hear the orchestra playing 'Moonlight Serenade'. It all seemed so trite, so soothing, so meaningless. Christ! If they only knew what was happening, that time was running. He wanted to shout out - to tell the world what he knew or what he thought he knew ... but it was hopeless without the right audience. He looked up and down the line of cars until he saw the large black Austin Princess with its Union Jack. Highly polished with huge headlamps, it was from a fine vintage. It spoke of the days when the map of Africa was predominantly pink. 'This way,' he said as he grasped Claudine's hand more firmly and hurried her towards the diplomatic limousine.

Gavin glanced inside and saw the chauffeur, in grey suit and black cap, fast asleep.

'Get in,' he commanded Claudine. So saying he pulled open the rear door and pushed her across to the far side, so that he was seated immediately behind the chauffeur. In his hand was the unsheathed knife. The driver awoke with a jolt as the door slammed shut. 'I'm a British Agent.' Gavin spoke out the words slowly and with deliberation. 'Take me straight to the High Commission in Sampopo. And quick.' He spoke with such authority that the African started to lean forward to fire the engine before seeming to change his mind. He twisted to look over his left shoulder, bewilderment on his face but words failing him. 'Here's my passport.' Gavin waved it in front of the man's frightened face. At the same time he jabbed the knife gently into the nape of the man's neck. 'I know the road well,' he bluffed. 'Any trouble from you, any attempt at anything stupid, and you'll feel this a damned sight harder.' As he spoke Gavin pushed the knife firmly, so that its point drew a trickle of blood which rolled down on to the man's white shirt. 'You and me have an emergency on our hands. Understood?'

The chauffeur said nothing but started the ignition and the 1953 Princess purred into life, its engine as sweet as the day it was built. 'Not too fast, not too slow. Just drive normally. Just imagine I'm the High Commissioner. Understood?' He saw the man shake his head in agreement. English was the second language of Sampopo, unlike Lumbola, with its French colonial heritage.

Hunched now over the steering wheel, a bubble of blood forming and then flowing into the rim of his crisp white collar, the chauffeur manoeuvred the vehicle out of the car park and away from the Palace. Within three minutes he'd turned onto the six lane highway for the short drive to the bridge. 'You will not stop at the checkpoint. You will slow down as if you're going to stop and then, at the last moment, accelerate straight through.' Gavin gave him a friendly jab in the back of the neck with the knife tip. 'Understood?'

'Yessir.' The chauffeur was respectful but distant, uncertain what to make of the turn of events.

Gavin watched as another trickle of blood ran down the thick bull-like neck which bulged over the top of the shirt. 'You keep behaving yourself and we're going to be good friends.' He spoke with reassuring precision. 'I'm Ok. You're Ok. You look after me, I'll make sure you get promotion. Ok?' He cast a quick glance at Claudine who was sitting the other side of the thick divide between the two rear seats. He could sense rather than see her tenseness and he hoped that she was drawing confidence from his tone. It was impossible to tell.

As the driver appeared ready to obey orders, rather than go for heroics, Gavin relaxed just a little and momentarily appreciated the rich smell of the pale grey leather upholstery and the walnut woodwork. Years of cigar smoke had permeated the leather. In the pocket built into the door panel was a small leather flask with a silver top. No doubt it contained a fine whisky or brandy for Sir Charles to swig as he whiled away the tedious minutes between the High Commission and the Polo Club. A huge cigar butt was jammed into the ashtray while on Claudine's side was a tartan travelling rug and a pair of designer sunglasses. 'You understand me?' repeated Gavin in the same tone of voice.

'Yessir.' Ahead, the giant framework of the bridge, floodlit now, appeared on the skyline, the flags of Lumbola and Sampopo clinging to their poles in the still night air. At the Lumbolan control point, a small white building, the guards were interested only in vehicles entering from Sampopo. They were waved through without ceremony.

At a steady twenty-five miles per hour, the Princess cruised southbound across the bridge. Miles of steel wire and 3,500 tons of metalwork carried the roadway eighty yards over the dark fast flow of the Sampopo. Gavin, sitting on the seaward side, had time to glance out to the Atlantic. He could see the lights of a number of ships twinkling and flickering across the water as they lay moored outside Dakalla harbour. Was one of them *Ryme Lady*? It was impossible to know. He bent forward to be close to the chauffeur, knife point at the ready.

His nerves were taut as the huge bulk of the car crested the bridge's high-point before descending the long, gentle slope towards the Sampopo guards. He felt Claudine's hand fumbling for his in the darkness and he found her silent presence reassuring. 'Slowly now,' he said to the driver. 'Take it steady.' The soldiers, about six of them, were standing chatting outside their guard-house. They looked up and saw the Princess, the Union Jack on the bonnet, and stood to attention, waiting for it to stop at the barrier. 'Slowly now,' he repeated. 'Make as if to stop during the last twenty yards but when you're ten yards from the barrier put your foot down.' The car slowed to ten miles an hour. 'Go,' he commanded as he jabbed the knife into the fleshy bulge of skin at the foot of the man's hairline.

The chauffeur jammed his foot down and the engine raced. The Princess responded with the dignity of an aged duchess whilst Gavin pulled Claudine down below window level, expecting shots to be fired. Nothing ..... nothing more then some muffled shouts of confusion and disbelief that the chauffeur had destroyed their brand new red and white barrier. 'You've done well,' Gavin told the driver. 'Now accelerate. Really fast.' The man did as he was told and drove the car over the bumpy road at fifty-five miles an hour, the springs doing their best to even out the worst of the pot-holes.

Though only the Sampopo River had separated the two countries, the contrast in wealth and efficiency was obvious. Since Sampopo had gained its independence from Britain, nearly thirty years before, the well-ordered and disciplined routines laid down by British civil servants had disintregated into a sea of corruption and neglect. The work of generations of Britons who had risked malaria and yellow fever had been cast away. Now what remained was the rotting decay of the old timber buildings, the Court House, the Parliament, the schools and the hospitals. Nowhere in sight was there any sign of progress or investment. 'You can see why Sampopo's the junior partner in the deal,' observed Gavin to Claudine, whose face was a mask with shell-shock over what was happening. He was looking at the Ministry of Defence. The roof-tiles were missing or broken, the clapboarding in need of paint, the windows grimy. Someone had stolen the knocker from the door and on the front lawn, where once there had been croquet and cucumber sandwiches, there was now a tethered goat and an abundance of droppings.

The car slowed and then turned down an even more rutted and pitted road until it came to a halt at a pair of black wrought-iron gates, hanging from massive white pillars with the words 'British High Commission' emblazoned on either side. The gates were floodlit, the impression created was of a well- manicured, lovingly preserved jewel in a slum of despond. The chauffeur sounded his horn three times. The gate-keeper appeared, immaculate in a white outfit and black cap with a red band. When he recognized the car, he opened the gates with a salute. Inside was a courtyard and to the rear was the timbered house. It was spanking white, low, with a verandah along its length, surrounded by luxuriant palms, shrubs and an abundance of flowers on every side.

Gavin jumped out and Claudine followed. 'Thanks. I'll put you up for the next vacancy for High Commissioner. Believe it or not, I really am on your side.' The driver sat in the car, rubbing the back of his neck with a sullen look on his face. The door of the building was opened by an official who had all the status of an over-dressed office boy. Gavin flashed his passport and IMB identity card. Despite the quizzical look at their strange and unexpected arrival, they were admitted to a small waiting room. The valet went in search of the man in charge that evening, telling them that he would be back in a moment.

'Still living in a bygone age,' commented Gavin as he looked round the room at the pictures of the Polo Match of 1929 and one of King George V shaking hands with a long-dead Governor. Claudine wasn't listening. She was staring through the window at the chauffeur who was mopping the back of his neck with a handkerchief and probably hoping that the two new arrivals would be thrown out.

She turned to look at Gavin. He was pacing nervously back and forth over the tiled floor. She could recognise in him all the determination of a Capricorn and all the intensity of a Scorpio. So why had he been born under Taurus? As she watched him gazing at the waste-paper basket made out of an elephant's foot, she tried again to firm up her thoughts. Take Carl. He wouldn't risk everything for this. Oh, yes ... he'd have had the chance but not the inclination. The influence of Saturn saw to that. And Mboro? She had no idea of his star sign. If only she could find out. 'What I still don't understand,' she spoke aloud in continuation of her thoughts, 'is how Edward and Sir Archie can both be Sagittarians. Everything else fits.'

There was a pause as Gavin tuned in to her conversation, switching his own confused thoughts which had centred on why the hell nobody else had any sense of urgency. 'I scribbled down the dates for you. Haven't you got the piece of paper?'

'Yes.' She fumbled in her small handbag, opened her diary and unfolded the note. 'There, Edward 27th November, Sir Archie, 6th December. Both Sagittarians. It just doesn't work, does it? Their characters don't match.'

'So you've said before.' His voice sounded resigned to an academic discussion. 'Look ... in different circumstances we could debate all this.' He smiled reassuringly before crossing the room to give her a friendly squeeze. He saw the scribbled note. 'Hold on! That isn't 27th November. That's 22nd November.'

'*Mon Dieu*! Your writing!

He felt her shiver of excitement and thought she was going to jump in the air with exhilaration. '22nd

November! A Scorpio! Edward's a Scorpio! Now that explains a great deal.'

'So what do I tell Walter Corbin? Is it good or bad news?'

Her face told him that this was no time for joking. 'Just listen to me.' There was a firmness in her voice. 'The Scorpio is intense, strong-willed, determined. The Scorpio can be highly sensitive with fierce, deep-seated passions. You say in England *dark horses*. No wonder he didn't get along with his father.'

From along the corridor came the distant sound of heavy footsteps. Gavin nodded thoughtfully. 'Tell me later what all this means.' He stole a quick peck on her cheek and then distanced himself from her, taking up a relaxed stance. He hoped he looked more confident than he felt. Carefully, he stood behind the Regency mahogany table, shoulders back, hands clasped together in front of him, ready now to advance and greet the new arrival.

He needed to impress, to get the upper hand right from the start. Claudine sat down in a faded blue moquette arm-chair, her own thoughts shuffling the astrological implications of the new information about Edward. Scorpios were sustainers and rarely initiators. Didn't that rule him out. So who *was* here in Dakalla? Sir Archie and Carl. No. Not them. Not unless Mboro was the *initiator*. Then there was the unknown Gonfleur.

The footsteps had stopped outside the waiting-room, cutting short her mental debate. The man who entered the room was short and stocky. As he introduced himself to Gavin but not Claudine, he revealed the slightest touch of North Country in his accent. Gavin judged the man to be around forty, about 5′ 8″, with neatly cut thinning sandy hair. Above his lip his moustache had just a touch of ginger in it. Wearing a dark brown suit with a large check pattern, he looked bulkier than he was. His hands were uncomfortably large and he seemed never to know what to do with them. 'The name's Tony Wilton. I'm number three here but tonight I'm playing Cinderella. Had an invitation to the do but someone had to look after the family silver.' There was a scoff in his laugh as he spoke. 'All the top brass are over in Dakalla. The PM and all that. Anyway ... I gather you arrived in some style. I hope you can justify what you've done. I'm sure it must be some sort of offence to hi-jack the High Commissioner's car. You told the driver you were an agent.' The freckled face was not unfriendly but the tone was formal and quizzically dry. The man was nervous, probably unaccustomed to being in charge. It spelled trouble. Except in physique the man appeared lightweight, best suited to an administrative post with nothing to administer. Gavin just hoped he was wrong.

'Thanks Mr Wilton. Look, there's no time to lose. Oh, by the way, this is Claudine Flubert who is helping my Bureau. Here's my card. No doubt you've heard of us.' Gavin knew that Wilton would never have heard of the Bureau and probably would not be man enough to admit it. He was right. Wilton nodded with undue enthusiasm. 'I'm going to tell you a crazy story but you've got to believe that I'm not mad.' He paused for a moment and looked for a chair. 'Mind if I sit down? What I'm going to tell you is sensational and urgent. But I'm serious, deadly serious. You may wish to sit down yourself.' Gavin said it for effect and was pleased to note that it worked.

'You'd better tell me.' Tony Wilton took a chair next to Gavin. Then he folded his arms in front of his chest so as to hide his ungainly fists and sat back to listen.

'My Bureau's been investigating shipping frauds. Our trail has led to Dakalla and everything centres round a ship that's under arrest there called *Cerne View*. That ship is moored next to the Presidential Palace. By midnight tonight, and probably at around 11.00 pm, in less than two and a half hours, that ship is going to blow up. It's going to be the biggest bang since Guy Fawkes stopped playing with sparklers. Everyone ... and I mean everyone ... in the Palace will be slaughtered beyond recognition. Blown apart. The United States President, our Prime Minister ... the lot.'

Wilton looked shaken and tucked his hands even more firmly under his armpits. 'Even Sir Charles? Our High Commissioner too?' He shook his head. 'This *is* serious. I'll fix some drinks.' He started to leave his seat.

'Sod the bloody drinks.' Gavin's retort was immediate. He leaped from his chair and stood in front of the startled civil servant. 'This is urgent. We're not dealing with a tea ladies' strike in Whitehall. I want action.' His voice was raised, his eyes wild with anger at the man's placid response to the crisis.

'There's *always* time for a drink.' Tony Wilton was not to be dragooned. 'You talk. I'll lay on some Pimms.' He walked to the door and summoned an assistant. 'And I'll listen. Really I will.' Wilton's tone showed that he thought he'd got a nutter on his hands - a troublesome one at that. Worse still, someone who wanted action and decisions taken. Decisions, for God's sake! 'Ah yes! We need some Pimms,' he told the young West African servant who had appeared, head bowed and full of respect for his great master. 'Strong ones.'

Chapter 51

The door of the cell opened, letting in a streak of light to the darkened room in which Art had been held in the army compound. A flourish of his machine-gun by one of the soldiers motioned him towards the door. Slowly he moved out of the windowless room into the corridor. The side of his face was blue and puffy where he'd been struck by the butt of a gun. His back was throbbing from the kick in the kidneys. Waves of nausea continued to overtake him, even though he'd vomited in the corner of the stinking little cell. In the darkness he had sensed but not seen cockroaches scurrying about their business, living off the faeces of a previous occupant.

Handcuffs secured his wrists in front of him as he was led down the corridor and into a brightly-lit room. There, Art was made to stand in front of an empty metal desk. Around the walls were three battered metallic chairs. Otherwise, the room was bare, the atmosphere stark yet foetid, the floor concrete, the light bulb naked. Even the slightest movement resonated round the dirty yellow walls.

Moments later, the door opened. A man entered and seated himself at the desk. Michel Mboro, resplendent in his evening dress, with a line of meaningless medals proudly displayed, eyed Art up and down. He noticed the American's mud-blackened face, the bruising and the blood which had congealed whilst running down the front side of his temple.

'I know who you are.' Mboro's voice was soft and gentle, surprisingly so for the tall, lean man which he was. 'I recognise your picture.' His English was good, the product of his three years in London. Smooth-shaven, with a long thin face and an air of quiet dignity, he looked every inch the Minister of the Interior. A waft of cologne filled the room. A glint of gold showed around the white cuffs. The evening dress suited him, adding to the elegance of his movements, the graceful flourishes of his wrists as he spoke. 'Art Lemman, ex-drug buster and now the hard man for the International Maritime Bureau.' The approach was soothing, yet deceptive. There was a sibilant condescension as the words hissed between the slender lips. He paused to look at his watch. 'I'm not pleased, Mr Lemman. Because of you I've been summoned from my dinner in the Palace. *Cerne View* is under arrest and therefore under my jurisdiction. Ships under arrest are not to be boarded.' A long delicate finger pointed accusingly and there was a pause as he waited for Art to respond.

Art said nothing.

'Mr Lemman ... what were you doing on this vessel?'

Art said nothing.

'Give him some encouragement.' It was an order to the two soldiers who were standing on either side of him. With no further word needed, one man held Art securely whilst the other placed a well aimed kick violently into his testicles. If he had been free to do so, Art would have buckled under the searing pain. As it was, he was held firmly upright, counter-balancing the rubbery feeling at his knees. The soldier lashed out again, this time striking him in the pit of the stomach so that he gasped for breath, eyes rolling, mouth sagging open.

'Stop.' Mboro had sat impassively through the attack. 'Now, have you changed your mind? Are you going to tell me what you were doing?'

'Sonovabitch!' Art shook his head and rather wished that he hadn't. His head pounded worse that ever, a reminder of the blows on his temple and cheek. For a moment Mboro fixed him with a hard stare. He was about to say something when the door opened. A young soldier entered carrying a piece of paper which he handed respectfully to the Minister. Mboro looked at it, smiled slightly and then looked up at Art. The eyes, which Art had judged to be brown, were now dark and lifeless. Mboro's face was gaunt, almost skull-like in its severity. 'Mr Lemman ... there have been some interesting developments.'

Tony Wilton had not enjoyed the last fifteen minutes. 'So, if you're right,' he said at last, 'we've got say two hours until *Cerne View* goes up. You reckon this ship *Rio Massu* is full of mercenaries who are going to fire the detonating shot into some luminous cross. That blast will not only wipe out the military HQ but the Palace as well. In the confusion, the mercenaries will storm the Palace, seize control and impose a new leader with a new regime. You have no idea who that leader might be, except you guess Michel Mboro, a distinguished Minister and a good friend of Britain, may be involved.' Wilton reached for his Pimms, wondering what he had done to deserve a problem like this.

'Outsiders have been beating the drums of fundamentalism. In the last couple of years, key government positions have been infiltrated by Moslem extremists.'

'I know. Yes of course I knew that.' There was a petulance in Wilton's voice as if there had been a personal slight at his knowledge of foreign affairs. Gavin felt sure that Wilton was not convinced, did not want to be convinced. 'So you're convinced then?' he enquired with a nod of the head and a positive inflection in his voice.

'No. Sounds pretty far-fetched to me. Sheer speculation.' The moustache seemed to droop in sympathy with the despair in his voice. The arms were restless again. 'Anyway ... what do you expect me to do?'

Gavin was exasperated. 'I'd have thought that was

bloody obvious. Intervene at once. Contact the Foreign Office in London. Alert the people at the Palace. Above all, stop *Rio Massu* entering harbour. Buy time till London can do something. Delay the ship till tomorrow and the coup will fail.'

'Why should someone want to blow up all these world leaders?'

'Listen, you stupid little man! We haven't time for a cosy chat about the semantics.' Gavin was about to leave it with this sharp retort but on seeing Wilton's scowl deepen, he decided he'd better speculate a little further. 'Independence Day has been scheduled for fifteen months. That means the coup could have been planned for just as long ... a prime chance to wipe out all the leading figures in Lumbola and Sampopo. 'However,' he clicked his fingers in emphasis, 'it was only recently that President O'Brien decided to come. That was the Ok for all the other me-too statesmen to follow, our very own Prime Minister included.' He saw Claudine's smile which gave him confidence. 'Maybe their presence is a bonus ... or an irrelevance. Anyway,' he sounded exasperated, 'we haven't got time to debate every detail. The simple question is what are you going to do?'

Wilton's hands hung down helplessly from the shapeless sleeves of his brown suit. 'How can I stop this ship?'

'For Christ's sake! I've risked my bloody neck tonight. My colleague's probably dead or in jail. I've hijacked the High Commissioner's car to get here. I'm not play-acting. I'd have gone to our consulate in Lumbola but the entire Lumbolan communications system has been put out of action by a fire. You'd call that coincidence, pure chance I suppose.' Gavin's frustration was turning to fury by the second. 'I assume your phone system here is working. We can ring London.' He expected Wilton to move towards the phone. Instead, he seemed to sink even further into a heavy-jowled sulk.

Gavin moved sharply towards the door. 'Come on Claudine. We'd do better talking to a tailor's dummy.' As he beckoned, Claudine rose from her chair and studiously ignoring the contorted anguish on Wilton's whiskery face, she crossed the room. 'My God,' concluded Gavin, 'I wouldn't want to be in your brown brogues tomorrow morning. The fate of countless ....'

'Wait.' Wilton's voice was a touch shrill. 'You mean stop er ... er ... *Rio Massu* by force?' The voice was incredulous.

'If necessary, yes, of course. We're dealing with mass slaughter, not boy scouts looking for badger tracks.' Gavin enjoyed that. Wilton reminded him of an effete scoutmaster from his childhood.

'Dear, oh dear! The High Commissioner won't like being dragged out of the celebrations.'

'If you do nothing, they'll be dragging him out feet first,' retorted Gavin, 'or what's left of him.' He grasped Claudine's arm, flung open the door and saw that the room opposite was the High Commissioner's office. On the desk was a telephone. 'I'll ring London myself.'

Wilton came as near to urgent action as was in his nature. He eased himself out of the chair like a man in a daze, his soft pink hands raised in protest. 'You can't do that.'

'Just watch me, Mr Wilton, I'll ring Walter Corbin. He's my boss. You'll speak to him and then he'll ring the FO. If you don't help then I wouldn't give a spit across Whitehall for your promotion prospects.' As she watched Gavin's face, Claudine saw the controlled menace, the twisted lip, the vein throbbing in his temple.

Wilton drained his glass, thought about his dilemma again. Then sheepishly his face darkened by the second as he joined Gavin at the High Commissioner's desk. 'Ah! It's ringing,' said Gavin. 'Walter! Thank God you're there. No, forget Claudine. That can wait. Here's what needs doing.' Briefly he outlined the position. 'Now I'm handing you over to Tony Wilton. He's our man in Sampopo.'

Ten minutes later, Gavin and Claudine were once again in the back seat of the Princess. The chauffeur's neck had stopped bleeding, his nape now covered with a plaster and his shirt stained dark crimson on the collar. Gavin was clutching a gold embossed invitation and was wearing an ill-fitting white tie and tails, a spare which Wilton had found in the High Commissioner's wardrobe. Claudine was wearing a navy blue ball-dress ransacked from the extensive selection belonging to the High Commissioner's second wife. 'Not exactly a perfect fit but good enough,' laughed Gavin. 'Cinderella will go to the Ball, leaving Cinderella Wilton behind yet again.' He laughed. 'Maybe I'll grow into mine over dinner.' He looked at his watch. 'No. No chance of that. Too late. Might get some cheese if we're lucky.'

'What happened while I was changing?'

'Wilton fired up his courage with a bucket of Pimms. Told me that if he got the all-clear from the Foreign Office *and* the Ministry of Defence, Sampopo's Air Force and Navy would be mobilized.'

'Will it work?'

'God knows. The Air Force is two old helicopters and the naval fleet is an old patrol boat. It's probably armed only with a loud-haler and a pea-shooter.' He fumbled in his inside pocket and pulled out a note written by Wilton. It was addressed to the High Commissioner, explaining the position. Wilton's warning to Gavin had been clear: His Excellency Sir Charles Wilberforce-Smythe would not be easy to convince when he's got his party hat on and has had a few drinks.'

'You said *Rio Massu* was full of mercenaries. How do you

know?' Claudine's question was whispered across the comfy rear seat. He turned and in the darkness could scarcely see her face but recognized her concern.

He reached out in the darkness and found her hand. It was cool, almost death-rattle cold, in contrast to his own. He gave a nervous laugh. 'A calculated guess. Art and I both think it's likely. If we're wrong then ... ' He ran his finger across his throat. 'In theory, stopping *Rio Massu* entering harbour if she's innocent should be easy - no bloodshed. If she resists, then ... who knows? Apparently Sampopo's Sikorsky helicopters are so old they were probably made by Igor Sikorsky himself.'

She gripped his hand tighter as they started to cross the bridge and approached the Sampopo checkpoint. Gavin leaned across and put his arm round her shoulder, pulling her towards him and lowering her head below the window line. He need not have worried. The twisted barrier was lying on the ground as their car sped past. Half a dozen soldiers were still standing round it, scratching their heads, voices raised as they recounted the event and didn't even notice the High Commissioner's car until it was too late. 'You're amazing. *C'est vrai.* So calm,' she said as she placed her hand on his arm. He loved it when she broke into French.

'And you're wonderful too. If ... I mean ... when we get through this ... we'll have a lot of fun.' He fell silent, thinking ahead to their arrival at the Palace. It was a bloody shame that Wilton was under orders not on any account to leave the High Commission. They really needed him for credibility. Still, he'd done his best, almost with good grace at the end, after talking to Corbin. A quiet smile played on Gavin's lips as he remembered the way in which Wilton almost stood to attention throughout the entire conversation. He'd lost count how many times Wilton had said *Yes sir*. 'That's it. We're over the bridge. Fingers crossed now for the Palace.' He kissed Claudine on the lips and she wiggled her slender hips along the seat until they were touching. 'This is what we're going to do. Using this invitation, we bluff our way in. Stay with me. Don't get separated. We make straight for Sir Charles. Show him the note from Wilton. Once we've persuaded him, it'll be his job to get the other top brass out.'

'How long have we got?'

'It's nearly ten. Anywhere between one and two hours. Plenty of time if Sir Charles hasn't got his party hat on.'

Art tried to read the note now lying in front of Mboro. It had obviously pleased the Minister. However the foreign language defeated him. He needn't have worried. Mboro spoke lovingly and with even more condescending ooze. 'Gavin Blair and a companion have just been arrested trying to enter the Palace. My staff had special instructions to watch out for him. They're now being held on *Cerne View* till I'm ready to see them. Just a few questions.' There was a lip-licking relish as he hissed out the words. 'I expect he'll talk when he sees what's happening to that woman with him.' His purple lips parted in a sinister smile. Art said nothing. He didn't believe Mboro would go anywhere near the ship. No. It was just a test, a trick set by Mboro. Trying to see his reaction to the mention of *Cerne View*.

There was a way of dealing with that. Art had learned many years before. *Think of something else.* Ignore the words. He did so, switching to the last moment touchdown by the Miami Dolphins in the Superbowl. He re-lived the cheers, the hot-dogs, the celebrations afterwards down at Buck's Bar. Somewhere in front of him, Mboro was droning on about what atrocities would befall Claudine but Art stood stony-faced, eyes and appearance impassive, the two guards beside him waiting anxiously for permission to beat his head in.

Slowly and with great deliberation Mboro scrumpled up the message. He screwed the piece of paper into a tight ball and then lobbed it with an arc of accuracy into the waste-bin. 'So you refuse to tell me anything?' He shrugged his shoulders. 'That's your decision. You will be taken to the prison.' He fired out some rapid instructions to the soldiers who nodded their heads with enthusiasm. 'The Prison Governor will see you when you arrive. Unless you co-operate you will be shot. Tonight. There will be no trial. No one knows we've arrested you.' He laughed in a manner which was funny only to himself but gave further encour-agement to the soldiers. 'Anyway, you are guilty of a seri-ous crime.'

Mboro rose from the desk usually occupied by the Army Commandant. He checked his watch. 'Yes. I should just be in time for the dessert.' He spun round on his patent leather shoes and was gone, leaving only the lingering scent of Paco Rabane to mask the stale sweat of the confrontation.

The Minister went out into the compound, glanced briefly back at *Cerne View* and gave a wry smile. Then he headed for the Palace with brisk strides, not that he'd be staying there long. The plan called for him to be well out of the way of *Cerne View*. Then ... all his dreams would come true. There would be an end to this western decadence. Soon there would be a return to fundamentalism, to the law of Sharia; soon West Africa would be dominated by similar regimes as one domino struck the next; soon all his political theory would become reality.

There was a manic gleam in his eyes.

Soon he would be President.

Chapter 52

Aboard *Cerne View*, Gavin could see across the harbour. Berth 17 was almost opposite. It was quiet, empty, giving not a hint of what was increasingly imminent. He felt like a fly, stuck in wet cement, awaiting the swatter. His right hand was handcuffed round the solid girder which supported a pair of built-in bunk beds. His left arm was strapped close to his body. He was able to stand up or sit down but not escape. His mouth was gagged but with the porthole shut, no one would have heard anyway.

He peered out again. Soon, across the strangely quiet stretch of water, *Rio Massu* would become reality. Her outline would fill the porthole and if Art's message were right, then he was trapped just ten feet beneath the luminous target. The thought of the cross just above him set him thinking. Why had it been necessary? Had the luminosity worn off during the voyage? Had someone judged the target too indistinct?

Ten feet! The proximity made him yank even harder at the pillar. It didn't budge. Although the cabin was in darkness, he'd seen that the upright was bolted to floor and ceiling, impossible to shift. He pulled even harder, hoping to secure at least a hint of movement. Nothing. The sole reward was the torn skin on his right wrist from which blood started to seep.

Quite out of reach was the cabin door, stout wood and noisily bolted when the guards had left. Beyond it was a narrow companionway, dimly-lit and leading to freedom. Behind another slammed and bolted door would be Claudine. He'd heard her screaming as she'd been bundled away. Then there was silence. Presumably, like him, she was gagged and manacled.

He looked out of the porthole. Shit! This was not funny. Just when success had been so near at the Palace. Less than an hour before he'd been full of hope, climbing out of the Austin Princess with Claudine. The gossip columns would have called them a 'handsome couple, made for each other,' as they were dropped by the main portico. There he'd flourished the invitation, addressed to Mr and Mrs Tony Wilton. He'd apologized to the officious flunkey for being held up. 'Affairs of State,' he'd said as they were admitted to the marbled hallway.

His arm in hers, he'd crossed the Ante-Room. Leading them was a subaltern, in black uniform with red stripes and a white cap. He could recall every detail - the noise of distant cutlery, the laughter, the orchestra playing 'In the Mood'. He could even smell the food, spicy and full of herbs. The chatter of a thousand guests filled the air. Soon he'd be in there. Then he'd get to Sir Charles.

It was not to be.

Just as the marquee came into sight, two men, strong, muscular and employed by the Interior Ministry, appeared. Clad in evening dress, they had quietly but forcefully diverted Gavin and Claudine into a small office, just to the side of the high-vaulted hall, its walls resplendent with a selection of Impressionists and Old Masters. The decor was white and blue with gilt on the embossed pattern of the ceiling. From their control room, with cameras to monitor every new arrival, Mboro's security team had picked out Gavin without difficulty. The likeness to his passport photograph left no room for doubt. Moments later, he and Claudine were being escorted none too gently through a side gate and across to the army compound.

'We're going to get a good view of the action,' Gavin had said as he saw where they were being taken. His touch of levity was not shared by his bowels which felt as if he'd eaten a lead pumpkin.

'Gavin, do something. You've got to do something. Get us set free. Tell someone.' The words were meaningless, frantic and her voice was raised. Claudine's face was ashen despite the make-up which she had hastily applied at the High Commission. The guard struck her cheek with a slap and motioned her to be quiet. She started to cry as she stumbled across the dusty parade ground and Gavin tried to get nearer to her to give comfort, to put his arm round her. It was impossible. When she looked imploringly across at him, he could scarcely meet her eyes in acknowledgement of his failure.

At gunpoint, they were pushed and shoved towards and then up the gangplank. 'We'll be all right. You see!' Though he sounded confident, he didn't feel it. Art must be a prisoner too, presumably somewhere on board as well. Now it was down to Tony Wilton. *Tony Wilton!*

In the darkness, as he pulled again at the handcuffs, he knew the real meaning of despair. It ripped at his guts, clouded his mind, clamped vice-like across his chest. If only they'd let Claudine free. She'd done nothing to deserve this. He'd have done anything, given everything to get her released. God! What must she be feeling. Unless it was a fix. Unless ... unless she really was on the other side and following a show of protest ... had been freed. How had he been recognized entering the Palace? No. Surely not. He'd back his judgment against Art's any day. She had given herself to him, she'd trusted him. He had to trust her. Well ... almost.

There was no light in the room other than what little of the night sky penetrated the thick, grimy porthole. The ship was silent. There was no one to bribe, no one to trick, no one to plead with. No one. Nothing. Nothing to do but wait for *Rio Massu*.

Suddenly he broke into a laugh, not his usual friendly

and infectious chuckle. Despite the gag, it was a mad, hysterical laugh as he remembered the Sampopo Air Force. Come on Gavin! Cheer up! There's the Navy too! Rescue's coming. It'll be like Desert Storm liberating Kuwait. He laughed again, this time the laugh fading into a sigh of resignation.

Rescue? Forget it. He could just make out the time on the clock on the desk. Maybe an hour to go, maybe less. Maybe Tony Wilton would be asleep in a chair too.

In the starry African night the temperature had dropped as four small dinghies, powered by outboard motors, made their way up the Sampopo River. Each contained six men and an arsenal of explosives. Their route kept them close to the steep banks on the Lumbolan side. Precisely on schedule they'd left *Rio Massu* half a mile out to sea. Since then they'd made slow progress against the strong flow of the river. Ahead and towering high above them was the bridge. About a quarter of a mile short of it, where the subtropical forest was at its thickest, falling right down to the water's edge, they pulled in. There they dragged the inflatables up the bank and out of sight.

The view ahead was awesome. Years of work, a masterpiece of engineering, the silhouette of the suspension bridge spanned the water in aloof splendour, the lights on its side flashing red and white in the darkness, an almost indecent mastery of man over nature.

Each of the twenty four had been selected with care, all had blown up bridges before, though none had tackled a giant such as this. It was breathtaking and more than one felt a hint of regret that something so magnificent should be destroyed. Others felt the shot of adrenalin pulse through them but whatever their feelings, their excitement was masked by professionalism as they gathered their materials for the final push. Semtex purchased in Naples from the

Red Brigade, wiring and detonators were soon ready to shift. Then they wound their way in single file through the thick undergrowth, under the command of a former officer from the SBS. Even his hands which clasped a machine-gun, were sticky in anticipation of the task ahead.

He looked at his watch. It was 10.31 pm, one minute behind schedule. There was a brisk confidence in his move-ment. The RT message of two minutes before had given the all-clear. The advance party, who had arrived in Dakalla a week before, had confirmed that it was *go*. The four guards at the foot of the bridge, on the Lumbolan side had now been eliminated.

Operation Mindblow had begun.

The three-ton army truck, its tyres bald, its engine knock-ing like a steamhammer, was a relic of the days of French colonialism and had been used at Suez in 1957.Creaking and complaining, it lurched and thumped along the un-made road from Dakalla to the prison. To Art, it seemed an age since he'd made the journey before. Hell ... surely it couldn't have been just yesterday? This time it was all so different: the handcuffs for a start. This time, it was a one way journey, ending up in that execution yard with his arms bound behind that single stake. A battery of shots at point-blank range. Then there would be the casual heave-ho onto a truck. Perhaps he'd bounce once before lying in a crumpled heap. Exit Art Lemman. No more booze and no more screws.

Fuck that!

No way was he going to give these bastards the pleasure! *No way* was he going to tell the Governor anything either. He looked over the tailgate. Behind the truck were the dis-appearing lights of Dakalla. Opposite him, machine-gun slung carelessly across his knees, was the guard. The two men were seated, facing each other across the gloom.

The man's face was placid, relaxed and his thoughts were whether the Governor would carry out the execution himself or whether maybe ... he'd get the treat ... get the chance to pump some bullets into this cocksure American guy. To Art's right and beside him was the tailgate, about twenty inches high. To his left were some crates containing God knows what and some old sacks. The air smelled of old socks and fousty hay.

In the front was the army driver, no doubt holding the wheel in the wrong place and swinging it from side to side as he bounced and rattled along the bumpy road on the mile or so left to the prison.

A mile or so!

The thought prompted greater urgency. Once at the prison, escape would be impossible - at least in the time available. He looked down at his raw wrists where he'd wrestled against the handcuffs and glanced across at the guard whose eyes were lowered now beneath his floppy hat. The African's lips were pursed in a tuneless whistle. The gun was aimed nowhere worse than the tailgate. Trouble was not in the guard's mind. If anything, he was more interested in the fireworks wooshing into the sky from the distant Independence Square.

Think man! Think! For Christ's sake! Oh! Sure, but it wasn't so easy to think ..... not when some black bastard had nearly kicked your balls up your ass and your head was swollen and suffering from the butt of a rifle.

A mile or so! That's it, he recalled. That first journey! The huge pothole. Remember it? That's right. The taxi driver. They'd been concerned about where he was taking them. Yes. There'd been that bend. On his side of the road too. Couldn't be far now. At 25 mph, there would be a chance. He'd have to be ready.

Art shifted slightly as the lorry rocked and rumbled on over the pits and ruts. None of them was the *big one*. Surely, it must be soon. Unless some ignorant fucker had filled it in. No. Not since yesterday. Not in West Africa, surely not. In the darkness, Art eased his hands forward, resting his elbows on his knees. Then, imperceptibly in the darkness, he worked his bottom across the sacking. He raised his hands to his face, spire-like, in front of him. Perhaps the guard would think it a gesture of prayer or despair.

Christ! The lorry was slowing! This must be it. Not too slowly boy. Drive like you normally do! For God's sake, you don't *own* this old heap.

The nearside front wheel of the lorry lurched into the deep pothole as it rounded the sharp left-hander. The whole vehicle sagged and flopped. Momentarily, the guard was caught off-balance and was jolted forward towards his prisoner. Art sprang across the narrow gap, locking his handcuffed arms in a vice-like grip round the soldier's neck. All in the same movement Art pivotted to his right, dragging the African with him. Together they tumbled over the tailgate and landed heavily in the road.

The guard's shout for help was muffled by the heavy throbbing of the diesel engine and scarcely had they hit the ground than the lorry had rounded the bend and disappeared from sight.

On impact, the soldier had slipped from Art's grip. Quicker witted and prepared for the situation, Art was instantly back on his feet whilst the soldier still lay on the ground, dazed and confused. In a surprisingly swift movement Art crashed down on him, kneeing him firmly in the stomach, crushing every ounce of air out of the lean and fit body. The savage pain made the guard drop his gun and for a moment he was nailed, gasping beneath Art, with his mouth opening and shutting like a beached fish.

Grabbing the gun, Art pointed it at the man's head. 'The key. You asshole! Give me the key! Don't you speak fucking English.' The guard spoke not a word and appeared not to understand. Art opened fire with a volley which hit the ground just beyond the man's head and ricocheted off into the night. Art leaned forward. 'The key, dick-head,' he shouted. It was useless. The guard understood nothing. He waved his padlocked hands above the man's head. Only then did a flicker of understanding cross the man's face. Eagerly he fumbled in his breast pocket and produced a set of keys. Art motioned him to undo the locks.

Seconds later, he was free. With the machine-gun, he frogmarched the soldier into the jungle. Hell! He couldn't risk the guard giving the alarm. Quickly he searched the man. Jesus! What luck! Another gun. Not his but a tidy looking snub-nose. Loaded too. He faced the guard towards a tree and faltered as he took aim. Then he thought of what was at stake. Sorry pal, not your day. Can't risk it, he decided as he squeezed the trigger and the guard fell to the ground in a lifeless heap. He pocketed the weapon, abandoned the machine-gun and started running towards the city.

Progress was uneventful, the approach roads all deserted as everyone, but everyone, had headed for Independence Square long before. Ahead were the bright lights and the colourful backdrop from the incessant fireworks.

For a moment he spared himself the luxury of thinking what he looked like. Get into the Palace? Like this? No chance. Without my ID card, clear the Palace? No way. Shoot my way in? Dream on baby. Not with those guards, the CIA security, the soldiers, the walkie-talkies, the gunmen on the roof. As he ran, his limbs cried out for relief, his head pounded, his lungs bursting with pain. Still he kept running, holding his head high, blowing hard.

The Palace came into sight.

It was 10.45 pm. Keep it going Art, you idle bastard, he goaded himself. Just a few more gallons of bourbon to sweat off. Keep it going ... but to where? Hell, if he couldn't save the Palace, then it had to be Gavin. He owed him one and sure, he might even have some ideas, some news too. His mind made up, he panted his way past L'Hotel Belle Marie and into the docks. The hole in the fence had not been repaired and he was quickly through it and into the compound. As he scuttled along in the shadows by the water's edge, he watched the single guard at the foot of the gangplank. He looked alert, watchful even. Art stopped, looked around and found what he was looking for. He picked up a lump of stone. This he threw beyond and behind the guard, so that it hit *Cerne View*'s hull with a heavy clunk.

The startled soldier turned to look away, giving Art the moment he needed to dart across the last few yards at a run. His Karate chop came down with a vicious thud across the back of the man's neck. The guard's knees buckled as he slumped to the ground. Art looked round. The barrack square was empty. No one seemed to have noticed. In a swift movement he tipped the dead soldier down into the murky water where he landed with a splash.

A few strides and he was up the gangplank and into the fo'c'sle where he shut the door behind him. The air was hot and stale and, in the darkness, he stood for a moment, hoping to hear a sound. There was none. He fumbled for a light switch. Goddammit, where the hell was it? Then he found it and the area was flooded with light. Ahead of him was a corridor, running across the ship. He recognised exactly where he was from the plan of the vessel which Edward had given to the Bureau.

Down one deck he went and over to the port side. There he saw the line of cabins. He flung open the first door. Empty. The second, empty. And the third. The fourth door was locked. 'Gavin?' He was rewarded with a grunt and the sound of movement. Across the wooden door were two heavy metal bolts. He pulled them back. 'Shit!' The key to the lock ..... someone had removed it. He took a couple of paces back and crashed his 190 lbs against it. At the second charge the door burst open, the light from the companionway flooding the cabin. Art saw Gavin's gagged figure manacled to the framework of the bunk-beds. 'Unlike a lawyer to be speechless,' Art commented as he pulled the greasy rag from Gavin's mouth.

'Unique. Have you found Claudine?' Gavin's jaw ached as he spoke.

Art was studying the way in which the beds were fixed to floor and ceiling. 'Fuck Claudine! I'll get a screwdriver or a hacksaw.' He turned to leave the oppressive little cabin. 'And don't go away.' Art's chuckle lingered after he'd disappeared as did the smile on Gavin's face. To Gavin it seemed an age before Art returned, brandishing a screwdriver from the Radio Officer's den.

'No sign of *Rio Massu* yet,' said Gavin.

'Just as fucking well! If I told you what was over your head, you'd empty your lunch into that fancy dress outfit.' As he spoke he was tackling the screws. 'Do you always wear this gear when chained to beds? Some kinda sex game?' He spoke between clenched teeth as he fought to get a screw turning.

'Wanted to die looking my best.'

'You think you're joking. Look out there.' Even as he was speaking, Art had glanced out of the porthole. '*Rio Massu*. *Ryme Lady*, if you like. Has to be.' He forced himself to work harder, faster, feverishly twirling the screwdriver. Three screws to go. Then he could pull down the support and slide the handcuff over the top. 'Now Mr Wise, tell me how we're going to get into the Palace.' Art really meant it.

'Ok. But first I've got to sort out Claudine.'

'Claudine! Listen, you stupid limey! You've gotta get out. This ship's going up. Your job is to clear the Palace, not go sniffing for your French tart.'

Gavin ignored the personal insult. 'There's no way you'll get near the Palace. Not looking that like. They're on to us. I got in but scarcely lasted a minute. Anyway, have you seen yourself! I've seen better dressed dossers crawl out of their cardboard homes.'

'I'll chance it. I'm not staying here. The Bureau doesn't pay good enough. Not to be blasted into little pieces and scattered over a 400 yard radius.'

'Christ, I should have told you! I've alerted the Sampopo Navy. And their Air Force. You wait and see.'

'Wait and see!' Art exclaimed. 'Thanks but no thanks.' He grunted with exertion as he worked away at the screws above his head. 'What's happening out there?'

Gavin looked out. 'Maybe one mile, one and a half miles to go. Then we're an easy target.'

'It depends on her guns. How big, how accurate. She can't get too close. Not unless she's on a suicide mission.'

'Thanks for coming.' Gavin looked up anxiously and saw that at last progress was being made. 'Look - if you're going to try the Palace, take my ID card. It may just help. Someone may believe you.'

'Yeah. We sure as hell look like twins.' The muttered words managed to show Art's appreciation as Gavin slipped his Bureau card into Art's pocket.

Across the water and out of sight of *Cerne View*, there was plenty of action on *Rio Massu's* deck. The guns had been uncovered, their crews were in position. What had once been an old cargo ship was now a fearsome weapon of war. Sitting in lines, machine-guns slung at the ready, were the mercenaries, some checking their grenades, others smoking a last cigarette before the battle ahead. In the air was a sense of grim determination. The plan was masterly, simple in concept: take out the bridge, detonate *Cerne View* and then move in, some to the army compound, some to the TV and radio stations, others to the telephone exchange. Yet for some of them, the final briefing had made them angry. Not everything was quite as it had seemed when they'd been recruited for a tidy wadge of US dollars. But hell ... the plan *was* masterly. *They'd been told it was.*

Back on *Cerne View*, sweat was pouring down Art's muddy and bruised face. His clothes were damp and smelling acrid from the stale sweat of his run through the jungle. 'Two gone,' he muttered as he set to work on the third screw. 'If I can't make the Palace, then I'm telling you straight, I'm getting as far from here as I can. If you're still here, I suggest you put your fingers in your ears.'

Gavin tried to laugh but it was not easy as he watched Art getting nowhere with the last screw, its head distorted, the grip gone. Art cursed as the screwdriver failed to bite at all. 'I'll have to pull the fucker out.' Art grasped the pillar, just below the ceiling, and yanked, twisted, pulled and pushed and yanked again. At first nothing happened but then the screw started to move, just fractionally, before suddenly it splintered itself free.

Gavin watched Art's contorted face as he stood on the lower bunk and grasped the post. Then he leaned back, all his muscly bulk urging it away from the ceiling. The top twisted over, just a little, and then bent violently, leaving a gap. At once Gavin climbed onto the bunk and stretched up his arm so that the handcuff slipped over the top. He was free. 'I'll find Claudine.' He glanced out. 'There's still time.'

'You won't make it.' Art's concern was deep.

'I'm not leaving without her. Want to wear these togs? Take the invite?'

'Me? Wear that?' He glanced out. 'You've got seven minutes I reckon. Ten at the most. I'll take the invitation.' As Gavin found it, stuffed into the jacket pocket, Art looked out again. Get that!' he shouted. 'The Sampopo Navy's arriving.'

Gavin nodded as he saw a small vessel gaining fast on *Rio Massu*. He saw the urgent flash of semaphore messages. 'Thanks,' he said as Art turned to leave.

'Be quick. Be lucky.' With a final nod Art was gone.

Chapter 53

Out in the harbour, close to the entrance, the Sampopo Patrol Boat flashed out another warning to *Rio Massu*. Again the instruction to stop was ignored. Both the Captain and First Officer were equally concerned as they looked at each other. Then the First Officer aimed his night-glasses at *Rio Massu*. For both men, this was the highlight of their careers for neither had ever had to fire a shot in anger. Opportunities for the Sampopo Navy were rare. 'London was right,' commented the First Officer as he lowered his night-glasses.' It's not a cargo vessel. It's a warship. Take a look.'

The Captain, who thirty years before had been a rare black cadet at the Royal Naval College, Dartmouth, quickly did so. He nodded pensively. 'Fire across her bows.'

One hundred and fifty yards of water was all that divided them when the first shot flashed across the front of *Rio Massu*. On the bridge, Colonel O'Hara looked over his shoulder at the fast approaching vessel. The warning shot screamed uncomfortably close. 'Don't stop,' he commanded the Greek Captain. 'Prepare to return fire,' he commanded a gun crew and watched as they swung their field-gun ready to attack.

Then he gave the order. The gun fired and the small bridge of the patrol vessel exploded in a blinding flash of torn metal. The low velocity field-guns which fired 75mm shells, weighing 14 lbs, had been selected for their task of triggering the explosion on *Cerne View*. The gun crews had adjusted the timers to give a micro-second of delay between impact and explosion, so that they would penetrate the containers and then explode from within. They were just as effective on the bridge of the patrol boat which was all but destroyed by the single shell.

The second shot struck at the water line, ripping a huge jagged hole. The effect of the shells on the small Sampopo vessel was devastating. Third and fourth shots followed. She stopped, listed and started to sink from the bow, fire blazing from her bridge. Her officers were dead, blasted to bits in the twisted metalwork. A couple of survivors jumped into the water.

Colonel O'Hara cursed that they'd been intercepted. How had that happened? Their approach should have been silent till they'd attacked *Cerne View*. Still, no time to worry. He checked his watch. Five minutes to go. The noise of the firing and the blazing ship must have attracted attention, even this distance from the Palace. 'Full speed. Make it four minutes,' he told the skipper and orders were given to the engine room. *Rio Massu* picked up speed.

Claudine's cabin had been next to his. Gavin forced her door, though with more difficulty than Art had encountered. Having flicked on the light, he'd found her sitting on the bunk, sobbing quietly. Handcuffs fixed her to the bed, just like his own had been. There was no time to ungag her. At once he was working on the three screws. 'We'll be all right. There's plenty of time,' though even as he said it, there came the sound of distant gunfire. An anxious glance through the porthole revealed the flames coming from the smaller vessel. 'So much for the Sampopo Navy. Air Force time now.'

The second screw was both a sod and a bastard. He struggled to make it turn, straining every sinew, wishing it had been as simple as the first one. Across the bay Claudine could see the patrol boat rapidly sinking. *Rio Massu* had left it far behind. 'Three minutes,' he'd said to himself whilst inwardly cursing whoever had put in two-inch screws when one inch would have been ample. 'I give up.' The second screw was hopeless, the head damaged beyond repair. He set to work on the third, his breath coming in violent, short pants, his eyes showing the stress whilst Claudine's palms were bleeding where her clenched nails had bitten into her own flesh.

In front of the Palace, Art tried to look dignified as he pushed his way up to the guard-post. All around him, happily shouting and jigging about to the heavy beat of tribal music, the throng had no idea that they had barely three hundred seconds to live. Cavorting wildly, they were unaware that an explosion was about to destroy the Square and rain down ten of thousands of tons of iron and metal which would crush and maim without discrimination.

The guards looked at Art. What they saw was an overweight man, his face greasy with perspiration, forehead swollen and blue, his hands bloodstained and grimy, his clothes torn, his hair spattered in mud. He flourished his invitation. 'Do you fuckers want to be killed? Let me in, you dick-heads.' The swing of the guns towards him was not promising. One of them made a great play of releasing the safety catch. 'If you don't ... you'll all be killed.' It sounded ludicrous. They didn't understand anyway. 'Don't you understand, you ignorant fuckers,' he shouted. They didn't.

A few yards away, beside the Palace portico, members of the American security team glanced across at the shouting. They were identifiable by their lean looking efficiency and American-cut suits. Each was holding a walkie-talkie. One of the men came forward and snatched the invitation.

'What's going on? Who in hell's name are you? You're certainly not Anthony Wilton Esq, of the British High Commission.' The laconic drawl of the man's accent was jokey but firm.

'I'm Art Lemman. I work for the International Maritime

Bureau. If I don't get this place cleared within three minutes, every single person here's going to be dead. You included.'

The man from the U.S. President's Secret Service team frowned and was about to comment when another voice sharply interjected, 'Art Lemman! Recognize that voice anywhere! Remember me? Matt Rees. Norman's Cay, Bahamas.'

'Matt! F'Chrissake, it's you! Bahamas drug bust. Sure. I was with the DEA then. Christ, Matt, you've gotta believe me. We're in the middle of a fucking coup. We've gotta ... '

His words were interrupted by a muffled explosion. The air reverberated.

'Think it's started?' muttered Rees.

'I'd guess.'

Six hundred yards away, Independence Bridge was crashing down. Twisted cable, chunks of tarmac, a lorry, the guards, a broken red and white barrier and thousands of tons of concrete disintegrated into the depths of the river. The ferocious blast at the base of the pillar on the Lumbolan side had worked to perfection.

'OK,' Matt gasped. 'I believe you. Thought I heard something out in the harbour anyway. Someone was checking. Let's go.' The last words were a shouted command to the other Americans. Together they ran across the floodlit courtyard, the crowd outside babbling excitedly at the sound of the distant explosion. It was better than the fireworks.

As he fought with the third screw, Gavin had no time to watch. Claudine however did. With his free hand he ungagged her so that she could report on the scene in the harbour.

'*Rio Massu's* nearly there.' Her voice was dry and distorted. Her jaw ached from being jammed open. Then she squealed in excitement. 'Gavin! Helicopters! Do you hear

413

them? They're diving towards the ship.'

'Keep talking. I like it. Keep bringing me good news.' Gavin spoke with a grimace on his face, his eyes like slits with the exertion.

'Listen! The first helicopter's going in now.' Claudine's face was pressed up against the porthole, her eyes were wide with excitement and fear. From seven hundred yards away came the heavy throb of the Sikorsky's engine and the swish of the blades as they cut through the night sky.

Down on the ship the gun crews had just completed final adjustments to strike at *Cerne View*. The arrival of the helicopters had changed all that. Across the water, 700 yards away and clearly visible in the searchlight from the helicopter, Claudine could see the silhouettes of men scurrying around. She was watching the Sikorsky hovering now, only about 200 feet above the water, when a streak of fire pierced the blackness. A single shell from the field-gun had smashed through the motor and cockpit, destroying the rotor engine. For a second it hovered, defying gravity. Then it exploded in a multi-coloured flash.

'Oh no! Oh no! The helicopter's crashing. They've shot it! They've shot it!' There was shrill hysteria in Claudine's voice. The palms of her hands started to bleed again as she dug her long nails into the skin.

'Bang goes half the Sampopo Air Force then.' Gavin gave a final twist to the screwdriver and the screw dropped out. 'Don't move. I'm going to force the upright.' So saying, he placed his feet on the bunk, clasped the top of the pillar with both hands and leaned backwards. Nothing. Plain nothing. Not an inch of movement. He needed Art's strength and weight, particularly the weight. More leverage.

'*Allez-y! Allez-y!* Go on! Go on.' Claudine screamed her encouragement at Gavin and at the second helicopter which had been hovering at a safe distance from *Rio Massu*.

Now it was dead set on a course fifty feet over the water which would take it just ahead of the ship. Blades swishing, engine revving, it seemed to hover as if there was some type of debate going on in the cockpit. Then, in a sudden movement, Claudine saw it change direction to fly straight over the ship. There it stayed, the big bulbous Sikorsky, its engine straining, its intentions unclear. It was an easy target, so close now to the men on the crowded deck who refused to be cowered by the violent down-draught and incessant roar of the engine.

'What's happening?' asked Gavin. Before she could answer, *Cerne View* shook with the blast of an explosion. It was a dull, resonant sound and the cabin reverberated.

'What the hell was that?'

'Nothing I can see. No change out there,' Claudine reported. 'Yes there is. Oh yes. They're going to kill them. Shoot it down.' She could see the outline of a field-gun being trained at the lumbering target which was positioned just above them.

Claudine was right. A split second later, the sky was lit by a flash just as the helicopter was revving and dipping to accelerate away. It was too late. The 75mm shell tore through the underbelly, smashing the controls. For a moment or two it fought for height. Then, as the fuel tank exploded, it plummetted onto the deck near the bow, scarcely twenty yards from the gun crews.

Unheard by Claudine, someone aboard the ship gave the command to fire at *Cerne View*. 'Oh no! They're turning the gun on us. It's aiming straight at us. They're going to fire. I can't stand it!' Her scream filled the cabin, whilst Gavin rocked back and forward, wrestling with the pillar. The bed support moved just a fraction. It wasn't enough. Gavin shook his head angrily. What did it matter? It was too late now. He'd failed.

Inside the Palace, Matt Rees led the way through the

ornate splendour of the Ante-Room. Each had been modelled on the White House. Each room had its careful sym-
metry, pastel shades and magnificent chandeliers.
Mboro's security team had abandoned the TV monitors at
the sound of the explosion from the bridge. They'd run into
the grounds to see what was happening, yet there was no
obvious sense of panic as the Presidential team raced
towards the red and white awning leading into the marquee. As they ran, Matt radioed to the President's personal
bodyguards so that when they reached the marquee, the
message was already seeping through.

The dignified banquet had been proceeding well. On the
flower-decked stage, the orchestra were playing a
Viennese waltz. The microphone had been put in front of
the President Elect of Lupopo, ready for his speech of welcome. The cheese had been cleared and, French style, the
dessert had just been served as the climax. Around the
room the guests were tucking into the Bombe Surprise
whilst the wine waiters topped up the glasses with vintage
Krug champagne.

Conversation had been interrupted by the muffled
explosion from the foot of the bridge. They'd heard it, had
been puzzled, had debated what it might have meant. No
one was going to panic. No one was going to be the first to
be *seen* to be panicking. Now, however, the guests near the
entrance to the marquee saw the six men appear. On their
faces was intense concern. Their actions looked sharp,
determined.

One of the men looked as if he'd just finished ten rounds
in a prize fight. And lost. Their look of urgency was infectious. The sound of further explosions in the distance
added to their unease. Some guests near the entrance started to stand up and shuffle about. No one knew what to do,
where to go. Like a Mexican Wave, the ripple of panic
swept through the thousand guests until only the Heads of

State at the top table maintained their dignity by remaining seated. National pride was at stake.

Claudine could scarcely bring herself to look through the porthole. Through tear-stained eyes she saw *Rio Massu* positioned to fire. From the glow of the flames, she could see both field-guns trained in their direction. Any second now their shells would be fired and *Cerne View* would rise out of the water like a giant, metallic soufflé. At that moment a puzzled look crossed her face. Suddenly everything changed. *Rio Massu* itself seemed to explode, shuddering and rocking in the water.

The four grenades which the helicopter's co-pilot had dropped down *Rio Massu's* funnel had struck deep into the heart of the ship. The fierce blast erupting from the depths of the engine room burst open the ship's stern just as the gun crews opened fire. The ship bucked and reared under the force of the destruction so that the two shells whistled harmlessly high over *Cerne View*. Still rising, their trajectory took them over the Palace and into the darkness beyond.

On the deck, which was splintered and split from the violence of the blast, the surviving mercenaries struggled to re-load. Around them lay the dead and wounded, their bodies maimed and blackened from the fierce fiery heat of the blaze. Flames from the stern were starting to spread along the deck. Near the bow, the burning remains of the second helicopter made the heat for yards around so unbearable that men were already jumping overboard. Only mid-ships, where the gun crews were situated, was there no fire. It was here that the survivors were fighting to retrain the guns on *Cerne View*.

The flames were a roaring mix of yellow, red and black, casting the faces of the men into a fierce, sharp perspective. The soldiers could feel their skin scorching but still they stuck to their task. A single shot on target was all that was needed. Then they'd be winning. Up on the bridge, Colonel O'Hara was shouting orders and encouragement down the intercom but the roar of the flames prevented anyone from hearing. The officer in charge of the gun crews lashed the men with his tongue, angrily shouting for quicker action.

Rio Massu lurched further to port and the stern started to sink. It wasn't much of a movement but sufficient to set the helicopter moving. The wreckage started to roll down the deck like a giant fireball, wrapping the nearest gun crew in a fearsome envelope. Their screams went unheard, even by the second team as they fought to train their field-gun at the cross on the container stack. As the list intensified and the stern sunk lower by the second, again and again they re-adjusted their sights, desperate to get their aim into the heart of the target.

Beneath the surface, the water was surging into the for'ard holds now. Besides the list, the stern was now down by over twenty degrees under the weight of water. Time was short. Too hastily, the gun crew fired again. This time the trajectory was too high and to the left of *Cerne View*. To the wrath of the officer he saw the fourteen pounder tear into the wall of the Central Bank of Lumbola, across Independence Square.

Matt Rees, with Art beside him, ran to the top table. It was heavy with candelabra, finest crystal glasses, gold-rimmed plates and shining Mappin and Webb cutlery. Together, they clambered onto the table between Lupopo's President-to-be and America's First Lady. Art fired his revolver into the red and white roof of the marquee. Women screamed, their arms raised with clenched fists fearfully placed in front of their mouths. The orchestra broke up in a cacophony of discord as violinists, pianists and percussionists stopped playing.

Rees grasped the microphone. 'Leave the Palace now,'

he shouted. His voice filled the public address system. 'Vacate by the south exit. I repeat, the south exit. Not the way you came in.' He was about to warn of the dangers of going to the front of the Palace when he was interrupted. The first pair of shells from *Rio Massu* screamed overhead, just thirty yards above the assembled gathering. 'Move,' he commanded. No one needed any encouragement now. A human tide of men and women were now pushing and fighting their way to escape without any pretence of dignity.

The bodyguards from many nations had quickly formed rings round their leaders. President O'Brien and the First Lady were cocooned by a solid circle of agents as they were hustled at the double towards the caterers' entrance. Art jumped from the table. 'I'll see you later,' he shouted to Matt as he ran back the way he came. Another shell flew over his head as he emerged from the Palace just in time to see it tear into the fifth floor of the Central Bank of Lumbola. All around was panic as the tightly packed crowd in the Square tried to stampede their way to safety.

Wherever that was.

In the cabin, Gavin had now removed his trouser belt. He'd looped it round the pillar to gain extra leverage. 'What in hell's name's going on out there?' The belt was helping. He was rewarded with an inch of movement. Another two would be enough.

Claudine fought to see through her tears and her hair which was clinging like wet hay across the smeared make-up. 'She's sinking. Back first.' She saw the helicopter roll its fiery path of destruction along the deck. Then it happened. The porthole was filled with a blinding flash of white light and *Cerne View* shuddered and shook as the harbour was illuminated and rocked by a huge explosion, the biggest yet. The Sikorsky had ignited the ammunition stack. *Rio Massu* could take no more. The vessel seemed to boil in the water, almost rising from it. Her back broken, the end came quickly. Amid a widening area of burning fuel, her two parts slipped rapidly below the surface into the depths of the harbour.

'Done it!' Gavin muttered in triumph. 'Stand up.' He raised Claudine's wrist to the ceiling and slipped the hand-cuff over the bent tubing.

She was free. He looked through the porthole. 'If that burning fuel reaches here, then the real show'll start. We've got to shift.' Hand-in-hand he dragged her along the corridor and out to the gangplank. The air was heavy with the smell of burning fuel as the clouds of black smoke rolled across the harbour.

The fireworks display was over.

When Art reached the entrance to the military compound, he found the guards had gone. The gates were open. The soldiers had fled at the sound of the first shells. Most had never run so fast in their lives. Art ran past the fuel depot and across the empty parade ground. Ahead of him the sharp outlines of *Cerne View* were clearly etched in silhouette by the flames which rose from across the harbour. A black plume of smoke was forming a pall in the still night air. He'd almost reached the gangplank when two familiar figures appeared just at the top of it.

'What kept you?' Art called.

'Sorry. Having a bit of a screw,' retorted Gavin with a grin.

Chapter 54

In the Square, the crowd had thinned. Screaming mothers, their eyes wide with terror, were fleeing with their babies, their belongings left behind. Fathers stumbled and pushed the elder children away from the harbour and towards the multitude of back streets. Beside them, the Central Bank of Lumbola was ablaze from top to bottom. Its front wall had fallen out, crushing the unfortunate dozens whose luck had run out. From everywhere came the sound of sirens as emergency services moved through the confusion.

Cavalcades of limousines, horns blaring, motor cycle outriders revving and using their sirens, added to the chaos. Foreign leaders, frail and all too human now, peered fearfully through the windows of their stretch-limousines, watching the mob who had now taken to looting the shops and turning over parked cars. The English Prime Minister watched in horror as a gang of young thugs clambered over the bonnet of his car in their haste to be first to chuck bricks at the windows of the jewellers by the Air France building. Happily, they seemed more intent on the display of necklaces and bracelets than in the cowering figures in the Austin Princess.

From overhead came the roar as a helicopter swooped down towards the Palace garden to pick up President O'Brien and the First Lady. Summoned by the Secret Service, the pilot, always on full alert, would have them back at the airport within three minutes. Already the crew of the presidential 747 had started the engine warm-up routine. Lance Bates, in personal charge of the President's own security team whilst on the tour, watched anxiously. Only when the 747 was clear of Lumbola would he feel that he had achieved his task. There was a worried frown on the young features. As it was, he could foresee months of Congressional investigations and enquiries.

He turned away to bark further instructions into his walkie-talkie as he watched the helicopter touch down near the ornamental gardens. Seconds later, he saw Cormack O'Brien and his wife scurry from the shadows, ringed by security. The door slammed, the helicopter was away. It had all taken a few seconds. Bates breathed a sigh of relief, wondering just what had been happening, just what was going on.

In Independence Square, people were none the wiser. Teenagers, reckless of the dangers, had run out to the quay on hearing the first shots fired. They'd climbed cranes, clambered over container stacks, to watch what was happening. Many of them had enjoyed a prime view of the battle between the helicopters and *Rio Massu*. The bravest had seen her explode, had felt the ferocious blast of heat. Most had been in time to see her slither out of sight, leaving only a skim of oil across the surface, much of which was now blazing fiercely, the flames leaping fifteen feet into the air. Two fire tenders were now racing across the harbour, hoping to dampen the flames and to prevent the fire spreading towards the fuel container tanks. Little did they know that the danger was much more extreme ... much nearer, in the shape of the hull of *Cerne View*.

As Art, Gavin and Claudine reached their hotel, they were still surrounded by the shouts of frightened people. Art led the way, barging through the crowd to the sweeping steps of the entrance. Once inside, it seemed strangely quiet, though the lobby was packed with journalists and dignatories who had escaped from the Palace. From outside could still be heard the distant shouts of the pillaging mob. As they waited for the elevator, it was Claudine who spoke. 'I've been meaning to tell you. I worked it out.

Edward's not just a Scorpio, he's a double Scorpio. Sun ...
and Moon. It's a sinister combination.'

As they stood watching the indicator monitoring the elevator's descent, Gavin gave her a bemused look and then
shrugged his shoulders helplessly in Art's direction. Her
timing was scarcely appropriate to the urgency now needed. 'Well, that's fine then. That solves everything. A double
Scorpio eh. Corbin will be pleased.' He put his arm round
her shoulder and from his right wrist, from beneath the
sleeves of Wilton's evening dress, the handcuff hung down
ludicrously.

'It explains a lot.' Claudine fought her corner and sounded resentful.

'Screw the stars!' Art's tone was not even kindly in his
impatience. To him Claudine was at best a liability, at worst
a danger. 'We'll check out Sir Archie's room, then maybe
Klodinsky's.' Once in the elevator, they left behind the
throng where the bar staff could barely keep up with the
demand for Black Label whisky. Nerves were tense and
suddenly everyone was talking, shouting, speculating.
Why they should feel safe now no one seemed sure as wild
rumour upon wild rumour spread through the bar.

At the fourth floor Gavin and Art got out. 'Claudine, you
go to my room. Stay there till I come back.' Gavin gave her
a perfunctory kiss on the cheek.

'You're always saying that,' said Claudine, uncertain
whether she was joking or angry at the flippancy of the two
men..

'Then do it this time.' It was Art who snapped the command as he ran down the corridor. There was no time for
pleasantries. Gun in hand, he approached Sir Archie's
room. It was locked. A single bullet sorted that out and the
door swung open. The room was empty. Lying on the bed
was Sir Archie's half-packed suitcase. 'He's gone.' shouted
Gavin. 'Didn't even have time to pack his case.' Gavin start-

ed to rummage through the suitcase when Art gave an excited whoop. He'd picked up a piece of notepaper. 'Listen to this - *Rio Massu. Ryme Lady*. Scrignac Lefebre/Mboro. Malacca. 200 men. Clifton Bridge. 11.25. Pei Fau Pang. Singapore. *Cerne View*. 11.30. *Paguera* - 12.30. Berth 27. Helicopter 02.00.' Art stopped reading and looked puzzled. 'Make anything of that?'

'Yes.' Gavin scarcely contained his excitement. He'd come alive, could see it all now. 'Come on, quick. It's Sir Archie's escape route. Must be. There's a ship called the *Paguera* at Berth 27. It was on Amadou Cayor's list of shipping movements. It was due to sail at 12.30.'

'Which is Berth 27?'

'Right up the far side, away from *Cerne View*. Well over a mile.'

Art looked at his watch. 'Gone midnight. No time for Klodinsky. Let's go.' Art was already hurrying along the corridor. Ignoring the elevator, they bounded down the stairs and rudely pushed their way through the babble of noise in the lobby.

The road running round the north side of the docks was full of cars, trucks, people, lights flashing, sirens wailing. Those who'd illegally parked their tenth-hand Renaults and Citroens in the docks were impatiently queueing to file out into the Square. Horns were tooted incessantly, a legacy of the days of rule from Paris. Nothing seemed to be moving into or around the dock road except emergency services. All that is, except for one car - a black stretch Mercedes, which had just turned into the docks in the general direction of Berth 27. 'That's a government car. Let's guess it's Mboro.' Gavin and Art looked at each other and nodded in agreement.

'Sure, but we need wheels. Let's grab a car,' was Art's suggestion. An ambulance, heading for the dock exit, came by at no more than walking pace as it forced its way through the queue. The African driver looked startled as Art opened the door and climbed in beside him, gun in hand. 'Turn round. Head that way.' He pointed in the direction of Berth 27.

The man replied in a torrent of meaningless angry phrases as Art summoned Gavin inside. 'Tell this dumb African to use his siren and to go like hell for Berth 27. He might understand your french.'

Gavin spoke to the man who seemed to comprehend the mix of french and body language. He nodded his head with reluctant acceptance. From the back of the ambulance came the sound of someone groaning. Art twisted round and peered through the curtain. He saw a young nurse crouching over a man lying on a bed. 'Keep the driver on course. I'm going into the back.' Art pushed through the curtain. The pretty nurse, intent on looking after the injured man, was surprised when Art appeared. He smiled at her reassuringly.

The young African woman, in a beautifully-starched uniform, continued her emergency treatment. The victim appeared to be losing an arm which was draped across his chest, Napoleon-like and held together by just a sliver of remaining bone. His denim top had been torn away and the remains were bloodstained and still dripping with salt water. The figure in the other bunk was covered over. 'Dead?' Art enquired, running his finger across his throat and pointing at the man. The nurse nodded. The injured man was still conscious, though obviously in pain. 'You speak English?' Art shouted.

'Yes.' It was more of an affirmative grunt than anything else. The patient's face contorted in agony as a nerve spasm swept through him. The nurse checked the tourniquet which she had fixed just above his left elbow and then continue to dab his brow and was about to inject some morphine. Art motioned her to stop and with a scowl at him, she did so.

'You on *Rio Massu*?' Art briskly barked at the patient. The man's hair was wet and oily, his white face which had once been camouflaged, was now also a greasy black from the smoke and scum. Yet beneath it all, in the bright lights of the ambulance, there was a deathly pallor to the skin. Art expected a positive response.

'Yeah.' The patient's face was expressionless. His muscles were lax.

'*Ryme Lady*. That's what it was called, wasn't it?'

'Just get me to hospital, for fuck's sake. Quick.' Art recognised the South African accent.

Art pulled out his gun and waved it in front of the man's nose. 'Don't tell me what to do, you bastard. Just start talking. Otherwise you'll never reach hospital. That ship was *Ryme Lady*?' Art saw the man nod in agreement. 'So who set you up? Who was paying you? Speak.' Art's face was almost nuzzled up to the man's ear, so that he could add zip to every word.

The mercenary, who was aged about thirty six, closed his eyes and kept his mouth tightly shut.

The nurse watched in horror as Art put his gun close to the man's head. 'OK. I'm counting to five. Then I fire.' Art clicked back the safety catch. 'One ... two ... three ... four ... '

The man opened his eyes, his breathing was difficult, his chest racked with pain. The shattered remains of his arm were throbbing. As the ambulance went over a bump he gave a squeal of pain. The nurse leaned forward to give him a jab of morphine but Art held her back. 'Colonel O'Hara recruited me in Hamburg. Big bucks. Overthrow the new government, he said. Detonate the ship, then move in and destroy. Piece of fuckin' cake, he said. Got us kitted up in Naples. Sailed from there.' The man's eyes turned to look at Art, seeking sympathy. There was none. 'Today this cunt O'Hara said we'd be killing the American President, the lot.' The man's eyes shut at the recollection. 'Shit! Crazy plan .... you gotta believe me.' He paused to wipe a bubble of dribble from his mouth with the back of his good arm. 'For Christ's sake, none of us knew about these big shots. We weren't hired to do that. Weren't paid to do that. Hell ... turning over some crappy African Republic's easy. Taking on the whole Western world ... no wonder it ... ended like this. Fuck knows who set it all up. But I'll get him. And that bastard O'Hara. That's if he survived.'

Art wasn't satisfied. 'Who was behind it? Tell me.'

'I don't know. I don't know!' The man's agitated face would have convinced most. Not Art.

Art fired into the pillow by the man's left ear. The mercenary jolted upwards and then slumped back. He groaned as he realized that he was unharmed

.'Libya? Is that it?' I'm counting to five. This time it's for real.'

'I don't know. But I did hear ... I don't know ... ' He faltered, his voice frightened. Art placed the muzzle against his temple. 'I did overhear O'Hara say something about North Africa. Something about someone wanting to become President.' The man groaned and then shrieked as a spasm of pain ripped through his arm. Art nodded to the nurse who injected the morphine.

Art returned to the front of the ambulance. 'How are we doing?' he asked before Gavin could enquire whether he'd shot the patient.

'There's the Mercedes up there.' Nearly four hundred yards ahead Art could see the tail-lights. 'They're still going in the right direction. That's Berth 25 we're passing now. Two to go.' In the harbour, the fire tenders were spraying foam across the burning oil. Beyond that, *Cerne View* lay silently, her secret danger unexploited. Behind her, the Palace lights filled the sky. It was 12.20 am.

Ahead, the dock road was suddenly empty of traffic

except for the Mercedes. The jams nearer the gates had been left behind. To their right were tumbledown warehouses, stacks of timber, trucks which had not moved in years, piles of sand and other debris. In the darkness rose the stark outlines of the container-hoists, the gantries, the giraffe-like crane jibs.

The brake lights on the Mercedes came on. 'They're stopping.' Art gripped his revolver as the gap rapidly closed. The Mercedes had pulled up by the *Paguera*, a 12,000 ton cargo ship, steam coming from its floodlit blue and green funnel. Fore and aft were gangplanks leading up to the deck.

'They're getting out,' said Gavin as they watched the doors fly open. Three black figures and a white man emerged just over 200 yards in front of them.

Art stared for a moment at the figures who had appeared in shadowy form. The dockside was in darkness and such light as there was came from the ship's deck, ten feet above the quay. 'Mboro and Sir Archie. Maybe the others are bodyguards.' Valuable seconds were wasted as the men gathered their belongings and ran towards the gangplank on their left. To the right were container stacks, a fork-lift, a broken down truck and a stack of sacks. High above them, the crane driver was ready to hoist the gangplank clear. The motor of the crane was running, the hook already fixed to the gangplank. A quick getaway was obviously intended.

'No sign of Klodinsky,' said Art, somewhat puzzled, 'just Sir Archie.' He turned to the driver. 'Stop by the Mercedes.' He motioned to the spot as Gavin translated. The ambulance screeched to a halt, blue light still flashing.

The four figures were now only thirty yards away, hurriedly crossing the large black cobblestones to the gangplank, as Art jumped out. Two of the black men stopped and then swung round, guns ready to fire. Seeing they were armed, Art dived behind the shelter of the Mercedes as two shots rang out. The bullets split the air just where he'd been. Crouching by the front off-side wheel, he peered round the bonnet. Mboro had reached the foot of the gang-plank, Sir Archie was a few feet behind, his portly body struggling to keep pace with the lithe African..

It was now or never. Art steadied his grip and squeezed. After what Mboro had inflicted earlier in the evening, the feeling was pleasurable. Most. The single bullet struck Mboro just above the nape of his neck. The Minister fell on the spot, his body crumpling across the cobbles. His body-guards didn't hesitate. Forget the Englishman! Not their problem. They ran full tilt towards the second gangplank, their feet pounding the twenty yards along the quay to safety. Art fired and was rewarded by one of the men falling in a stumbling dive. Seconds later, the other was up the gangplank but already Art's attention was turned to the Englishman. He was the danger. He was the key figure.

'Sir Archie ... stop!' He shouted across the twenty-five yards of open ground between them. The Englishman fal-tered. A few paces ahead lay Mboro in a rapidly widening pool of blood.

Gavin joined Art crouching behind the car. The white-suited figure was close now to Mboro's body. 'I said stop. Turn round or I'll fire.' In the half-light, the man turned.

Art was shaken. 'F'Chrissake!' It was not Sir Archie. It was Edward and he had a gun. Despite the immediate dan-ger it was Claudine's astrology which first sped across Gavin's mind. A fleeting smile creased his face before his thoughts turned to the similar build of father and son, both bulky and of nearly equal height. So where the hell was Sir Archie? On board already? Maybe. God! The old boy was getting away with it.

Both Art and Gavin could see Edward's face now, saw that it was mean and dangerous. He had nothing to lose. If arrested, he'd be facing a firing squad. They watched as he picked his way carefully backwards, retreating towards Mboro's body and the chance to get aboard the ship. It was his only chance.

'We'll confuse him,' whispered Art. 'You run that way, towards those sacks.' He was pointing to cover available no more than five yards away and in an area where the light was murkiest. 'I'll go the other way.' Art had chosen the dangerous route. He paused for a moment to watch the gun which was still poised ready to fire at them. 'Now!' On the command, Gavin ran to the right and Art to the left and towards Edward. The brace of simultaneous rapid movements surprised Edward. He wasn't sure which way to fire and his shot missed them both.

Art levelled his revolver without hesitation and aimed at Edward's chest, fat and panting beneath the white linen suit. He squeezed. There was a click and no more. The chamber was empty. All six bullets had been fired. He felt naked and exposed, standing just twelve yards from Edward's gun. Art could see the snarl on Edward's face which the shadows helped to exploit. He saw Edward raise his gun again and take rapid aim, pointing it unmistakably towards his heart.

A single shot rang out. Utterly helpless, Gavin saw Art fall to the ground. There the body lay, still and lifeless. He felt sick, he wanted to hide. Didn't want to be a hero. Then, a split second later, from the corner of his eye, he saw too that Edward had collapsed, the top side of his scalp blown off. From behind the sacks of grain where he'd taken refuge, Gavin could see the severity of the injury. He'd heard the single shot and had seen both men fall. For a moment he stayed where he was, watching the scene. Then slowly Art started to move, lifting his head. 'Christ! You've got him,' shouted Gavin. 'You've got him.'

Art started scrambling to his feet. 'I didn't fire, for

Christ's sake. My gun was empty.' He looked round. 'Who the hell did?'

'It was me.' From between a pile of crates the figure of Sir Archie appeared. In his hands was a Mauser pistol. He walked towards them as if in a daze, the pistol clasped uncertainly now. His eyes were cold and without compassion as he looked briefly at his son. The top part of Edward's head had been blown clean away.

Art looked at Sir Archie. 'Your own son? *You* killed him?'

'No.' Sir Archie shook his head. 'He was already dead. Dead ever since he killed Ingrid.' He wiped round his neck with a spotted hankie and tried to sound calm. It wasn't difficult. Inwardly, he felt relaxed, relieved of the burden.

'You mean ... ' Gavin's voice was incredulous.

Sir Archie sighed. 'No. Not literally. He told Ingrid about me and her sister Chrissie. The snivelling little bastard knew Ingrid couldn't take that.' His florid face was dispassionate. 'Oh God! He knew she couldn't take that,' he repeated. His ice-calm was melting. The automatism was passing, the anger was subsiding. His eyes became downcast. His shirt collar was sweaty, his cuffs soaked by the stress of it all but in his left hand was the gun, the same hand which had won him the Olympic Gold back in 1952. 'He knew she'd jump, *wanted* her to jump, wanted her shares.' He looked at each of the listeners in turn. To him, that was the important point, not the coup, not Mboro. 'He wanted the *power* of her shares. It was a way of getting at me. That's why he told her.' Momentarily his eyes flashed from his reddened face and he raised the gun to pump another bullet into Edward's inert body. Gavin gently placed his hand on Sir Archie's arm, pushing it downwards. 'Till he told her...... Ingrid and I were happy. Blissfully happy. We understood each other ...... our little needs. Except for Chrissie. Her sister. That was the blind-spot. Once Edward found out ...' his voice trailed away in disgust.

'Let me have the gun,' said Gavin. With a look of mournful resentment on his face, Sir Archie handed it over as if it were a child's bag of confiscated bubble-gum. And then it started ... the unburdening.

'Despite everything, I really loved Ingrid, d'ya see? Hard to believe, eh? But I did. And all this,' Sir Archie flourished his arm towards the two corpses and vaguely in the direction of the city, 'because of his greed.'

'Let's go back to the hotel. No point staying here,' said Gavin as Art took a final look at Mboro and Edward. Gently again he steered Sir Archie towards the car. They climbed into the ministerial Mercedes, with its tinted glass windows, its key still in the ignition. 'Might as well travel in style.' Then, Gavin shouted across to the bewildered ambulance driver that he could go. Moments later, the two vehicles were speeding back towards the city centre. The bank was still blazing furiously but the fires in the harbour were now dampened down and controllable. *Cerne View* was no longer a danger, though the luminous cross shone eerily in the blackness across the harbour.

Sir Archie produced a flask of brandy from his pocket and took a swig. 'Little bugger nearly succeeded, didn't he? Fooled me for long enough. Did everything possible to frame poor old Carl Klodinsky, d'ya see?'

'The USA trip?' Gavin speculated.

Sir Archie nodded, his eyes looking tired, his skin hanging loosely on his cheeks. 'The IRA stuff? That's when I started to suspect what was going on.' He took another swig as the car cruised with a gentle purr along the quayside. 'The message apparently received by our New York agents about the IRA connection ... Edward wrote that himself - to keep you away from here. God knows why. I found his draft wording on a scrumpled piece of paper. In his office.'

As he listened Gavin's mind thought back. Suddenly it all made sense. Edward *had* known of his hotel in Paris. With Mboro's French connections, arranging for the bribe and death threat parcel would have been easy. And the kidnapping. Just the thing to throw suspicion on Klodinsky. Which it did. And the explosions at Wickham and his flat? Someone had set them up. Why not Edward? And the South Bronx? What better place to fix the rendezvous than a derelict building controlled by a Klodinsky company? Neat. But why? What did Edward get out of it? *Ryme Lady*? *Cerne View*? He couldn't be clear yet. 'What about Susannah?' he asked Sir Archie.

'Nothing to do with her. Edward acted alone. She and Edward have never been close.'

'So you decided to come out here to see what Edward was up to?'

'I didn't know Edward was coming.'

'He hadn't got a visa,' said Art. 'How did he get here?'

'With Michel Mboro as a friend? Going back to their London School of Economics days? Who needs a visa?' Sir Archie's face showed the simplicity. 'So what was going on? I can't explain. I spoke to Carl Klodinsky this evening. Always trusted him. One of the chaps really,' he said before qualifying it rather hastily, 'as Americans go.' He didn't notice the sardonic look on Art's face at the comment. 'Didn't want Edward to know where I was, d'ya see. Reckoned he was a danger to me, to everyone. Didn't know what he was up to. Just knew it was no good.' He twisted in his seat to look back at Gavin, as if he blamed him more than Art. 'I had no idea you were here. You never told me. If I'd known, I could have told you that Edward flew in this morning.'

Gavin wanted to explain with an apology and Art, sensing this, motioned him silent with a chopping action of his right arm. 'Count Brads out of all this,' continued Sir

Archie. 'It was Edward working alone, d'ya see? Funny business, *Cerne View* being arrested. Didn't make sense. Not till I got here. Don't know why she was arrested. But I found that Mboro has been to the London School of Economics at the same time as Edward. Then it all became clear. They'd been friends for over ten years.'

'So you think Mboro and Edward set up *Ryme Lady*?' prompted Gavin.

'I do. Greed again. Most West Africans know about shipping fraud. It's rife. Mboro would have thought this was a quick way to easy money. So who better to turn to than his old pal, Edward. Edward who was down on his luck, Edward who's got a rusting old ship. So they set up the disappearance. Mboro no doubt had enough hot money to pump-prime the venture. Edward could never have afforded that. Edward saw the chance. Fill up the old dear with valuable cargo, get the ship to disappear and flog off the goods for cash. Everybody wins. The cash from the cargo would have been enough to keep Edward and Mboro rich for ever. D'ya see? What's more, Brads had the chance of an insurance claim for the hull value of *Ryme Lady*. It was insured for one million. Insurers never paid though. Still, that was small beer if they flogged off the cargo.' He exhaled noisily after another swig of brandy.

'So you think the cargo went aboard?' prompted Gavin. 'Can't prove it. Just my hunch.' Sir Archie laughed contemptuously. 'Mboro's plan, whatever it was, gave Edward power. Money and power.' He shook his own head in agreement with the point which he was making. 'That's all Edward ever wanted.'

Art, who was driving, looked across at Sir Archie as they waited in the queue still filing out of the gates. 'And *Cerne View*?'

'I spoke to Alberto Forensi. I never thought that he would do anything ... corrupt. He told me he was suspicious and so we came here together.'

Gavin felt his palms dampen with anxiety. He knew this was where he had missed a point. 'Hadn't he sold out his Pinetto company to someone?'

'Yes and no. He's getting on a bit. He'd made over control to his son-in-law, Hugo Gonfleur. Alberto told me yesterday - he loved Pinetto as if it were his own son. He was angry at the arrest. Had no idea what it was all about.' The expansive wave of the arms sent a dollop of cigar ash tumbling over the upholstery. 'Of course it was a set-up. He didn't know why she was arrested. Mboro could have told us. Now we'll never know.' The listeners could have explained a great deal but chose not to, anxious to let the Chairman's unburdening continue. 'Tonight, the three of us, that's with Carl, were due to have drinks. Alberto didn't turn up. I don't know why.'

Gavin was about to volunteer but felt it might stop the flow of information and speculation. 'But suppose we'd recommended chartering *Cerne View* to Klodinsky. That would have buggered Edward, wouldn't it?' Gavin was in the back seat, leaning forward in the cavernous space of the luxurious car.

'I'd say he knew *Cerne View* was going to be arrested whoever chartered. If you'd advised Klodinsky to be the charterer, then he'd have been discredited, d'ya see? What Edward wanted was to be consistent in his anti-Klodinsky stance. Kept all eyes on him. As it was, Pinetto are clean. Forensi's persuaded me of that.'

'And Hugo Gonfleur is his son-in-law.' It was less of a comment, more a sigh of relief. Gavin was realizing that Sir Archie's earlier comment had let him off the hook.

A turnip-shaped face like Sir Archie's could never be described as gaunt. It was altogether too round, too heavily jowled for that. Nevertheless, it came close to it as his tumbling thoughts surfaced. Hatred of Edward, tinges of remorse about Ingrid coloured every thought and every word. 'So anyway,' Sir Archie continued, 'once I knew Edward was in Dakalla, I checked out his room number. As soon as I saw his key hanging at the front desk, I went through his room.' From the hip pocket in his baggy grey trousers he produced a single piece of paper. He handed it to Gavin who flicked on the light and read aloud.

'Pei Fau Pang. 200 men. Bridge. 11.25. CV 11.30. *Paguera* 12.30. Berth 27. 02.00 Helicopter.'

'Snap,' said Art. 'Except on your note you wrote 'Clifton Bridge'.'

'You're right. I assumed that the reference to *Bridge* was to Clifton Bridge.' Sir Archie frowned. 'How did you know what I wrote?'

'Same way as you got hold of Edward's note.' Art laughed loudly and, after a moment, Sir Archie did too.

'I'd guess he was referring to the Sampopo Bridge which was blown up this evening.' said Art. 'If *Ryme Lady*, I mean *Rio Massu* had not been sunk, *Cerne View* would have gone up too.'

Sir Archie's voice came out like a squawk from a throttled parrot. '*Ryme Lady*?' His voice contained both an exclamation mark and a huge question mark at the same time. 'That was *Ryme Lady* in the harbour?' The tone was incredulous. 'That was her which was sunk?' Sir Archie's eyebrows nearly reached his hairline. His voice was equally raised in amazement. 'And *Cerne View*? You mean she was going to be blown up?'

'Yes. We'll explain later.'

'Just as well she wasn't. After seeing Edward's note about CV ll.30, I waited as near as I could, down by the military compound. I thought I'd see whatever was going to happen from there.' It was his turn to laugh. 'I wondered what those shells were. Couldn't make it out at all. That's when I buggered off to the next rendezvous at the *Paguera*, d'ya see?'

As Gavin listened, he was angry that Edward had been busily framing Klodinsky and that he'd swallowed it. Now Edward's intentions were obvious. By attacking Klodinsky's credibility, he was defending Brads against a takeover which would have cost him his job. Better still, it kept the Bureau wrong-footed at the same time. Attacking Klodinsky was a double-pronged defence mechanism, a good ploy. He thought of Claudine, who'd been kid-napped because of Edward; who'd nearly died at Wickham, of how Gilbert and Alison had been murdered, how Janie and his neighbours had been blasted to their death in Barons Court. The image of Edward lying on the quayside was no recompense. 'So was Captain Scutar aboard? And my crew?' Sir Archie queried, disturbing Gavin's thoughts.

'We don't know. I doubt it. Put them down to 'lost at sea'.' Gavin's tone was positive. 'Edward's doing, I guess. Make any sense?'

Sir Archie shook his head in the negative. 'No. Not real-ly. I did go through our telephone account the other day. A defending lawyer would have a field day on this as evi-dence but at the time that *Ryme Lady* went missing, the long distance calls to Malaysia and Singapore were up 800%.'

'After she'd disappeared or before?' Gavin continued the questioning as Art deftly manoeuvred round a lorry and into the snarl of the square.

'Before. Maybe you can work on that.'

Art lit a cigarette and drew on it heavily. They were now thoroughly stuck as a traffic policeman waved his arms frantically to little effect. 'So who set all this up?'

Gavin's response was immediate and overly lawyer-like.. 'I've no evidence. Claudine was adamant it was not Klodinsky. So are you. It wasn't just because she knew him.

437

It was because he was a Capricorn.' He waited for Art's groan of disbelief but it never came. 'Edward, as a Scorpio, she'd said was bound to clash with you as his father. Reckoned a double Scorpio meant danger. He had the ego, the greed.' Gavin found himself talking freely. 'That leaves Mboro. Obviously he must have approached Edward as an old friend. But was someone else behind Mboro and his ambitions?'

Art was quick to comment. 'The mercenary in the back of the ambulance wasn't too sure. Muttered something about African politics. We'll go through them all down at the hospital tomorrow. What's left of them.'

'That fits two ways. Fundamentalism is rife. Mboro could have been the front-man for shit-stirrers from North Africa ... or the Middle East, come to that. What's more, many a cargo has been sold for cash in Libya.' Gavin was increasingly confident that the pieces fitted.

'You mean?'

'If *Ryme Lady* had a genuine cargo and she changed her name, then the cargo could have been sold off in Libya before going on to Naples. Would have raised plenty of millions to get the cash flow. There would have been time.'

Art looked round. He even appeared slightly impressed. 'Sure. That could have financed the coup. Kitting up *Ryme Lady* as *Rio Massu*; orchestrating the cargo on *Cerne View* so that she was a floating bomb; paying the mercenaries and lining Edward's pockets. That ... above all.'

'And putting Mboro into power. Anyway, let's leave the detail to the CIA. We've done our bit.' Art double-parked in front of the hotel. The commissionaire gave them a respectful salute as he saw the ministerial car. Art switched off the ignition and looked across at Sir Archie. The man's face was impassive, calm and contented. He seemed to have found peace with himself at last. 'Before we go in I must ask this. What about the options? I know you keep saying that Klodinsky's not involved. You may be right but he lied to the Bureau. He denied any knowledge of the options.'

Sir Archie nodded. 'Four people knew about the options. Ingrid was one. To admit knowing about the options would have meant admitting that he'd found out from Ingrid.' Art did not reveal that Klodinsky had already confessed his feelings about Ingrid. 'Ingrid told him. Pillow talk, d'ya see?' Slowly Sir Archie's head turned to face Art. 'Klodinsky admitted to me tonight that's how he found out. And yes ... he told me that he *has* been stalking our company. He wanted to pick up the shares cheap when we ran out of money but he denies, denies absolutely, trying to engineer the situation.'

'So he denied knowing about the options because it would have compromised him in two ways.' Gavin could see the force of the explanation.

'Frankly, I'm now resigned to Klodinsky picking up Brads. I've fought to save the company for long enough, too long maybe. No doubt he could have Edward's shares and mine ... at a suitable price.' Sir Archie's hip flask was empty. He looked at it thoughtfully. 'Can we go into the hotel now? I could do with another drink.'

The noise in the bar was louder than ever. Everyone seemed to have a story to tell, a slant on what they thought they knew. Carl Klodinsky was sitting on a bar stool pensively looking at his Campari-soda. He saw the trio and walked across. 'Want a drink?' The invitation was extended to Sir Archie in particular but all three went across to join him at the bar. 'Is it true what they're saying? That there was an attempted coup tonight?'

'That's what we heard,' said Art slowly. 'Seems that Edward Crawford and Michel Mboro intended to re-write history tonight, Mboro greedy for power, Edward just greedy.'

'I guess you two owe me a few apologies?'

Gavin was about to agree but Art cut in. It wasn't in his nature to apologize. 'Didn't you invite us over for a drink? Mine's a large scotch. No ice.' He turned to Gavin. 'I think you ought to see Claudine, don't you?'

Klodinsky's eyes narrowed as he screwed up his face. 'Claudine? She's here?'

Gavin smiled in agreement. 'Yes, I must go up.'

'One thing's troubling me,' said Klodinsky. 'Besides why in hell's name Claudine's here at all. About the kidnapping, as you call it. That postcard and the phone call.'

'Claudine's told me. She was forced to write the card and to phone you. Edward's handiwork again. Someone working under orders in Paris for him and Mboro.'

Sir Archie wasn't listening. He was craning his neck, peering round the crammed bar which was doing a roaring trade. 'Where's Alberto Forensi? It's his round.'

Gavin was about to volunteer but the look on Art's face told him to say nothing. 'I'll see you later,' he said as he nodded his goodbyes, thinking now about the London School of Economics. It had been a hotbed of youthful politics, not least at the time when Mboro and Edward had been there together. Mboro must have turned to him as someone able to help his ambitions and make himself rich at the same time. No wonder Edward had been so keen for Brads to cling on. He'd known that cash was coming, a soft loan maybe, from a secret offshore company under his control, which would have saved Brads from Klodinsky and would have given the funds for the options to be exercised. He'd have put Sir Archie out to grass.

A drunken journalist in the other side of the elevator stared curiously at Gavin who had been muttering to himself during his inward debate. Proving that Edward had set up *Ryme Lady*'s change of name and change of crew would have been difficult. Academic now. Proving his involvement with the coup might have been nearly impossible. His every move had been calculated to distance himself from Dakalla. So why had he come at the last moment?

Gavin stepped out of the elevator, still puzzling over that point. Maybe he'd never know but a best guess was that Mboro had summoned him on learning of the arrival of the men from the Bureau. But Mboro had failed, Edward had failed and Brads would survive if only at the grace and favour of Klodinsky. And *Ryme Lady's* crew? He guessed Captain Scutar and his crew were dead, unless they'd been bribed to disappear. Possible. More pump-priming by Mboro and Edward.

Too exhausted even to appreciate the moment of triumph, he walked slowly to the bedroom door. He entered the room and found Claudine leaning on the balcony rail. The Square had been cleared now, roped off, and only the emergency services remained. She never saw Gavin come up behind her and she jumped as he gently put his arms around her shoulders. 'I'm back, it's all over.' Standing firmly behind her, their heads close together, they surveyed the scene. *Cerne View* was in darkness. She was still inviolate, still menacing, her secret intact. 'We'll have to get her shifted but first we'd better do something about these handcuffs. We must look a right pair.' He raised a hand and their handcuffs jangled in unison.

'Can't that wait?' Her face was soft, her smile beguiling and her voice pleading. 'Can't we have a few minutes together? Just the two of us? You're always leaving me.'

Gavin tightened his grip and held her, face to face. 'It really is all over. I'm not dashing off anywhere. As for the handcuffs ... you're right. They can wait. Let's send down for a bottle of champagne and sandwiches. We've some catching up to do.'

'What about Walter Corbin? Shouldn't you get a message through?' Claudine regretted making the suggestion even before she'd finished saying it.

'No. Impossible. We can't cross the bridge to Sampopo and there are no phones here. Anyway, we need more time to work out what to say. We've a bit of explaining to do. Some careful thinking.'

They entered the bedroom and Gavin was about to call Room Service when the telephone rang. 'Mr Blair?' The receptionist's voice was respectful. 'The problem at the exchange has been overcome. There's a call for you. A Mr Walter Corbin.'

COMING SOON!

The Dallas Dilemma

by

DOUGLAS STEWART

*A Novel of Fraud in
The Drug Industry*

**THE BOOK THEY TRIED
TO BAN!**

FURTHER READING

As confirmation that the sea is rife with fraud and intrigue, readers will find abundant guidance in these books:–

'MARITIME FRAUD'
by Barbara Conway
(Published by Lloyds of London Press Ltd)

and

'PIRACY AT SEA'
Edited by Eric Ellen Q.P.M.
(Published by ICC Publishing S.A.)

For my research (and enjoyment) they
have been invaluable

Douglas Stewart
London
January 1993